Herod

The Secret History

A novel of ancient Judea based on the works of Josephus Flavius, Plutarch, Suetonius, and Cassius Dio, as well as the Gospels of Matthew and Luke.

Kelly Conatser

ISBN: 979-8-9909043-0-9 (paperback)
ISBN: 979-8-9909043-1-6 (ebook)

Timeline of Events

72 B.C.   Birth of Herod

66 B.C.   Aristobulus replaces Hyrcanus as king of Judea

63 B.C.   Jerusalem captured by the Romans

48 B.C.   Julius Caesar victorious at Pharsalus, appointed dictator of the Roman Republic

47 B.C.   Caesar secures the throne of Egypt for Cleopatra; Antony governs Italy as Caesar's deputy; Herod appointed governor of Galilee

44 B.C.   Caesar assassinated; civil war erupts in Rome

40 B.C.   The Parthians invade Judea; Herod flees to Rome and is named King of Judea

37 B.C.   Herod marries Miriam and conquers Jerusalem, ending the Jewish civil wars

35 B.C.   Murder of the high priest Aristobulus

31 BC.   Octavian defeats Antony in the Battle of Actium

29 B.C.   Trial of Miriam, Herod's queen

25 B.C.   Two years of famine devastate Judea

19 B.C.   Herod rebuilds the Temple

7 B.C.   Trial of the two princes in Beirut

4 B.C.   Magi arrive in Jerusalem; death of Herod

The Royal House of Judea

In the Generations Before and After Herod

Principal Figures

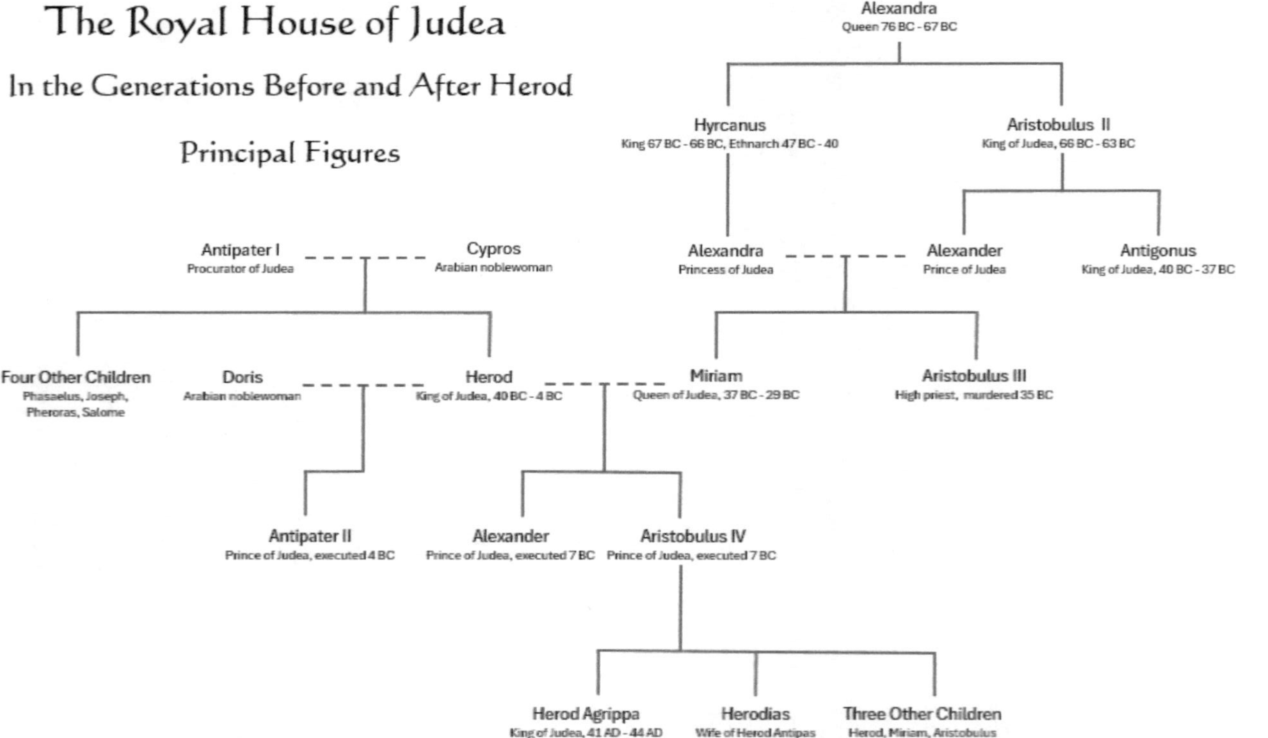

Herod's Wives and Family

Wives

Doris	Arabian noblewoman, first wife, mother of Antipater II
Miriam	Jewish princess/queen, second wife, mother of Alexander and Aristobulus IV
Miriam	Jewish noblewoman, third wife, mother of Herod II
Malthace	Samaritan woman, fourth wife, mother of Herod Antipas and Archelaus
Cleopatra of Jerusalem	Noblewoman of Jerusalem (different from Cleopatra of Egypt), mother of Herod Philip
Pallas	Background unknown, mother of Phasaelus
Phedra	Background unknown, mother of Roxana
Elpis	Background unknown, mother of Salome
Cousin	Name, background unknown, no children
Niece	Name, background unknown, no children

Family

Antipater I	Idumean nobleman, father
Cypros	Arabian noblewoman, mother
Phasaelus	Brother, governor of Jerusalem
Joseph	Brother, prince of Judea
Pheroras	Brother, ruler of Perea
Salome	Sister, princess of Judea

For more information about *Herod: The Secret History*, go to
www.HerodTheSecretHistory.com.

This web site includes a study guide that provides additional
information, including references to the historical sources for
the events in the story and to the scriptural passages cited in
the text.

Cover art and interior map by Enrique Fuster.

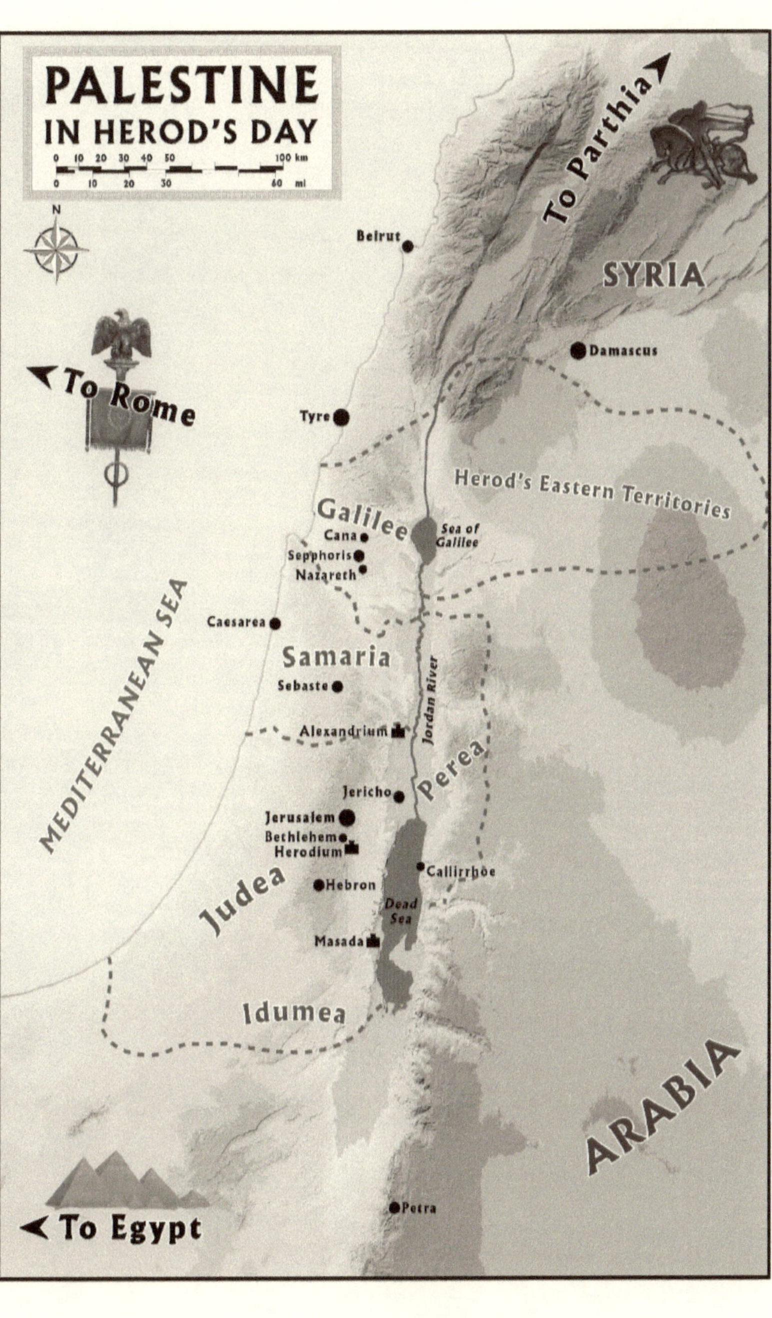

PALESTINE
IN HEROD'S DAY
0 10 20 30 40 50 100 km
0 10 20 30 60 mi
N
To Rome
To Parthia
SYRIA
Belrut
Damascus
Tyre
Herod's Eastern Territories
Galilee
Cana
Sepphoris
Nazareth
Sea of Galilee
Caesarea
Samaria
Jordan River
Sebaste
Alexandrium
Perea
MEDITERRANEAN SEA
Jericho
Jerusalem
Bethlehem
Herodium
Callirrhöe
Hebron
Dead Sea
Judea
Masada
Idumea
ARABIA
To Egypt
Petra

Chapter 1

"Come away from the window, maid."

Joanna considered this for a moment. Then she stood on tiptoe, straining for a better view.

"No one can see me through the lattice," she said quietly.

"No one can see you, but the lattice won't help you if a stone comes flying from the street."

The housekeeper was tiny, and frail with age, but her voice was firm. The girl stepped back from the window, reluctantly obedient. She was midway through her teenage years, on the cusp of womanhood, with dark hair and wide, intelligent eyes that continued to probe the darkness in the street outside.

"Is it always like this here?" she asked.

"There are disturbances from time to time. But never like this." The housekeeper shook her head. "All Jerusalem is in an uproar."

"But why?"

"They say a new king has come."

At this the girl turned away from the window.

"A new king!" she said. "But Herod is our king. Has he—"

"No. Herod lives, and more's the pity." The housekeeper's wizened face took on a defiant look. "Nonetheless, they say there is a new king."

"Who says there is a new king?" Joanna demanded.

"Wise men," the old woman replied. "Men from the East. Magicians."

"Magicians!" The girl's voice quivered with quiet awe.

"Men who read the stars," the housekeeper nodded. "They've come asking for the king of the Jews, so they can worship him. No one knows what to make of it."

"But why would men from the East come here to worship? Why would they worship the King of the Jews?"

The housekeeper shrugged.

"My uncle will know," Joanna said confidently. "My mother once told me that he was an important man in the affairs of Judea."

"That was years ago," the housekeeper said briskly. "Your uncle is an old man now, retired from the affairs of Judea. Long since forgotten by those who once relied on his counsel. And the Lord be praised for that."

She turned her attention to a bit of kindling that had fallen from the hearth. Joanna watched as the old woman stirred the fire, momentarily brightening the dim light in the room. It was a simple dwelling, but not shabby, located on a narrow side street on the hillside that sloped from the Upper City, which housed Jerusalem's elite, to the more commonplace districts below. Its walls of stone and masonry seemed massive, impenetrable. But the girl knew how quickly walls could crumble.

A moment later the heavy wooden door that opened from the courtyard to the interior of the house swung open. An old manservant, as wrinkled as the housekeeper but considerably less composed, stepped inside. He pushed the door shut behind him and sagged against it, his face haggard.

"It's madness out there!" he panted. "All Jerusalem is in chaos!"

"Madness indeed!" the housekeeper scolded. "You should not have taken part in it."

"I wasn't taking part in it!" the man protested. "It took me three hours to cross the city! I could barely move. Every street is packed. Every square is jammed. Men are crammed so close together that I couldn't make my way between them. And many of them armed!"

"Armed!" the housekeeper exclaimed. "Herod's soldiers?"

"No, Edna, no. Citizens. Men with clubs, stones, bricks. Blacksmith's tools! Earthen water jugs! Anything they can lay their hands on. Men that we know. Elias, Hodaviah. Others."

"Men who should know better." Edna shook her head.

"Men who should know liberty," the manservant retorted. "Men who should know freedom from the tyranny of Herod! And they will! Suddenly no one is afraid! Innovation is in the air. Herod will no longer be king!"

"You should not have been out," the housekeeper repeated. "Herod's spies were among that mob."

"Oh, Herod's spies, Herod's spies!" the old man cried. "I'm sick to death of Herod and his spies!"

"We all are. But we must take care."

"Oh, yes, we must take care!" the manservant cackled contemptuously. "Careful what you say! Guard your tongue! It'll be the rack for you, or worse! Well, no man was guarding his tongue tonight, that was certain. 'Messiah has come,' every man was saying. 'There's a new king of the Jews!'"

"Yes, we've heard the cries," Edna said. "I've even repeated them myself, though I don't really believe it."

"Beware, Edna, beware!" the old manservant mocked. "Herod's spies, you know!"

"Within these walls I may say it as many times as I like," Edna said defiantly. "There are no spies here."

"If only we could be sure of that," the old man said sourly.

The girl had followed this exchange with wide-eyed wonder. Now she looked down.

"Old fool!" Edna rebuked him. "How can you say such things, Irijah? This girl has no part with Herod. Do you think she wants to be here? She has no family now, except for our master. Where else could she go?"

"Where else could she go? I don't know. I don't care! Anywhere but here. She arrives here this very day, the same as these mysterious magicians, and who knows what it could mean—"

A clatter in the courtyard interrupted Irijah's querulous reply. Moments later a heavy pounding shook the door on which the old manservant was leaning. He seemed certain to swoon but recovered himself just in time to step away from the door before it abruptly swung inward. In the doorway stood a large man in uniform and helmet: an officer of the palace guard. In the courtyard behind him a half dozen soldiers stood at the ready.

"His Majesty Herod, King of the Jews, sends for Aduel of Sepphoris," the officer announced. "Let him come forth."

Irijah was too terrified to speak. But Edna had her wits about her.

"My master is not here," she said quickly.

"Where, then?" The officer peered skeptically at Irijah.

"On a journey!" Edna temporized.

"A journey! A journey where?"

"To Jericho."

"Jericho!" the officer scoffed. "That old man hasn't gone to Jericho."

He motioned to the soldiers. "Search the house."

The soldiers, evidently in a foul mood after fighting their way through the Jerusalem mob, wasted no time pushing their way past Irijah, who offered no resistance. Edna and the girl remained rooted in their places, their eyes downcast, under the suspicious gaze of the officer. They could hear the soldiers rummaging through the house, tramping up the stairs to the upper rooms, and then up the ladder to the rooftop verandah. After a few minutes they returned.

"There's no one here, sir," a soldier reported.

"Are you certain?" the officer demanded. "You searched the rooftop?"

"We searched everywhere, sir."

"Very well."

The officer lingered in the doorway a moment as the soldiers assembled in the courtyard.

"I shall report to His Majesty that your master has travelled to Jericho," he said to Irijah. "Perhaps the king will send us to look for him there."

He smiled a cruel smile.

"And if we do go to Jericho, I hope very much that we find your master there. For your sake."

At this he wheeled from the open doorway and with a curt signal crossed the courtyard to the outer gate. The soldiers fell in behind him and the troop filed into the street. Irijah remained motionless. Edna crossed the room and quietly pushed the door shut. As she fixed the bolt in place Irijah's strength left him entirely and he sank onto a nearby bench.

"We're doomed," he moaned. "Doomed."

Joanna looked to Edna, but the old housekeeper silently turned away.

"Doomed?" repeated a new voice. "Perhaps. But perhaps it is not so bad as that."

A man had appeared from a little nook in the corner of the room. It was a place that the soldiers had searched thoroughly just moments before. But the man seemed to have appeared from a wall of solid stone.

"Uncle Aduel!" Joanna cried. She hurried toward him. He took her hands with a placid smile. His maroon robe was trimmed with beige embroidery and was of the rich linen favored by the ruling class, but a little frayed around the edges. He was much older than the girl, about the same age as Edna and Irijah, but his serene, bearded face displayed none of the terror that gripped the two elderly servants.

"You have nothing to fear, my child," he reassured her. "Herod has no business with you."

His assurance did more to confuse the girl than to calm her.

"But what business does he have with you?" she demanded. "Why would he send for you?"

"That is a very good question," Aduel mused. "One that I can't answer at present."

"I can answer it!" Edna interjected. "He wants your counsel."

Joanna stared at the servant woman and then at her uncle, astonished.

"Counsel?" she asked. "Herod wants your counsel?"

"That remains to be seen," Aduel shrugged. "One never knows with Herod."

"But why?"

"I had not intended for you to know, but I suppose it can't be helped," Aduel replied. "You see, I once was a member of Herod's court."

"Herod's court!" The girl was stunned. "Why did no one tell me?"

"It isn't as important as it sounds," Aduel demurred. "The palace employs a great number of people. Hundreds, in fact."

"But what did you do there?"

"Why, whatever I was told, of course," Aduel chuckled. "Copying correspondence, composing decrees. All manner of tasks, great and small. For a time I held a place of some importance, but toward the end it was of lesser importance. And that," he concluded with a twinkle in his eye, "is why I am still alive today. Happily pensioned off to a comfortable retirement with my scrolls and my two loyal servants and oblivious to the affairs of Herod and his court."

Joanna stared at her uncle in stark amazement.

"Rather chilly this evening, isn't it?" Aduel said casually. "Irijah, more wood for the fire, please."

Irijah did not stir. Edna quickly unbolted the door and darted into the courtyard, returning a moment later with an armful of firewood. Aduel motioned Joanna toward one of the two chairs in front of the fire and took the other himself, prodding the dying embers to life and carefully arranging the fresh wood on top of them.

Finally he leaned back in his chair, satisfied.

"A least we will be comfortable as we await developments," he said.

Edna, who had bolted the door again and was leaning against it, had a different idea.

"You should flee!" she urged him. "You should flee at once.

You should leave this house before they return. We all should flee."

"We could," Aduel shrugged. "But where would we go?"

"To Jericho!"

Aduel smiled. "After your statement to the palace guard, I think Jericho might be the first place they would look."

"Arabia, then."

"The friends I had in Arabia are long since gone," Aduel replied. "Murdered, most of them."

"Then here. Jerusalem. There are those who would take us in."

Aduel shook his head.

"Wherever we might go in Jerusalem, I assure you Herod would know of it before daybreak," he said. "His spies are a subtle thread woven throughout the fabric of the city. No, Edna, no. The night is too cold for futile misadventure. I think we shall remain here and enjoy the hearth."

The rekindled fire had overcome the chill that had pervaded the house, and on any other night it would have made the girl feel cozy, relaxed. But tonight she was too agitated to feel drowsy. She studied her uncle's face, impassive as he stared into the flames, lost in thought. It seemed heartless to rouse him, to remind him of the tumult that surrounded them, the danger. But she could not help herself.

"Will Herod send for you again?" she asked.

"Perhaps," Aduel replied. "But events seem to be moving quickly. Perhaps he will have other things to occupy him."

"What will you say to him if he does send for you?"

"I have no idea." Aduel's countenance radiated the tranquility of a man who had encountered many things over a long and varied life.

"Did you ever speak to him before, when you were in the court?" she pressed.

"Oh yes, many times. Although mostly Herod spoke to me."

"What did he say to you?"

"All manner of things, from the brilliant to the insane. Plans and schemes, plots and counterplots. If it was something especially unholy, I would try to employ some subtle stratagem to subvert it."

"So you did give him advice."

"In fact I did, from time to time, though in all the time I spent in his service I don't think he ever took it," Aduel smiled. "Although there was one instance..."

His voice trailed off for a moment, as if a forgotten memory had suddenly returned.

"Yes, once, in the matter of Cleopatra. He did take my advice in that case, and I believe that he was later quite glad of it."

"Cleopatra?" Joanna demanded. "What did you tell him?"

"Why, I told him not to murder her," Aduel said, with a wry smile. "He had quite decided that he would. He said it would be a favor to his friend Mark Antony, and that Antony would thank him for it. I advised him that Antony's response might be a great deal different than he imagined. At last he relented, but he left us guessing until the very end."

"Cleopatra!" Joanna murmured. "I've heard so many tales of her."

"Have you?" Her uncle smiled indulgently. "Well, perhaps I can tell you one or two more. Provided I survive this night."

"But Herod wouldn't really kill you, Uncle," Joanna said bravely. "Would he?"

"Hard to say," Aduel shrugged. "In all my years in Herod's

service, the one thing I learned is that I could never predict who would be killed and who would be spared. The more monstrous the murder, the more likely Herod was to approve it. I think that argues in my favor, does it not? An old, forgotten civil servant, long since pensioned off and never highly regarded to begin with, hardly merits torture and death, does he?"

The girl shook her head weakly, resolving to ask no more questions about Herod. She studied the fire, staring in silence as the flames methodically consumed all that they touched. By and by the fascination overwhelmed her.

"Tell me about him," she said.

"Tell you about whom? About Herod?"

"Yes. Tell me everything."

"Tell you everything," Aduel mused. "Do you know, child, how long I have been waiting to tell someone everything about Herod? Quite a long time! I thought it would be best to wait until he was gone from the scene. Fallen from the favor of Augustus, stripped of power. Dead of old age, if nothing else! But none of these things has come to pass, despite the prayers of a people, the hopes of a nation."

Aduel stirred the fire, arranging it again, moving the kindling this way and that. Joanna could see that he was again lost in thought. There was a long silence before he spoke.

"Perhaps I have waited too long. Perhaps I should begin, before my time runs out. Yes, I will begin. But as I go on, remember this: For the many things that may be said about Herod that are strange, cruel, and horrible, not all are such. He brought order to Judea, order from chaos, a chaos that had lasted a generation. He also brought sorrow, and the most unspeakable oppression.

"He is quite possibly the most gifted man of our time. He is also quite possibly the most wicked. And with that in mind—"

There was a noise in the courtyard. Joanna gasped. The knock at the door a moment later was loud and firm, but it was not the brutal pounding of the officer of the guard.

Irijah whimpered pathetically but did not move. Aduel rose silently from his chair.

"Perhaps my time has run out," he sighed. He signaled to Edna to answer the knock.

"Eyes down," he whispered.

"Should I go?" Joanna whispered fearfully as she quickly covered her head.

"No. They saw you here before. If they don't find you it will give them reason to search the house again. Now, eyes down. And keep them down until they have gone."

Edna took her time unbolting the door. Joanna did her best to follow her uncle's admonition, but she raised her gaze just enough to take in all that was happening. In the doorway was not a brutish officer of the guard, but a more sophisticated man dressed in the fine blue vestments of the palace elite. Behind him, in the courtyard, was the same troop of soldiers. Her uncle had vanished.

The man took a step forward, into the doorway.

"I am Nicolaus of Damascus, minister to His Majesty Herod, King of the Jews," he announced calmly. "I have come for Aduel of Sepphoris. I understand he has returned from Jericho this very hour."

Edna, overwhelmed, shook her head but said nothing. Nicolaus of Damascus smiled slightly.

"May I?" he asked.

Edna opened the door more widely. Nicolaus stepped inside and motioned for her to shut the door, which she gladly did.

"Ah, a roaring fire!" Nicolaus said cheerfully. "The perfect welcome for your master after his long journey."

The same slight smile remained upon his lips. He was clearly a man accustomed to navigating delicate circumstances.

"My—my master—" Edna began to stammer.

Nicolaus motioned her to be silent. He now raised his voice somewhat, speaking more loudly than necessary to be heard by the girl and the two servants.

"You see, although our friends of the palace guard were ready to set out for Jericho this very hour, His Majesty the King told them to return at once to this house. Their orders are to retrieve your master so that His Majesty can confer with him, or to retrieve his severed head on the end of a pike. I accompanied the guard in the hopes that I might help your master to make the wiser choice."

Joanna shuddered. Nicolaus seemed to have taken no notice of her, and she stole a searching gaze at him. His robes were the finest material, and he had an air of importance about him, not unlike the magistrates she had seen from time to time in Jericho. But this man was somehow more sophisticated than even the leaders of Jericho—and more dangerous. His eyes were not cruel, but nor were they kind, and she realized that they were the kind of eyes that take in everything at a glance.

"I do hope it will not be necessary for the soldiers to search the premises," Nicolaus announced.

There was a slight movement near the little nook in the corner. Again Aduel had appeared seemingly from nowhere.

"I am here," he said simply.

"Aduel." Nicolaus bowed slightly, not in the least surprised. "It has been many years."

"Only three," Aduel replied. "I had hoped it would be more."

Nicolaus ignored the insult.

"No doubt you thought that His Majesty had forgotten you," he said patiently, "but he still holds you in some regard. It was a rash act for you to refuse his summons."

"I did not refuse," Aduel shrugged.

"Of course," Nicolaus smiled. "You were on a journey from Jericho. I had forgotten."

"And now the soldiers have come back for me," Aduel said. "And strangely enough, you with them. Why?"

"Perhaps I have come to repay a debt," Nicolaus shrugged. "A debt to a man who stifled my haughty words and pulled me back from a rash act that would have meant destruction. Should I not repay such a debt?"

Aduel said nothing. Nicolaus leaned forward and spoke in a low tone.

"To refuse Herod again would be fatal."

"Undoubtedly," Aduel replied. "But why send me for me after all this time? You are his trusted advisor."

"Perhaps. But there is a difference between us." Nicolaus smiled his cynical smile. "I, and all of those like me, have always told Herod what he wants to hear, whereas you always told Herod the truth. And Herod, as mad as he is, still has wits enough to know which of those is more valuable in a crisis."

Aduel sighed a deep sigh.

"I will go," he said.

"No, Master, no!" Edna blurted. "Do not go!"

"I have no choice," Aduel said. "My heavy cloak, please."

"But—Herod!" Edna implored. "Do you not fear?"

"In the Lord I trust and shall not fear," Aduel replied. "What can flesh do to me?"

Her lip trembling, Edna fetched the cloak. Aduel took it from her, then took her hand in both of his.

"The girl is in your care now."

Edna nodded. Waiting near the door, Nicolaus seemed to notice Joanna for the first time.

"Why Aduel, who is this?" he asked. "Some relative of yours?"

"My niece. From Jericho."

"A comely young maiden," Nicolaus commented. "Is she betrothed?"

Aduel hesitated a moment. "Of course," he said.

"Interesting." Nicolaus seemed to make a note of it.

He opened the door. In the courtyard, the waiting soldiers snapped to attention. Moments later the clatter of pikes upon paving stones faded into the tumult of the street as the troop began its return to Herod's palace with Aduel in their midst.

Once again Edna shut the door and bolted it firmly. Only now did Irijah stir from his stupor.

"A curse is upon us!" he wailed. "A curse has fallen upon this house today!"

"Quiet, old fool!" Edna spat. But Irijah paid her no heed.

"Wise men from the East!" he moaned. "Magicians! Curse them and their magic! 'Messiah has come!' Bah! Rubbish! They've brought disaster with their talk. Oh, what will become of us? What will become of our master? And the young maid!"

Joanna stared at him, astonished at his sudden concern for her welfare.

"Oh yes, the course of your life has altered tonight," Irijah muttered, as he struggled up from the bench. "Up to this day all has been well with us, but the course of our lives has altered. It has altered for each of us, but most of all for you. Mark my word, you'll remember this night for the rest of your life."

He tottered away toward the back of his house, heading to the servants' quarters on the other side of the courtyard. Joanna made no response. She sat motionless, tears streaming down her face, the old manservant's malevolent prophecy ringing ominously in her ears. Her life, difficult enough in Jericho, had seemed to hang by a thread in the days since her widowed mother had died. And now that thread was about to snap: Her uncle—her last surviving relation, her only guardian and her final hope—taken away by Herod's soldiers! Why had her mother not told her the details of her uncle's connection to Herod? And why had her uncle told Nicolaus that she was betrothed when she was not? It was incomprehensible, disastrous. She tried to recite a psalm, to bravely proclaim triumph over fear, but the words would not come. Terror of Herod—his madness, his tortures, his murders—had seized her; catastrophe seemed inevitable. She sank deep into her chair, exhausted, as before her the fire in the hearth, fanned by the fresh draught from the courtyard, danced wildly.

Chapter 2

Joanna groaned and shifted in her chair, bargaining for a more comfortable position. She had fallen asleep in front of the blazing hearth, but now the fire had burned itself out. Aduel's house was dark, and still. She peered into the shadows, trying to make out her surroundings, but in the faint glow of the dying embers everything was gloomy and indistinct. She closed her eyes and pulled the folds of her mantle more tightly around her, hoping to fall asleep again, but it was no use. She had awakened enough to remember where she was—and why.

A room had been prepared for her—a musty pantry adjoining the kitchen, in which items had been shifted and stacked to make room for a narrow bed. She knew the house well enough to find her way there, but whether she could do so without upsetting something in the dark was a different matter. She clambered out of the chair and groped her way to the basket of candles near the door, submerging one in the ashes of the hearth until it lit.

The flame flickered and grew, bathing the room in golden light. She squinted as her eyes adjusted. The window that looked out to the street had been shuttered, but nothing else had changed. On one side of the window was a low table, surrounded by cushions; on the other was the bottom of the stone stairway that led to Aduel's chamber on the upper floor. In the opposite corner, farthest from the street, a low doorway opened to the little kitchen at the back of the house.

The girl made her way toward this, then stopped. By now she was fully awake—and curious. When her uncle had appeared so unexpectedly earlier that night, it had not been in this doorway, but instead in a little nook in the other corner, where the stone staircase reached its highest point. She reasoned that there was another door there—a door that she had not noticed before. She made her way carefully along the wall until she reached the nook.

There was no door, nor even the hint of one.

Joanna stared, puzzled. Absently she ran her fingers along the wall. It was a mystery, this little nook with no apparent purpose, but not one that needed to be solved in the middle of the night. As she was about to turn away her fingers encountered a tiny gap between two stones. Holding the candle close to the wall, she discovered that the gap was actually a seam that ran from the top of the wall to the bottom. Instinctively she pushed against it—and gasped as the wall silently gave way. Before her was a narrow door, partially obscured by a tapestry and cleverly disguised to match the masonry.

She thrust the candle into the opening and peered inside. Before her, at a right angle to the door, a secret stairway descended, mirroring the stairway above her head. Her heart beat faster as she stepped through the doorway, holding the candle before her, and crept down the stairs.

On the bottom step she stopped. Before her was a room, not much bigger than a closet, whose existence she had not suspected. A single glance told her that there was nothing intrinsically fascinating about it, but still there was the thrill of a secret place—especially now, late at night, as she stood upon the threshold alone. Before her was a small, square table with a sturdy wooden stool in front of it. Its smooth, polished surface held candles, ink, a roll of blank papyrus, and several styli, and she recognized it at once as a simple writing desk. Above it, covering the breadth of the wall, were three broad wooden shelves, uniformly subdivided into compartments that were filled with dozens of papyrus scrolls, neatly stacked. To the side, high in the adjoining stone wall that comprised the side of the house, was a horizontal slit that served as a window. A quick calculation told her that it opened to the outside just above the level of the street, where it would not attract attention. It was all so clandestine—and yet would have been all too obvious to anyone who stopped to look for it.

Joanna's eyes glittered as they roamed over the scrolls. There were dozens of them; she had never seen such an extensive collection. She set her candle on the table and selected one of the largest, holding it close to the light as she unrolled it a little way:

The vision received by Isaiah son of Amoz concerning Judah and Jerusalem.

She set it aside and opened another:

The proverbs of Solomon son of David, King of Israel, by which men will come to wisdom and instruction.

She knew that these were scriptures—books that were familiar to her, though she had never read more than a few lines of them. Before he had been taken by the pestilence, her brother, like many ambitious boys, had received instruction in the basics of literacy. Late at night, by the light of a candle, he had taught Joanna much of what he had learned. They had told no one—not even their mother—for there were many in Jericho, and elsewhere in Judea, who held that to teach a girl to read was a waste of time, or worse.

Intrigued, she selected another scroll from a different section of the shelf. This scroll was shorter, with smaller writing that was more precise. She squinted to make out the words in the flickering light of the candle:

Herod: A Secret History, by Aduel of Sepphoris. Book the First.

Joanna's mouth dropped open. A day earlier she would have stated with certainty that this was a different Aduel of Sepphoris, that her quiet old uncle could have nothing to do with any secret history of Herod. Now she was not so sure. Quickly she closed the scroll and replaced it on the shelf along with the other two she had removed, wiping her hand on her sleeve as if she had touched something dangerous. Because it was something dangerous. She understood little about Herod and his network of spies, but she knew that to possess such a scroll might be considered a crime, possibly treason.

She glanced nervously at the narrow window slit high in the wall. Was the night beginning to give way to the first faint rays of the new day? She could not tell, but it didn't matter. She should not be here. Her uncle must never find out that she knew of his secret chamber—and especially that she knew of the secret history, no matter who had written it. She glanced about to make sure that everything was just as she had found it.

And then she stopped. Her gaze had come to rest on the writing materials on the corner of the table. Fascinated, she reached for one of the styli and slowly rotated the slender, sharpened sliver of reed between her fingers. She had never put ink to papyrus. Tolerant enough of her progress with reading, her brother had drawn the line with writing. The ink was too difficult to mix correctly, he told her, the papyrus too precious. And so she had watched in silent envy as he had traced out the letters of his rudimentary lessons—roughly, at first, but then with increasing confidence and precision. What was it like to write your own words, with real papyrus and real ink?

She glanced at the window again. Surely there was enough time for a single quick experiment with the stylus. She had no illusion that she could write words, or even a single character. But how thrilling it would be to write anything—even to trace a meaningless line or curlicue! Hesitantly she reached for the inkpot and removed the lid, then rolled out a tiny section of the blank papyrus. Her hand trembled a little as she prepared to slice off a section with the scribe's knife she had found on the table. It occurred to her that she was taking the papyrus without permission, but this hardly seemed worth worrying about, for she would be removing a sliver so slender that it would never be missed.

A moment later the deed was done. It was a clean cut and she relaxed a little. But the papyrus scroll, which she had stretched out for the operation, unexpectedly rolled up on her hand. Startled, she batted it back—and upset the little ceramic inkpot.

Joanna gasped. She set the inkpot upright but it was too late. Some of the ink had spilled onto the table—and a small bit had leaked into the tight coils of the papyrus scroll. Impulsively she blotted the puddle with her bare hand, leaving her fingers a sticky, blackened mess. A stain remained where the puddle had been. She moistened it with saliva and rubbed it with the sliver of papyrus she had cut. This helped, but the stain remained. She scanned the table, hoping to find other stains that would make this one less egregious, but its surface was immaculate.

Joanna's heart pounded. It seemed that no amount of rubbing would completely remove the stain on the table. She glanced at the window again. Now there could be no question: daybreak was near. Frantically she put everything back where it belonged. But the scroll of blank papyrus had been ruined, an inky blot on each successive coil. And what of her hand? There were rags in the pantry, where her bed was located, but they would wipe away only the worst of the mess. That stain would remain, possibly for days. How would she explain it?

She hurried up the secret stairway and stepped from behind the tapestry back into the little nook, shutting the door noiselessly behind her. Only a few moments more and she would be safely in the pantry, with time to concoct a plan.

But as she stepped from the nook, the door to the courtyard opened. It was Edna, bringing in fresh kindling for the hearth. Startled, the old woman's gaze travelled from Joanna's candle to her face, then back down to the inky hand clutching the crumpled wad of blank papyrus. After an initial expression of astonishment, her face hardened to an angry glare.

"What are you doing there, maid?" she demanded. "Where have you been?"

Chapter 3

Joanna stared, speechless. It was an innocent misadventure, hardly the stuff of criminal intent, but she was at a loss how to explain herself.

"Do you think you be free to do anything you like?" Edna dropped the firewood with a clatter and crossed the room, regarding Joanna's inky hand with disgust. "Prying into the master's private quarters, and using his materials just as you pleased? Did you have his permission for that? No, I hardly think so. But I suppose to you it doesn't matter, with him marched off to stand before Herod and likely never to return."

"No!" Joanna protested. "I was only—it was just—it was just that I—I woke up and—"

She stopped suddenly. Edna had not had time to bolt the door, and it had opened again. In the doorway, alone, stood her uncle.

"Uncle Aduel!" she cried.

The two women hurried across the room, their confrontation forgotten.

"Goodness, child, goodness!" Aduel exclaimed softly, as Joanna embraced him with one hand. "You look as though you've seen a ghost."

"Perhaps she thought she had," Edna said tearfully. The old housekeeper clutched Aduel's arm, as if to make sure of it herself. "When the soldiers came again, we thought we had seen the last of you. And then Irijah, with all his talk of curses and doom—"

"Irijah!" Aduel chuckled. "When did you begin listening to Irijah, Edna?"

Edna smiled through her tears.

"Yes, despite Irijah's prediction of doom I have lived to see another sunrise," Aduel said, "and have returned in the flesh."

"And no one with you?" Edna asked fearfully. "No soldiers? No Nicolaus of Damascus?"

"No soldiers and no Nicolaus of Damascus," Aduel confirmed cheerfully. "No, I believe I am finished with the affairs of the palace, this time for good."

"But what did they want?" Joanna demanded. "Why did Herod send for you?"

"It was as Edna surmised," Aduel replied. "He wanted my counsel."

"And?" Edna pressed.

"I gave it to him," Aduel said. "I affirmed the course of action that they had already decided upon. Then I added one small caveat which immediately disarranged all their plans."

He grinned impishly.

"And now, I would like to sit," Aduel added. "I have been standing before Herod much of the night. Dear me, it looks as if the fire has completely gone out. And you, child. It seems you've had a nighttime encounter with my inkpot."

Joanna looked down, her cheeks burning. She felt her tears rising but she fought them back. She would not try to conjure his sympathy with tears. Better to take the tongue-lashing and whatever other punishment was due. But what would that be? She did not know what to expect. Her uncle seemed a gentle man, but she did not know him well. During their journey from Jericho he had spoken little. He often seemed lost in his own thoughts.

Thankfully, on this occasion punishment did not seem to be among them.

"Go, child, go," he said. "Clean yourself up. You'll ruin your clothes if you aren't careful."

"Uncle Aduel?"

"Yes, child."

"I spilled ink on your writing table, too."

"Did you? Hmmm."

Aduel shrugged and shooed her away. By the time she returned he had rekindled the fire and made himself comfortable in one of the chairs. He motioned her to sit, then lapsed into his usual silence. Joanna waited for what she considered to be a respectful amount of time before speaking.

"What were Herod's plans?" she prompted. "And what did you do to disarrange them?"

"Herod's plans were simple," Aduel responded. "He had called in the entire religious leadership of the nation to tell him where the Messiah could be found. And cursed traitors to the faith, they told him! Vipers! To betray their own Messiah to please a mad king! They told him that Scripture foretold that the Messiah would be born in Bethlehem, less than two hours' march from here. After that, the course of action became obvious. Herod's army would descend upon Bethlehem at the break of day and slaughter every single inhabitant of the town, and all in the surrounding area. What could be simpler? But still, Herod was uneasy. Something was nagging at him, and he couldn't tell what it was. And none of his advisors could tell him, or perhaps none would. That is why he called for me. He remembered me from long ago, saying things that others would not."

"And of course you told him not to do it," the girl said confidently.

"No, I fully agreed with the plan," Aduel smiled. "Much to the surprise of all who remembered me, especially Nicolaus of Damascus. And that was that, except for one small detail."

"What detail?"

"I observed that in the current state of things, Herod would need to make sure that the Jerusalem rabble did not follow the soldiers in search of this Messiah," Aduel said. "I pointed out that for the army to conduct such a slaughter in full view of the populace would have led to a revolt, one that Herod and his army might not have survived.

"So, after much discussion, an alternate plan was adopted. Herod will secretly summon the magicians from the East, and request that they find this Messiah and then come back and notify him of His exact location. Herod will tell the magicians that he wants to worship the Messiah, to put their minds at ease. Then a small, precise military operation, one that will attract no notice, will suffice to end the life of this Messiah and his immediate family, thus confirming Herod and his descendants on the throne."

"Then how did that help?" Joanna wondered. "Will not the Messiah be murdered either way?"

"Perhaps," Aduel shrugged. "If the men from the East do as Herod requests, then certainly the Messiah will be murdered, and my efforts will have come to nothing. But I like to think that perhaps I have purchased for this Messiah, if he indeed exists, a bit of time to escape."

"It seems a slim hope," commented Edna, who had returned from the kitchen to a place near the hearth.

"Slim indeed," Aduel agreed. "But better than none. The

will of the Lord will be done, Edna. Of that you may be sure."

Edna nodded and left the room. Joanna waited a few moments before venturing a request.

"Uncle," she began.

"Yes?"

"Last night you said that Herod was the most wicked man of our time."

"I did say that. But I also said he was possibly the most gifted. Which is somewhat less memorable, I suppose."

The girl let this remark pass.

"You said you would tell me the story of how he got that way," she continued.

"Yes, I suppose that I said that as well."

"Then perhaps..."

"Perhaps what, my child?"

"Perhaps tonight you can tell me the story of Herod."

Aduel chuckled.

"Tonight? It will take more than one night to tell you the story of Herod," he said.

"Then perhaps you could begin tonight."

Aduel was silent for several moments. He seemed to be pondering something. Then he peered at the girl.

"Tell me, my child," he said. "Tell me. Do you know how to read?"

Joanna looked down.

"No."

Her uncle looked at her intently.

"Not even a little?" he asked.

Joanna looked up again, searching his face.

"Maybe a little," she admitted.

"I thought as much," Aduel nodded.

"My brother was learning to read the Scripture," Joanna explained quickly, as if making excuse for herself. "He taught me the letters, and many of the words. He showed me at night, by candlelight, so no one would know."

"Of course," Aduel nodded. It was some time before he spoke again:

"Would you care to complete your education?"

"My education?"

"Your reading," her uncle explained. "Would you like to continue to learn? Not just the letters and the simple words, but all of it. Our language is complex, but it is a thing of great beauty. I should like to teach it to you."

"But I'm not supposed to—"

Joanna stopped abruptly.

"Not supposed to what?" her uncle prodded. "Not supposed to read?"

Joanna shrugged.

"Who says that?"

"It says in the Scripture that the sons should be taught," Joanna offered weakly.

"Yes. 'Do not forget the things you have seen, and do not let them pass from your minds as long as you live, but teach them to your sons and your sons' sons.' But where does it say that the daughters should not be taught? Does it say that in the Scripture?"

"I don't know."

"It does not. The great scribe Ezra read the Law to both the men and the women of Jerusalem after they had forgotten it for so long. No, the prohibition you speak of is a tradition promulgated by the Pharisees. And search as you might throughout Judea and Galilee together, you will never find a greater collection of more flatulent fools."

Relieved, Joanna could not suppress a smile.

"Scripture isn't enough for a good Pharisee," grumbled her uncle. "He must add his own rules, and rules on top of rules, each more ridiculous than the last."

"But why?"

"Because the Pharisees think the favor of the Lord comes from following rules. And the more you follow, the more favor you will find. Or so they seem to believe. Thus they continue to add rules, the better to find favor."

Joanna was confused. The favor of the Lord was a vague and uncertain thing to her, but had she been asked to summarize it, her response would have been rather similar to the philosophy her uncle had just described.

"But—don't you believe that?" she ventured.

"The laws of the Lord are the laws we must follow," Aduel said. "Not the precepts of men."

Joanna nodded. What had seemed an impenetrable mystery a moment ago was suddenly obvious. She leaned back in her chair. She would learn to read Scripture, she decided. She would learn to find such answers for herself.

"I would like to complete my education," she said.

"Then we have much work to do," her uncle smiled. "We'll get started at once."

"But Uncle, you must be weary."

"I should be, but strangely I am not," Aduel responded. "Rather, I am invigorated. I have been given new purpose. I will tell you the story of Herod, as I promised last night. I will also teach you to read. And I will accomplish both at the same time. Come along, then."

He got up and led her to the little nook, pushing open the

concealed door.

"No need to initiate you to the mysteries of the house, since you have initiated yourself already," he commented dryly as they descended the steps.

"This is where you were when the soldiers came," Joanna said.

Aduel nodded.

"But how did they not find you?"

"They were not clever enough to look," Aduel shrugged. "Nicolaus of Damascus would have found me in a minute."

"You heard his voice, so you came out."

"Yes. He knew I was in the house. There was no use hiding from him."

"But how did he know?"

"Nicolaus is the kind of man who knows things without being told," Aduel said. "The kind of man it's best to be wary of. But that is for another time."

They had reached the bottom of the stairs. Aduel glanced at the stain on the table but said nothing.

"For the present you have come for a different purpose," he continued. "You have come to hear the story of Herod. Although...hmm. It seems that you may have already begun."

Joanna's mouth dropped open as he selected a scroll from the shelf.

"How—how did you know?" she stammered.

"Because this book belongs on this shelf, and these two belong over here."

"I'm sorry, Uncle. From now on I'll ask permission."

"From now on you will not have to ask. I would like for you to read these books, and learn."

"Then I have permission?"

"You have permission, today and tomorrow and forever." Aduel smiled a wry smile. "For who knows how long I will be here to grant permission."

Joanna was about to contest this morbid sentiment, but Aduel interrupted her by handing her the scroll.

"That story begins here," he said. "As you already know."

"I only read the first line," Joanna protested.

"This time we'll go a little further, if the Lord is willing."

Hesitantly Joanna unrolled the first part of the scroll. The inside was covered in small, precise lettering arranged in a series of neat, uniform panels each about as wide as her hand.

"Did you write this?" she asked.

Her uncle nodded.

"It's beautiful," she said.

"As an official of the royal court, one makes a habit of writing beautifully," Aduel said. "Or one learns to shovel the stables. Let's see what you can make of it. Start here."

He pointed to a paragraph just below the introductory line. Joanna turned to make better use of the daylight filtering through the window slit.

"'The story of Herod begins with two brothers...'", she began haltingly. She stopped.

"Princes," her uncle prompted.

"'...princes of Judea,'" the girl continued, "'whose...'"

"Struggle."

"'...whose struggle for the...throne...'"

"Involved."

"'...whose struggle for the throne involved the Romans in the affairs of our nation in a way that neither of them could have...foreseen?'"

"Correct. 'Foreseen,' Aduel said. "Very good. Pray,

continue."

"'I will not dwell upon the details of this struggle, for it was before the time of Herod. But I will describe it briefly, for it led...'"

"Indirectly."

"'It led, indirectly, to Herod's...'"

"Control."

"'control and...'"

"Domination."

"'control and domination of our nation.'"

Joanna looked up from the manuscript, fatigued. It had taken her nearly five minutes to read three sentences.

"I'm sorry, Uncle," she apologized. "I wish I knew more."

"Nonsense. You read far better than I expected," Aduel said. "You clearly comprehend the grammar, and many of the difficult words are already familiar to you. Your brother taught you well. Continue."

Joanna unfurled the scroll to its full length, looking dubiously at the panels of tiny lettering that covered it, then at the dozens of scrolls that remained on the shelf.

"Are there more?" she asked.

"Yes, many more," Aduel said. There was more than a hint of pride in his voice.

"All of these scrolls contain the story of Herod?" Joanna pressed.

"Not all of them," Aduel replied. "Some are written by others; I keep them for my own study and enjoyment. Many are Scripture. But many of them contain the history I have written."

Joanna took a deep breath, realizing that the enterprise she had embarked upon was far more daunting than she had thought.

"Perhaps I should help Edna with the housework," she suggested. "Before she grows tired."

"Edna has managed the housework for many years without growing tired."

"But with Irijah on his sickbed—"

"Presently we shall roust Irijah from his sickbed and set him back on his feet, however unwilling those feet may be," Aduel interrupted. "Now you shall read."

Joanna was dismayed. There was an insistence in her uncle's voice that she had not expected. She ran her gaze along the scroll, back to the place she had left off. The neat panels of tiny letters, so intriguing a few minutes ago, now seemed an impenetrable wall. Suddenly overwhelmed by the events of the previous night, she felt her eyes blur. She wiped them quickly with her sleeve, mortified at the thought that an errant teardrop might smudge even one of the precisely penned characters.

"Tears," Aduel said, surprised. "Are they tears of intimidation or tears of defeat?"

"I don't know," Joanna sniffed. "I don't know."

Aduel waited until her frustration had subsided.

"Perhaps would be best to pursue this in a different manner," he said at last. He held out his hand for the scroll. Joanna rolled it up and held it out to him, only half unwillingly.

"I will read the entire scroll, from beginning to end, answering any questions that you might have," Aduel said. "Then I will give it to you, to study as diligently as you think fit, and again I will answer any questions you might have. Any word, any phrase, any expression that you do not understand,

I will explain to you. When you feel you are ready, you will read it back to me, from beginning to end."

"But what if I can't read it back to you?" Joanna fretted.

"Then I shall read it again, in its entirety, and we will repeat the process."

"But if we do it over and over and I still can't read it back to you, what will happen then?"

"Then you can help Edna with the housework," Aduel said curtly. "Or, if you prefer, you can help her now."

Joanna could tell that her uncle was becoming exasperated. She dreaded the possibility of failing him. Perhaps it would be better for her to live simply, to forget the fraught business of literacy. After all, no one would expect it of her. Some might even despise her for it.

But after a few moments she had mastered her fear.

"No," she said quietly. "I'm ready."

Aduel had resumed his placid demeanor. He unrolled the manuscript.

"I shall read from the beginning," he said. "Are you listening?"

Joanna nodded.

"Very well. Herod: A Secret History, by Aduel of Sepphoris. Book the First."

The story of Herod begins with two princes of Judea whose struggle for the throne involved the Romans in the affairs of our nation in a way that neither of them could have foreseen. I will not dwell upon the details of this struggle, for it was before the time of Herod. But I will describe it briefly, for it led, indirectly, to Herod's control and domination of our nation.

The two princes were the sons of Queen Alexandra, a pious

woman who had proven most capable in uniting Judea and strengthening its army. In outlook and temperament these two could not have been more different. The elder, Hyrcanus, was quiet, bashful, and indecisive, seemingly unable to master the intricacies of government. By contrast, the younger, Aristobulus, was bold, impulsive, charismatic—a natural leader of men. But Alexandra perceived that Aristobulus could be impetuous, and fearing that he might in some way jeopardize the authority of the royal family that had ruled Judea for nearly a hundred years, she gave him few official duties. Hyrcanus, on the other hand, she appointed high priest, which at that time was a largely ceremonial role that was within his capabilities.

After she had reigned for nine years, Queen Alexandra became dangerously ill. When she realized that her death was imminent she took a decisive step, naming Hyrcanus as her successor to the throne. Aristobulus slipped away from the palace that very night, telling none but his wife what he intended. At first Alexandra assumed that there was nothing amiss, but soon came reports that Aristobulus and his supporters were taking control of the military installations throughout Judea, first one and then another. Within half a month he had gotten under his control twenty-two fortresses throughout the country, and it was evident to all that he intended to declare himself king, which he very shortly did.

It was obvious that war was imminent. The loyalty of the people, from the aristocracy to the common rabble, was divided between the two brothers. Those who preferred Hyrcanus pointed out that as the elder son he was the rightful heir to the throne and in addition had been explicitly chosen by Alexandra. Those who preferred Aristobulus responded that he was the natural leader, who had over the years of Alexandra's reign taken great pains to cultivate goodwill and loyalty among many of the leading citizens.

The two sides with their respective armies confronted each other near Jericho, but as the battle was joined many of Hyrcanus's soldiers deserted to Aristobulus. Hyrcanus fled back to Jerusalem, where he took refuge in the citadel that adjoined the Temple. In that same citadel were the wife and children of Aristobulus, who had been imprisoned there when Aristobulus declared himself king. Before any sort of siege could begin in earnest, Hyrcanus sent messengers to Aristobulus to negotiate. Soon everything was settled. Hyrcanus would recognize Aristobulus as the legitimate king of Judea, and would retire to a life of private luxury, free from the cares of government, in Jerusalem. The brothers met in the Temple and swore to this agreement, giving each other their right hands and embracing in front of the multitude. After that, they departed: Aristobulus to the palace, and Hyrcanus to the house of Aristobulus, which would now become the house of Hyrcanus, a private citizen. And with that there was peace within the house of Asamoneus, which had endured for nearly a hundred years. Moreover, there was peace throughout the land of Judea, and it seemed that this peace might endure for generations to come.

"Thus ends Book the First."

Aduel had come to the end of the scroll. He glanced at the girl.

"So there was no war?" she asked incredulously.

"No war," Aduel replied.

"Not even a siege?" Joanna insisted. "None of the hostages' blood was spilled?"

"Not a drop."

"The Lord be praised!" Joanna exclaimed. "What virtuous men! To truly act like brothers! To put their families, their nation, above their own selfish ambitions! Oh, I do hope they led long and happy lives after this!"

Aduel said nothing.

"Did they?" Joanna demanded.

"They might have," Aduel sighed. "They so easily might have."

"But they didn't, did they?" Joanna asked, crestfallen.

"No."

"But why?"

"You know the story of the serpent in the garden, do you not?" Aduel began.

"It was Herod, wasn't it?" Joanna cried. "It was Herod, I know it! Oh, I hate him! I hate Herod! I hate him!"

"Hush, child, hush!" There was alarm in Aduel's voice as he glanced up at the narrow window. "You must speak quietly when you say such things. It was not Herod, at least not at first. But it will not be long until he enters the story. You will meet him in the next book."

Aduel took his time rolling up the scroll.

"But first," he said with a wry smile, "you must learn to read this one."

Caught up in her excitement, Joanna was brought short by this reminder. But she hesitated only a moment.

"I will learn to read it," she said resolutely. "When should I start?"

"Whenever you like."

"I shall start now."

"Very well."

Aduel handed her the scroll. He got up from the stool and began to shuffle, somewhat stiffly, toward the stairway. The girl's voice arrested him.

"Uncle Aduel?"

"Yes?"

"You told Nicolaus of Damascus..."

Her voice trailed off.

"I told Nicolaus of Damascus that you were betrothed," Aduel said, turning to face her.

Joanna nodded.

"But you are not," Aduel added.

Joanna shook her head.

"So why did I tell him that you were betrothed when you are not? Is that what you would like to know?"

Joanna nodded again.

"Because Jerusalem is not like Jericho," Aduel said. "The influences of Greece and Rome are strong here. The most disgraceful political maneuvering takes place daily, hourly. Lives are traded for the smallest consideration. In the wrong situation, a comely maiden who is not betrothed could easily become a bargaining chip, a favor."

Joanna's face had clouded as she began to understand her uncle's meaning.

"But Nicolaus could find out, could he not?" she worried. "He could find out that I am not truly betrothed."

"He could," Aduel admitted. "Though not right away. He will assume that you are betrothed to a young man in Jericho. If he believed my statement in the first place, that is. I must confess that I hesitated a bit before answering him."

"But if I truly were betrothed, then he could do nothing. Is that correct?"

"There are some men who might try to interfere with a betrothal, but Nicolaus would not think it worth the trouble. He is wily and morally malleable, but he does have his limits."

"Then I should be betrothed, as quickly as possible,"

Joanna concluded.

Her uncle regarded her with surprise.

"Do you wish to be betrothed?" he asked.

"I think that I do," Joanna said. "Because then I would know…"

Her voice trailed off.

"Because then you would know your future," her uncle said. "At least more of it than you know now, which is all uncertainty."

"Yes," Joanna said. "But I also think that I do not, because…"

"Because when a husband is chosen for a maiden, it may not be a husband she wants," Aduel said. "It is a peculiar arrangement, is it not, that the maiden should have no voice in her betrothal? And often not the young man either. Their lives together: chosen for them, often arranged when they are children! Yes, it is a peculiar way of doing things, decidedly imperfect. But, my child, you must consider this: There are so many things that are uncertain in life, so few things that are promised. In this one thing, then, our people choose certainty and stability."

"But it seems such an important thing," Joanna objected.

Aduel considered this.

"I shall make inquiries," he said. "Discreetly, of course. But I must tell you plainly: I am not a man of means. What little I can offer for a dowry is most inconsequential. It would not merit the consideration of a man of rank or influence."

"I care nothing for rank or influence," Joanna declared. "Only that I can have a man of wisdom and honor."

"My child, may the Lord bless you with such a man!" Aduel exclaimed. "You yourself have clearly been blessed with these things.”

His lip trembled. It was the first time the girl had observed in him any emotion other than quiet amusement.

“I shall see what can be done about a betrothal,” he said presently. “And, if possible, I shall contrive a way for you to have some say in the matter. Although I confess that I do not know how I might accomplish that. But I will try.”

“Thank you, Uncle.”

“Children are a reward from the Lord,” Aduel murmured. “A reward that I have never received, until now. You are my child, now, and I will do all that I can for you.”

He cleared his throat and pointed to the stool.

“Now,” he said, “you have work to do. Sit.”

“But should I not stand as I read?” Joanna asked.

“You honor me, child,” Aduel chuckled, regaining his usual composure. “But this is hardly a sacred text. No need to weary yourself standing. You have much work before you. Now sit. Read.”

Chapter 4

It was nearly a month before the girl was proficient enough in the Hebrew language to read the first book of Aduel's history without grinding to a halt. It had been tedious, difficult work, but more often than not Aduel had been at her elbow with hints and explanations. For the times that he was not there he had instructed her to write out the unknown words and incomprehensible phrases for him to review, and he was only mildly surprised to learn that she had never put ink to paper. He instructed her on the use of the stylus and gave her the spoiled scroll of blank papyrus to practice. After many days she had begun to master it. It was not the precise, beautiful calligraphy of a trained scribe, but it was legible.

Her sixth attempt at reading the scroll from beginning to end was a laborious effort that consumed an entire afternoon, but it proceeded with only a few interruptions. When she had finished, she closed the scroll carefully and set it on the desk before her uncle, who sat impassively on the stool.

"Tomorrow," she said with an exhausted sigh.

"Tomorrow?" Aduel asked. "What will happen tomorrow?"

"Tomorrow I will read it perfectly."

"Tomorrow you will not read it at all."

The girl peered at her uncle, crestfallen and a little fearful. "But why?" she asked.

"Because tomorrow you will be reading Book the Second," Aduel smiled.

"Oh, Uncle!" Joanna clapped for joy. "Are you certain? Maybe we shouldn't be so quick about it. I want to understand the first book perfectly."

"The way to understand the first book perfectly is by studying the second," Aduel replied. "Tomorrow when I read the second book much of it will already be familiar to you. You will recognize words and phrases that you did not know before. You will see the words and letters in your mind."

"Oh, Uncle," pressed the girl, swept up in the excitement of it. "Do you think you could..."

"Do I think I could what, child?"

"Do you think you could read it now?"

"Now?" Aduel was taken aback. "But the day is almost gone."

"But you read so quickly and so well," Joanna coaxed. "You can finish before the light fails. And if darkness falls we can always light the lamp."

"You want to find out what happened, don't you?" Aduel chuckled.

"Of course!" Joanna exclaimed.

She paused.

"Although in some ways I don't," she reflected. "It all seemed to have been settled so perfectly. Each brother got what he really wanted, what suited him best. And yet somehow it all went awry."

"This has been the history of mankind from the very beginning," Aduel commented.

"You did say there was a serpent," Joanna recalled.

"Yes."

"But that it wasn't Herod."

"Correct."

"Who was it, then?"

"The serpent's name was Antipater," Aduel said. "The father of Herod. Let us find out more about him."

Aduel returned the first book of his history to the shelf and selected another, motioning Joanna to take his place. The girl settled herself on the stool, leaning back slightly against the wall, making herself comfortable for that most satisfying of luxuries, the first reading of a new book. Aduel cleared his throat:

"Herod: A Secret History, by Aduel of Sepphoris. Book the Second."

The solemn peace agreed upon by Hyrcanus and Aristobulus in the Temple did not endure for long. During their conflict, the nation of Judea, and especially the city of Jerusalem, had split into rival factions, some taking sides with one brother and some with the other. While most were content to put aside these differences and to unify again under the kingship of Aristobulus, there was one who was not content. This one was Antipater, a wealthy and influential man from the land of Edom, which bordered Judea on the southeast.

"Antipater was an Edomite?" Joanna blurted.

Aduel's eyes snapped up from the scroll so suddenly that Joanna dropped her gaze. It was hard to tell which of them had been more startled by her interruption.

"Yes, Antipater was an Edomite, or what the Greeks call an Idumean," Aduel said, a little irritably.

"But didn't you say that he was Herod's father?"

"Yes, of course."

"Was Herod's mother an Edomite as well?"

"No, Arabian."

"Then Judea is ruled by a foreigner!" Joanna exclaimed.

"Judea is indeed ruled by a foreigner," Aduel confirmed. "Shall I continue?"

The girl nodded quickly, and Aduel resumed.

Antipater had served as Queen Alexandra's military governor for the territory of Edom, and thus he sided with Hyrcanus, the queen's chosen heir, when it appeared that a civil war was imminent. When war was averted by the compromise in the Temple, Antipater immediately set about to shatter the peace for his own purposes. He began by trying to stir up discontent with the settlement among the leading citizens who supported Hyrcanus. But when that led nowhere, he turned to Hyrcanus himself, trying to convince Hyrcanus that Aristobulus intended to kill him. At first Hyrcanus, being of mild temperament and enjoying life as a private citizen, brushed aside these claims. But Antipater's warnings were ingenious, relentless, and terrifying, and soon Hyrcanus was persuaded that his life was in danger. By night he fled Jerusalem, seeking asylum with the king of Arabia, a special friend of Antipater's.

But this was just the beginning of Antipater's scheming. Next he turned his efforts to the king of Arabia, imploring him to make war upon Aristobulus on behalf of Hyrcanus. At first, the king of Arabia, like Hyrcanus before him, brushed aside these entreaties. But Antipater persisted, and in time the king of Arabia sent forth an army of horsemen and foot soldiers numbering fifty thousand. With the forces of Judea divided, Aristobulus was decisively defeated and most of his supporters defected. He quickly retreated to the Temple in Jerusalem and was besieged there by his opponents.

"It's the exact opposite of what happened before!" Joanna interjected.

It was the second time she had impulsively interrupted her uncle's narration, and once again he peered at her over the scroll. But this time he was less peevish.

"You seem to be paying attention," he said.

"Of course I'm paying attention, Uncle."

"Good. I write of Hyrcanus, Aristobulus, Antipater, and the Romans because they play a part in this story. It would take a dozen more books to record all the twists of fate that befell the brothers and the surviving remnants of their royal line as Herod rose to power. As it is, we will meet the usurper very shortly."

The girl nodded. Although curious about the details of world events, she was thankful that the story of Herod would not require her to parse a dozen additional books about them.

Aduel lifted the scroll and continued:

Thus began a long series of negotiations with the Romans, who had just conquered Armenia and had come into our region with dreams of further conquest. Each brother sent emissaries to the Roman commander with accusations and claims, arguments and counterclaims—and with bribes. Three hundred talents of gold, four hundred talents of gold, a fabulous crown worth five hundred talents of gold! In the end it was Hyrcanus who prevailed—not so much because his bribery was superior to that of Aristobulus, but because Aristobulus and his followers offended the Romans with too much finery and too little flattery. The Roman army captured Jerusalem and took Aristobulus and his family back to Rome as captives, leaving Hyrcanus the victor. After more years of turmoil,

Antipater ingratiated himself with the great Julius Caesar, now dictator of the entire Roman world, and was appointed procurator of Judea and the surrounding area. Nominally he was under the authority of Hyrcanus, who ruled as ethnarch, a designation of royalty less sweeping than king, but the real power lay with Antipater. And so it was that through the selfish strategies of one man, Antipater, the nation of Judea came under the dominion of Rome.

Antipater married the daughter of an Arabian noble and she bore him five children: four sons and a daughter. In time, each of these children would play a part in the history of our nation. In the remaining books of this history we shall encounter each of these offspring and learn the part that they played, although naturally the leading role will belong to Herod, who rose to become the most powerful, the most terrifying, and the most tormented of them all.

Aduel rolled up the scroll.

"And thus concludes Book the Second," he said.

"That's all?" Joanna objected. "That's the end of Book the Second?"

"It's one of the shorter books in the history," Aduel shrugged. "That is why I agreed to attempt it today. As it is, there was barely enough time to read to the end."

For the first time the girl noticed that the light in the room had faded to a faint gray glow.

"But what of the two brothers?" she insisted. "Will we hear of them again?"

"Oh yes," Aduel assured her. "Each of them will play a part in the story of Herod, as will their children and grandchildren and even their great-grandchildren. That is why I took pains to introduce them to you. Although I must warn you that the parts they play will not be happy ones."

"Aristobulus will be the first to die," Joanna predicted. "He and his family will be executed in Rome."

"Aristobulus was the first to die," Aduel confirmed. "But not in Rome. In fact, after some years in Rome, Aristobulus gained the favor of Julius Caesar, who sent him back to Judea with two legions at his command to take control of Judea."

"But in the text you said it was Antipater who gained the favor of Julius Caesar," Joanna objected.

"In the text it was indeed Antipater who gained the favor of Julius Caesar," Aduel confirmed. "But only after Aristobulus had been poisoned. Antipater, who had been opposing Caesar, then switched sides."

"But who poisoned Aristobulus?" Joanna demanded.

"I think you know the answer to that," Aduel replied.

"Antipater!" Joanna cried.

"Antipater indeed," Aduel nodded, "although in victory Caesar's partisans were quite gracious. They embalmed the body in honey to preserve it until it could receive a proper burial in the royal sepulcher."

The girl shook her head at the ghastly image.

"It seems strange to us now, but in those days even the most bizarre events seemed common," Aduel explained. "Turmoil and chaos prevailed. For years there was constant civil war—uprisings and betrayals, relentless suffering and death—throughout our nation. Our people, from the greatest to the least, were asked to choose sides, again and again and again. This brother or that brother? Revolt or remain loyal? Rise up or lie down? Say what you will about Herod, about his spies and his persecutions, about his greed and his madness, but at least he has removed from us the curse of internal chaos and strife."

Joanna sighed.

"I wonder…" Her voice trailed off.

"What do you wonder, my child?"

"I wonder," Joanna mused, "if there will there ever be a land where people live in peace and contentment, without the terror of a cruel king hanging over them to keep them from tearing each other to pieces."

"I think there will be such a land, someday," Aduel said solemnly. "Although I will not be the one to see it. It will come in the future. Perhaps in your future. Perhaps beyond. But it will come."

"You mean when the Messiah comes."

"The government will be on his shoulders," Aduel nodded.

"Do you think the Messiah truly was born in Bethlehem as the magicians from the East proclaimed?"

"I do not know."

"But what did the magicians tell Herod after they found the Messiah?" Joanna asked. "Did they tell Herod where to look? You never told me."

"I never told you because I know nothing for certain. It's said that the magicians never returned to Herod, that they left the country secretly by night."

"Then the Messiah lives!" Joanna said excitedly.

"Perhaps," Aduel shrugged.

"But you said it would be too risky for Herod to slaughter all the inhabitants of Bethlehem," Joanna reminded him. "He didn't do that, did he?"

"No, not exactly."

"What, then?"

"He restricted the slaughter to the male children two years

old and younger. A few dozen at the most. It was a secret military operation—not widely known at the time, but it has since become known."

"Then the Messiah does not live," Joanna said gloomily.

"The Lord will accomplish his purposes whatever men do," Aduel reassured her. "But now we find ourselves in darkness. Let us make our way upstairs before we break our necks on the steps."

He put the scroll back on the shelf and turned to the stairway. Before he could mount the first step, the girl's voice arrested him.

"Uncle?" she asked.

"Yes?" Aduel peered at her but could not make out her features.

"When you said I would not be reading Book the First again, you frightened me," Joanna began.

"Frightened you!"

"Yes. I—I shouldn't have been frightened, of course. But I was. I couldn't think of the reason. I thought it might be…"

"You thought it might have something to do with the matter of your betrothal, perhaps?" Aduel ventured.

Joanna looked away, but her embarrassment was evident even in the darkness.

"Yes," she said finally.

"Indeed," Aduel nodded. "We have spoken of it but once, and that was the day you began to study the first scroll. Doubtless your thoughts have wandered from grammar and spelling from time to time."

Joanna reddened but said nothing.

"I have not spoken of it again because thus far I have had little to say," Aduel continued. "By design, my inquiries have proceeded slowly. They have already raised eyebrows among those who know me, or have heard of me. Old Aduel, once the secretary to the king, now a recluse who has renounced the society of men. But hark! Suddenly we see him tarry in the marketplace, in the courtyards of the Temple! Inquiring after men's families—after sons, their ages, their temperaments, their connections. Their betrothals! What could it mean? Yes, my inquiries have raised eyebrows indeed. I must be careful not to raise suspicions as well."

"But whose suspicions do you fear, Uncle?" Joanna asked.

"Herod's spies, of course," Aduel replied. "They gather and report every aspect of life in Jerusalem. Doubtless some with whom I have already spoken are in secret service to the king."

Joanna sighed at the seeming hopelessness of it all.

"But fear not," Aduel continued. "My labors may yet bear fruit. I have been able to identify two eligible young men, both from good families. Additional inquiries will establish whether the youths themselves possess these characteristics that you so fervently desire. If so, then we will proceed."

"How?" Joanna demanded.

"Leave that to me, child," Aduel said. "I have spent much time considering how such an unusual circumstance might be brought about, but my deliberations are not yet complete."

"Are you saying you don't know how?"

"That's exactly what I am saying."

Joanna leaned back against the wall, digesting this new information.

"But you said I would be consulted," she murmured.

"I said that if at all possible you would have some say in the matter," her uncle reminded her. "It is still not clear to me how that will be managed."

Joanna stood up straight, suddenly galvanized.

"You must make no agreement without my consent," she said firmly.

"Indeed!" Aduel raised an eyebrow. "I see that the topic has crossed your mind from time to time. As well it might for one so astute." He pondered for a moment. "As a free woman who has reached her majority, you have the right to refuse any arrangement I might make. You understand that, do you not?"

"Yes."

"Then perhaps we should wait. In time, as you settle into life here in Jerusalem, you will be able to investigate for yourself. Then you can choose as you like, and I will assist with the arrangements."

Joanna deliberated.

"I think it would be better not to wait," she said finally.

"Very well. It shall be as you wish. I will proceed, but cautiously. When the time comes you will be consulted."

Chapter 5

The conquest of the second book of Aduel's history was accomplished much more quickly than the first. As her uncle had predicted, the girl's proficiency in the Hebrew language had increased rapidly, thanks to her natural aptitude and hours of study each day. Within a week she was able to read the second book with only a few interruptions, and with a wordless nod of approval Aduel returned it to the shelf and retrieved the next scroll. A glance at the small window high in the wall told him that ample daylight remained, and after unfurling the first part of the scroll he cleared his throat to read.

"Herod: A Secret History, by Aduel of Sepphoris. Book the Third."

After Julius Caesar had appointed him procurator, Antipater wasted no time consolidating his control over the region. His first son, Phasaelus, he made governor of Jerusalem and the surrounding area. His second son, Herod, he made governor of Galilee. Herod planned to make the government a good deal more active than it had traditionally been and quickly set about setting up his administration in Sepphoris, the provincial capital.

Sepphoris was home to a large archive that housed historical, legal, and genealogical documents from the towns and villages throughout Galilee. Adjacent to the archive was a school, where young men were trained to become professional scribes. As the final stage of their training, the most advanced of these were employed creating and copying documents for the archive.

Shortly after his appointment as governor, Herod made his way to this school. News of his visit—and its purpose—reached the building before he arrived and the schoolmasters and the other apprentices took this opportunity to quietly make their way out through a back door. Thus the only person Herod encountered was an apprentice scribe, sixteen years of age, engrossed in his work, oblivious to all that had taken place.

"You there!" Herod called out. "What are you doing there? Where is everyone?"

The apprentice looked up, startled. Although he had not yet laid eyes on the new governor, he did not need to be told who it was.

"You, answer me!" Herod demanded. "I need a scribe, perhaps two or three. Where is everyone?"

The apprentice bowed slightly, not averting his eyes from the riveting countenance before him. At this time Herod was just twenty-five years old—practically a contemporary of the apprentice. He was a man of average stature, but his thick black hair, heavy beard, and piercing eyes gave him something of a wolfish appearance—a resemblance that was accentuated by his habit of pulling his thin lips back to expose his teeth. It was an expression that made him seem to be smiling, although the apprentice would quickly learn that he usually was not. In all, it was a countenance that promised activity, intrigue, and adventure all at a single glance, and although it was not an especially handsome face, there was something compelling in it, something hypnotic.

"I don't know, Excellency," the apprentice replied. "All of the masters seem to have left their work."

"All of them but you," Herod grumbled. "Well, you'll do. Come with me."

Joanna raised her hand to get her uncle's attention.

"Was it you?" she asked excitedly. "Were you the apprentice Herod asked to be his scribe?"

"I was indeed the one, but there was no asking involved," Aduel said with a rueful smile. "I had very little say in the matter, as you will soon see."

He resumed reading.

"If Your Excellency requires a scribe, I can have a master sent to the governor's palace," the apprentice said. "What kinds of documents does Your Excellency require?"

"All kinds. And as for these masters, where are they? You seem to be the only one here. You'll do."

"But Excellency, I am but an apprentice. I have not completed my training."

"You haven't? Then what are you doing? Here, let me see your work."

The apprentice was in a quandary. It was not customary for a document to be read by any except those who had commissioned it, or by a master who was checking the accuracy of an apprentice's work. But Herod did not seem to have heard of this custom—or, if he had, he seemed not to care. He strode to the writing table where the apprentice had been working and examined the document.

"Hmm. It's quite good for an apprentice. What more have you to learn?"

"I wish to become a scribe of the Law," the apprentice explained, "devoted to the study and observance and teaching of the Law of the Lord—"

"A scribe of the Law!" Herod interrupted. "Ha! It will be years before you'll be a scribe of the Law. Don't waste your time! Taking a bath every time you write the name of God, and washing your stylus besides! Nonsense! There are other kinds of scribes, you know. Much better to be a scribe of the governor. I'll have you writing history, heroic deeds and glorious exploits!"

He chuckled at his own hubris.

"I assume you know Greek," he continued.

The apprentice nodded slightly.

"Aramaic too, obviously. Latin?"

The apprentice shook his head, for Latin was little known in Sepphoris at that time.

"Hmph!" Herod grunted. "You'll learn. Come with me."

The apprentice felt panic rising within him, but he remained motionless.

"If Your Excellency requires a scribe, I can have a master sent to the governor's palace," he repeated. "What kinds of documents does Your Excellency require?"

Herod turned to the official who had accompanied him.

"This one dares resist me," he commented. "I like that. He looks me in the eye. We'll see about that."

His companion, well-practiced in dealing with aristocracy, chuckled more loudly than was necessary.

"Enough of your questions!" Herod commanded the apprentice. "Come!"

At this the apprentice's resistance crumbled and he followed the governor and his companion into the bright Galilean sunshine. The two soldiers who had attended Herod fell in behind them. As they made their way along the dusty main street of crushed limestone the apprentice looked this way and that for any of the master scribes who might rescue him from this predicament. But these had hidden themselves away, although he thought he saw one of them eyeing him discreetly from a shadowy doorway. The common folk of Sepphoris, on the other hand, did not attempt to avert their stares, and the apprentice could see the curiosity in their eyes as they gawked. He reminded himself to hold his head high and meet their gazes so that he would not be mistaken for a criminal.

Soon the little group had reached the gates of the governor's palace. As palaces go it was a modest building, having nothing close to the grandeur of the royal palaces that Herod would later build in Jerusalem, Jericho, and other places, but it was easily the most imposing building in Sepphoris. At the base of the steps, Herod spoke:

"Do you ride?"

The apprentice, not thinking the question was directed at him, said nothing. Herod's companion, following a half-step behind him, turned and struck the apprentice in the face.

"Dumb brute! Answer when the governor asks you a question!"

"Apologies, Excellency!" the apprentice blurted. "I did not hear the question."

"Are you deaf, then?" Herod spat. "Have I found myself a scribe who writes beautifully but hears nothing?"

"No, Excellency."

"Very well, then," Herod said irritably. "I said, do you ride?"

"Ride?" The apprentice was all confusion now. "Horses?"

"Yes, horses!"

"No, Excellency. Never in my life."

"Then you will learn," Herod said. "You will be asked to record certain events that do not take place in the palace. Perhaps many such events. There will be one such not many days from now."

He turned to one of the soldiers.

"Teach him to ride," he ordered. "By tomorrow."

"Yes, Excellency."

The soldier and his comrade, enjoying the spectacle of physical abuse that accompanied the pique of a tyrant, grinned at this absurd command. But before the sun had set they had taught the apprentice to mount a horse and guide it slowly around the courtyard. Then, with a few gruff instructions about how to care for the animal they told him to return it to its stall. By the time the youth emerged from the dark, musty stable, the last light of day was fading in the western sky. The two soldiers were nowhere in sight. Relieved, he resolved to slip away before anyone else could notice him. But the only way out of the palace complex led him around the corner of the building past the sentry near the front steps. The apprentice walked as nonchalantly as he could, trying to imitate the manner of a palace official, but the sentry was not fooled.

"You there!" the sentry called out. "Where are you going?"

The youth turned to face him.

"Home."

"No. You live here now."

"There must be some mistake," the youth objected. "I'm just a scribe. An apprentice, really."

"I know who you are," the sentry replied. "And I say you live here now. The governor may call for a scribe at any hour."

"But my mother," pleaded the youth. "She will wonder where I am."

"Your mother!" The sentry laughed derisively. "Let her wonder."

"What's this?" came a voice. "Whose mother? What will she be wondering about?"

The sentry wheeled, then snapped to attention. The voice belonged to Herod himself. He had just emerged from the palace in his usual whirl of energy. Several officials trailed behind him, apparently accompanying him upon some new errand in the city.

The sentry swallowed hard.

"My mother, Excellency," the youth spoke up. "Your sentry said I am not to return home tonight."

"That is correct," Herod nodded. "Quarters have been arranged for you. Modest quarters, but better than the barracks. The steward will show you. As for your mother, well now. We can't leave her wondering, can we?"

He snapped his fingers. One of the men standing behind him stepped forward.

"Send a messenger to this scribe's mother," he commanded. "Inform her of the great honor that has befallen her son." He paused. "And with the message include thirty shekels of silver, to console her for the loss of his companionship."

He turned back to the youth.

"Spare no worries for your mother," he said. "You will see her from time to time, but not often. You'll be quite busy in my service. She will receive half your pay, and she will be cared for if you do not return."

The youth looked at him in alarm.

"Return!" he stammered. "But—where am I going?"

Herod, suddenly in motion again, was already in the street.

"The same place the rest of us are going," he said over his shoulder. "You'll see."

Aduel rolled up the scroll.

"Why are you stopping?" Joanna demanded.

"That concludes Book the Third," Aduel replied.

"But where are they going?"

"That you will learn in Book the Fourth," Aduel said. "First you must read Book the Third."

"Couldn't I read two books at once?"

"Soon," her uncle smiled. "But Book the Fourth is one of the longer ones. For now, I think we will read only one."

"Hmph!" For the first time Joanna did not attempt to hide her annoyance. She held out her hand for the scroll.

"I would like to begin now," she said.

With a look of approval, Aduel handed her the scroll and turned to leave. But Joanna forestalled his exit with an abrupt question:

"Will there be an expedition of some sort?"

"In Book the Fourth? Yes. And after that, a second expedition that includes a trial."

"Who will be on trial?"

"Herod."

"Herod? Good. But what of your mother? Will we hear more of her?"

"No. At this point in the story we leave my mother behind."

"Oh." For some reason Joanna had not expected this. "I suppose we leave her behind because you left her behind."

Aduel nodded slightly.

"Of course you had no choice," Joanna added hastily. "Was it hard for you?"

"For me?" Aduel thought for a moment. "No. In the presence of Herod there was no time for such thoughts. Each day brought a whirlwind of unexpected developments. As an apprentice in school I had thought that I was immune to a young man's love of adventure, but I found that I did not know myself as well as I had thought. Those early days were…well, they were exhilarating. I soon forgot the domestic comfort of my mother's simple home."

Joanna considered this. Not long ago she had been parted from her own mother, and the pain still pierced her. She tried to imagine what it must have been like for Aduel's mother those many years ago—the tranquility of a simple life suddenly shattered by the whim of a foreign interloper.

"At least Herod sent her money," she remarked.

"Yes," Aduel said. "Unexpected, and from his standpoint quite unnecessary. Men in his position are accustomed to doing as they please and letting others struggle with the consequences. He needn't have sent a messenger at all, much less money. In a way it was quite generous of him."

"What do you mean, 'In a way?' You said that Herod didn't have to give her money at all."

"That is correct. He did not."

"Then why do you say 'In a way?'" Joanna pressed. "Wasn't thirty shekels of silver a great deal of money?"

"It wasn't a great deal, but it wasn't a trifle either," Aduel said. "It was more than a young apprentice could possibly have expected, and I can assure you that my mother was happy to have it. But there was a little sting in it as well. You see, in the marketplace of human chattel at that time, thirty shekels of silver was the price of a common slave."

Chapter 6

Joanna spent only one day poring over the third book in her uncle's history before reading it to him in full. The recitation was remarkable for its clarity and accuracy—there were only a few small errors—but Joanna was impatient with her uncle's interruptions and curt with his corrections. The relief and gratitude she felt at being succored in her time of need was giving way to restlessness—discontent, even. She was thrilled with the rapid progress of her learning and enthralled by the story, but suddenly she wanted something more. But she did not know what.

When she had concluded her reading she closed the scroll and handed it to her uncle with a gaze that was just short of a challenge:

"Well? Was it good enough? May we proceed to Book the Fourth?"

"Perhaps we will proceed to Book the Fourth later today," Aduel said placidly.

"Later?" Joanna said irritably. "Why not now?"

"The Lord has created a beautiful day for us. Even though winter still lingers the sun makes things warm to the touch. I think perhaps we will spend some time out of doors to enjoy it."

The girl's mouth curled to a pout.

"I think I'd rather read," she said pointedly.

"But today is Thursday," her uncle remarked. "The marketplace will be in full operation."

"The marketplace!"

This was something different. The marketplace was open every day except the Sabbath, but Mondays and Thursdays were prime market days, when vendors large and small packed the stalls to offer every imaginable ware. These two days were the highlight of everyday life in any Judean community, down to the smallest village. And the marketplace in Jerusalem! That was something not to be missed. Since coming to Jerusalem more than a month before, Joanna had been out of doors daily—but only in the small courtyard of Aduel's house, helping Edna with the chores or simply enjoying a few precious minutes in the fresh air. It was a welcome alternative to the interior of the house, but she had yet to venture beyond its gate.

"Yes, a visit to the marketplace would be a welcome diversion today," Aduel said. "Come, we will go when you are ready."

Five minutes later they were in the street, and it was with some trepidation that Joanna watched her uncle close the courtyard gate behind them. The chaos of her first night in Jerusalem, the strange inquiry of Nicolaus of Damascus, and her uncle's chilling warning about the treachery of the capital had filled her heart with fear of this turbulent city. Moreover, the oddity of this unexpected expedition did not escape her. Aduel's household, though not destitute, lived simply. There had been no impromptu excursions to the marketplace while she had been there, particularly by her uncle. If necessities were required, it had always been Irijah who was sent—and only after much discussion and planning.

But gradually her fear subsided. Life in the Judean capital had returned to its normal rhythm; the tumult occasioned by the magicians from the East was seemingly forgotten. The narrow streets, shaded by the buildings on either side, gave way to a wider, more-crowded boulevard, and soon they found themselves in the bustling hive of the marketplace. They plunged into the throng, the girl a half-step behind. Open-air booths of every description lined the street: Pottery, leather goods, glass, jewelry, clothing, footwear, animals, and foodstuffs of every kind were on display, as well as many things she had never seen before. Hawkers scurried beside them offering all manner of goods, from colored fabrics to Mesopotamian spices. All around her was the same pleasing commotion as the marketplace she remembered in Jericho, but on a much grander scale. Certain that people were staring, she tugged at the ribboned net that lightly veiled her face—while at the same time constantly reminding herself to tear her own eyes away when they had lingered too long on a face or a figure. Her first real taste of Jerusalem!

But Aduel paid no attention to any of it. He strode purposefully onward, turning neither to the right nor to the left. Soon they had left the market street behind and had entered the New City, a suburb of Jerusalem that had expanded to the northwest as the city had grown. Here they encountered another hive of commercial activity that Joanna soon recognized as the smiths' bazaar, though it was far more extensive than anything she had seen in Jericho. The sounds of commerce were still evident, but they were quieter here, and they were mingled with the sounds of industry—of workers in gold, silver, copper, and brass diligently molding lumps of metal into things of breathtaking beauty.

Finally Aduel seemed to have found something that interested him. Joanna followed closely as he turned aside into a shop that featured silver articles of every description: bowls, pitchers, goblets, and utensils of all types. In the middle of the shop, on a long table, were three wooden cases that contained smaller, more delicate items. Near these a youth sat on a low stool, deep in concentration over some object on a workbench. After a moment, he took notice of them and left off what he was doing—a little grudgingly, Joanna thought. As he stood Joanna noted that he was taller than most but no more than eighteen years of age, with curly black hair and the makings of a heavy beard under the smooth skin of his face. He seemed too young to be the shopkeeper, but there was no one else in the shop.

He watched wordlessly, his dark, expressive eyes turning from the old man to the girl and back again, as Aduel wandered about the shop, seemingly without purpose. Joanna wondered at the youth's strange behavior. It was a shopkeeper's duty to engage a customer at the first opportunity, to direct him to some item that might result in a quick sale. But the youth did not seem to be a typical shopkeeper. He seemed content to wait.

Aduel finally paused in front of the wooden cases. Only now did he and the youth make eye contact.

"May I help you, sir?"

The youth's voice was deep, but he had not fully grown into it.

"Yes, I've heard of this place and I thought I'd come to look around," Aduel replied. "A lot of attractive wares you have here."

The youth simply nodded.

"Quite a variety, all shapes and sizes," Aduel continued. "From the smallest trifles to that platter over there that could feed ten men."

The youth did not respond. Joanna was puzzled. It was not like her uncle to make idle chatter.

"This piece, for example," Aduel said. "May I see it?"

He pointed to a narrow bracelet in the center case that seemed different than the rest. It was a strip of silver tapered at either end, worked to smooth perfection. Up each side ran an intricate etching of a flowering vine, expanding outward with the width of the bracelet, utterly lifelike in its fine detail.

The youth removed the bracelet from the dowel that secured it in the case, glancing at the girl as he did—or perhaps it was more than a glance. Joanna averted her gaze, adjusting her veil slightly to better admire the bracelet and the strong, deft fingers that held it.

"This one is remarkable." Aduel took it and held it up to the light. "Look at the delicacy of the work, the symmetry. A thing of beauty, is it not?"

Joanna nodded.

"Where is the silversmith?" Aduel asked the youth. "I should like to compliment him on his work."

"He isn't here now, sir."

"He isn't! He's left you here to manage all this?"

"I am his apprentice."

"I see. Where is he? At the Temple?"

The youth nodded.

"The best smiths are often engaged at the Temple," Aduel explained to Joanna. "Creating ceremonial objects or decorative elements."

He turned back to the youth.

What's the price of this piece?"

"Twenty-five shekels," the youth said.

He paused, in the time-honored method of the shopkeeper.

"For you, fifteen," he said.

He glanced at Joanna.

"Ten," he said softly.

Joanna felt her face flush. She looked down.

"Hmph! Ten shekels!" Aduel bargained. "It's a bit thin for ten shekels. I might pay five for it."

"Five! I paid nine for the silver alone."

"You paid!" Aduel said. "You paid for the silver? You made this piece?"

The youth, having unwittingly revealed the authorship of the bracelet, said nothing.

"Well, I might pay ten for it," Aduel shrugged. "I'll think about it. Come along, maid."

He handed the bracelet back to the youth and without another word walked away from the shop. Joanna followed. She knew that if the bracelet were worth less than ten shekels the youth would pursue them for another round of bargaining.

But he did not pursue. Aduel and Joanna made their way further along the bazaar, glancing occasionally at the wares in some of the other stalls, before turning into a side street to start their journey home. They had proceeded a little way before Aduel spoke.

"Well, what did you think?" he asked casually.

"It was beautiful."

"What, the bracelet? Yes, it was beautiful. The lad has all the makings of a master. An ornament like that would have attracted the notice of Cleopatra herself had it been made of gold instead of silver."

"Cleopatra! How do you know what would have attracted the notice of Cleopatra?"

"Well, I saw what she wore," said Aduel, a little miffed. "I should think I might be able to predict what she might like."

"You never saw Cleopatra," scoffed Joanna. "Did you?"

"Saw her? Why, yes, I did. I encountered her many a time. In her palace in Alexandria, and in Jericho. I never tutored her children, the way Nicolaus did, but I did encounter her."

"Nicolaus of Damascus?" The girl was stunned. "He taught Cleopatra's children?"

"Why, of course. He's a very learned man when it comes to that sort of thing. One of the most learned in the East."

"Cleopatra's children!" Joanna marveled. "Why didn't you teach them?"

"Me! Teach Cleopatra's children?" Aduel shook his head in disgust. "Certainly not. I had enough on my hands with Herod, and he with Cleopatra herself."

Joanna's eyes grew wide as she began to grasp more fully how near her uncle had once stood to the most powerful people in their world. "Was she as beautiful as they say?" she asked.

"Beautiful? Who? Cleopatra? Bah! She was the plainest Greek harpy I ever set eyes on."

This shocked the girl for a number of reasons.

"Greek!" she objected. "But Cleopatra was queen of Egypt."

"Yes, Cleopatra was the queen of Egypt, but Cleopatra was a Greek. Macedonian, actually—the last in the line that had ruled Egypt since the death of Alexander the Great. She was different than those that had gone before, though. Do you know that of all those generations of Greeks that had ruled Egypt for centuries she was the first to learn how to speak to the Egyptians in their own language? And she could speak six or seven others besides."

"She was intelligent, then."

"Oh, she was beyond intelligent. She was brilliant. And cunning. And voracious. And beyond all that there was something else about her, something spellbinding, something that captivated the greatest men of the Roman world! First Julius Caesar, and then Mark Antony! I never understood it. Of course, she never had occasion to employ her charms on me."

They had reached Aduel's house. He glanced over his shoulder as he closed the courtyard gate behind them, then leaned down and spoke in the girl's ear in a low voice:

"Herod never understood it either. He hated her passionately."

"Is she in your history, Uncle?"

"Oh yes, we'll encounter her soon enough. But you still haven't answered my question. What did you think?"

"I did answer your question, Uncle. I said I thought it was beautiful."

"Not the bracelet. What did you think of the young man who made it?"

Joanna caught her breath. Again she felt her face flush— not in a quiet wave this time, but a rush. She could feel her heart pounding.

"Do you mean..."

"That's exactly what I mean. You said you wished to be consulted."

Joanna suddenly felt dizzy. She sat down on one of the rough wooden benches that were scattered about the perimeter of the courtyard.

"Oh, Uncle," she said. Suddenly her breath was coming in short gasps. "Do you—would I—do you think it's even possible?"

"I do indeed," Aduel replied, taking a seat next to her. "I would not have taken you on such an errand if I thought it were not possible. The young man is indeed the silversmith's apprentice. He is also the silversmith's son."

"But—you couldn't approach them now! Not after—after going to look him over like goods in the marketplace! He would hate me."

"Bah! He knows nothing of it. He knows neither who I am nor what I am about. I have made my inquiries discreetly and gotten my information indirectly. To him it was simply a chance meeting, an old man considering a purchase for a favorite daughter. Or granddaughter, more likely. If I were to reappear to propose a betrothal, we would take a cue from our friends the Greeks and mark it down to Fate. Happy, beneficent Fate. It did seem to be a propitious encounter."

"But—I didn't think I would have to—it's all so soon!" Joanna stammered. "When must I decide?"

"You have time," Aduel reassured her. "There is another for you to consider."

"Another!"

"Yes, I told you I had identified two possibilities, did I not? As it turns out, both of them are reported to be young men of excellent character, so both are eligible for consideration. Unless you would rather stop now."

"I—I don't know! No, I—I suppose I should see both."

"Very well, I shall try to manage it. Although arranging the second encounter might be more difficult than the first. But we will manage it, one way or another."

Chapter 7

After a brief midday meal the girl and her uncle retired to the secret subterranean room to resume the reading of Aduel's history. In truth neither of them was in the mood for reading, but neither was willing to admit it. Aduel took his time opening the scroll, letting his eyes wander back and forth over different passages, while Joanna, who usually leaned forward in eager anticipation, slouched backward on the stool, lost in reverie. Her mind was a cacophony of a hundred different thoughts—or rather, a hundred different variations on a single thought: the silversmith's son. She knew that he could not be all of the virtuous things she imagined him to be—then eagerly convinced herself that he could. Strong, quiet—masterful, in a mysterious, brooding way. An artist, a maker of beauty! A seer of things beyond, things that could not be seen—not some chattering, money-grubbing, shopkeeping pest! And handsome. Oh yes, quite handsome. Possibly the most handsome man she had ever seen and possibly not, but certainly handsome enough.

She tried to rid her thoughts of him as her uncle finally cleared his throat to begin:

"Herod: A Secret History, by Aduel of Sepphoris. Book the Fourth."

The city of Sepphoris had been chosen as a regional capital a few years prior to Herod's arrival due to its location. It sits on a very high hill in the midst of Galilee, a location that provides a clear view of everything for miles around. An hour's journey to the south, the town of Nazareth. Beyond that, the plain of Megiddo, where great battles have been fought in the past and likely will be fought in the future. An hour the opposite way, Cana. To the east, the Sea of Galilee. And to the west the great sea, the one the Romans call Mediterra. But the Romans had chosen Sepphoris for more than just strategic reasons: they had chosen it as a symbol of their power. For it was a place that could be seen for miles around, a city that could not be hidden.

Despite these advantages Sepphoris was of limited importance. Galilee was an agricultural backwater, far removed from the center of Judea, and its government was a sleepy provincial administration, quite limited in comparison with the international government in which Herod's new scribe would later serve in Jerusalem. But for Herod it offered one indispensable advantage: It was the type of base upon which an ambitious political leader could build, and Herod used his tenure in Sepphoris as the first stepping stone on his ascent to the Judean throne.

It was not many days before the young scribe began to live out his role in Herod's unlikely ascent. One night he was roused from the servants' quarters in the palace long before dawn by an old man named Neriah. Many years of experience under previous governors had made Neriah adept in the business of government and upon Herod's arrival he had been appointed the governor's personal secretary. The young scribe had been placed under the supervision of this seasoned civil servant and was therefore not entirely surprised to find the old man at his bedside, candle flickering in the darkness.

"Get up, get ready, you'll be going soon," Neriah growled as he shook the youth.

"Going?" the scribe mumbled sleepily. "Going where?"

"To Syria," the old man replied.

"Syria!" The scribe sat up in his bed. "What will I be doing in Syria?"

"It's a military expedition of some sort," Neriah replied. "I'm not privy to the details. You'll be responsible for the governor's correspondence from the field. And, of course, you're to chronicle any great acts of bravery and conquest that might happen along the way."

Even in the darkness, the youth could see the old man rolling his eyes.

"Will His Excellency be attacking Syria?" the scribe asked.

"I hope not, since Syria is a Roman province," Neriah muttered. "You'll find out soon enough. Now up with you, out of bed! Get your things. You must be ready in the courtyard in ten minutes."

"But where will you be?"

"Here, of course. You don't expect an old man with gout to ride out to arms, do you?"

To arms! There was a thrill in the words, and terror. In his wildest dreams the scribe had never contemplated such an existence. He had always expected his life to unfold in an unremarkable way, in the orderly hush of documents and letters. But there was no time to think of such things. In five minutes he was in the courtyard, shivering in the night air while an entire century of soldiers milled about him. Soon he was accosted by one of them, the same one who had spent the past three afternoons molding him into a passable horseman.

"Where have you been?" the soldier barked. "Would you keep

the governor waiting, you idle scribe?"

"Are we attacking Syria?" the scribe asked.

"Shut up! Bridle your horse!"

The scribe was puzzled as he made his way to the stables. There were not nearly enough horses to accommodate all of the soldiers in the courtyard, and the night air carried the sound of the other centuries in the cohort mustering nearby. Slowly the situation became evident. The soldiers were infantry; they would march. Only Herod and his trusted officials would have mounts for this expedition, but accompanying these would be Herod's scribe—an aide de camp with papyrus and palimpsest, standing ready to compose dispatches and any other documents the governor deemed necessary.

It was a full day's march to the scene of the action, and the scribe was thankful that the pace of the infantry did not put his equestrian skills to the test. He rode at the back of the mounted group, at a respectful distance from Herod and his officers—studiously silent, but his mind full of conjecture. As the sun set over the Mediterranean Sea, the detachment stopped in a desolate place— somewhere, the scribe guessed, on the border between Galilee and Syria. One of Herod's men quietly guided his horse to the top of a low bluff among the rocky hills and paused, searching the landscape below. After a minute or two he rejoined the mounted group, reporting to Herod in low tones that the scribe could not make out.

Evidently Herod had found what he was looking for, for he gave a brief signal to the commander of the infantry that waited a hundred yards behind them. The scribe, unversed in military tactics, looked on in wonder as the troops divided into three groups and silently moved out. It was Herod himself who put an end to the scribe's speculation, beckoning him with a peremptory flick of his finger.

"I take you know what this is about," he said when the youth had joined him.

"No, Excellency."

"Ride quietly to the top of the bluff and then report what you see."

The scribe did as he was told. The bluff overlooked a narrow wadi, a rocky canyon with a trickle of water still flowing in the bed of the stream that had cut the narrow channel, but as the scribe peered down its length he could make out nothing unusual. Suddenly, in the distance, a slight movement caught his eye—a man moving among the rocks. Then there was another, and another still—men emerging from the concealment of nearby caves, coming down to the stream to wash.

The scribe returned to the foot of the bluff.

"Well?" Herod demanded. "What did you see?"

"I saw men," the scribe reported. "It seems to be an encampment of some sort."

"It is an encampment. Do you know whose?"

"No, Excellency."

"I take it you've heard of Hezekias."

"Hezekias the Marauder?" The scribe's eyes grew wide. "Of course, Excellency. Are those his men?"

"They are. What do you know of them?"

"They are the scourge of Galilee," the scribe replied. "They terrorize all who travel the roads, and the villages as well. They pillage and spoil and take whatever they will. None but the largest cities can resist them."

"Yes, they are a terror throughout Galilee, and throughout much of Syria as well. They make their raids and retire to this wilderness to divide their spoils while your rulers remain quaking behind the city walls. They are more than bandits; they are rebels. They have made a mockery of your government. They will not mock me."

The scribe pondered this in silence.

"We shall fall upon them unaware, just as they have fallen upon others unaware," Herod added.

"Will they not be alerted to our presence and melt away into the night?" the scribe wondered.

"Did you notice a sentry as you stood at the top of the bluff, in full view of their camp?"

"No, Excellency."

"No, you did not. They have not bothered to post sentries. They have operated with impunity for so long they have grown complacent. We might even take them without a fight."

"You intend to capture them, then."

"I intend to butcher every last one of them," Herod said with grim satisfaction. "You know your place in this, do you not?"

The scribe gulped. Even though he was seated on a horse, his knees suddenly felt weak.

"No, Excellency," he croaked.

"Your place is to record all that occurs," Herod said. "When we return victorious, accounts of our triumph will be dispatched to Jerusalem and to the Roman procurator in Damascus. Your report will be the basis of these accounts."

"Yes, Excellency."

The scribe breathed a sigh of relief as Herod turned to rejoin his officers. But he was not entirely free from anxiety. He knew that Hezekias's band had horses of its own, and he wondered if he would be able to manage his own mount in headlong flight if the fight did not go Herod's way.

He need not have worried. Herod's soldiers executed the governor's plan to perfection. At sunset they fell upon the camp from three directions after the outlaws had emerged from the caves to take their evening meal. As Herod had predicted, Hezekias and his band were captured without a fight, and within a half hour every one of them had been bound hand and foot—well over a hundred men in all. Herod, who had been surveying the operation from a nearby outcropping that overlooked the wadi, rode to the clearing where the troops had gathered the bound prisoners, followed by his officers. As usual the scribe trailed behind at a respectful distance.

Herod stopped in front of the motley crowd and surveyed them silently for several moments before nodding to the senior centurion who stood at attention nearby. The centurion stepped forward.

"Awaiting your orders, Excellency," he said. "Shall we march them to Damascus for trial, or to Sepphoris?"

Herod seemed to consider this for several moments.

"There's no need to trouble these men with such an arduous journey," he said finally.

There were nods and a few guffaws from the captives: the rough camaraderie of brutal men. Herod's intent seemed clear: There would be a slap on the wrist; the soldiers would complete a wholesale theft of the bandits' plunder; and then all would continue more or less as before.

Then Herod raised his voice. "Slay them here."

A collective gasp escaped from the bound men. Even the centurion seemed shocked.

"Which ones, Excellency?" he asked.

"All of them."

A cacophony of cursing and pleas for mercy arose from Hezekias and his followers. Herod smiled his smile that was not a smile, those thin lips revealing that wolfish grin, and wordlessly turned his horse back to Sepphoris. His officials followed. The scribe turned his horse to join them, then stopped. He had been ordered to record all that occurred.

The soldiers wasted no time in carrying out their commission. By the light of a large fire of brushwood the scribe witnessed the gruesome, piteous spectacle until he could bear no more. He once again turned his horse toward Sepphoris, but he had not gone far when he realized that he was not exactly sure where Sepphoris was. Herod and his mounted party had long since disappeared into the darkness. The scribe cast a backward glance over his shoulder, hoping that the moon would guide him, and directed his horse slowly over the rough terrain.

It is not an easy task to find one's way through unfamiliar terrain by the light of the moon, and it was not until the middle of the next day that the scribe and his haggard mount staggered into Sepphoris. He was famished and exhausted; every bone in his body cried out for relief from the torture of the saddle. But mostly he was terrified—terrified at the fury that he was sure Herod would unleash due to the delay of the report of his remarkable triumph.

But there was no need for a scribe to publicize the results. The news had preceded him. A festival atmosphere prevailed in Sepphoris; the streets were packed with jubilant citizens offering thanks for the cleansing of the land and singing praises to the man who had brought it about. Not long afterward, as if to mark the occasion with a memorable capstone, the cohort returned to Sepphoris. Remarkably cheerful for men who had been marching for a night and most of two days, most had not bothered to wash away the blood they had spilled during the mass execution of the outlaw band, which reddened their sandals and was caked up to their ankles. It was resounding confirmation of the victory that had taken place, and the first confirmation of the ruthless control that Herod would exert throughout a career that no one at the time ever would have thought possible.

"And thus concludes Book the Fourth."

It was several moments before Joanna realized that her uncle had stopped reading and was looking at her intently.

"I'm sorry, Uncle."

"Your thoughts are far away," Aduel remarked. "In the smiths' bazaar, perhaps."

Joanna smiled weakly.

"It's all I can think about," she said quietly.

"Perhaps I have been too hasty in this matter of betrothal," Aduel said. "I thought you wanted me to act quickly."

"I did," Joanna said. "It worried me."

Her voice trailed off.

"It worried you that you are not betrothed?" Aduel prompted. "Why? Because of what Nicolaus said?"

"Yes. It seemed so odd that he would ask such a thing."

"It was odd," Aduel agreed. "Nicolaus is not the kind of man who asks such questions without a reason. And yet we have heard nothing more from him. This is something to give us hope."

"Hope that he has forgotten?"

"I doubt that he has forgotten. Rather, we can hope that he is too consumed with more important matters. And hope that he stays that way for some time. In any case, we have come to the end of Book the Fourth. We shall resume tomorrow, perhaps, or the next day, when you have had a chance to read it yourself."

He patted her shoulder and turned to the stairs. When Joanna interrupted him, he paused as if he had expected it.

"Uncle?"

"Yes?"

"When must I choose?"

Aduel turned to face her.

"You must choose when you know in your heart what you want," he said. "And even then there is no guarantee that it will come to pass. Just because these young men are eligible does not necessarily mean they will be amenable. Their families may object. There may be other arrangements that I was not able to discover. Any number of difficulties might arise."

"Then we should not delay."

"You should not make a rash decision because of one remark by Nicolaus of Damascus."

"No, but…"

"But what?"

"After Nicolaus left that night—and you with him, with the soldiers—Irijah said…"

"What did Irijah say?" Aduel asked sharply.

"He said that the course of my life had altered that night."

"And this worries you?" Aduel prodded.

"It haunts me." The girl's voice was barely a whisper.

"Has Irijah said anything else to you?"

"No. We try to avoid each other."

"A good idea," Aduel said, "although somewhat difficult in this small house. Do your best to forget the words of Irijah. He speaks foolishly when he is overwrought, but he has been a faithful servant to me these many years. If the inquiry of Nicolaus of Damascus is at the heart of your anxiety, it might be better to address it directly. I shall go to see Nicolaus, and find out exactly what he had in mind."

"No!" Joanna seized her uncle's wrist, panicked.

Aduel stared at her, astonished.

"But child, it might be for the best," he encouraged.

"Nicolaus still seems to regard me as a friend—a comrade, anyway—for a kindness that I showed him long ago. Though he has far surpassed me in power and influence, he still seems to regard himself as being in debt to me. I might be able to bring some influence to bear."

"No, please, I beg of you!" Joanna shook her head vehemently. "Do not remind him. It might have been a chance remark. He might have forgotten."

"Possibly he has," Aduel considered. "Very well, then. It shall be as you wish. Try not to let it trouble you."

"Thank you, Uncle. When I know in my heart I will tell you."

"Good. But not a moment before."

"Not a moment before," Joanna repeated. "But...if I should choose, and then..."

"And then what? Change your mind?"

Joanna blushed.

"You may change your mind up to the moment the marriage contract is signed," Aduel said solemnly. "Although," he added with a rueful smile, "it would be better for all concerned, especially me, if it did not come to that."

Joanna nodded. She had a vague understanding of the importance of a marriage contract. Under the law of Moses, a man in Judea could divorce his wife for almost any reason, and this provision was sometimes invoked frivolously, even cynically. The marriage contract, especially when crafted by a cagey guardian such as Aduel, would stand as a deterrent to such a disaster by providing for her financial security.

Aduel patted her hand and turned away a second time.

"Uncle?"

"Yes?"

"What if he will not have me?"

"Who? The young man?"

Joanna nodded. Aduel turned and took both her hands in his.

"My child," he smiled, "that is the least of my worries."

Chapter 8

Joanna leaned back on her stool in dreamy meditation as her uncle's shuffling steps receded up the narrow stairway. In a single day her view of her life had changed completely. Terrified by the words of Nicolaus and Irijah, for weeks she had been content—grateful, even—to remain safely inside the walls of Aduel's house. It was a refuge in the midst of this turbulent, intimidating city—a refuge from chaos, from the prying eyes of strangers, from a possible chance encounter with Nicolaus or someone like him. But suddenly all these terrors seemed remote—ridiculous, even. She was seized by a sudden, searing thirst for life; again she found herself beset by a longing so deep that she could not explain it. She could not remain shut up inside these walls forever. Her life was out there, somewhere. She resolved to go and find it.

But how? She knew that the leading families of Jerusalem actively discouraged unmarried daughters from ever leaving their homes, relying on servants to perform necessary errands and chores. In Aduel's simple household this was one luxury she that actually enjoyed, though now she no longer valued it. But the fact remained that as a maiden and a stranger she could not traipse the city alone, the way she might have in Jericho, a city she had known all her life, without attracting the kind of attention that she still viscerally feared. She must be accompanied at all times. But those opportunities were limited. Her uncle and his servants were not venturesome people. Regular market days were only twice a week, and even those often passed without anyone from the household in attendance. Her uncle sometimes attended the Temple to hear the reading of the Torah, but his recent missions had been undertaken with an ulterior motive—one that would have been evident had she accompanied him.

The reality of it was inescapable: Patience would be necessary. But suddenly patience was in short supply. She would do what she could. She would take every opportunity to venture beyond the walls of her uncle's courtyard with Aduel, or Edna—or even with crotchety old Irijah, if necessary.

Until then she would wait. She would have to. But it seemed intolerable. Her uncle's house, until recently so cozy, now felt impossibly small—the tiny underground room like a cell. She glanced up at the window. At least three hours of daylight remained, and there was more than half a week until the next full market day! Would this day never end?

She cast about for something to distract herself, but the little room offered only the familiar meager inducements: The scrolls, the styli, the papyrus, the ink. She picked up a stylus, fingered it idly for a moment, then dipped it in the ink and began to doodle languidly. It was a shameful waste of papyrus, even spoiled papyrus, and she confined it to a corner. Then, without her really intending it, her fingers started tracing out letters—letters more precise and beautiful than any she had ever written.

Silver.

Smiling sheepishly, she dried the ink on her finger and smoothed her robe. Her uncle had left the fourth book of his history upon the table. She knew that her attention had drifted as he was reading; the description of the executions of the rebel band, though brief, had sickened her. But the story of Herod still fascinated her. And her uncle's part in it! So vivid, so compelling! And yet so terrible for a youth unwillingly plucked out of a simple, respectable life! Surely a quiet life would be preferable to one filled with trial and terror, but was there such a thing as a life that was too quiet?

She closed the fourth book tightly and placed it on the shelf. She wondered how many remained in her uncle's secret history. From the looks of it there were about a dozen more. She took one down and glanced at it. It was Book the Fifth, the next in the series. She wondered how much of it she could read without having heard it first. Aduel had previously mentioned that there was another expedition that involved a trial, and she had paid enough attention to the fourth book to know that he had not read anything about a trial.

She glanced up at the window. The light had not changed. She had no better way to while away the remainder of the afternoon; there was no reason that she should not continue with the story, at least a little way. She seated herself again and unrolled the papyrus, allowing herself to be drawn back into the remarkable tale.

Herod: A Secret History, by Aduel of Sepphoris. Book the Fifth.

Once back in Sepphoris, the scribe ignored his exhaustion and set to work at once on his account of Herod's expedition. Impatient for the authentication of his triumph, the governor himself soon appeared in the small room where the scribe sat huddled with papyrus and ink. But rather than the fearsome rant the scribe expected, Herod was buoyant—playful, even. The success and adulation that had come his way made him too jubilant to be angry.

"What say you, boy?" he demanded, looking over the scribe's shoulder to peruse what had already been written. "Can't you work any faster?"

The work was not half done, but the youth thought better than to make excuse.

"Yes, Excellency."

"Not too fast, though," Herod cautioned. We can't have any blotting or mistakes."

"No, Excellency."

"Have you been about the city yet?" Herod exulted. "Have you heard them singing in the streets?"

"Yes, Excellency. I just returned an hour ago. All Sepphoris is overjoyed."

"As well it might be! Saul has slain his thousands and David his ten thousands, but Herod has rid the land of a plague! What do you think, boy? Will Herod take his place among the great leaders of our nation?"

"Certainly, Excellency," the scribe nodded, careful to keep any trace of sarcasm from his voice.

"They're singing it in Syria too, you mark my words. I want that report finished by sundown, do you hear me?" Already he had left the room, his rapid stride fading quickly down the corridor. "No later than sundown," he called out, "or you will answer to me!"

But Neriah, the ancient palace administrator, was less sanguine. He too had heard the singing in the streets, and before the scribe had finished his report the old man was at his elbow, glancing nervously about him to make sure they were alone.

"Is it true?" he whispered. "Did Herod really execute Hezekias and his band without so much as a trial?"

"It's true," the scribe replied.

"That is something he should not have done." Neriah shook his head. "Only the Great Sanhedrin in Jerusalem can pass the sentence of death in Judea."

"The Great Sanhedrin in Jerusalem are three days' journey from here," the scribe shrugged. "They know nothing of it."

"They will know of it, of that you may be sure," Neriah muttered. "It remains to be seen what they will do about it."

"They will do nothing about it," the scribe retorted confidently. "Hezekias and his band were worthless, brutal men. No one will complain."

Neriah made no reply, but shaking his head darkly he left the scribe to finish his report.

By the end of the day the account was read in full to Herod, who nodded his satisfaction and ordered copies to be sent immediately to Jerusalem and Damascus. Already he had begun making plans to pursue other rebellious bands, smaller and less infamous but no less dangerous, that had defied the civil authorities and plagued the countryside. Within days these too were either summarily executed or melted away into the rural villages before they could be hunted down. Next Herod turned his attention to complaints of government corruption and oppression in Galilee; these were investigated and the most egregious were rectified. Week by week the scribe was called upon to commit these deeds to official documents which comprised a good deal of Herod's correspondence. Herod's brother Phasaelus, who was governor of Jerusalem and the surrounding areas, was inspired to initiate his own campaigns, and these were hailed with equal enthusiasm by the citizens under his authority.

Thus in a very short period of time Antipater and his sons came to be held in the highest regard throughout the regions of Judea and Galilee, although they were still nominally under the authority of

Hyrcanus the ethnarch, who many still regarded as king. It was a time of prosperity and righteousness throughout the land, and people being what they are, such a situation could not endure. The letters that came back from the royal palace in Jerusalem were congratulatory at first, then less so. Old Neriah, Herod's official secretary, was worried. He had privately received word that a faction in Jerusalem, jealous of Antipater's popularity, was attempting to provoke Hyrcanus into a confrontation with Antipater, Phasaelus, and Herod.

After a few more weeks, the rumors proved correct. The scribe was finishing his work one afternoon when Neriah cornered him at his writing table. The old man's hand was shaking as he held out the letter that a special courier had just delivered from Jerusalem.

"What is it?" the scribe asked.

"It's a summons," Neriah quaked. "Hyrcanus has summoned Herod to Jerusalem to stand trial!"

"Stand trial!" the scribe exclaimed. "For what?"

"Murder!"

The scribe scanned the document, which had just been unsealed by the old secretary. It was brief, but shocking. Herod was indeed being accused of multiple murders—the murders of Hezekias and his band of outlaws!

"You must inform His Excellency at once," the scribe said.

"Yes, yes, I must," Neriah said, his voice trembling and distracted. "You must accompany me."

"Me!" the scribe balked. "Why me?"

"I do not trust myself," Neriah said. "To read such a letter before Herod!"

The scribe unwillingly followed the old secretary through the administrative wing of the governor's palace, hoping that Herod would not be on the premises, but they found him conferring with his senior military officers. The scribe knew that this was not the place that such a letter should be read, but Herod had noticed Neriah and had already summoned the secretary to stand before him. As the old man had predicted, his voice failed him as he tried to read the letter. The scribe stepped forward, but before he could take the letter from Neriah, Herod himself had taken it.

"What is it that's tied your tongue, Neriah?" Herod inquired. "Must be something important."

"From His Majesty Hyrcanus, ruler of Judea," Neriah managed.

The scribe watched with trepidation as Herod read the letter. Within moments the governor's eyes were blazing; his thin lips had pulled back in that fearsome grin of his. Suddenly he burst out laughing.

"So! It seems I am accused of murder!" he grinned.

Those in attendance murmured in shock.

"By the mothers of Hezekias and his outlaws!" Herod exclaimed. "Can this possibly be true?"

The murmurs of the officers swelled to outrage. Neriah made a gesture of helplessness.

"The mothers of a band of murdering outlaws have accused me of murder for bringing their sons to justice!" Herod seemed to be enjoying the absurdity of such a charge. "I am to take my trial before the Great Sanhedrin in Jerusalem at the first opportunity! Well! This requires a response."

He cleared his throat and began to dictate:

"Hyrcanus: I will certainly appear in Jerusalem to defend myself in this ridiculous matter. I will come at the time that seems right to me, since I must settle matters in Galilee so that the province does not revert to the same disorder that prevailed before I arrived here. In good time I will appear. Herod."

He looked pointedly at Neriah.

"See to it immediately."

As soon as Neriah and the scribe were out of Herod's earshot, the old man clutched the scribe's shoulder in a frantic gesture.

"Did you hear His Excellency's response?" he demanded.

"Of course."

"Then you must write the letter."

"Me!" The scribe had grown accustomed to writing official correspondence, but never anything of this import. "You are the governor's secretary."

"My hand shakes so, see how it shakes!" Neriah implored. "I am an old man now. This letter, this one time, you must write for me."

The scribe nodded wordlessly. Back at his writing table he sat for a minute, composing his thoughts. Herod would want the letter immediately, but it must be in the scribe's most elegant hand—and there must be no mistakes. Finally he took a sheet of the finest parchment and began to write:

To His Majesty Hyrcanus, High Priest of Israel, Benevolent Ruler and Supreme Authority of all Judea and Galilee: Hail, our most excellent ruler! I am in receipt of your summons and I will hasten to appear in Jerusalem to explain my actions in this most important matter concerning those who have flouted your authority in Galilee. There may be some small delay as I will require time to settle matters in this province so that disorder does not break out again during my absence. I eagerly await the day that I will appear in person to pay homage to my most generous benefactor. With many thanks for your gracious forbearance in this matter, I remain your faithful servant.

Herod, governor of Galilee under the authority of Hyrcanus, High Priest of Israel and Ruler of Judea.

Neriah, who had been pacing fretfully in the corridor, hurried in as soon as he heard the scribe push back his stool from the writing table. He snatched up the parchment—carefully, blowing on the newly written words to make sure that the ink would not run—and read it with darkening countenance.

"What is this?" he demanded.

"It's the governor's response to Hyrcanus," the scribe said, puzzled.

"This is not what His Excellency dictated," Neriah scolded.

"It's exactly what His Excellency dictated," the scribe contradicted. "I just put it into diplomatic form."

"Diplomatic form!" Neriah scoffed. "Is that what you call this? 'Supreme Authority....most excellent ruler...most generous benefactor. Faithful servant!' Herod said none of these things!"

"No, but if Herod intends to affront Hyrcanus, I doubt he wants to do it in this letter," the scribe reasoned calmly. "To send such a letter as His Excellency originally dictated would be nothing less than a declaration of rebellion—"

"Rebellion?" demanded a voice from the corridor. "What rebellion? Where is my letter? Have you completed it?"

Neriah and the scribe froze. With customary impatience Herod had come to check on their progress.

"No, Excellency," Neriah stammered.

"No? Why not? What have you been doing all this time? It wasn't an oration. It should be ready by now. What's this, then?"

He snatched the letter from Neriah's trembling hand.

"Deepest apologies, Excellency," Neriah stammered. "Our scribe, fearing that it would appear as if you intended to affront His Majesty Hyrcanus, has altered some of the wording of your reply, setting it into what he feels is a more diplomatic tone."

"I did intend to affront His Majesty Hyrcanus," Herod replied.

"But it seems our scribe takes a more strategic view of the matter. It's a good thing, too. This business is more serious than I first perceived. I need to proceed carefully, or the bootlickers who whisper into the ear of that fool Hyrcanus will have me in chains the moment I set foot in Jerusalem."

He quickly finished reading the letter.

"This is good," he muttered. "It's very good. Close it up and I shall seal it. The messenger awaits."

He turned to the scribe.

"You're smarter than I thought, boy," he said. "Hyrcanus and the Sanhedrin will think me chastened. Much better than having them on their guard."

He clapped the terrified Neriah on the shoulder.

"What do you think, old fellow? This young scribe may have something to teach us both!"

Herod took his time getting ready to go to Jerusalem, but finally he did go. The scribe was not surprised to be included in the travelling party, for although Neriah remained the governor's official secretary, he never missed an opportunity to remind Herod of his incapacity for travel. Herod's attitude toward the proceeding, on the other hand, was a surprise. Defendants who were called to trial before the Sanhedrin invariably did their utmost to appear penitent and humble—clothed in mourning, their countenance disheveled—but Herod took the opposite approach. He ordered multiple sets of expensive new clothing, and included his personal barber in the travelling party so that he might look his best. Apparently this advice had come from Antipater, Herod's father, who provided frequent updates from Jerusalem. Neriah had handled these letters, so the scribe was not privy to their contents, but their advice resonated with Herod, who could never have mustered the humility to rouse the pity of the Sanhedrin. If there was any doubt about Herod's posture, it was erased when it was learned that the travelling party would include the governor's personal guard. This consisted of an entire century of soldiers—not enough to threaten rebellion against Hyrcanus, but enough to serve notice that Herod would not be punished without a fight.

Word of the impending confrontation had captivated Judea for some weeks, and there was no little stir when the governor and his party—the scribe included—arrived in the capital. Even at this time Jerusalem was a remarkable city, though it had little of the splendor it would later achieve under Herod's rule. The scribe knew it well, having made the required pilgrimages since he had come of age, but this journey was different. Without the tens of thousands of pilgrims that attended the annual festivals the city was far quieter than the scribe remembered, and in that quiet the tension of the upcoming trial hung ominously. Antipater and Phasaelus had met the party outside the gates and had conducted them to Antipater's palatial estate in the Upper City, quickly bringing Herod up to date on the latest developments. Antipater was an older, wiser version of Herod, a man who was born to rule yet knew that he would never rule. A shrewd, calculating taker of chances, he understood that the only way that he would ever exercise power would be to become the deputy of a weak, indecisive ruler, and had rightly perceived that Hyrcanus could be that ruler. He was a handsome man and ceaselessly active, always silently scheming beneath a beneficent countenance. By turns jovial and brutal, merciful and ruthless, he seemed effortlessly to win the loyalty of soldiers and the adulation of the crowd. Phasaelus, his eldest son, was in many ways his double, though even greater in stature, in strength, and in physical comeliness. Seeing the three of them together, even if only for a few minutes, the scribe could tell that the father had passed down his most vital traits to both of his sons, with Phasaelus having received a double portion of many of them.

Based on Herod's direction, the scribe had expected a sojourn of several days, if not weeks, in Jerusalem. But there was little time to strategize. The Sanhedrin—the council of seventy-one priests, Pharisees, and leading aristocrats that acted as the supreme court and governing body of the Jewish nation—had already convened.

When Herod emerged from Antipater's residence an hour after his arrival, the grit and grime of the recent journey were gone. The governor was newly shaven, his hair neatly trimmed, and he was wearing dazzling robes of deep purple. It was a daring declaration, resembling nothing so much as a regal procession, and passersby marveled at the spectacle as the soldiers, officials, Antipater, Phasaelus, and the imperious governor of Galilee strode through the city. Outside the meeting place of the Sanhedrin, Herod paused for a moment, allowing twelve hand-picked soldiers to assemble around him. Then, with his usual decisive stride, he marched forward into the chamber—not alone, as everyone expected, but with his troops in a crisp square around him, marching in lockstep.

The rest of the party remained outside, watching from the entrance. The scribe strained for a better view. The Sanhedrin, assembled in a semi-circle inside the chamber, sat in stunned silence. The large space in the midst of the gathering, meant to isolate and diminish a lone defendant, was barely enough to accommodate Herod and his party; the dusty sandals of the soldiers brushed against the revered fringes of the long robes of the judges. No one knew what was to be done; no defendant had ever dared such affrontery. Everyone looked to Hyrcanus, seated at the center of them all. In addition to being the nominal ruler of Judea he was also the high priest, and thus the president of the Sanhedrin—but he could only stare, as motionless as if he had been turned to stone. The silence continued for what seemed an hour. Finally, Shemaiah, an elder of the Pharisees who had been one of the leading voices within the Sanhedrin for many years, rose to speak:

"O you who are judges with me, and you who are my king, I have never known such a case, and nor do I suppose any one of you can name its parallel, that one who is called to trial ever stood before us in such a manner. But this admirable man Herod, who is accused of murder, stands here clothed in purple, with his armed men around him. Yet I do not make this complaint against Herod himself: He is, to be sure, more concerned for himself than for the laws, but my complaint is against yourselves and your king, who give him license. However, know this: That this very man will one day punish both you and your ruler himself."

All who sat in judgment understood the wisdom of this statement—and felt it the more keenly due to the ominous prophecy with which it concluded. There was murmuring, and then a clamor, and even before Herod was allowed to make his defense there were calls for an immediate verdict. Hyrcanus, who secretly admired Herod for the very brashness that would one day lead to his own demise, arose amidst the uproar and abruptly adjourned the trial. Immediately all was confusion, and Herod, not awaiting further instructions, strode silently from the chamber with his armed men about him.

That night there arrived at Antipater's mansion a letter from Hyrcanus, a letter so secret that it was placed directly into Herod's hands. In it, Hyrcanus advised Herod to flee Jerusalem at once, warning that he would not be able to prevent a conviction if the Sanhedrin reconvened the trial. Herod and his retinue departed from Jerusalem within the hour—bound not for Sepphoris, but for Damascus. There Herod made an alliance with Sextus Caesar, cousin of the great Julius Caesar who was then ruling in Rome, who—in exchange for a great deal of money—placed at Herod's disposal a large army. With this Herod set his sights on revenge against Hyrcanus, his rage growing with each passing day as his army proceeded toward Jerusalem. The city was in a panic, certain of invasion, but Antipater and Phasaelus once again met Herod outside the gates and implored him to reconsider. Although Hyrcanus had indeed been maneuvered into calling Herod to trial, they reminded him, he had also been the instrument of Herod's deliverance. By degrees Herod's temper was cooled, and finally he marched back to Sepphoris, having made his show of strength before the nation.

All of this the scribe witnessed with his own eyes. During this time he played almost no part in the proceedings; there was very little in the way of correspondence, either sent or received. He was never so glad as on the day he returned to Sepphoris, for he was certain that the expedition he had just completed would be the one great adventure of his life and that now he could settle down to a quieter and more predictable existence. Little did he understand that this was but a foretaste of all that he would experience in the service of Herod. And as the events of the ensuing years rapidly unfolded, he would note with astonishment that the prophecy of Shemaiah did indeed come to pass. For when Herod later became king of Judea one of his first acts was to slay every member of the Sanhedrin who had sat in judgement against him—every one of them, that is, except the bold and righteous Shemaiah.

Joanna rolled up the scroll and replaced it on the shelf, exhausted and a little amazed. She had read the entirety of Book the Fifth with barely a stumble; for more than two hours the silversmith's son had been absent from her thoughts. Suddenly she was glad that there were so many more books in her uncle's secret history of Herod. She would escape the confinement of the house whenever possible, but meanwhile reading and writing were the only things that would save her from the slow torment of agonizing over her future. Again she arose and smoothed her robe, noticing as she did the prominent ink stain on her forefinger. She glanced down at the papyrus she had marked before she had begun to read and carefully blotted out the word she had written before feeling her way up the secret stairs.

The ground floor of the house was quiet and empty. Although winter had loosened its grip on Jerusalem there was still a chill in the air, and she hoped that Irijah would soon get on with the business of building a fire. She opened the door to the courtyard and peered out, but Irijah was not there. Nor was anyone else. She glanced at the sky. There was still some daylight left—perhaps an hour, perhaps less. Enough time to venture into the city, just a little way—perhaps in the direction of the smiths' bazaar.

She shook her head. It was a crazy idea. Surely she should wait. Patience was necessary.

No, she decided. She would bide her time no longer. The silversmith's son was out there, somewhere beyond these walls, and she would move toward him—if only in the most vague and harmless sort of way. What was the worst that could come of it? She would veil herself heavily in the unlikely event that she should encounter him. She was certain she knew the way. She had walked it just this morning. And if she should become uncomfortable, or uncertain, then it would be a simple enough thing to turn around and come home.

At the gate she hesitated, looking around to make sure no one was watching. Then she lifted the latch and stepped out: into the street, down the hill, and into the market street. The market crowd was thinning and almost immediately she attracted unwanted attention. A little man with a leathery face rushed up to her, displaying a large basket of onions.

"Look! Look! Onions! You want? Good price," he said, addressing her in the pidgin Aramaic of the countryside.

Joanna shook her head and walked more quickly, but the man was not deterred.

"Good onions, real good price," he repeated. "I give you good deal."

"I have no money," she said apologetically.

"No money, it's okay," the man said agreeably. "I come back tomorrow, you pay then."

"No."

"You take half, then. I give you really good price. You take half. Good onions. Really good."

She shook her head again. She understood his desperation. To bring the onions to the marketplace, he had paid Herod's heavy tax at the city gate. If he took them away and brought them back tomorrow, he would pay the tax again—probably more than the onions were worth.

He continued to follow her, thrusting the basket at her with more and more distressing entreaties. By now Joanna was feeling a little desperate herself. At the first opportunity she broke away from him, heading down a side street away from the marketplace. He called out after her, in a pathetic, accusatory tone, but she ignored him. She sighed as his complaints faded behind her. Her adventure into the city had ended almost as soon as it started. At least she would be able to return to Aduel's house well before nightfall.

She hurried along, intending to turn at the first opportunity and to double back along side streets in such a way that she would cross the market street at some distance from the man with the onions. But the street she had taken went on for some time without interruption, twisting and curving in unexpected directions. Finally she was able to take a turn to the right, and then another, but soon she found herself in the opposite predicament, for the farther she walked in this new district the shorter and more random the streets seemed to be, splitting off in all directions.

Joanna looked about nervously. She could not get her bearings. Buildings crowded on either side, blocking out all but a tiny sliver of the sky. There were no street signs or markings; one either knew one's way or one didn't. Landmarks were the way one navigated the cities of Judea, and if Joanna had been interested in this neighborhood she would have made note of several already. The house ahead, for example—tall and narrow with an unusual adobe awning that jutted out over the street. She had seen one like it a few minutes before, on a similar street. But this one had a small etching next to the door, a palm tree in terra cotta. The other house had not had an etching like that. Or had it? She could not remember.

She hurried along, becoming more uncertain with each new intersection. The unfamiliar streets were deep in shadow; impassive eyes examined her from dark doorways. She pressed ahead, her heart pumping faster. Any minute now she would stumble upon the market street; she was sure of it. Perhaps this next intersection would be the one that led her to safety.

Her mouth dropped open as she turned the corner. Landmarks were the way one navigated the cities of Judea, and just ahead there was one: A house tall and narrow, with an unusual adobe awning that jutted out over the street. She walked slowly toward it, unwilling to admit the chilling reality. But it was undeniable. There, next to the doorway, was a small palm tree, etched in terra cotta.

She began to panic. She had been walking in circles for twenty minutes, possibly longer. The daylight was nearly gone. She knew that if she were found alone in the streets after dark, she would be presumed a woman of loose morals, or worse. The shame would be intense, unbearable—not only for herself, but for her entire household, her uncle and even the two servants included. The silversmith's son would hear of it, somehow, and then all her hopes would be dashed. All because of one foolish, flighty impulse!

There was just enough light left for her to make it home before nightfall—but only if she made all the correct turns.

"Direct my steps, Lord," she prayed. "Show me the way."

Her only hope, she knew, was to retrace her steps to the market street. She took a deep breath to steady herself, then set out with firm, purposeful strides. Before her was a building she recognized; surely she had turned here. She turned to the left, and then to the left again. She was on the long, winding street now. Surely this was it. Yes. There was the market street ahead.

She wondered whether she would encounter the onion man again. She had a few choice words for him if she did. But he was nowhere to be seen. The market street was nearly empty. Soon she was headed up the hill toward Aduel's house.

She paused outside the courtyard gate to give her fluttering heart a moment to calm down. She prayed another prayer—that no one would be in the courtyard, and no one would hear her open the door to the house. But this prayer was not answered. Aduel was seated on one of the wooden benches. She approached him quietly. He appeared to be deep in meditation, or possibly asleep. Silently she skirted past him, hoping to enter the house without rousing him.

"So." Aduel was not asleep. "You have a taste for adventure now."

Joanna stopped in her tracks, too mortified to speak.

"A little adventure goes a long way," Aduel continued quietly. "Take it from one who has had more than his share."

"I know, Uncle, but Jerusalem is so…"

"So what? So exciting? So full of possibility?"

"Yes. Yes."

"I understand."

For a moment Aduel seemed ready to lapse into one of his long silences. But he continued: "Lift up your eyes to the heavens, child, and consider who created it all! The Lord leads out the stars one by one and calls each one by its name. Through His power and might, not one is missing!"

Joanna did not know what to say to this. She seated herself next to him and cast her gaze skyward. Aduel was right. As the deep violet of dusk faded to black, she could see the stars appear, one by one. It was a majestic procession, profound in its own simple way, and yet she had never noticed it.

After several minutes their reverie was broken by the opening of the courtyard gate. It was Irijah, who regarded the two of them curiously but said nothing. The old servant gathered up some wood for the hearth and disappeared into the house. Aduel looked upward again, seeming to search the sky. After several moments he broke the silence.

"What are we that the Almighty should remember us?" he said. "What are we that God should care for us?"

Joanna looked down. She never knew whether her uncle

was quoting Scripture—and was vaguely ashamed that she did not know. But she knew that she could not be blamed for it. Soon she would be able to read it for herself—and she would. She raised her head defiantly and cast another glance at the sky—a quick glance this time, as was her custom. The procession was complete; the heavens were now a starry blanket—hardly worth a second thought when there were more pressing matters at hand.

"Uncle?"

"Yes?"

"You said earlier that in the matter of..."

She stopped. Now more than ever the word felt strange and fantastic on her lips.

"In the matter of your betrothal," Aduel prompted.

"Yes. You said in that matter that there was another to be considered, and that you soon hoped..."

Her voice trailed off again.

"That I soon hoped to arrange it so that your decision would become clear to you."

"Yes."

"When will that be?"

"Soon, my child."

"Perhaps tomorrow," Joanna suggested. "I could accompany you."

"A second adventure in as many days," Aduel remarked. "Or in your case, a third! Well, perhaps it could be arranged. If these old bones will permit such excitement two days in a row, that is. Now, help me up. I've grown stiff with the cold. Let's go inside and see if Irijah has kindled the fire."

Chapter 9

The nighttime chill remained in the air the following morning as the girl clambered up the ladder to the rooftop, a bundle of clothing slung over her shoulder. Shortly after her arrival from Jericho, she had settled into a routine of helping Edna with the household chores—grinding, sweeping, mending, and many other small tasks similar to those she had performed in her mother's home in Jericho. Today she had been tasked with the washing, using a small basin that she would fill from the rooftop cistern. It was a duty Edna had been only too happy to relinquish, for the old woman's hands were dry and cracked and during the course of the winter the water had grown frigid, almost painful to the touch. But Joanna did not complain. In the weeks since she had come to the household the two women had shared a wary coexistence, a tension which Joanna had worked to alleviate at every opportunity. Moreover, in Aduel's household the chores were not onerous—especially since most of the outside errands were delegated to Irijah—and were usually completed before midday, while Aduel was reading or writing in his room below the ground. Joanna was surprised, therefore, when the gate to the courtyard below swung open and Aduel entered from the street.

"Good morning, Uncle," she called.

Her greeting startled Aduel, who was not accustomed to being hailed from the rooftop.

"Oh! It's you, child," he said, shielding his eyes from the bright morning sunshine. "Come down from there. We are going to the Temple."

"The Temple! Now?"

"Yes, now. You're craving adventure, are you not?"

Joanna nodded vigorously.

"Then dry your hands," Aduel said briskly. "I promised you an excursion beyond these walls. There is something I wish to see as well."

Joanna hurried down the ladder. Soon she and her uncle were making their way through the streets of Jerusalem, but not at Aduel's usual leisurely pace.

"Is there something happening at the Temple, Uncle?" Joanna asked, hurrying to keep up.

"Perhaps," Aduel said. "This morning I went to see a man about drafting a document, but he was not at his place of work. They said that all the young men of good education had gone to hear some teaching in the courtyard of the Temple. Quite unusual! I want to see what it is that has taken them all from their work."

"Oh." Joanna could not hide her disappointment. She had hoped that her uncle had been about the business of the second suitor.

"A bright young man, this fellow I had hoped to see," Aduel commented. "A future scribe of the Law, it seems. Too young to be ordained at present, of course, and currently of humble means, but certain to rise in society if what I have been told is correct. Also currently unencumbered by a betrothal."

"Oh!"

"Four or five years older than the previous candidate," Aduel said, glancing sideways at the girl. "Would this be acceptable?"

"I—I don't know." Joanna, already a little short of breath, was now panting. She found herself shrinking from the thought of life with a man several years older. Such pairings were not uncommon in Judean society, but they were often among family members—between cousins or in-laws who already knew one another. The differences usually faded over the course of years, she knew, and even if the betrothal were to be completed soon, the marriage itself would not take place for some time. Still, the idea of betrothal had suddenly transformed from a fevered daydream to something very real. To leave the comfort and relative independence of her uncle's household to move into the family home of a man six or seven years older just because of a single remark by Nicolaus of Damascus? It seemed the height of folly.

By now they had reached the base of the Temple Mount. Aduel led the way to the far end of the wide southern steps, where a steady stream of visitors was ascending toward a triple gate. The steps were irregularly spaced—by design, it seemed, for the girl noticed that Aduel, like all those around him, had slowed to a more solemn and deliberative pace. At the entrance to the gate the girl noticed the suspicious glances of the Temple guard; imitating the action of a woman a few paces in front of her, she lifted the hem of her robe slightly to show that there was no filth on her sandals. There were more stairs, a great many more, as they ascended through a tiled, arched tunnel that rose through the base of the great wall.

As they emerged, Joanna stopped suddenly, momentarily

blinded. Before her, across an enormous plaza, the Temple rose majestically above a dazzling surface of polished stone. She had seen it once before, from a distance, when she and Aduel had rounded the Mount of Olives on their approach from Jericho. Even from a distance it had been a remarkable sight, like a glistening snowy peak capping Mount Moriah, but it had not prepared her for this. It was the largest building she had ever seen, a hundred cubits tall and equally as long, and though she had heard tales of its splendor, she could not have pictured such magnificence in her wildest imagination. Her first impression had been only a glimpse, for the brilliant morning sunlight gleaming from the wall of polished white marble—overlaid with glinting panels of beaten gold—had caused her to shield her eyes with both hands. As her vision adjusted, she realized that she was alone—Aduel had plunged into the crowd in the plaza—but she was too awed to panic. She stood perfectly still, her mouth agape, taking in the sight as the crowd milled about her.

Gradually she began to make sense of her surroundings. The plaza before her was a hive of activity. Behind her, a massive portico, its roof supported by four rows of gigantic columns, rose to the height of several men. There was the sound of animals, and of clinking coins—the Temple sacrifices for sale, and the money changers who facilitated the transactions.

Suddenly Aduel was at her side.

"There you are, child!" he exclaimed. "I found that I was speaking to you and getting no reply. Then I looked back and you weren't there. Ah! Overcome by the magnificence of the Temple, are you?"

"It's so beautiful," Joanna murmured.

"Isn't it, though?" Aduel said. "And you know whom we have to thank for it, don't you? Herod. All of this is his doing. He has built fortresses throughout Judea, an enormous harbor that rises up out of the sea, a completely new city, but this is his crowning achievement. He wanted Jerusalem to take its place among the great cities of the world. I would say he has succeeded, wouldn't you?"

Joanna nodded silently, amazed that such a feat could be accomplished at the whim of one man.

"For our purposes we have arrived too late," Aduel said. "The teachers who have captivated the youth of the city seem to have finished their lessons. Perhaps we shall hear them another time. But for now you will see the Temple in all its splendor. Come, we'll have a look at the inner courts."

She hesitated for a moment as he guided her into the plaza. Even the pavement beneath her seemed magical—an intricate mosaic of perfectly cut, carefully polished stones in a variety of colors. It seemed profane even to touch such a beautiful surface—much less to walk on it—but Aduel did not seem to give it a second thought. In the center of the plaza a low wall formed a perfect rectangle around the Temple and the buildings that adjoined it. At the eastern end of the wall Aduel pointed to two signs posted near the entrance.

"Observe the proscriptions."

The girl squinted and shook her head. The stone tablets were clearly written, but she could make no sense of them.

"What do they say?" she asked.

"The first, as you probably know, is in Greek," Aduel replied. "It says, 'The Gentile who passes this boundary will bear the responsibility for his resulting death.'"

"You mean a Gentile would be put to death just for going

past this wall?"

"Exactly."

"But why?"

"Because beyond this wall is the sanctuary, ground that is sacred to the Jewish people," Aduel explained. "You are now in the Court of the Gentiles. All are welcome here. Even Gentiles may offer a sacrifice to the one true God if they wish. But only those who belong to the nation of Israel may pass beyond this point."

"And what of the second sign?" the girl asked.

"It is the same, but in Latin."

"Such strange letters!"

"Strange to us, but necessary. People from all over the world come here to worship, or simply to admire. Even now you see them, though it is not yet the time for the Passover feast."

"Maybe we shouldn't go any further," Joanna demurred, glancing at the swords of the guards she had seen posted at every gate.

"You needn't worry," Aduel chuckled. "No one is going to mistake you for a Gentile. Come."

They made their way up some steps and through an ornate gate, emerging into the raised area that housed the central part of the Temple complex. Inside was a separate courtyard, perfectly square—spacious enough in its own right but much smaller than the Court of the Gentiles, with porticoes on either side. Across this courtyard were fifteen semicircular steps leading to yet another gate—this one enormous, with two massive doors that gleamed in the sunlight. Behind these the Temple loomed above all, with a cladding of thick gold plates adorning its façade. Above its outer gates hung ornate golden vines with clusters of grapes that were as tall as a man, and through these open gates the girl could just make out the thick veil of scarlet, blue, and purple that marked the boundary of the most holy inner sanctum at the back.

In the center of the courtyard Aduel stopped, allowing the crowd to swirl past them.

"Look around," he instructed the girl. "This is as far as we can go together, the Court of the Women. All Israel is welcome here. The men of Israel may proceed through the Great Gate with their sacrifices."

"Do they take them into the Temple?"

"Oh, no," Aduel replied. "Only the priests may go into the Temple. The men of Israel can go only as far as the Court of Israel. There is a smaller, interior courtyard surrounding the Temple itself which may only be accessed by the priests. That is where the sacrifices take place, visible to those watching from the Court of Israel. In fact, when this Temple was built Herod had to train a thousand priests to be masons and carpenters so that regular workers did not defile the innermost sanctum."

"Did the priests make those enormous gates?"

"No, those are not part of the Temple itself, so they did not have to be made by the priests. A good thing, too, since they are made of Corinthian bronze! Fifty cubits tall, shipped here from Alexandria. Herod had intended to have them plated with gold, like all the other gates, but they shone so brilliantly that he left them as they were."

"I don't understand how one man could pay for all of this," Joanna remarked.

"Well, the people of Jerusalem contributed what they could, as they usually do when it comes to the affairs of the

Temple," Aduel said. "But the vast majority of the funds came from Herod. Herod is a hard man when it comes to taxes, but he can be generous with his money if it suits his purposes. Which reminds me, I have a shekel here. Could you put it into one of the treasury chests?"

There were several chests stationed around the Court of the Women. Joanna deliberated for a moment, then walked to a chest marked "Voluntary Sacrifice" and tossed in the shekel. Near it was a slender column of polished stone that towered into the sky, taller than the nearby portico and even than the huge gates of Corinthian bronze. Looking about she noticed that there were three more like it in the Court of the Women, one each corner.

"I see that you noticed the menorahs," Aduel commented when she returned.

"Those are menorahs?"

"Yes, the largest in the world. Giant torches that are lit during the Festival of Booths, in the autumn. Their fire illuminates the Temple, and much of the city as well, reminding us of the pillar of fire that guided our people during their journey through the wilderness. It's quite a spectacle. You'll enjoy it. Come, it's time for us to be on our way."

Aduel turned to go, much to the girl's disappointment. There were so many things to see, to learn! These would have to wait for another time. But she could not resist the impulse to tug at her uncle's sleeve just once.

"Uncle, what is that?"

She pointed to a large golden statue that surmounted the great gates of Corinthian bronze.

Aduel glanced in the direction the girl had indicated and quickly turned away.

"Hmph, the eagle!" His proud demeanor quickly changed to disgust. "That represents Rome."

"Rome!"

"Yes, Herod has placed it there to honor the emperor and his legions. Perhaps it is best not to speak of it here. I'll tell you more about it presently."

Joanna followed in silence as Aduel led the way out of the Court of the Women and across the wide Court of the Gentiles. They exited through a different gate on the west side of the southern portico, descending through a domed tunnel similar to the one through which they had entered. Not until they had cleared the Temple grounds did Aduel clear his throat and begin to speak.

"The golden eagle that Herod installed atop the Great Gate is a source of tremendous controversy," he explained quietly as they made their way along a side street. "Our law clearly states that there must be no images of any kind in the Temple. That is why you cannot spend Roman money on the Temple grounds, or even donate it to the Temple treasury, because it bears the image of Caesar. And yet Herod has chosen to mar his greatest achievement with just such an image."

"Why would he do that?" Joanna wondered.

"Why, indeed?" Aduel mused. "This has been Herod's dilemma ever since he ascended the throne. He is intent upon impressing the Romans but at the same time he must appease the Jews. Not an easy task for two peoples so fundamentally different! But the eagle was an obvious mistake. The Romans care little about it, but it has infuriated the Jews. However, that is one of the flaws in Herod's nature. He has an irrepressible urge to show the Romans that he is one of them, that he is somehow their equal."

They pondered this in silence all the way back to Aduel's house.

"I wonder what he will do next," Joanna mused, as Aduel opened the gate to the small courtyard.

"Herod? You might not be wondering long." Aduel lowered his voice. "There are reports that Herod is dying."

Joanna drew her breath sharply.

"Soon?" she asked.

"No one knows. This is something that has been going on for some time now. They say that it is an internal fire that glows slowly. The doctors have not been able to stop it. But knowing Herod, he will not go quietly. No, he will make a monumental struggle of it."

"If he does die, what will become of Nicolaus of Damascus?"

"My child, you must stop worrying about Nicolaus of Damascus."

"I'm not worrying," Joanna insisted. "But...if Herod should die, what would become of him?"

"That is unclear. There has been great turmoil in the house of Herod in recent years, as you will find when you come to the end of my history."

"Will there be a struggle for the throne?"

"That depends on many things. The first of them is whether Herod actually dies. I would not put it past our king to spread the rumor of his own demise in a bid for his enemies to reveal themselves."

"Did he look ill when you were called to court a few weeks ago?"

"Not terribly ill. But he did not look well, either." Aduel gestured to the door. "Come, let us go inside and shed these sandals. Too many steps can be hard on the feet of an old man!

Perhaps we can find Edna and see if she will give us something to eat. Then we shall rest."

"Actually, Uncle, I was hoping…"

"Hoping what? That you might read this afternoon?"

"Yes."

"Ah, our little excursion has whetted your appetite for Book the Fifth."

"Book the Sixth, actually."

"Book the Sixth! Then you have already finished Book the Fifth?"

"Yes."

"And you understood it all?"

"I think so. Except for a few words."

Joanna looked down, suddenly realizing that her uncle might not approve of her unauthorized foray into a new installment of his history. But Aduel seemed amused, even a little delighted.

"Well, as long as I am not the one standing, I think a bit of reading this afternoon would be just the thing," he chuckled. "But first we must eat. Something very tempting is calling to me from Edna's griddle. I do believe there may be a cake of figs waiting inside for each of us."

Chapter 10

Aduel's senses had not deceived him; the aroma of baking was fully evident as soon as he and the girl entered the house. But something besides cakes was waiting for them. In the corner of the room, a young man was seated on one of the cushions at the low table near the window.

He rose as they entered. Joanna was taken aback; in the time she had lived in the house, there had been no callers—other than the soldiers and Nicolaus of Damascus. She had removed her veil in the courtyard, and now in her confusion she forgot to put it back on. The young man regarded her with interest but did not acknowledge her in any way, in keeping with the Jewish custom. Instead he bowed to Aduel:

"Your servant, sir."

Joanna looked to her uncle, but Aduel seemed equally confused.

"I summoned no servant," he said irritably.

"In the matter of a contract," the young man prompted.

Joanna's eyes widened. This was the second suitor Aduel had mentioned, the scribe. It had to be! But he had taken them by surprise. To have him here in Aduel's house was hardly the surreptitious introduction her uncle had intended. For their purposes, in fact, it was a disaster. She knew that there was little chance of a marriage contract with this young man now. Still, she took another look at him before pulling her shawl low over her forehead. He was fair skinned and of average height; his robe, though not elegant, was neatly kept. His face was not remarkable, but nor was it ugly, and the clear, piercing gaze of his light eyes seemed to convey a love of clarity, reason, and order. It was a marked contrast with the swarthy, smoldering countenance of the silversmith's son.

"Ah, yes," Aduel said hastily. "I came to see you at your place of work, but they could not find you."

Joanna attempted to edge out of the room to leave the men to their business, but Aduel was blocking the way and, in his consternation, seemed rooted to his place. So she remained where she was, casting her gaze downward.

"Most humble apologies." The young scribe bowed again. "Important business required my presence at the Temple."

"Business!" Aduel scoffed. "I've heard about this business. I went to the Temple myself, to find out more about it. My niece and I have just come from there. Unfortunately we were too late to hear the business being discussed."

"I believe you would find it enlightening," the young scribe said. "Two teachers, passionately dedicated to our Law, with a strict devotion to the Lord our God, hold forth in the Court of the Gentiles for all who care to hear."

"For all who care to incur the wrath of Herod," Aduel replied. "One man's passion for the Law might be another man's sedition. I would be careful to spend too much time with these teachers if I were you."

The youth acknowledged the admonition with a slight bow, and an awkward silence descended upon the room.

"There was the matter of a contract," the scribe reminded Aduel.

"Yes, yes, the contract," Aduel said. He clearly was flustered. "What I require is, hmm. What I want is a marriage contract, one that conforms to the most up-to-date interpretation of the Law. Yes, that is what I want. That is exactly what I want. I have been told that despite your lack of years you are considered an authority on this subject."

The scribe acknowledged the compliment with a nod.

"I can make note of the names and all the other details," he said.

From a pocket in the sleeve of his robe he drew out a small palimpsest, but Aduel waved it away.

"The names and other particulars will be left blank for the time being," he said.

"A blank marriage contract?" The scribe was perplexed. "That is most unusual."

"Perhaps, but I'm concerned mostly with the form. The details can be filled in easily enough. I want to make sure that all requirements are strictly adhered to in accordance with the strictest interpretation of the Law. I wish to review it in draft before any formalities are discussed."

"Very well. It shall be done as you say."

"When?"

"It will be ready in two days' time. Shall I deliver it here?"

"No, no, I'll have my manservant pick it up."

"Very well, sir. Will there be anything else?"

Aduel shook his head irritably. The scribe bowed deeply to him, ignoring the girl as was proper—except for a glance that told her that she was not ignored. Then he was gone.

Not until they heard the gate of the courtyard clatter behind the departing visitor did Aduel heave a sigh of exasperation.

"What a stroke of ill luck!" he moaned. "I did not anticipate that he would take the initiative to call on me here, unannounced. There can be no question in his mind that the marriage contract is intended for you—you and another man. To attempt to engage him now would offend him immensely."

"It's all right, Uncle," Joanna consoled him. "He's so much older."

"Recall that he is but twenty-two or twenty-three," Aduel reminded her. "Such composure for one so young! And a sincere regard for our laws and the pursuit of righteous living! Well, it cannot be helped."

Edna appeared from the back of the house, carrying a tray of freshly baked cakes. She looked at Aduel and the girl with surprise.

"Where is our visitor?" she asked.

"Gone," Aduel muttered. "Gone for good, I'm afraid."

"Already?" Edna was puzzled. "I left him for just a few minutes, to prepare the refreshments. I thought he would be here for some time. He said he was here to discuss business."

"Yes, yes, the business has been discussed and concluded," Aduel snapped.

"Well, there are cakes for you at any rate," Edna said. "More than enough, now."

"I'm not hungry," Aduel grumbled.

Edna turned and offered the platter to Joanna.

"I'm not hungry either," she said politely.

"Nonsense, eat!" Aduel said. "Eat mine as well. I deserve no reward for bungling this business."

With that he stalked off. The girl shrugged at Edna and wasted no time helping herself to one of the fig cakes. She followed the old woman to the kitchen where the overpowering aroma of the warm, gooey pastry induced her to take another, and then a third. She contemplated the awkward encounter with the young scribe as she ate. She perceived that he was her uncle's first choice for her as a husband, and that Aduel was grieved that now the union would never take place. She herself was not grieved. The young scribe had intimidated her. It was his manner of speaking, his gaze—the intensity of it. It was the gaze of one who would always be reasonable, and fair to her—likely even gentle and kind—and she knew that this was the most that a young wife in Judea could dare to hope for. But it was intimidating indeed—that gaze, the clarity of it, because she was uncertain that she would have the mettle to return it.

Three of Edna's cakes remained on the platter. Joanna contemplated them for a moment but after just having consumed three others the temptation was quickly overcome. Instead she took the platter and made her way down the stairway to her uncle's room underground. Aduel was kneeling on a thin cushion under the tiny window slit, his back to the door. Noiselessly she set the platter on the writing table and turned back toward the stairway. But Aduel's voice arrested her:

"I'm sorry, my child."

Joanna turned back, surprised that he had heard her. Slowly, stiffly, Aduel rose from his prayer mat. The struggle pained her; she hurried to him and took both his hands in hers, regarding him with mild alarm. For a moment she was supporting him, grasping his hands firmly. For the first time he seemed old to her.

"There's nothing to be sorry about, Uncle!" she comforted. "You've done so much for me."

"Only what any man might be expected to do for the child of his sister," Aduel grumbled. "I had hoped to do more."

"Oh, nonsense!" Joanna reprimanded gently. "You've done more than I could ever have asked."

"Hmph! Perhaps, but then to mismanage a key part of the business...Hmph! Help me to the stool, child. Ah, that's better."

Aduel situated himself comfortably, leaning back against the wall. In an effort to hide his frustration he adopted a businesslike tone:

"As to the business of your betrothal, obviously it has just become a good deal simpler," he said. "The silversmith's son it shall be, if that is your desire. And, of course, if that is his desire."

"Of course," Joanna said amiably.

"An admirable match, from what I know of the situation," Aduel continued, trying to sound cheerful. "When the contract is ready I will examine it carefully. Then, if you are sure, I will visit the silversmith. At that point we will know what will or will not be done."

Joanna nodded.

"Then it is settled, at least this part of it," Aduel concluded. "Now, we have the entire afternoon ahead of us. You had mentioned that you would like to do some reading."

"Oh, no, Uncle, not today. We've already been so busy. I should not have interrupted you. You wish to be alone."

"No. The last thing I want right now is to be alone. To hear you read my little work will be a balm to my soul. Here." He handed her a scroll. "Book the Fourth. And, if I am satisfied with your recital, Book the Fifth. And then, perhaps, if enough light remains, Book the Sixth as well."

"Three books at one reading?" Joanna smiled. "We'll see."

"Yes, we shall see." The familiar twinkle had returned to Aduel's eye, although it had a discouraged aspect to it. "There are three cakes here. Let's see if I can make them last for three books."

Aduel listened with his eyes closed, hardly moving, as Joanna read through Book the Fourth with little trouble. He was so still that as she approached the end of the book, with the gruesome executions of Hezekias and his rebel band, she wondered whether he had fallen asleep. But as she closed the scroll he nodded approval and wordlessly took it from her, handing her another. Once again he settled himself comfortably, and she proceeded though the fifth book. This too went smoothly; even the words that had puzzled her the day before now seemed clear. Aduel was alert now, following the story with interest, as if remembering things long forgotten, nibbling at the fig cakes and helping her with the few words she could not interpret.

When she had finished Aduel nodded approvingly.

"You have done well, my child," he said. "Do you have any questions?"

Joanna reflected for a moment.

"Do you think Herod was jealous of Phasaelus?" she asked.

"Do I think Herod was jealous of Phasaelus?" Aduel repeated. "Now that is a question I have never considered. Why do you ask?"

"Because the way that you described them, it seemed that they both were like their father, but Phasaelus more so. He seemed more level-headed and careful. It makes sense that Antipater would favor him."

"For the most part Phasaelus was the more level-headed

and careful of the two," Aduel agreed. "And certainly those are desirable qualities when it comes to governing a nation as fractious as Judea. But to my knowledge Antipater never showed any favoritism between his sons. The two brothers remained fast friends until Phasaelus met his death."

"But Antipater appointed Phasaelus to remain in Jerusalem with him to govern, while Herod was sent to Galilee."

"True, but that was to be expected," Aduel shrugged. "As the elder, Phasaelus would receive the better portion. But perhaps you have perceived something in the text that was not evident to me. It would explain much. Herod has always been eager—desperate, even—to gain the notice of others. Perhaps that is an impulse that was sparked very early in life."

The two of them contemplated this in silence for a few moments.

"Did Phasaelus live a long life?" Joanna asked.

"No, Phasaelus died at a young age. He will meet his end rather soon, I am afraid."

"In Book the Sixth?"

"Yes. You will find that he was not as careful as he might have been."

Joanna glanced at the window. The Sabbath would begin at sunset; there would be no reading on the morrow. She also remembered that she needed to go to the roof to collect the washing she had spread out to dry that morning. But they had gotten an early start and the days were growing longer. It seemed that there was plenty of daylight left. Aduel seemed to read her thoughts.

"Surely you are tired now, child, or at least thirsty."

"No, Uncle, neither."

"Very well, then."

Aduel rolled the fifth book more tightly and replaced it on the shelf. After rummaging about for a moment, he handed her another scroll.

"Book the Sixth," he said. "It's one of the longer ones. With luck we'll finish it by sundown. But when the Sabbath begins, the reading stops."

Joanna nodded and cleared her throat.

"Herod: A Secret History, by Aduel of Sepphoris. Book the Sixth."

It was about this time that events in Judea became inextricably entwined with the affairs of Rome, as they remain to this day. The assassination of Julius Caesar, who had ruled the Roman Republic as dictator for three and a half years, initiated a period of great instability throughout the Roman world and especially in Judea. It was during this time that Antipater, the father of Phasaelus and Herod, was poisoned by a rival. The two brothers avenged their father's murder with the full approval of the Romans, who reaffirmed the brothers' control over the affairs of Judea. Although Hyrcanus remained ruler, Herod, with the backing of Rome, was given command of an even larger army, and thus assumed the same role that Antipater had played, effectively in control of the nation, with Phasaelus his loyal partner in charge of Jerusalem.

Due to the turmoil in Rome in the wake of Caesar's demise, the province of Syria had been wrested from Roman control by the Parthians, rulers of a great empire to the east that had once belonged to the Persians. It was not long before Pacorus, a Parthian prince, attempted to pry away Judea as well. The first sign of trouble was an urgent dispatch indicating that a Parthian force had invaded Galilee and was headed south through Samaria. By this time the scribe from Sepphoris, despite his tender years, had become Herod's official secretary and was at his side in Jerusalem when the dispatch was read.

"I knew it!" Herod spat. "Pacorus has Syria and now he wants Judea as well."

He handed the dispatch to Corinthus, a captain of the guard, who happened to be standing by.

"Surely this is just a raiding party," said Corinthus, after perusing the dispatch. "The Parthians would never attack Jerusalem. For them to challenge Rome in such a way would be madness."

"They've already challenged Rome, and taken Syria," Herod replied acridly. "Is that the kind of madness you're talking about? No, the Roman world is divided at present, with two would-be emperors circling each other like wild animals—Octavian in the west and Antony in the east. It's the perfect time to make an attempt on Judea."

"Still, Excellency, it seems unlikely," Corinthus argued. "The Parthians have extended themselves too far. With the forces that you and Phasaelus have together, the Parthians haven't the troops for to take Judea."

"They would if they could stir the people to revolt against us."

"The people would never rally to a foreigner."

Herod's face darkened, and the young secretary held his breath. Corinthus was a military man, unsubtle in matters of politics, and in his agitation over the news of the Parthian incursion he had forgotten that this was the very complaint the people had against Herod—that as a man of Idumean and Arabian ancestry he was a foreigner who controlled the nation behind the facade of a puppet king. But after a moment Herod allowed the unintended insult to pass.

"No, but they would rally to a Jew, especially one of royal lineage," he mused.

"The only Jew of royal lineage is Hyrcanus, and he already occupies the throne," Corinthus said.

"Hmph! Hyrcanus! Aren't you forgetting someone?"

"Who, Excellency?"

"Antigonus."

"Antigonus!" exclaimed Corinthus. "The son of Aristobulus, the brother of Hyrcanus? Surely Antigonus would not ally himself with the Parthians against his own uncle!"

"Yet there are reports that he has."

Herod snapped his fingers.

"Notify Phasaelus, at once," he directed the secretary. "Tell him what we know and ask whether he has any similar information. We must determine whether these reports are true."

The reports were true. Within the hour another dispatch had arrived, and then a third, and soon many more. The news was grim. In the north of Samaria, in the region near Mount Carmel, a great number of Jews had joined the party of Antigonus. Thousands more, stirred by the party spirit that had arisen during the fraternal rivalry between Hyrcanus and Aristobulus years earlier, were joining each day as the Parthian force made its way south. And then, before anyone fully comprehended what was happening, this rabble descended upon Jerusalem. They besieged the palace of Hyrcanus but were driven off by the forces of Herod and Phasaelus, precipitating a great battle in the midst of the marketplace, near the Temple. The brothers' troops proved victorious, yet they were unable to drive the rebels—and their leader, Antigonus—from Jerusalem.

For a time there was an uneasy truce, broken by repeated skirmishes throughout the city, but neither side could prevail. Soon it was time for the Feast of Weeks, which the Greeks call Pentecost because it takes place fifty days after the Passover. Jerusalem was filled with thousands of pilgrims from the countryside—all of them armed, it seemed, and all supporting Antigonus and his Parthian allies against the ruling party of Hyrcanus, Phasaelus, and Herod. There was another great clash, with Herod and Phasaelus again victorious—yet again unable to complete the victory by driving the rebels out of the city.

Herod was inspecting the fortifications of the palace with his officers, preparing yet another assault, when he received yet more bad news, delivered to him by the secretary. It was a message from Phasaelus.

"The fools!" he exclaimed, crumpling the papyrus in his hand.

"What now, Excellency?" asked Corinthus.

"Hyrcanus has persuaded Phasaelus to admit the Parthian prince into the city with five hundred horse!" Herod exclaimed. "Come quickly. We must put a stop to it."

They hurried to the palace, but it was too late. The five hundred Parthian horsemen were already arrayed outside. It was an impressive assembly, but Herod ignored it. With a shocking disregard for court etiquette, Herod and his officials barged into the grand audience chamber where Pacorus and his retinue were being received in a formal ceremony. On the dais Hyrcanus was seated on his throne, his flabby face looking exhausted and harassed, flanked by Phasaelus and numerous court and military officials. Facing him was Pacorus, backed by several officials of his own. The Parthian prince was a thin, wiry man with a hawkish face and large, darting eyes. But the most notable thing about him was his manner of dress. His brightly colored tunic was belted at the waist and worn over a peculiar garment of a kind rarely seen in Jerusalem, one that covered each leg with a separate sleeve of fabric.

Herod, still wearing his breastplate and armed with both dagger and sword, wasted no time waiting for an introduction.

"Phasaelus!" he barked. "What is the meaning of this? To allow enemy cavalry to enter the city unchallenged! Are you mad?"

Phasaelus opened his mouth as if to reply but seemed uncertain as to what to say. His hesitation gave Pacorus an opening.

"Enemy!" the Parthian objected, addressing himself to Hyrcanus. "We are not the enemy of Judea. Quite the contrary. We come as friends. We hope only to restore peace to your land."

"Make no mistake, Majesty," Herod said to Hyrcanus. "These are your enemies. They have been fighting Rome for more than fifteen years, and we are allies of Rome."

"Rome!" sneered Pacorus. "What is Rome? A broken lance, an empire wracked by civil war! Where are your Roman allies now, King Hyrcanus? You have barely enough troops to defend your palace, let alone your capital. To say nothing of your nation. Rome will not help you now. The Romans have been busy fighting other Romans these four years now."

Hyrcanus, as weak and indecisive as ever, shifted his troubled gaze from Pacorus to Herod and back again.

"Phasaelus admitted the Parthian force to the city at my command," he said to Herod. "It was suggested by Antigonus, in the interest of establishing peace in the city."

"Antigonus!" Herod exclaimed. "The viper who would depose you? He cares nothing for peace in the city. His only interest is in your throne."

"But what is the alternative, Herod?" Hyrcanus cried. "These repeated battles within Jerusalem, with dozens killed each day and nothing decided, cannot continue. What do you propose?"

"I propose that we fight this sedition until we defeat it!"

"The babble of junior officers can be most entertaining,"

Pacorus chuckled. "Perhaps this youth does not understand that your resources are limited, and that you are far outnumbered."

Herod bristled at the insult, which was all the more pointed because Pacorus was in no way an elderly man, and was, in fact, Herod's junior in years.

"What, then?" Hyrcanus asked Pacorus. "What is it you suggest? How will you restore peace to the land?"

"A conference," said Pacorus.

"A conference!" Herod was incredulous.

"A conference," Pacorus repeated placidly, "involving all interested parties: Antigonus, King Hyrcanus, and the king's military commander Phasaelus. Perhaps even this junior officer here, if he can be taught to hold his tongue. I offer my services as mediator."

"Out of the question!" objected Herod. "To allow Antigonus to set foot here would be the same as handing the throne to him directly."

"The conference would be held in a neutral place." Pacorus continued to address his remarks to Hyrcanus, pointedly refusing to recognize Herod. "Galilee, perhaps. Halfway between Jerusalem and Syria. The Parthian governor who now commands our territory in Syria would join us. He is most experienced in these sorts of negotiations."

"An obvious trap," scoffed Herod. "Dismiss this deceiver at once, Hyrcanus. Or kill him now, before he can do any serious harm. I'll kill him myself, if you give the order."

He took a step forward, his hand on the hilt of his sword. Alarmed, Hyrcanus raised his hand, but words failed him. Suddenly Phasaelus found his voice.

"No, Herod," he said, stepping forward. "Pacorus is the crown prince of the Parthian Empire. He will someday be their king. I think we can trust him."

"He will be the chief liar of a nation of liars," Herod snarled. "Already he outdoes himself with this absurd proposal. You must not go."

"But what is the alternative, Herod?" Hyrcanus fretted.

"The king will decide," Phasaelus said simply.

"Yes, I will decide," Hyrcanus sighed. "And I will go. Phasaelus too, to advise me. If he consents."

"I do consent."

"You are fools, both of you!" Herod cried. "You sign your own death warrants, as well as the death warrants of all who have supported you! But I will not sign mine. They will have to take me by arms, not by trickery!"

He wheeled from the audience chamber, his astonished retinue hurrying after him, and departed the palace for the nearby barracks. It was here, not long afterward, that Herod saw Phasaelus for the last time. In the final meeting between the two, Herod's elder brother made an earnest effort to persuade him to accommodate this powerful enemy from the east.

"The Parthians can be bargained with," he told Herod. "If we manage them skillfully, we can use them to our advantage."

"That might be true if we were indeed managing them, but they are managing us," Herod retorted. "Can you not see that our only hope of victory is to remain united in Jerusalem?"

"But we have tried that, and failed," Phasaelus reminded him. "There have been ambushes and slaughters every day, with both sides depleted and nothing decided. It cannot go on."

"It must go on, and we will be victorious," Herod said.

"No. It is time to strive for peace. I believe we can trust these Parthians. They have agreed to leave two hundred of their horse in the city—hostages, of a sort."

"Two hundred enemy horse in Jerusalem is two hundred too many," Herod growled. "By drawing you away from the city, the Parthians undermine our only hope of success. Can't you see that?"

"All will be well, Herod," Phasaelus reassured him cheerfully. "You'll see."

"All will not be well," Herod snapped, "and as for seeing, I fear this will be the last time we shall look upon each other's faces."

Phasaelus—powerful, confident, and seemingly invulnerable in his armor—merely smiled and clasped his brother in a manly embrace. Mounting his magnificent horse, he turned away and joined Hyrcanus and their Parthian escort as they made their way out of Jerusalem.

Regular dispatches travelled between Herod and Phasaelus as the royal party made its way north through Samaria and on into Galilee. At first nothing seemed amiss, but Herod's suspicions did not abate. Then, when the procession reached the port city of Ecdippa, near the border of Galilee and Syria, things changed. There Phasaelus learned of the Parthians' true intentions: They had always been in league with Antigonus, as Herod had suspected. They had bargained with the rebel leader for a payment of one thousand talents of gold—and, even more disgracefully—for five hundred women of Jerusalem. These women would be deported to the Parthian empire and distributed to the Parthian nobles as spoils of war, never to return to Judea. They would be taken from the leading families of Jerusalem—including those of Hyrcanus, Phasaelus, and Herod.

Phaesalus's most trusted friends implored him to flee at once on horseback, to a ship that waited to transport him to safety. But Phasaelus, a man of integrity to the last, refused to abandon Hyrcanus, and instead, after sending a messenger to Herod to apprise him of the way things stood, went to the Parthian governor to confront him directly. This man swore to Phasaelus that he was mistaken, then immediately afterward had both him and Hyrcanus arrested and bound hand and foot.

All of this Herod learned not from Phasaelus's official messenger, who had been detained immediately by the Parthians, but by others who had fled from Phasaelus's camp. One of these, having taken a roundabout route through rough territory to avoid capture, arrived disheveled and exhausted in the council room of the palace the following day. Herod listened stone-faced as the man gave his account. When he had finished, there was a long and terrible silence.

"Oh, my brother, my brother, your trusting nature has put you in the power of ruthless men," Herod moaned finally. "Why did you not listen?"

At that moment, an official from the Parthian camp was announced and was escorted into the chamber.

"Good news, excellent Herod," the man said, bowing deeply. "Messengers bearing letters from Phasaelus have arrived and await just outside the city."

"If they are just outside the city, then why do they delay?" Herod demanded. "Bring them to me at once."

"The messengers say they cannot travel further," the Parthian said smoothly. "You must come outside the city to meet them."

"Bring me the letters they carry from Phasaelus. That will be sufficient to tell me whether Phasaelus has met with any treachery."

"There has been no treachery," the Parthian said evenly. "But these men claim that they have secret instructions from Phasaelus that they may speak into your ear only. You must go to them."

"Well, if they carry secret instructions, I suppose I must," Herod mused. "But not now. The day is almost gone. Tomorrow. Expect me at the Gate of Ephraim at midday. Then you may conduct me to these messengers."

The Parthian official bowed and was escorted away. When he was gone, Herod turned to his officers.

"I have bought us a little time, but only a little," he muttered. "They will wait until morning to see if I am as trusting and foolish as my brother. If I do not accompany them beyond the walls of the city, they will attack us here."

"And we will fight them, and win!" cried Corinthus, the commander of the guard.

"No." Herod shook his head. "We will not fight them. Even if Phasaelus were here with his men, we could expect nothing but defeat. Without them, the battle would be over in minutes."

"What, then?" asked Corinthus. "Do we quit the city and attempt to free Phasaelus and his men?"

"Phasaelus and his men are lost to us," Herod said grimly. "They have placed themselves in the power of the enemy. If we were to go to them, our small force would be surrounded and crushed. What am I to do? What am I to do?"

No one answered. The room was silent as Herod paced distractedly.

At this moment, Alexandra, the daughter of Hyrcanus, burst into the room. She was a striking woman of about forty, with an intelligent, royal bearing, but a slight downturn of the mouth hinted at the trouble lurking behind that beautiful façade. Indeed, she was in the habit of indulging in disgraceful histrionics that made her detested among Herod's men. However, she had inherited a good deal of the political acumen that had marked the reign of the famous queen—her grandmother—after whom she had been named. Herod, though often provoked by her outrageous behavior and her pronounced lack of deference to him, had always chosen to endure it in order to gain the benefit of her counsel.

Despite her royal pedigree Alexandra, like Herod, had little concern for the niceties of court protocol when it suited her.

"Herod!" she exclaimed breathlessly. "Herod! I've just had word that Phasaelus and my father are taken prisoner by the Parthians!"

"Yes, we have heard the same," Herod replied grimly. "Word travels quickly here in the palace."

"Well, what are you going to do about it?" Alexandra demanded. "Stand here chattering with these useless knaves and boobies? You must go to them!"

Herod peered at her irritably but for a moment said nothing. In addition to being the daughter of the king, Alexandra had an even stronger claim on him. Her eldest daughter Miriam, the most beautiful young woman in all Judea, was betrothed to Herod himself. By consenting to this, Alexandra had paved the way for Herod to marry into the royal line of Judea that stretched back to the Maccabees more than a century before.

"Hmm," Herod seemed to consider. "Leave our fortifications with a handful of men to march straight into the Parthian forces that await us? I think not, Alexandra. We would be cut to pieces before we got a mile outside the city walls. And you would be left to your fate, with whatever Parthian prince would have you."

"Parthian prince!" Alexandra spat. "You disgust me, Herod. No Parthian would dare to touch the daughter of the King of Judea. Find out what he wants. If Antigonus is offering him money, offer him more."

"According to the messengers we have had from Phasaelus, that has already been tried," Herod said. "Antigonus has offered one thousand talents to the Parthians, and Phasaelus, before he was taken, offered more to buy them off. But it seems that the money was not enough. No, the Parthians have their eyes on something...hmm, how shall I say it? Something more stimulating."

"What, then?"

"You."

"Me!" Alexandra, that prodigy of shocking statements, was herself genuinely shocked.

"Yes, you, and four hundred ninety-nine others like you." Herod's eyes glittered. Even in these dire circumstances, he could not resist the timeless pleasure of needling his prospective mother-in-law. "You are the chief inducements Antigonus has offered the Parthians. Five hundred women of Jerusalem, to be handed off like gifts, like prize cattle, to the most favored Parthian lords. And you would be one of the greatest prizes, no doubt, despite your years. A daughter of the King of Judea."

Alexandra paled as she saw that Herod was not joking. Her own words rang mockingly in her ears as the horror of Antigonus's vile bargain became fully apparent to her.

"The wretch!" she cried. "The fiend! He bargains our lives— our honor—for the throne!"

"He does indeed," Herod said. "And as things stand now, he's very close to completing his bargain. So. Since you have presumed to advise me, I beg you, advise. The Parthians say that messengers from Phasaelus await me outside the city, and that I must go to them. Shall I leave the city? Shall I go to the Parthian camp and offer them more money?"

"No! You must not go to them! The Parthians are liars, all of them."

"At least we agree on that. But what, then? What?"

"I don't know, Herod," Alexandra taunted sourly. "You're the leader here. You're the one who has usurped the authority in my father's kingdom. You wanted power; you've gotten it. You must decide. You are the leader."

Herod remained deep in thought for some time, while the

others awaited his decision.

"Yes, I must decide," he said at last, his voice rising from a low growl to a frenzied shriek. "I will decide! I am the leader!"

A sudden rage came over him, a rage of the type that was to grow more frequent and more uncontrollable as the years progressed. He quivered and roared incoherently, and then without warning drew the dagger from his belt and plunged it into the table before him. All in the room uttered a collective gasp and a shudder, and then there was again silence as he paced the room distractedly.

Finally he halted at the doorway and gazed wordlessly at them. He had become calm again. Replacing his dagger, he seemed to have reached a conclusion. But it was Alexandra who broke the silence.

"We must leave Jerusalem," she said mournfully.

"We agree on that too," Herod said calmly. "Yes, we will leave this city, and we will leave it tonight."

"But where can we go?" Alexandra demanded. "Where?"

"To my ancestral homeland," Herod replied. "South, to Idumea. I have sent much of my treasure there, in case of an emergency such as this, and I have supporters who will shelter us. For a time, at least."

"But what of the women?" pressed Alexandra.

"Why, the women will come with us," Herod said. "It is for their sake that we flee. Were it not for them we would stay here, and fight, down to the last man, and then leave the city to its fate."

"But how will we choose?" Alexandra exclaimed. "Five hundred women! Which ones will we take?"

"All of them, of course. No one who wishes to leave Jerusalem will be left behind."

"All of them?" Alexandra asked incredulously. "You propose to evacuate five hundred women from Jerusalem in a single night?"

"Five hundred women and their families," Herod reminded her

sententiously.

"But what of the Parthians, Excellency?" fretted Corinthus. "Will they not take notice of such a procession?"

"The two hundred horse of the Parthians have been sent to Bezetha, in the northernmost part of the city. They will know nothing of what is happening as long as we do things quietly."

"Indeed, Excellency. But will they not pursue us?"

"Likely they will. Their main objective is Jerusalem, but they'll want the women as well. That is why we must get as much as head start on them as possible."

"Yes, Excellency."

"I myself will rally the soldiers," Herod continued. "Corinthus, you will see to the transports. Carts, wagons, horses, mules— anything you can muster. As for you, my dear Alexandra, you will organize the women."

"Me! I am the daughter of the King of Judea!"

"Yes, and you seem to have a talent for giving orders. Perhaps you should put it to good use."

"I never said—"

"The women may take with them only what they can carry about their persons," Herod interrupted. "There will be no one to assist them, not even those of the highest rank."

"Herod, there are at least two women who have just given birth," Alexandra snapped. "They are in no condition to walk for miles, or to be transported on donkeys or carts! And what of their children? They are infants, only a few days old!"

"The mothers will carry their infants. They will ride with them if possible."

"Ride with them! To Idumea on some broken-backed mule? It's impossible!"

"It's their choice," Herod said grimly. "They can go with us to

Idumea, or they can go with Pacorus to Parthia."

Alexandra had a grim retort of her own, but perceiving that her sharp tongue would benefit her nothing she fell silent.

"Come, then!" Herod clapped. "We have not a moment to lose! We leave by the second watch!"

Alexandra pushed past him, with a baleful gaze that Herod endured stoically. The military officers and court officials filed out quickly. The secretary was the last to leave. Herod pulled him aside.

"Burn all the papers in the royal archives," Herod said in a low voice.

"All of them, Excellency?"

"Everything there is. Tomorrow the Parthians will have this place, and all Jerusalem with it. They must not find anything of importance."

"Yes, Excellency." The secretary hesitated. "Shall I accompany you to Idumea?"

"Of course you shall accompany me! Do you think I would arrange safe passage to five hundred wailing women and leave behind a valuable servant who knows how to hold his tongue?"

"Many thanks, Excellency."

The secretary hurried away to Herod's bidding, wondering whether thanks were really warranted. It would not go well for him, he knew, should he remain in Jerusalem after it fell. But he had no doubt that the Parthians would pursue Herod's party on the road to Idumea. Herod was the last remaining obstacle to Parthian control of Judea. Which would be worse, to be slaughtered in a bloody battle in the middle of a doomed escape, or to take his chances by remaining incognito in the city? It did not matter. Herod was going, and the secretary would go with him, serving faithfully, as he had since that fateful day in Sepphoris seven years before.

Though it had seemed impossible, the fugitives set off at the start of the second watch, just as Herod had commanded. By this time there were far more than the five hundred women and their families; all partisans of Herod, Phasaelus, and Hyrcanus knew that their freedom, and most likely their lives, would be forfeit once Antigonus and the Parthians had taken the city. Herod moved ceaselessly among them, offering words of hope and encouragement. A remarkable change had come over him since his fury in the council room; he seemed gentle, even cheerful, as he encouraged those who had stumbled and exhorted the rest to make haste.

It was a miserable, ragged procession that departed Jerusalem through the southern gate. Despite the commotion—the weeping and muffled lamentation, the clatter of the carts and animals, the cries of frantic mothers trying to keep their confused and frightened children from straying—there was no indication that the partisans of Antigonus within the city had alerted the Parthians to the surreptitious exodus. Outside the city walls began a mountainous descent, lit only by torches and faint moonlight. It was here that calamity nearly befell the entire enterprise. Most of the soldiers had been stationed at the back of the caravan as a rear guard, but Herod's family rode in the front, in rough carriages improvised from wagons and carts while Herod's civilian officials made their way on foot. Suddenly the wagon carrying Herod's mother—Antipater's widow—lurched into an unseen declivity in the road, overturning completely and spilling its driver and his passenger into the road. Herod's retainers hurried to the scene, and moments later Herod himself rushed up.

"What is it?" he cried. "What's happened? Set that wagon upright and get moving! Wait! Is someone hurt? Who is it? Mother? Mother! Is she dead? Mother! Mother!"

He gathered up the frail, crumpled body and laid it tenderly in another wagon nearby. The soldiers lighting the way in the vanguard of the column had rushed back with their torches, and those of Herod's inner circle leaned over the wagon, straining for a glimpse. There was no sign of life. Herod turned away, distraught.

"Why do you delay?" he demanded of his officers. "Get everyone moving! We have not a moment to spare!"

"The overturned wagon is blocking the road, Excellency," an officer reported. "We cannot proceed until it is removed."

"Well, then, remove it!" Herod roared.

He clenched his fists in rage, and the same frenzied mood that had come over him in the council chamber a few hours before now took hold again.

"Fool!" he bellowed into the night. "Coward! I am a fool, to attempt this! I am a coward to abandon Jerusalem! How much better it would have been to stay and fight! The Parthians will have our women no matter what course I choose! They will take them here, amidst this wreckage on a mountain road, without even a battle! But they will not take me!"

With this he drew his sword and was about to plunge it into his breast when the secretary, who was standing nearby, grabbed his arm. The secretary had not the strength to overpower Herod, but within moments the others had rushed up and restrained him. He struggled with them, but they were too many for him, and were most earnest in their intention to deter him.

Corinthus had come up from the rear to investigate the delay, and having witnessed all that had happened began to task Herod severely with his horrid intention.

"What is the meaning of this, Excellency?" he demanded, picking up the sword which had clattered to the ground. "We have no time for jesting!"

"It is no jest!" Herod roared. "Unhand me! Let me finish what

I have begun! They will not take me! They will not take me!"

"Of course they will not take you," Corinthus soothed. "But you must finish what you have begun. All of us have put our lives in your hands. Without you to lead us, there is no hope for any of us."

Among the men who still held Herod in their grasp, there were murmurs of agreement.

"Our fate is in your hands, Excellency."

"Take heart, Excellency, all is not lost."

"You are our leader, Excellency. It would be the height of cruelty to abandon us now."

"This accident with the wagon is but a small setback in what will be remembered as a glorious escape," Corinthus continued. "Just as this escape will be but a small setback in what will be remembered as a glorious career. Let no man say that Herod, son of Antipater, did not fight to the finish."

At these last words Herod's eyes flickered, and his look of wild despair began to give way to his customary bearing, so clearly inherited from Antipater, of reckless courage. At this moment, his personal physician, who had been attending to his mother in the wagon, approached.

"Well?" Herod demanded gruffly. "Is she dead?"

"Your mother lives, Excellency," the physician said. "She will recover."

"Your mother lives, Excellency," Corinthus repeated, straining to remain calm. "You will live. We all will live, if we have you to lead us."

Herod had ceased struggling.

"Well," he muttered, "If indeed my mother lives, perhaps it is a sign. Perhaps I do have a duty to her."

"A duty to all these," Corinthus said boldly. "To mother, to sister, to wife, to betrothed, and all these others besides. Now, unhand him."

Herod's officials, having committed the capital offense of touching him, were only too glad to do so. Corinthus stepped forward and handed Herod his sword. All around him held their breath as they waited to see what he would do with it. But after a moment's hesitation he sheathed it, and after attending to his mother, barked orders for the caravan to move on.

With daylight came the expected pursuit from the Parthians, but Herod held them off with ease. More troublesome were the natives of the land, the Jews who were partisans of Antigonus. A great party of them engaged Herod's troops at a place on the edge of the desert about eight miles from Jerusalem, but again Herod was victorious, fighting like a man possessed at the head of his troops. Here, many years later, when he had become King of Judea, he built a great palace, and a city around it, to commemorate this victory, and named it after himself: Herodium.

After this Herod's caravan made its way unimpeded, but the number following him had grown to more than nine thousand. It was far too many to be accommodated at his intended destination, the mountain fortress called Masada. Thus, when he had reached Idumea, at a place called Thressa, he divided the multitude, taking with him only eight hundred, including the women so greatly desired by the Parthians, and sending away the rest, distributing to them all the gold he had, and advising them to make their way as best they could in Idumea.

And thus concluded the one great reversal of Herod's career, though in the end it was to lead to greater worldly glories than Herod himself had ever envisioned. But for the time being, Antigonus was crowned king of Judea, and his control over the nation was complete. Phasaelus, though uplifted by the news of Herod's escape, knew that his own life was forfeit. Though his hands were bound in his prison chamber, he contrived to kill himself by dashing his head against a rock rather than being made sport of by his enemy. The attempt was not entirely successful, for Phasaelus continued alive, but Antigonus instructed the doctor who attended him to pour poison into the wound, and by this means the valiant Phasaelus met his end. As for Hyrcanus, Antigonus cut off his ears—some reports said that Antigonus himself bit them off—so that he could never be high priest again, for the law of the Jews requires that all priests be without blemish in any part of their bodies.

Joanna had come to the end of the scroll. She peered dubiously at her uncle.

"He didn't really do that," she said skeptically.

"Didn't do what?"

"Bite off his ears," Joanna said with disgust. "No one could be so foul."

"You might be surprised at how foul people can be," Aduel shrugged. "It's certainly possible. Antigonus was a ruthless, vicious sort of man."

"Then Herod was right."

"Right about what?"

"About everything. About Antigonus, the Parthians."

"Oh yes, Herod was right about many things. He was quite shrewd in matters of politics. Perhaps even shrewder than his father Antipater."

"And yet it seemed as if he almost went mad."

"What, the incident with the sword?"

Joanna nodded.

"That was the start of it," Aduel confirmed. "He had always been unpredictable, volatile, but the incident with the sword was something new."

"Do you think it was because of his mother's accident?"

"Undoubtedly. He genuinely cared for her. And coming on top of the strain of events, a strain that had built up over days and weeks and had culminated in such urgent danger, the event was too much for him. It suddenly became more than he could bear."

"Still, it seems so strange," Joanna mused.

"What seems strange, child?"

"To think that a man like Herod would actually care for someone."

"Yes, we think of him now as nothing more than a deranged tyrant, and that he is," Aduel agreed. "But remember, child, the text you just read describes events of thirty-five years ago. Much has happened during the intervening years to darken Herod's heart and embitter his soul. He cared for many people at times in his life, those who were close to him and the commoners in the street. That is the side to the story that no one sees anymore. That is the side I wish to tell. Along with the rest, of course."

A silence fell over the darkening room. Joanna glanced at the window. Suddenly there was a blast of trumpets: Three distinct calls. She gasped.

"What is it, child?" Aduel asked, concerned.

"The Sabbath has started!" Joanna exclaimed. "I thought I had more time!"

"More time! Time for what?"

"To gather the washing," Joanna replied guiltily. "I left it out to dry on the roof when we went to the Temple this morning."

"Oh, the washing," Aduel laughed. "Never mind the

washing. No doubt Edna has gone up to get it, and if not it can wait a day. Come, help me up these steps. Now it is time to celebrate our day of rest. You for one certainly have earned it."

Chapter 11

The Sabbath day of rest had come at a good time for the girl and her uncle, for the preceding day had taxed both of them. For Joanna it was nothing more than an annoying hoarseness, but for Aduel it was more serious. He remained in his bed the entire day with a cough and a fever. The following day he emerged from his bedchamber on the upper floor to sit in front of the hearth, a blanket wrapped around his thin frame to ward off the chill of the early spring morning. Having finished her morning chores, the girl sat next to him in one of the little home's two chairs. They were luxury items in Judea, these sturdy pieces of furniture, and although they were not exactly comfortable the girl never ignored the opportunity to sit in one. In the turbulent recent months she had left behind most of the fantasies that accompanied childhood, but sitting in a chair in front of the hearth it was only too easy to lapse a little, to close her eyes and pretend that she had been transported to a palace.

They had sat for some time in silence before Aduel stirred himself, clearing his throat and calling for Irijah.

"Fetch my purse, Irijah," Aduel said, when the old manservant appeared. "I have an errand for you."

Irijah disappeared, silent and morose as usual. Joanna leaned toward her uncle.

"Are you sending Irijah to fetch the marriage contract?" she asked quietly.

"Yes."

"Uncle." Joanna held her breath for a moment before venturing her request. "May I accompany Irijah?"

"Accompany Irijah?" Aduel was surprised. "What on earth for, child? Do you hope to see the young scribe again?"

"No, I hope not to see him," Joanna said. "I could remain outside while Irijah conducts your business."

"Why, then?"

"I don't know, exactly," Joanna confessed. "Because...well, I want to see more of the city. The people."

"It's just as I feared," Aduel rasped darkly. "A taste of freedom has done nothing but whet your appetite for more."

"I'm sorry, Uncle." Joanna was embarrassed, though she hardly knew why. "It's just that I..."

Her voice trailed off.

"It's just that you what?" Aduel prompted.

"It's just that I was never meant to live shut away in the house like the noblewomen of Jerusalem."

"No, that is not the life for you," Aduel admitted. "You are too full of vigor, of questions. And in any case I am not in a position to provide you with that kind of a life."

He seemed darkly amused at the thought of it.

"Yes, you may accompany Irijah," he said. "Though I warn you, he will not like it."

"I won't be a burden to him," Joanna promised. "I won't say a word."

Irijah reappeared with the purse, a leather pouch that seemed to contain a substantial amount of coinage. Aduel drew out two shekels and a half-shekel coin and told Irijah where to find the scribe's place of work, at an address off the main market street near the Temple.

"The maiden will accompany you," he added.

Irijah cast a sharp look of disapproval at Joanna but said nothing. He turned immediately to the door. The girl was prepared for this; she quickly donned her veil and followed him. But in the few moments it took her to lace her sandals, Irijah had already disappeared. By the time she bolted through the courtyard gate the old manservant was far down the bumpy street and was walking quickly away, making it clear that he had no intention of waiting for her.

Joanna knew that it would be undignified to run after him—a confirmation of the dour old servant's opinion that she should not be allowed out of the house—so she hurried down the hill as best she could. Fortunately, a commotion in the wide market street ahead had slowed Irijah's progress. Streams of people, mostly young men, were surging through the market street, all of them moving in the direction of the Temple. In their excitement, they were hurrying forward, pushing—some even running to try to get ahead.

At the street corner Irijah had seized a young man by the arm. He was interrogating his unfortunate captive as Joanna caught up to him.

"What is it?" the old man demanded. "Where are all of you going?"

"To the Temple!" the young man panted. "They're cutting down the eagle!"

"What eagle? The golden eagle? Herod's eagle?"

"Yes!"

"Who?" Irijah was astonished. "Who is cutting it down?"

"The scholars!" the youth cried. "The young men of the city!

Come, see for yourself!"

"But Herod will kill them!"

"Herod is dying," the young man exclaimed as he broke away. "All Jerusalem knows it! He may already be dead!"

Irijah stared with a look of utter amazement. Suddenly, without a second glance at the girl, he bolted into the surging crowd. Caught up in the excitement and unsure what to do, Joanna hurried after him. Quickly she wished she had not. For a short time Irijah's tall, lanky frame was visible in the jostling crowd ahead of her, but soon even that was lost from view. The street curved as it approached the Temple, and the crowd became more tightly packed. Joanna thought of pushing her way out, but she was hemmed in on all sides and could do nothing but move forward. She began to panic. She had encountered crowded streets in Jericho, but nothing like this. There were no other women anywhere in sight. The men around her had been careful to respect her person, leaving a little space around her, but it was very little. They themselves were packed tightly against one another and the crowd was getting thicker each moment. Soon they would press against her; she would be crammed against shouting, shoving men. The thought alarmed and disgusted her. It was not proper for a young woman of Judea to be in such a situation.

Just when it seemed that the crush would envelop her, the street turned abruptly to the right and the crowd began to thin. After a moment more, the girl could see why. The street had opened onto the broad paved area at the base of the Temple Mount. Joanna recognized the wide steps that she and her uncle had ascended three days earlier as they made their way into the Temple complex. With more room to maneuver, the men around her began to run unabashedly. Buffeted and shaken but otherwise unharmed, she made her way to the side of the thoroughfare as the crowd streamed past. Some ran for the triple gate, which was the usual way to enter the Temple, but it was the farthest and others made for the nearer double gate which was generally used as an exit. Still others took a third route, up a wide stone staircase to the left that turned and turned again to deposit them in the southwest corner of the Temple complex.

Safely out of the maelstrom, Joanna paused to ponder and to catch her breath. She wished to return to the safety of Aduel's house, but she was not certain she could find it. Some other time she might have attempted it, relying on her wits to take her safely home, but after her misadventure a few days earlier she decided that this was not the day to try. The Jerusalem that seemed so civilized and inviting just three days ago now seemed chaotic, crazed. The crowds surging up the various sets of steps had begun to ebb. No doubt most of them had already reached the great glittering plaza that encompassed the Temple complex. Irijah was certainly among them. It would not be hard to find him, she reasoned. The crowd would be immense but it would not be so turbulent, and Irijah's tall form would not be hard to pick out. Moreover, she wanted to see if the youth's report about the eagle was true. Even if Herod were truly dying or already dead, could it really be possible that anyone would dare such an affront? How would they even manage it? She wanted to see for herself. If it really was happening, her uncle would be amazed, overjoyed. She wanted to share the experience with him in all the vivid detail that Irijah would be sure to leave out.

Convinced that the bulk of the crowd had passed, the girl joined the latecomers who were racing to catch up. Walking quickly, she made her way to the triple gate—an extra distance that few of the stragglers were bothering to traverse. She made her way up the wide stone steps, carefully negotiating the irregular intervals as she had with Aduel, and entered the arched, cavernous tunnel that led further upward to the Temple complex.

She was not prepared for the sight that greeted her when she emerged. The vast Court of the Gentiles, which had seemed so busy on her previous visit when it was filled with a few hundred people, was now jammed with thousands. Clearly it would be only by a stroke of luck that she would find Irijah. But she no longer thought of turning back. Her only thought now was to see whether the young men of Jerusalem truly intended to cut down Herod's eagle, and how they would accomplish it.

She took a moment to size up the situation. Even from the edge of the Court of the Gentiles, she could see that the assault upon the eagle was well underway. The giant statue had seemed invulnerable, perched atop the Great Gate, fifty cubits tall, that marked the west end of the Court of the Women. But not far from the brilliant brass gate was the Temple, whose majestic facade rose to twice that height. Atop the Temple were several young men who had somehow contrived to fix a thick cord from the roof of the Temple to the top of the gate below. She watched, spellbound, as one of them clambered over the top of the Temple wall and, after testing the cord, began letting himself down its length, hand over hand, in a slow diagonal progression toward the gate. It was a spectacular feat, unprecedented in living memory, and the crowd murmured in amazement. Any mishap would mean certain death. Suddenly the cord slipped; the crowd gasped as one. But the cord held, secured and stabilized by the conspirators on the roof of the Temple, and after a moment the young man dangling midway along it resumed his efforts. Before long he had transited the entire distance and had alighted upon the great brass gate. He steadied himself, seemingly unsure that he had achieved his objective, then took a few steps along the top of the gate and thrust his hands to the sky in a moment of triumph.

Pandemonium erupted. For a few tense minutes the daredevil's fate had hung literally in mid-air. Now he seemed safe, and the breathtaking assault upon Herod's authority would continue. Another young man soon followed, moving hand over hand from the Temple to the gate, all while carrying a second cord held firmly in the belt around his waist. This too was fixed to the top of the gate, creating a second bridge, and before long several young adventurers had appeared at the top of the Temple wall, waiting their turns.

Joanna perceived that the center of the drama would soon shift to the Great Gate, and she pressed forward to obtain a better view. A great swarm of people still stood between her and the Court of the Women, but most of them took little notice of her, transfixed as they were by the spectacle of additional youths attempting the death-defying transit from the Temple to the Great Gate. Small and lithe, she squeezed through the gaps in the crowd, threading her way across the Court of the Gentiles without being challenged.

Soon she had passed the low wall, with its ominous warning to Gentiles, that surrounded the central area of the Temple complex. The signs had given her pause—for she still had an irrational fear of being mistaken for a Gentile—but only for a moment. Already she was at the base of the fifteen tall steps that ringed the elevated surface of the Temple's inner courtyards. She worked her way to the eastern side, where she intended to access the gate that she and Aduel had used to pass from the Court of the Gentiles to the Court of the Women. But this would not be so easily done, because others in the Court of the Gentiles had also begun crowding toward the eastern gate. The eastern gate was of modest proportions, not nearly as wide as the Great Gate, and the crowd that was funneling into it was already quite dense. The Court of the Women was filling rapidly; it seemed that not many more would be able to get in. And yet Joanna decided she would attempt it, that she would risk the crush of unfamiliar bodies that had seemed so repugnant just a few minutes before.

By the time she attained the third step, however, her halting progress came to a stop. The Court of the Women seemed to have reached its capacity. Every few seconds one or two people on the top step managed to squeeze through the eastern gate, and by careful observation and impeccable timing she was able to advance three more steps. Suddenly a great cry went up from inside the court. A few more at the top of the steps pushed through the gate; Joanna advanced to the seventh step. There was another great cry, and then, as it subsided, another sound: the chopping of an ax. At this there was another push from the top of the steps—frantic, this time, as those at the entrance fought to witness the seditious event—and Joanna advanced to the eighth step.

But having gotten halfway was no use at all. The eastern wall of the Court of the Women, through whose gate she was trying to pass, was blocking her view of everything inside. From her previous vantage point at the far edge of the Court of the Gentiles she would have at least been able to see some of what was happening at the top of the Great Gate. This realization seemed to have occurred to many of those in front of her, for suddenly they began to disperse, pushing their way down the steps back to the Court of the Gentiles, or laterally along the steps in hope of finding lesser crowds at the north or south gates to the Court of the Women. With this Joanna saw her chance. Darting through the tiny gaps created by the shifting crowd—and ahead of any who showed a moment's hesitation—she quickly advanced to the thirteenth step, and then, as the crowd congealed again, the fourteenth. Fortunately none of the men around her, though visibly agitated at the sight of an interloper pushing past them, was prepared to transgress the strict customs of Judea by challenging her physically. Without pausing to consider, she pushed these scruples to their limits, claiming a foothold on a tiny sliver of space on the fifteenth step and vaulting herself into it, forcing the men around her each to fall back by a few inches, thus securing her place just in front of the gate.

From here she moved inexorably forward, inch by inch, as those remaining on the steps pushed insistently from behind. Soon she had reached the gate, and then she was beneath it. The chopping sound continued but she could see none of it. Her forward progress had stopped; it seemed impossible that the people in the courtyard could be any more tightly packed. And then suddenly, somehow, she was through. She had gained a place in the Court of the Women!

The Great Gate was directly opposite her; she had a clear view of all that was happening. She had arrived just in time to witness the climax. Several young men at the top of the gate were pushing the statue, which wobbled upon its base. A youth with an ax stepped forward and aimed a few more blows, and then the others began to push again. Someone looped a rope around the eagle's neck, and several of those pushing the statue hurried to the opposite side to pull on it. The combination of forces soon took effect. The statue began to rock—a little at first, and then more and more—until finally it toppled.

Joanna's heart was beating wildly—partly with the thrill of the moment and partly at the delirious celebration that had erupted all around her. The roar was intense, palpable—a swelling release of rage that vibrated throughout her body in waves that seemed to roll back and forth throughout the courtyard. Some of the men around her raised an arm in triumph. But Joanna could not; her arms were pinned to her sides. She began to feel dizzy. Although the courtyard was open to the sky, the cheering and bellowing seemed to have sucked out all the air. And just as it seemed that the frenzy had reached its peak, there was more: The youths at the top of the Great Gate had dragged the eagle to the edge of their lofty platform, where all Judea could witness its fallen glory— and moments later had heaved it into the air, where it plummeted to the semicircular steps below with a spectacular crash.

No one was standing on the steps, but the crowd had pushed up to the base of them and then had moved instinctively backward at the plunge of the great idol. This, combined with the incessant pressure from the rear, began to crush Joanna like a vise. Desperately she looked about but she could barely turn her head. There were more women in the courtyard than there had been outside it—evidently those who had come to worship and to pray, expecting this to be a normal day—but they were in no position to help her. Nor, she realized, was anyone else. All in the courtyard were trapped in the same predicament; not even the strongest man could push his way out.

Young men with axes, confederates of those who had cut down the eagle, rushed forward through the Great Gate from the Court of the Israelites. Oblivious to the disaster that was taking shape in the Court of the Women, they quickly set to work upon what remained of the eagle, hacking at it from every side. Joanna hardly noticed. She could not breathe; her vision began to blur. The panic that had visited her momentarily as she followed Irijah on the packed market street now flooded in. She tried to push back, to fight for even an inch of freedom, but she had no strength. She tried to cry out but she could not draw breath. A strange awareness of her own mortal existence, so solid and yet so precarious, began to envelop her. The uproar in the courtyard began to recede; she felt as though she were floating, though in what direction she could not tell.

And then, suddenly, she felt herself falling backward. With a jolt, she realized there was space behind her. Someone grabbed her under the left arm and steadied her on her feet. She was grateful, yet at the same time indifferent. Let her fall! As long as she had the room to do it! The crowd behind her was receding rapidly, but she did not know why. She stood still for a moment, trying to make sense of it. From outside the Court of the Women, somewhere in the Court of the Gentiles, a cry had been taken up, and it was growing louder and more insistent by the moment. Now she could make out the words, and the terror of their message:

"Run! Run! The king's guard is coming! Run!"

Chapter 12

The king's guard? What did it mean? Joanna's mind was still hazy; she tried to focus. But those around her were quicker to perceive the danger. Almost as one they turned away from the dismemberment of the eagle and began to flee. Standing near the gate in her dazed state, Joanna was quickly knocked to the ground. A man tried to help her up and he too was knocked down, and as he scrambled to his feet his companions dragged him away toward the exit. The crush was upon her; she covered her head with her arms. She sensed that they were trying to avoid her, but they could not. Feet and ankles and knees were all about her, scuffling, vaulting, tripping. She was being trampled: A horrible, terrifying death at the hands of her own panicked countrymen. Suddenly there was a second man trying to help her, standing above her, holding his arms to either side to shield her, but soon he too was knocked down. This man did not try to get up again, but instead remained on hands and knees, hunched over her, using his body to shield her as best he could. Looking up from the pavement Joanna could see his body reel, again and again, as the crowd battered him from all sides, even using his back as a stepping stone. But he did not yield, and those taking flight began to make their way around him, like a rushing river dividing around a great rock.

Soon the flow had ebbed to a trickle, and then the courtyard was eerily silent—except for the sound of axes still hacking at the eagle. Joanna lay still upon the paving stones of the courtyard, barely conscious of what was happening around her. The man who had protected her was now kneeling at her side; she felt him put his ear to her face to listen for sounds of life. From across the courtyard she heard a voice—a woman, it seemed—imploring the ax-wielding rebels to take flight along with everyone else. She knew that she too should flee, but she remained where she was in dreamy defiance. What a luxury it was just to lie there, stretched out upon the pavement! To breathe!

After a minute more, she heard a voice again—the same voice that had rebuked the young men across the courtyard. It was closer now, and she could tell for certain that it was an old woman who was speaking:

"Is she dead?"

"No, she lives," replied the man who had sheltered the girl.

"Thanks to you. Come, you must flee. Both of you. Herod's guard will be here any moment."

"I have nothing to fear from Herod's guard," the man stated simply.

"Indeed you do! Woe to those who have destroyed Herod's eagle! Look at them, the fools! Even now they remain, though the soldiers will be here any minute!"

"But I am not one of them."

"That matters not!" the old woman cried. "You look like them, and that's enough! They'll take you too! Woe to him who falls into the hands of Herod! A terrible death awaits!"

"But the maiden!" the man objected. "I can't leave her here."

"Quick then, pick her up! Bring her to my chamber!"

There was a moment's hesitation, then Joanna felt herself being lifted, gently, from the pavement. Now she was being carried, and she knew not where, but there was something that puzzled her far more: the voice of the man who was carrying her. It seemed as though she had heard it before.

There was the sound of a door opening, then shutting.

"There," the woman's voice said. "In the corner."

Joanna felt herself being lowered into something that felt like a low pallet bed. She felt the gentle, caressing touch of wrinkled fingers on her face, removing her veil. Her eyes fluttered open. She quickly shut them again. The man and the old woman were bent over her, but she seemed to be hallucinating. For the man she had seen was a young man, and the face was a face she had seen before. It was the scribe Aduel had hired to draw up the marriage contract!

She opened her eyes and blinked hard. She had not been mistaken. It was indeed the young scribe. From the look on his face she could see that the astonishment was mutual. After a moment he recovered his wits:

"You're the niece of old Aduel, are you not?"

She murmured an assent.

"But what are you doing here?" he asked gently.

"Yes, what?" the old woman demanded. "Caught up in such a rabble! You might have died!"

Before Joanna could reply the clatter of men at arms could be heard. The old woman hastened to the door and cracked it open.

"Herod's soldiers!" she hissed. "Keep quiet! I will stand at the door so they do not enter."

"No," said the scribe. "I will stand guard."

"No," the old woman stated defiantly. "You must not let them see you. I will not allow it."

"At least stay inside the chamber!" the young scribe reasoned with her. "They will not harm you if they do not see you."

"Harm me!" the old woman exclaimed. "How can they harm me? The Messiah has come, and I have seen His face! Let them harm me! Let them do as they wish! My life is complete!"

She stepped outside the door, swiftly shutting it behind her. The girl and the scribe had looked away from each other after the old woman had left their sides, as propriety demanded, but at this shocking statement their eyes locked.

"Who is she?" Joanna whispered.

"I don't know," the young scribe whispered back. "I've seen her here before, praying in the Court of the Women."

Their eyes met again, for a lingering moment. But it was not proper for the two of them to be alone together in the closed room. The scribe got up and went to the farthest corner of the room—behind the door that the old woman was guarding from the outside—and stood silently, listening to the commotion in the courtyard. Joanna closed her eyes. The memory of her first tumultuous night in Jerusalem, and the strange tidings that had occasioned it, had faded from her memory. Now it returned with a crash. The Messiah, again! Had He really come, to rule and to reign? To set things right after decades of oppression under Herod?

There was a commotion outside the door: The rough voice of a soldier and the old woman's querulous reply. The young scribe lifted his hand as if to open the door, but suddenly there was silence and he refrained. There were additional sounds from farther away—officers of the guard shouting commands, it seemed—but eventually these too subsided. It was some time before the door opened and the old woman slipped inside.

"They're gone," she said tiredly. "Finally."

"Herod's guard?" the young scribe asked. "They're gone?"

"Everyone is gone," the old woman said. "The soldiers, the scholars, all of them. The courtyard is completely deserted."

"Were any of the scholars taken?"

"Oh, yes, quite a number of them." The old woman shook her head angrily. "Forty, I heard one of the soldiers say. They could have run! At least some of them would have escaped! But no! They chose to remain! They said they would take responsibility for their actions. The fools! They'll soon see what Herod does to those who take responsibility!"

She looked at the scribe, and then at the girl.

"You must go, too," she said. "Go now, before the Levites come to search the premises."

"But the maiden may be injured," the young scribe objected. "Surely the Levites will not hand us over to Herod."

"The Levites will do whatever suits them at the moment," the old woman scoffed. "Go now, I tell you, before they come out of hiding. I cannot keep you here."

She knelt at the side of the low bed and took Joanna's hand.

"What say you, maid? Are you badly hurt?"

Joanna blinked. While there had been danger in the courtyard she had not thought to assess her own condition.

"I don't think so," she said slowly. She sat up—and winced. "Oh!"

"What is it?" the old woman demanded.

"My leg," Joanna replied. "Someone stepped on it."

"Where?" the old woman said. "Show me."

The girl pointed to her leg. The scribe averted his gaze as the old woman pulled up the hem of Joanna's tattered robe a few inches. Above the left ankle the flesh was puffy and swollen, and a livid bruise had already taken shape.

"Is it broken?" Joanna asked tearfully.

"Hard to say," the old woman said. "Can you stand?"

"I don't know."

"Can you try?"

Joanna swung her feet out of the bed and slowly stood up, with the old woman and the scribe each holding one hand. Gingerly she shifted her weight to the swollen leg. It was painful, but manageable.

"Well?" the old woman asked gently. "How is it?"

"It hurts," Joanna said. She took a cautious step. "But it isn't too bad."

"Then it's likely not broken," the old woman said. "You should walk if you can."

"Yes," Joanna said bravely. "I can walk."

"Nonsense!" the scribe declared. "To walk all the way home from the Temple on a leg that might be broken? It's not a good idea. So many stairs. I can hire a litter."

"A litter!" the old woman scoffed. "Won't that attract attention!"

The scribe shrugged helplessly.

"Then what do you suggest?" he asked.

"I suggest that she walk, and that you assist her. Wait here a moment. I'll get something that will help."

The old woman hurried out, leaving the scribe still holding the girl's hand for support. There was a long, awkward silence as the two of them studiously avoided each other's gazes.

"I don't think it's advisable—" the scribe finally began.

Before he could say more the old woman returned, holding a crutch. Joanna stared at it. It was not the crude, stick-like thing she had seen on the streets of Jericho, but a smooth, polished specimen of oak. The old woman chuckled at her amazement.

"Beautiful, isn't it? Here at Herod's Temple we have all the best that money can buy, even in crutches. Here, see if you can walk with it."

Joanna took a few awkward steps with the crutch.

"Well?" the old woman asked. "Can you do it?"

"Yes. I can do it."

"Good." She turned to the scribe. "You must hold her hand to steady her, especially on the steps."

The scribe nodded.

"If you encounter any of Herod's soldiers, or the Temple police for that matter, do not engage them in any way," the old woman continued. "Do not even look at them. Act as if you are husband and wife."

At this Joanna blushed and looked down, deeply embarrassed by the suggestion of such familiarity, even in pantomime. But the old woman reached out her wrinkled hand and raised the girl's chin until their eyes met.

"It is a matter of life and death," she said quietly. "If they think the young man is one of the rebels, they will arrest him immediately. And then Herod will kill him. Do you understand?"

Joanna nodded with frightened eyes. The old woman opened the door a crack and peered out. But before she could open it further, the young scribe pushed it shut again.

"Wait!" he said. He seemed as flustered as Joanna, but for a different reason. He looked intently at the old woman.

"You said," he began, and then he stopped, as if he was about to repeat something scandalous. Suddenly he blurted, "You said you had seen the Messiah."

"Yes," the old woman nodded.

"But what did you mean?" the scribe demanded. His voice was agitated. "When? Where? In a dream? In a vision?"

"Not in a dream," the old woman replied. "Nor in a vision. Here, in this very courtyard, not forty days since!"

"But that's impossible!" the scribe objected. "If he had been here in this courtyard, many would have seen him. All Israel would know!"

"He is but a babe," the old woman replied. "Not all who have seen him understand who he is. But some day He will return, with many signs and wonders, holding the power of heaven! Our deliverer, the great teacher and judge of all Israel! I will not live to see that day, but you will, both of you. I can see it!"

The scribe and the girl stared in silent amazement. The old woman opened the door and looked out.

"Now go," she said. "Go! If you encounter any soldiers, say nothing to them. Do not even look at them!"

The scribe passed over the threshold first, offering assistance as Joanna followed. The old woman pulled the door shut and stood in front of it, watching as they made their way haltingly across the courtyard. The Court of the Women was deserted—a remarkable sight on any day, but especially today. As they passed through the gate on the south side of the courtyard they could see that the vast Court of the Gentiles was equally vacant. The thousands that had packed the Temple grounds such a short time ago had vanished without a trace.

As the scribe had predicted, the steps were the greatest challenge. It was slow going—agonizingly slow. Each step, hardly worth a second thought under normal circumstances, now required meticulous care, and Joanna could not help looking up every moment to scan for danger. But the scribe made no demands of her, offering only his strong arm of support and words of encouragement. The girl marveled that he could seem so unworried about the possibility of capture. His only concern seemed to be for her. Her heart pounded— mainly from fear and exertion, but partly from something else. The unusual warmth she had felt in the injured part of her leg seemed to have spread throughout her body—especially to the hand that the scribe was holding.

Finally they reached the smooth, level paving stones of the Court of the Gentiles. Joanna was becoming accustomed to the crutch and soon they had reached the great portico on the south side of the Temple complex, where the steep tunnels led to the double gate on the south side of the Temple Mount. There were more steps here—a great many of them—but she was less fearful. If Herod's soldiers should return, they would likely come across the wide bridge that connected the west side of the Temple complex to Herod's palace. She leaned against the wall to catch her breath. The scribe caught her eye for a moment, then looked away. She did not know what to make of his strict decorum. It seemed so impersonal, and yet his care for her was so real! She wondered what he really felt.

Navigating the remaining steps was an arduous process that required several brief pauses for Joanna to steady herself. By the time they had reached the bottom of the Temple Mount people had begun to venture out again; slowly life in Jerusalem was returning to normal. The scribe led her down quiet side streets to avoid the hectic foot traffic of the market street. Her leg throbbed with each step, but the pain was bearable. After more than an hour of slow progress they had reached Aduel's street.

"We turn here," the scribe said.

He had been silent for several minutes. He seemed to be contemplating something. As they began the short ascent up the hillside he began to speak.

"As soon as we have returned you to your uncle's home I will fetch the marriage contract he requested," he began.

"Yes."

"You understand, I assume, that as a woman who has reached her majority you have absolute right of refusal over any arrangement your uncle might negotiate."

"I trust my uncle more than anyone in the world," Joanna said. "He will do what is right for me."

"Yes, but you might ask at least to consult with him as to his intention," the scribe said. "So that you might make the choice that suits you best."

He glanced at her and saw that she was blushing deeply.

"I—I speak only in a professional capacity, of course," he stammered. "I simply want you to understand the law."

Immediately her heart stopped racing.

"Yes. Of course."

They said no more as the scribe helped her into Aduel's courtyard. He held the door as she entered the house. Aduel was in the same place Joanna had left him hours before, in his chair before the hearth. At the sight of the scribe—and the girl's crutch—he leaped to his feet.

"Good heavens, child!" he exclaimed. "What happened?"

Joanna stared blankly. Suddenly the intense emotion

of the day overwhelmed her and she could find no words. She burst into tears and fell into her uncle's arms, sobbing. The scribe remained in the open doorway, holding the door.

"There was a riot at the Temple," he explained briefly. "There was a panic. Your niece was injured in the chaos."

"He saved me!" Joanna sobbed. "He...saved...me!"

The scribe looked on impassively. Aduel regarded them both in rank consternation.

"But what was she doing at the Temple?" he demanded. "I did not send her to the Temple! And where is Irijah?"

"I do not know why your niece was at the Temple," the scribe said in his businesslike, matter-of-fact way. "And I know nothing of Irijah."

"Irijah ran ahead of me," Joanna said, trying to catch her breath between sobs. "I couldn't—I couldn't keep up. There were so many, all running to the Temple. One of them said that Herod was dying, or dead. I followed them, and then... then, I wanted to see it."

"Wanted to see what, my child?" Aduel soothed. "What was it you wanted to see?"

"I wanted to see—I wanted to see them cut down the eagle."

"What! Herod's eagle?"

"There was a great disturbance," the scribe confirmed. "The eagle has been destroyed, and many of those responsible have been arrested."

"But is Herod really dead?"

"I know nothing of that," the scribe replied.

"Then Herod is not dead, you may count on it." Aduel shook his head darkly. "I will know it when Herod dies. I will feel it in my bones."

The scribe did not respond to this.

"I should go now," he said. "I will fetch the marriage contract you requested and return with it at once."

Aduel waved off this suggestion.

"No, no, there's no hurry about that. Tomorrow if you please, or the day following. You have already done enough for one day. For many days. Thank you, my son. Thank you for…whatever it is you have done."

The scribe bowed. Joanna turned. She did not want him to leave so soon. She wanted to exchange Aduel's embrace for his, to fall into his arms—those arms that had protected her from a gruesome death, that had carried her to safety. But that was not the way things were done in Judea. She settled for a brief parting glance. And then he was gone.

Aduel helped the girl to the chair he had been sitting on, then placed a small table in front of it and propped her leg on it.

"May I examine it?" he asked.

Joanna nodded.

"It's badly bruised," Aduel concluded, "but I don't think it's broken. I don't think you would have been able to walk here all the way from the Temple. Still, we will call the doctor to be sure. Edna! Where is Irijah?"

Edna appeared from the back of the house.

"I haven't seen Irijah since morning," she said. "I thought he had gone on an errand for you—"

She stopped short when she caught sight of the girl.

"Good heavens, maid!" she cried.

The wall of mistrust that had stood between the two women since Joanna's first night in Jerusalem crumbled away instantly. Joanna's tears began again as the old servant clasped her hand and stroked her hair. She watched nervously as Edna examined the injury, gently turning her foot this way and that, while Aduel briefly explained the circumstances.

"Does it hurt at all?" Edna asked.

"A little," Joanna said. "Mostly it's just numb."

"I should think so!" Edna said. "Look at the swelling! You're a nesh thing, maid! You must take more care! I don't think it's broken. But this won't do. The leg must sit higher."

She fetched a couple of cushions from the other side of the room and gently propped them under the girl's foot.

"Hmph! Not enough."

"No doubt you are correct, Edna, but I want to be sure," Aduel said. "Irijah is not here, so you must fetch the doctor. Then go to the marketplace and get whatever is required to make her comfortable. Find my purse and take whatever you need."

"I will go at once."

After she had gone, Aduel settled into the chair next to Joanna. When she had recovered her composure, he leaned forward and peered at her keenly.

"Now, child, if you can, I want you to tell me everything," he said. "Everything that has happened to you since you left the house this morning."

Aduel sat spellbound as Joanna recounted the day's events in detail, omitting nothing but remaining dispassionate in her description of the actions of both Irijah and the young scribe. After she had described the momentous events that had taken place in the Court of the Women, she paused as if puzzled.

"An old woman was there," she said slowly. "She sheltered us in a small room near the courtyard. The scribe said he had seen her at the Temple many times before. The room…she said…she said it was her chamber."

"Ah!" Aduel said. "Old Anna. She has lived on the Temple grounds for many years—for decades, I think—praying and fasting each day. Some say she is a prophetess."

"A prophetess!" Joanna exclaimed.

"Yes, a prophetess," Aduel chuckled. "Although I am unaware of any specific prophecies she has given, or whether they have been fulfilled. Why do you look so, child? Did Anna foretell a glorious future for you while you were in her chamber?"

"I—I don't know," Joanna said haltingly. "She said…"

"She said what, my child?"

"She said she had seen the Messiah."

"The Messiah!" Aduel, who had become teasing, even playful, in his relief at the benign outcome of the girl's misadventure, was suddenly all seriousness. "When did she see the Messiah? Where?"

"She said she saw him there, in the Temple, not forty days since. She said he was but a babe."

It was some time before Aduel spoke.

"Just as was told by the wise men from the East," he murmured. "Did Anna say anything else?"

"Well, yes. She said that the scribe and I…"

"Yes?" Aduel leaned forward. "She said what about you and the scribe?"

"She said that we would live to see the Messiah, to witness his return, in power and in glory."

At this Aduel sank back, deep in thought. Joanna watched him, impatiently, for she wanted her uncle's opinion of this bizarre prediction. All Israel awaited the Messiah—had awaited him for centuries! Would she really see him? First the wise men from the East, and now this! What did it all mean?

She shifted herself into a more comfortable position, with her leg stretched out before her, and prepared to wait. After several minutes the door opened, startling Aduel from his reverie. It was Edna, returning with three dun-colored cushions. The doctor would arrive, she informed them, within the hour.

She quickly set about arranging the cushions under the girl's injured ankle. They were luxurious things, stuffed with the softest lamb's wool, and the girl's foot sank into them, helping to relieve the throbbing.

"Was there any sign of Irijah in the marketplace?" Aduel inquired.

"No," Edna said irritably. "I do not know where he is or what he is about."

"I suppose we will wait until sundown before making inquiries," Aduel began. "No doubt there were others injured in the riot. If Irijah was one of them—"

The door opened abruptly. It was not the doctor, but Irijah himself. He was not injured. He looked from one to the other of the reproachful faces that confronted him, silently sizing up the situation as he shut the door slowly behind him. His eyes lingered for a moment on Joanna—her foot, the cushions, the crutch—and his initial expression of relief was replaced by one of worry as he began to comprehend the trouble he was in.

"Irijah!" Aduel broke the silence. "Were you at the Temple today?"

Irijah nodded.

"Did I send you to the Temple?"

Irijah shook his head.

"Yet you went there anyway, leaving the maid to fend for

herself. You can see what happened. She was trampled in the chaos. She nearly died."

"They were cutting down Herod's eagle!" Irijah protested. "Nothing like that has ever happened in Jerusalem!"

Aduel ignored this.

"Irijah, do you wish to remain in my service?" he asked severely.

Irijah, simultaneously shame-faced and defiant, took a moment to answer.

"Yes."

"Then you will treat all those under my roof with the same care and respect with which you treat me," Aduel said sternly. "This transgression I shall overlook. I shall not overlook the next one. Do you understand?"

Irijah nodded.

"Out of my sight, then. Get about your work."

Without another word Irijah turned and went back to the courtyard. Edna gave a loud snort of disgust, and opening the door after him, spat on the ground behind him. Joanna was shocked. She would not have imagined that the gentle old housekeeper would ever do anything so vulgar. She had always assumed that Edna and Irijah were a long-married couple, indentured to Aduel while he was in Herod's service and later freed, but now she was not so sure. Aduel's stern rebuke of Irijah made her wonder all the more. If there was no formal bond between the two servants, it would be much easier to turn Irijah out of the house. Now Edna, who always seemed irked by him, was infuriated, and even Aduel, that wellspring of patience, seemed deeply disturbed. Joanna did not know what to think. Before today she would not have been sorry to see Irijah go, yet now she found that she could not be angry with him. His abandonment of her had been callous, even cruel, but in one of those peculiar twists that life sometimes takes it was Irijah who had opened a door for her— a door to an undreamed-of world of possibility, and desire.

Chapter 13

Soon after Irijah's ignominious exit the doctor arrived to confirm the wisdom of the elders. Anna, Aduel, and Edna had been right: Joanna's leg was not broken, only badly bruised. She was to remain as immobile as possible, with her foot elevated as Edna had recommended, until the swelling began to recede—three days at the least. After that, there would be two additional weeks indoors—with no ladders, stairs, or steps of any kind.

The doctor had ordered bed rest and Joanna had dutifully complied—but only for a short time. It was barely mid-afternoon, and the day's events had stimulated rather than exhausted her. Soon she was limping back to the front of the house, where Aduel remained seated, staring into the hearth. He made no remark as she took a seat next to him and heaved her leg up onto the pile of cushions. Already the throbbing pain had begun to subside, replaced by a dull ache.

Two weeks of convalescence! She wondered how she would endure it. Throughout her first month in Jerusalem she had not left the confines of the house, yet she had kept busy: Helping Edna with the housework, fetching things for Aduel, climbing the ladder to the roof, descending to Aduel's cellar to read and to study. There would be none of that now. She could not imagine how she would pass the time. In Jericho she and her mother had spent many an indoor hour spinning wool into thread—it had been the family's primary source of income—but there was no wool in Aduel's house. Now more than ever she needed an outlet for the nervous energy of an active mind, because now, stimulated by the day's events, that mind was racing faster than ever. Disconnected thoughts of the scribe leaped wildly through her brain. The fearlessness of his resolve as he protected her from the crush of the madding crowd. The strength of his arms as he carried her to safety. The steadfastness of his hand as he guided her down step after step on the perilous descent from the Temple Mount. The earnestness of his voice as he confirmed that she understood her rights under the Law. *So that you might make the choice that suits you best.* Surely he had been speaking of himself!

But had he? She could not be certain. She could not collect her thoughts. The chaotic inferno might have consumed her had it not been for his clumsy addendum: *I speak only in a professional capacity.* Why had he said such a stupid thing? What had he meant by it? His intention would have been clear if not for that confounding statement. He had ruined everything. But immediately she pivoted and rose to his defense. What man did not say stupid things, and repeatedly? Only her uncle, and his was a wisdom achieved over many grueling years; he had alluded many times, in casual conversation, to various blundering remarks he had made over the course of his youth. No, she would make allowances for the scribe. She could not have framed it in words, but her intuition told her that for all his impressive knowledge he was completely unversed in the fickle art of beguiling the feminine mind.

She sighed deeply, despairing at her confusion. Aduel

noted her discontent, though he only vaguely suspected the reason for it.

"We're a fine pair of invalids, coughing and sighing and staring at the fire," he remarked. "Perhaps there is something that might help us forget our infirmities, at least for a while."

He got up and shuffled away. A few minutes later he returned with a scroll in his hand.

"Book the Seventh," he announced, as he settled back in his chair. "A doorway to another place and another time, if you would care to step through it."

"I would."

"Good. Here you will meet Cleopatra, so perhaps it is appropriate that we shall peruse it in a place of leisure, rather than in a place of study. So. Which of us should have the honor of our first reading before the hearth?"

"I think you should, Uncle."

"Very well, then," Aduel said, but his quiet delight at the prospect of reading his work was shattered by a sudden fit of coughing.

"Perhaps a trip below ground was more exertion than I am ready for," he smiled weakly. "The Seventh is one of the shorter books from this point forward, but nonetheless I think you will do the reading."

"Certainly, Uncle."

Aduel handed her the scroll and coughed again, for some time, before clearing his throat.

"Edna!" he called weakly. "Some water, please!"

"I'll get it, Uncle," Joanna said, automatically beginning to rise from her chair.

"No, my child," Aduel clasped her wrist and smiled, nodding at her ankle. "You will keep still, and read."

Edna appeared with two cups of water. Joanna took one and took a long draught before unrolling the scroll. Then she cleared her own throat and began to read.

"Herod: A Secret History, by Aduel of Sepphoris. Book the Seventh."

Herod's flight from Jerusalem was the start of the most harrowing phase of his career, a phase that ended in glory—as much to Herod's surprise, perhaps, as to all those who depended on him for succor and hope. He quickly secured his family and most loyal followers, as well as many of his troops, in the impregnable fortress of Masada, which he had provisioned beforehand with supplies that would last a year. He then headed south, accompanied by a small group of soldiers and advisors—his secretary among them. His object was the city of Petra, from which his longtime ally, Malichus, ruled the desert kingdom of Arabia.

But Malichus had been warned by the Parthians to have no dealings with Herod, and being the kind of ruler who changes alliances with the shifting of the wind (and additionally, hoping to be rid of the debts he owed to Herod), he sent messengers to refuse any discourse. Herod and his party then turned westward, toward Rome's most powerful and most loyal ally: Egypt. At Pelusium, the great fortress and naval base that guarded the entrance to Egypt from the east, Herod prevailed upon the naval captains, who had great regard for him, and he and his retinue were soon conducted by sea to the capital, Alexandria.

That great city was the jewel of the Mediterranean, second in size and in splendor only to Rome itself. It had been created from nothing nearly three hundred years earlier, when Rome was still a small republic of little consequence, on the orders of Alexander the Great. It was a center of both commerce and culture, with the world's largest library and two great harbors that could accommodate the largest of ships. A stupendous lighthouse, more than two hundred fifty cubits in height, stood as a beacon that could be seen for thirty miles, thanks to great mirrors of polished brass that were illuminated by the sun during the day and by fire at night. Lining one of the harbors were the palaces of the Ptolemies, the Macedonian pharaohs who had ruled Egypt ever since Alexander's kingdom had been divided at the time of his death. It was here, amongst the lavish gardens and brightly colored buildings, that Herod would meet Cleopatra.

By this time the exploits of this clever, daring woman were already legendary. Her claim to the throne of Egypt had been validated by the great Julius Caesar years earlier, around the time that Herod was beginning his career as governor of Galilee. While Caesar still lived she had borne him a son, but more recently she had seduced Mark Antony, one of the successors to Caesar and now master of the Roman East. Crossing the Mediterranean to Asia Minor, she had sailed up the River Cydnus to Antony's military headquarters on a gilded barge powered by sails of purple and silver oars. She herself reclined under a canopy of gold, reports said, while boys dressed as the Greek god Cupid stood on each side to fan her and her maids, dressed as sea nymphs, worked the rudder and the ropes. Antony, who awaited her at his tribunal in the marketplace, found himself alone as the crowd rushed away to see the fantastic sight. He sent for her, inviting her to dinner, but she declined, preferring that he come to her. By the time Antony arrived darkness had fallen, and he found the vessel lighted by thousands of candles strategically placed in all sorts of ingenious arrangements.

It was a spectacle like none that had ever been recorded, and Antony was instantly captivated. Like a lovesick swain he soon followed her back across the Mediterranean to Alexandria. There they spent the winter in drunken revels with a group of select companions, often traipsing through the city disguised as servants and initiating brawls with unsuspecting citizens. It was during this time, while Antony dallied with Cleopatra far from Rome's eastern frontier, that the Parthians had been emboldened to seize Syria and then Judea.

But by the time Herod arrived in Alexandria, Antony was long gone. He had set sail months earlier, intending to return to Asia Minor to rally his army against the Parthians. But he soon turned his force of two hundred ships toward Italy, for his wife and his brother and those Romans who were allied with them had precipitated a confrontation with Caesar's other successor, Octavian, for full control of the Roman world.

Thus no one knew what to expect when the Egyptian warship bearing Herod and his officials arrived at the dock in Alexandria. Egypt at this time was still a sovereign nation, and like Herod, Cleopatra was a staunch ally of Rome. And even with Rome on the brink of another episode in its ongoing civil war the two were in agreement: In the clash between Antony and Octavian they both backed Antony. But even among allies there is seldom perfect harmony, but rather a subtle jostling for future advantage. Cleopatra's reputation for getting what she wanted was well known, and one of the things she wanted was Judea. Even the brash Herod, so accustomed to facing down powerful adversaries and wading into seemingly impossible battles, was intimidated by her. He was in a position of extreme weakness—a wartime refugee routed by a superior foe, a political pariah with a shattered power base. All those around him were greatly downcast, for it was hard to know what he could possibly hope to salvage from the wreck of his prospects, other than a minor military command under the watchful eye of a domineering queen. And even that was far from certain.

But the delicate dance of diplomacy that was expected to take weeks or even months was over almost as soon as it began. Cleopatra did indeed receive Herod with great splendor, installing him and all his retinue in the nearby palace of a former pharaoh. (Alexandria's harbor was lined with palaces, for the riches of Egypt were so great that each new monarch of Egypt would build a lavish new palace, rather than occupy an existing one.) But no sooner had the customary welcoming ceremonies and feasting been completed than word arrived from Italy that there had been a reconciliation between Antony and Octavian, with Antony to rule the Roman East and Octavian the West. Herod understood at once that his destiny now lay in Rome, and brushing aside Cleopatra's ominous warnings about the ill winds that would blow with the coming change of the season, he set sail as soon as he could.

Cleopatra had not exaggerated the perils of sailing the Mediterranean in winter. Herod's ship encountered fierce storms as it beat its way north, and more than once all those aboard had given themselves up as lost. As a last resort, the crew tossed most of the cargo overboard and the ship was able to struggle into port on the Greek island of Rhodes. Eventually the party arrived at Brundisium on the southeast coast of the Italian peninsula and hurried along the Appian Way to Rome. There Antony, a curly-headed bull of a man with a lively countenance, welcomed Herod with open arms, and resolved to reattain for him the government of Judea at the expense of Antigonus and the Parthians.

Antony at this time was still a vigorous man, active in the affairs of government and not yet hopelessly lost to a life of luxury and dissipation. Away from the presence of Cleopatra he had broken free of the spell she seemed to cast upon him. He had always been easy in speech with the most sophisticated aristocrats and the lowest soldiers, and in many ways he was not unlike Herod's deceased brother Phasaelus. This may have been why Herod fell so easily into friendship with him, as had his father Antipater before him.

The only obstacle was Antony's co-ruler, Octavian. By nature a deeper and more circumspect man, Octavian might have objected to installing one of Antony's partisans in so strategic a position. But Herod's reputation as an ally of Rome was well known to him, and he was keen to preserve his newly established peace with Antony. So along with Antony he convened the Roman Senate to ratify their choice, and after the necessary speeches and deliberations the matter was settled. Antony and Octavian paraded out of the Senate chamber with the highest magistrates of Rome before them and Herod between them. Antony feasted Herod on this first day of his reign, and within seven days Herod departed Italy, having procured a prize far greater than he had expected—for he had actually come to Rome to advocate that the younger brother of Miriam, Herod's betrothed, should be named king.

All this time Antigonus had besieged those whom Herod had left behind in the mountain fortress of Masada, which was still well-stocked with all the things necessary to maintain a resistance except one: Water. The situation had become dire, and one of Herod's younger brothers, Joseph, whom Herod had left in charge of the refugees, decided that he would try to break the siege the following day. But that night there was a great rainstorm that filled the cisterns of the fortress, and all those who were besieged took it as mark of divine providence, resolving to hold out until Herod returned.

Herod made haste to go to them, with a large force both of his countrymen and foreign mercenaries. As he marched through Galilee, a large part of the population, which had been so eager to see him ejected the previous year, sensed the dramatic turn in his fortunes and rallied to his side. As Herod's army drew closer to Masada the besiegers melted away, and soon Herod and his men were reunited with those they had left behind so many months before.

But the conflict was by no means over, for the partisans of Antigonus were still abundant and were fully capable of waging war. It took two more years of fighting throughout the land before Herod prevailed; not until Pacorus, the perfidious Parthian prince, was killed in battle with the Romans, did the tide begin to turn in Herod's favor. One by one Herod's forces overcame the garrisons loyal to Antigonus—the most important of those being Sepphoris, which capitulated during a driving snowstorm.

Herod himself was in the front lines of nearly every engagement, tirelessly waging war in both body and spirit, and more than once his disdain for precautions nearly cost him his life. In the final year of the conflict he was wounded by an arrow in fighting near Jericho, and soon after, when he had returned to Galilee and established his base in the village of Cana, he engaged the main forces of Antigonus. In this decisive battle Herod's forces prevailed, as Herod himself ran the utmost hazards. When the defeated enemy troops took refuge in the houses of a nearby village, Herod ordered his soldiers to pull down the houses one by one, so all who ran out were put to the sword and all who remained within were crushed in heaps. When the slaughter was complete, Herod dismissed all his troops and his officers except for one servant, and, hot in his armor, entered one of the buildings that had not been destroyed to bathe himself. But no one had thought to scout this house for enemy soldiers, and there were three who had lain there for some time, waiting for night. Not realizing that Herod had entered the house, these men thought to make good their escape. The first of them, with sword drawn, came upon the king, unclothed and unarmed, just as he was about to get into the bath. But the man fled in terror, and the second and third, following close behind, did likewise, wanting nothing more than to escape into the darkness. Because of this deliverance from a near-certain death, and several similar events, many in Judea concluded that Herod was favored by God, and still more of them rallied to his side.

After this there remained but one final prize to be won: Jerusalem. This was by no means certain, for the city had endured many a siege in the thousand years since David had made it his capital. The advantage lay with Herod, for Antony, after vanquishing the Parthians and settling the affairs of Syria, had sent his army to Judea under the command of a general named Sossius, adding eleven legions and six thousand horse to the thirty thousand men of Herod's own army. Still, preparations dragged on for months, into the summer of the following year. When the assault finally commenced the defenders refused to surrender, fighting courageously in brutal battles outside the walls and in the cramped tunnels that Herod's men had dug underneath. After fifty-five days of fighting, Herod's troops and his Roman allies stormed the city. The Romans, enraged at the difficulty of the siege, swarmed like madmen, cutting down people of all ages, both indoors and out, until every street was filled with the dead. Herod sent messengers throughout the city, imploring the Roman soldiers to spare the common people, but without effect. Fighting his way through the chaos with his personal guard, he found the Roman general, Sossius, and demanded an end to the bloodshed.

"Will your soldiers empty the city of both money and men?" he cried. "Will you leave me the king of a desert?"

"The plunder is justly permitted," Sossius snapped, "after what they suffered during the siege."

"But those being slaughtered are not soldiers!" Herod pleaded. "Even dominion over the whole habitable earth would not be compensation for such a murder of my citizens!"

To this Sossius merely shrugged.

"If it's money they want, they shall have it!" Herod said desperately. "I will pay them out of my own treasure! And you as well, if only you will call a halt to this madness!"

At this Sossius took notice, and gave the command that the slaughter should stop, and thus Herod saved Jerusalem from annihilation. He made good on his promise, awarding a handsome payment to each Roman soldier, with higher amounts for the officers and an enormous bounty for Sossius, so they all went away full of money. With them went Antigonus, in chains. The defeated king was taken to Antony, and was later beheaded at Herod's behest, thus securing Herod's kingship of Judea with the full support and favor of the Romans.

Joanna closed the scroll and frowned.

"Is that all?"

"That is the conclusion of Book the Seventh," Aduel said, a little disconcerted. "Did you expect more?"

"I thought there would be more about Cleopatra."

"We saw very little of Cleopatra during this visit. Or Alexandria, for that matter. Which was a pity, since I never went back. What an amazing city it was! Ten times bigger than Jerusalem, if not more. And did you know that the Egyptians have built an enormous hill right in the middle of it? Around it goes a spiral path, so walking to the top you can see for miles in any direction."

Aduel sighed wistfully and drifted into silence. Joanna stifled a sigh of her own. She could not manage even a pretense of interest in a hill with a spiral path.

"Don't worry," Aduel smiled. "Cleopatra will reappear more than once in the coming books."

"I wish I had been there to see the barge," Joanna remarked.

"Those who did see it never tired of talking about it," Aduel chuckled. "They told the story again and again, even years later. That was how I knew so much of it. It was a perfect illustration of how she managed the greatest men of the Roman world."

"Did she greet Julius Caesar on a barge as well?"

"No, that was rather a different sort of introduction," Aduel said. "It was years earlier, when Cleopatra's hold on the throne was not yet secure and she was being hunted by her rivals within Egypt. She judged Julius Caesar to be her only hope, so she sneaked through enemy lines on a tiny fishing boat and had herself smuggled into his chamber in a rolled-up bed covering."

"She did not."

"She did indeed! Imagine the astonishment of the great Caesar as the bedclothes unfurled themselves before his eyes and a beautiful queen appeared! He fell under her spell that very night."

"But you told me she wasn't beautiful," Joanna reminded him.

"She wasn't, really," Aduel admitted. "She was a striking woman, but not beautiful. But she had a way of making herself irresistible, although I never really understood what it was. Of course, she had no reason to direct her charms toward me. Or toward Herod, for that matter. Not at this juncture, anyway."

"So Herod met her again."

"Yes, several years later. In that instance I believe that she did mean to seduce him, with an ulterior motive. But we shall come to that presently. For now—"

He was interrupted by a pounding at the door that made Joanna jump. Aduel frowned and rose stiffly from his chair but Edna had hurried from the back of the house to open the door before him. It was a soldier—not an officer accompanied by a troop, as on that tumultuous night the girl had arrived in Jerusalem, but a single infantryman. Nonetheless she shrank back instinctively. Even one member of the king's guard was enough to be frightening.

"I come for Aduel of Sepphoris," the soldier announced roughly.

"I am Aduel."

"You have been summoned by the king. Come!"

"Come? Come where? To the palace?"

"To the theater."

"The theater!" Edna exclaimed. "He is recovering from an illness. He cannot sit outdoors in the theater!"

"You will come to the theater," the soldier repeated. "The king has called the leading citizens of Jerusalem to account for the riot at the Temple this morning."

"The leading citizens!" Aduel scoffed. "Look around you, man! Do I look like one of the leading citizens of Jerusalem?"

"You have been summoned. Will you come willingly, or shall I have you bound and taken in chains?"

"No, no, I'll go," Aduel grumbled. "Wait just a minute. Edna, my cap and heavy cloak, please."

He closed the door and spoke quietly to Joanna as Edna hurried to fetch the clothing.

"So, Herod is not dead," he mused. "Just as I thought."

"But surely he must be dying, Uncle!" Joanna whispered. "Don't you think at least he must be dying?"

"I don't know, my child," Aduel replied. "But I suppose I'll find out soon enough. As for you, when I return I expect to find you just where you are now. Remember what the doctor said. No scampering about while I am gone."

"But Uncle, what about your own health?" Joanna objected. "You've been coughing all afternoon."

"Oh, the cough is much better than it was," Aduel said, putting on the cloak that Edna had brought. "A touch of catarrh, that's all. It comes and goes and was not so very bad this time. The theater is not far, and there is some daylight remaining. Perhaps Herod will be able to conclude this business, whatever it is, before the torches burn too late into the night. Yes, the historian in me thinks I will be very glad to witness this firsthand. It might make an interesting postscript to my work."

Chapter 14

Joanna sat motionless for some time after Aduel's departure, reliving the events of the day over and over in her mind. Irijah, the Temple, the scribe, the soldier! It was overwhelming—years' worth of vivid emotion packed into one chaotic day—and soon she had fallen into an exhausted sleep. When Edna shook her awake and insisted that she not sleep sitting up, she did not argue but groggily hobbled off to her makeshift bedchamber where she collapsed into the narrow, simple bed.

When she awoke, she could not tell how long she had slept. She lay there for some time, becoming aware, with each passing minute, how stiff and sore she felt. She stared into the darkness as she lingered over the events of the previous day with dreamy detachment. So many crises, and nothing resolved! The most pressing was Herod's summons to Aduel. What could the king possibly have wanted? Had her uncle really been taken to an audience in the theater with the leading citizens of Jerusalem? And more important, had he returned? She wondered how long it would be until morning, when she would have the entire story from his own lips.

She thought she heard Edna moving about quietly somewhere outside her door. She knew that the old woman arose before daybreak and decided to get up—but slipped back into sleep. When she awoke again she felt certain that it must be morning, but she could not tell, for it was pitch dark in the little room and her candle had long since burned out. Finally she swung out of bed, wincing a little as she tested her injured leg. With the help of the crutch she ventured into the kitchen.

Edna was nowhere to be found, but in the front room Aduel was in his chair before the hearth.

"Uncle! You're home!"

"Yes, I am home. The business with Herod took rather longer than I had hoped. It did not conclude until the fourth hour of the night. But finally it did conclude."

"But why are you up so early? You need a good night's sleep!"

"I have enjoyed a good night's sleep," Aduel chuckled. "You, on the other hand, have enjoyed that and more. Do you know that it is almost the sixth hour of the day?"

"The sixth hour! Why didn't you wake me?"

"You have nothing to do today but rest and recover," Aduel said. "Why should we wake you?"

"But I could have been helping Edna in the kitchen," Joanna apologized. "The crutch is a nuisance, but I can still knead, I can still clean—"

"Nonsense, child," Aduel interrupted. "If I had awoken you, Edna would have used that crutch of yours to deliver me a severe beating."

He grinned at the thought of it.

"But where is Edna?" Joanna asked.

"She is on the roof, attending to the washing."

Joanna groaned at the thought of the old woman plunging her hands into the frigid water.

"Sit, child, and stop worrying," Aduel admonished her.

"Edna is glad to be of service to one who has been of so much service to her. Presently she'll come down, and we can all enjoy our midday meal."

Realizing that there was nothing to be gained by protesting, Joanna gingerly seated herself in the empty chair. Aduel himself got up to prop up her injured leg and arrange the cushions. She waited until he had finished and taken his own seat before she spoke:

"So Herod still lives."

"Yes, barely. He was so weak that he could not stand. He lay upon a couch to address us all."

"What did he say?"

"A great number of things. He enumerated all the labors he had endured on our account, particularly the building of the Temple, and how much it had cost him. He reminded us that no one since Solomon had performed so great a work for the honor of God. He said that he had adorned the Temple with the golden eagle to leave for himself a memorial after his death, and that although the young men who had torn it down claimed that they had done it for the glory of God, they had really done it with no other purpose than to affront him while he still lived. He said that those who were responsible, including the two teachers who had urged the young men to such boldness, had been sent to Jericho in chains to await their fate."

"And what is their fate?" Joanna asked quietly.

"That was the question that Herod put to the assembly: What should be done with those arrested for the crime? Of course, most of us there were secretly delighted with the destruction of the eagle, but none dared say it. All were in fear of Herod's fierce temper—in fear that in his rage and disappointment he would inflict punishment on those who had nothing to do with it. So none dared say anything at all in favor of the young men—no request for clemency, no suggestion of mercy. Quite the opposite. Those who dared to respond said that what had been done had been done without their approval, and that those responsible might well be punished for it.

"This seemed to pacify Herod, although he continued to cry out that though he had done great works for our nation, he was hated and abused by all. And then, his anger still not spent, he passed sentence on those who had been arrested and sent to Jericho."

"Are they to be executed?" Joanna asked.

"Executed on the morrow," Aduel confirmed. "They are to be burned alive."

"Burned!"

"Yes. A barbarous punishment, is it not? But Herod seemed to feel that it would have a purifying effect."

Joanna shuddered. She was thinking of the young scribe—of how close he had come to this horrible death. Had it not been not for the old woman in the Temple, he might now be counting out the last hours of his life. And all because he had dared to risk his own life to save hers.

"Were any others sentenced or accused?" she asked.

"No," Aduel replied. "Herod's raillery continued for some time, but eventually he grew weary and was carried back to the palace, leaving those of us who had assembled in the theater free to go home."

"But why did he summon you?"

"I don't know," Aduel said. "I have been puzzling over that question all morning."

"He didn't speak to you?" Joanna asked.

"Not a word. He didn't even notice me, as far as I could tell. I was one among hundreds."

"Why, then?"

Aduel simply shook his head.

"Were Herod's advisors there?" Joanna asked.

"Yes, all of them." Aduel paused, then decided it would be unkind to force the girl to ask.

"And yes, I did see Nicolaus there," he added, "though I don't think he noticed me either."

Joanna pondered this.

"Surely Herod will not live much longer," she said.

"No. From what I observed last night, a few weeks at most," Aduel said. "And then there will be chaos throughout the land, you can be sure of that."

"What will we do?"

"We will do what seems right at the time."

A fretful gloom descended over Joanna; the peace of her long slumber had vanished. Aduel had anticipated this. After leaving her to her thoughts for a minute, he produced a tiny ceramic pot with an equally tiny lid, sealed lightly with wax.

"On a more pleasant note, this is for you," he said.

She took it carefully and looked at him questioningly.

"You may open it," he nodded.

The moment she lifted the lid a powerful, pungent odor assaulted her nostrils. She quickly replaced the lid and looked at Aduel with astonishment. She knew that myrrh was a powerful balm, and expensive.

"Thank you, Uncle."

"Oh, you needn't thank me," Aduel said breezily. "I had nothing to do with it. It was delivered earlier this morning.

Along with this."

He held up a bound scroll. Joanna gasped.

"Is it…" Her voice trailed off.

"The marriage contract," Aduel confirmed.

"The scribe delivered the marriage contract?" Joanna hesitated, wanting to presume nothing.

"And the myrrh," Aduel nodded.

"But—is it for me?" she stammered.

"I think that it is," Aduel smiled. "It came with this."

He held out a small piece of papyrus that had been cut from a scroll with a scribe's knife. It had been folded inward upon itself into a perfect square and sealed with a dab of plain wax. On the outside was a brief inscription:

For the maiden.

Joanna's heart pounded. Hesitantly she took the note, staring at it as if it were a summons from Sinai. Everything else in the room seemed to fade.

"I believe I hear Edna coming down the ladder," she heard Aduel say. "I'll fetch Book the Eighth, in case you would care to read this afternoon, and ask her to prepare us something to eat. And to apply the myrrh, of course."

Joanna made no response. She placed the little pot securely in her lap and stared at the note, turning it over in her hands. Should she open it? Of course she should! But she hesitated, because now, while sealed, its possibilities were infinite. She wanted to wait, to treasure it just as it was, while it was still the perfect embodiment of all her hopes and dreams. But what were those hopes and dreams? She did not even know.

She glanced about. She wanted to be alone when she opened the note. She could hear Aduel clumping down the stairs to his subterranean chamber and Edna clattering about in the courtyard. Condemned as she was to a regimen of recuperation, this might be the only solitude she would enjoy all day. To retreat to her musty little bedchamber would not be an option until nightfall, since that room was pitch dark and she could never justify lighting a candle while daylight abounded. Could she wait until night? She decided she could not. Glancing about once more, she broke the seal and unfolded the note.

"Dear Maiden," it read, in a supremely elegant hand, "I have never encountered a woman with such admirable strength of character. I fervently pray that this balm will speed your recovery."

She stared at the note in disbelief. *Strength of character?* She felt her cheeks begin to burn. *Strength of character?* Was that all he could think to say to her?

All at once her unbridled emotions were racing again, hurtling her across an unfamiliar landscape. She glanced at the note once more, to make sure she had not missed something, then angrily tossed it into the hearth. Immediately she wished she had not, but it was too late. The papyrus ignited instantly and burned quickly, stoking her fury. The words had been hopelessly prosaic—but the penmanship! So elegant, so precise, so beautiful! It was like a tiny work of art that she had held in her hand. And now she had destroyed it! Oh, why had she done it? But it was his fault! Why had he muddled things with such a mundane message? Why could he not make it perfectly clear? Strength of character! What kind of courting was that?

She did not realize that in the scribe's mind this was the highest compliment he could have paid her.

She wanted to leap from the chair, to rush through the streets of Jerusalem, to find him, to grasp him by the tunic and make him tell her what he really thought. But of course this was impossible. She did not even know where to look for him. Besides, she was not supposed to go anywhere at all. She could not slip away to seek solitude on the rooftop, or even pace the courtyard and shake her fist at the sky. All she could do was sit and smolder. She thought of the silversmith's son. What might his note have said, had he written one? She did not even know if he could write. But he could speak, she knew that. And if he did, he would not speak about strength of character. No, his words of wooing would be passionate, irresistible. She was sure of it. But still—what would such words really mean? Were not actions more important than words? What had the silversmith's son ever done for her? He had offered her a bangle at a bargain price. Intriguing, yes, but how many other maidens had received the same offer?

She heard Aduel coming back up the steps. Quickly she wiped away the tears of consternation that had been streaming down her face. As Aduel sat down their traces did not escape his notice, but he said nothing. Their awkward silence continued until Edna opened the door from the courtyard. The old woman's eyes lit up at the sight of the girl.

"You be awake, maid!" she cried gladly. "Just when I thought you might sleep the whole day through!"

Joanna smiled in spite of herself.

"I almost did," she said. "You should have woken me."

"And disturb the slumber of the innocent?" exclaimed Edna. "Not I! Your uncle might do such a thing, for he is a hard man, but never I!"

"Oh, nonsense, Edna," Aduel chuckled. "You gabble like a

dizzy old woman."

Joanna found herself drawn into the quiet mirth, despite the turmoil in her heart.

"He said if he had tried it, you would have beaten him with my crutch," she told Edna.

"Indeed I would," Edna affirmed. "He knows me well, your old uncle."

She was already busily plumping the cushions and rearranging them under the girl's leg.

"There. Is that better? Is it more comfortable?"

"Much more comfortable."

"Of course it is. Never leave it to a man to make things comfortable. But what is that odor? It smells like myrrh."

"Perhaps it is myrrh," Aduel grinned, nodding in Joanna's direction.

The old woman looked at her quizzically. Sheepishly she produced the little ceramic pot from the folds of her robe.

"But who went to get it?" Edna demanded. "Surely neither of you has gone out this morning."

"Not I," affirmed Aduel.

"And certainly not you, maid," Edna said. "Was it Irijah?"

Aduel laughed out loud at such an absurd suggestion.

"No, not Irijah," he said. "After what happened yesterday, such a thing would have been an inspired penance. But Irijah is not known for his inspiration."

"Nor his penance," added Edna. "But who, then?"

Again she peered at Joanna, who blushed and looked down.

"An admirer, perhaps," Aduel hinted.

"Ah, an admirer." The old woman smiled slyly. "An admirer bearing precious gifts. An admirer with an eye for beauty."

An admirer who waxes poetic about strength of character,

Joanna thought peevishly. But her anger quickly crumbled. Her mind was racing again—this time focusing on the unexpectedness of the gift—and the lavishness of it.

"Would you like me to apply it?" Edna asked.

"Our invalid had hoped you would bring her something to eat first," Aduel interjected. "I believe she said she would hardly fancy a meal that tastes like myrrh."

"I believe she said no such thing," Edna said wryly. "However, I can easily believe that her uncle might have said it. Very well, just wait a moment. I have already prepared something that you both seem to enjoy."

She returned a minute later with the platter she had used a few days earlier. Again it was heaped with cakes of figs. Joanna sat up taller; a pang of hunger had gripped her. The cakes had been baked hours earlier and the aroma had faded, but Edna had kept them warm and they were delicious even to the touch.

Aduel took a cake of his own and rose from his chair.

"Join us, Edna," he implored. "Sit and eat."

"I have already eaten," Edna replied. "Pray, sit back down and enjoy your meal. I will fetch some water. Then I will apply the balm."

Joanna was voracious. She could not stop until she had consumed six of the cakes. Aduel himself had three. Edna stood by contentedly, refilling their cups with water until she was satisfied that both had eaten their fill. Then she took away the platter, with its lone remaining cake, and returned to kneel and apply the myrrh. The room filled with a smoky, spicy scent as she gently rubbed a few drops of the resinous liquid over the girl's bruised, puffy leg.

The soothing effect was immediate. Joanna leaned back

with a sigh of satisfaction.

"Better?" Edna asked.

"Much better," Joanna murmured.

"I'll apply it again at sundown, and once more before bed." Edna straightened up and gently draped the girl's robe back over her leg. "Meanwhile, I'll store this in a safe place."

She regarded the little pot with a mixture of wonder and amusement.

"Brought by an admirer, you say," she remarked. "We might all be so lucky as to have such an admirer! Not every admirer would have thought to indulge you with such a remedy. Not I, certainly, nor your uncle either."

"Thank the Lord for the inspiration of youth," Aduel commented placidly.

The room lapsed into silence as Edna departed. Joanna closed her eyes, lulled by the food and the scent. Incredibly, she felt herself drifting back into sleep. When she awoke a half hour later, she noticed that Aduel seemed to have drifted off as well, though his eyes were open. Book the Eighth was open on his lap.

"Uncle?"

"Yes, child." Aduel's voice was barely a whisper.

"Have you stepped through a doorway to another place and another time?"

"Yes. Oh, yes."

"May I join you?"

"If you wish. But you should know that it is a place of bitterness. And a time of sorrow and strife."

"A place that you have been?"

"A place that I have seen with my own eyes and felt with my own heart."

"Is it really so very sad?"

"Oh, not at the beginning, I suppose," Aduel reflected. "Much of what is to come is actually rather entertaining. But I must warn you. Up to now, we have followed Herod to the pinnacle of his success. From here it is a long, terrible descent, a descent that ends in the raving ruin that I witnessed last night."

Joanna nodded solemnly.

"I think I would like to go there with you," she said.

"Very well," Aduel said. "You will experience it through my eyes and my heart—the knowledge without the pain, if I have done my work well. That is why I wrote these words, after all. For people to know, and to understand. Besides, there is someone in Book the Eighth that I would like you to meet."

"Who?"

"The most enchanting woman I have ever encountered."

"Cleopatra? I've already met her."

"Not Cleopatra. Miriam, Herod's second wife."

Joanna leaned forward, her interest piqued.

"Would you like me to do the reading today, Uncle?"

Aduel stared at the scroll in his lap for a long time before handing it to her.

"Yes," he sighed. "Perhaps that would be best."

Joanna's eyes gleamed as she took a moment to bask silently in the immaculate block of text that made up the first panel of the eighth book. Her injury, the gift, the note, the scribe—all were forgotten in the anticipation of the story. She drew a deep, luxurious breath and began to read:

"Herod: A Secret History, by Aduel of Sepphoris. Book the Eighth."

With the capture of Jerusalem Herod had achieved his life's ambition, and at a relatively young age, for he was at this time only about thirty-five. He was now the unchallenged ruler of Judea, a kingdom which included not only Galilee and the traditional tribal lands of Judah and Benjamin, but much of the surrounding territory as well—territory that would be further augmented as his reign continued. The end of the civil war and the prospect of a unified nation were a source of great hope for all Jerusalem—all, of course, except the partisans of Antigonus who had survived the sack of the city. Forty-five of these were summarily executed, their property and possessions seized, and Herod even went so far as to set guards at the gates so that nothing of value could be carried out with their dead bodies. In fact, each of the thousands of corpses that had accumulated in the devastation was searched for articles of value, and anything that was found was confiscated. In this manner Herod heaped up huge amounts of silver and gold, all of which he sent to Antony and his friends—thus planting, at a very early stage, the seeds of resentment and hatred that would quickly sprout and continue to entangle him throughout his rule.

In a like manner, though no one could have suspected it at the time, he sowed the seeds of far more excruciating trouble—the one, in fact, that would drive him to madness. He took for himself a second wife: Miriam, the granddaughter of Hyrcanus, to whom he had been betrothed four years earlier. She was said to be the most beautiful woman in all Judea, and never was anyone heard to dispute this claim, even in the most confidential conversation. She was a raven-haired temptress, tall and slender with a thin, smooth face accentuated by high cheekbones, an exquisite mouth, and defiant, laughing eyes. Unlike Herod's first wife, who was of the Arabian nobility, Miriam was pure Jewish royalty. Not only was she the granddaughter of Queen Alexandra on her mother's side, but also a great-granddaughter on her father's side—for her father was Alexander, the long-dead brother of the recently deposed Antigonus and the son of Aristobulus, who had two generations earlier contended for the Judean crown with his own brother Hyrcanus. The marriage provided Herod, who was still regarded as a common usurper by many Judeans, a conclusive way to legitimize his own claim to the throne.

There was an additional element, though, one often absent from the annals of royal matrimony: Herod loved his new queen passionately. The feeling on her side may have been less fervent, though it is not known whether her thoughts on the matter were ever expressed. In any case, she bore her royal heritage well. She was a queen from the crown of her head to the soles of her feet: generous, impetuous, haughty. She could be compassionate and kind, but also quick to deride any who displeased her. Unfortunately the latter included most of Herod's birth relatives, particularly his mother and his sister Salome. Yet they all were housed under the same roof, in the palace formerly occupied by Antigonus and before that Hyrcanus, and this arrangement would cause no end of domestic conflict for the king.

The trouble began over the high priesthood. The obvious choice was Aristobulus the Younger, the brother of Queen Miriam and the grandson of Queen Alexandra. Aristobulus was still a youth, only sixteen years old, but as one of the two remaining members of the royal line he was popular with the people. Fearful that appointing Aristobulus to the high priesthood would provide the youth with a stepping stone to the throne, Herod summoned an obscure priest from Babylon to fill the post.

This was too much for Alexandra, the scheming, histrionic mother of Miriam and Aristobulus, whose opinions Herod alternately desired and detested. In her mind, the dignity of the high priesthood could be conferred on only one individual—her son, Aristobulus—and she was not long in formulating a campaign to overcome Herod's resistance. She began by writing to Cleopatra, with her letter being carried in secret to Egypt by a court musician, desiring the Egyptian queen to intercede with Antony on her son's behalf. Her attacks from within were more direct. She enlisted her daughter, Queen Miriam, who badgered Herod continually on the matter, laying at him vehemently in shouted arguments that rang throughout the halls of the palace.

After many months of this Herod relented. Calling together his friends and his highest officials to his audience chamber, he summoned Alexandra, Aristobulus, and Queen Miriam to appear as well.

"There has come to my attention," the king began, in a low, steady voice, "a conspiracy against my royal authority."

There was a shocked murmur among those assembled, which Herod allowed to linger.

"I am told that there are those in this chamber," he continued, "who would deprive me of the government by means of foreign intervention."

This was a dangerous moment for the royal secretary, who as one of the assembled court officials had been standing off to the side. He never lost an opportunity to gaze upon the beautiful countenance of the queen, but had always been careful to do it with the utmost discretion, when he would not be noticed. At this utterance of Herod's, when all those assembled had looked at each other with questioning glances, her eyes had happened to snap to his first, and there could be no question but that she had caught him staring at her. This was a serious offense, an affront to the king, and it would have been entirely within her right to reprimand him in front of all those assembled, to lodge the accusation that would leave him humiliated at best or more likely dismissed from the king's service and scourged. But there was no angry reproof, and in the moment before he tore his eyes from hers he could have sworn that there was a bond between them, an unspoken affinity. It was the most tenuous of connections, a gossamer strand of astonishment and mystery—thrilling to be sure, but also terrifying beyond all measure.

"A certain party here before me has seen fit to engage in a private communication with the monarch of another nation, namely the Queen of Egypt, in the matter of a royal appointment," Herod said.

With this everyone in the chamber knew exactly who and what he was talking about, and all eyes turned toward Alexandra. Well known for her ability to assume any guise at a moment's notice, she displayed no emotion. But she did tremble slightly.

"All of which was unnecessary," Herod went on, "for I have always intended to appoint Aristobulus as high priest. I have forborne to do it until now due to his young age. Now, though, I see no reason to wait any longer, if that meets with the approval of all those assembled here today."

At this Alexandra abandoned her impassive posture and gave a loud cry as she fell weeping to the floor.

"Majesty, oh Majesty!" she wailed. "Wisest of all rulers! Most beneficent of all kings! What a fool I have been! I should have known that you acted only in the best interests of the young prince! I thought only of the disgrace of having another appointed in his stead! But as to the kingdom, not true! What you say is not true, for he has never desired it, nor I for him, and if it were offered he would not accept it! For it is evident to all that you are the one best suited to rule our fractious nation. I can only implore you to make allowance for me, if the nobility of my family has caused me to act precipitously and imprudently in this matter! I am overcome by your beneficence, and from this day forward I will always act in obedience to your wishes."

Through it all Herod sat impassively. When she had finished, he silently regarded her prostrate form before him. The chamber was deathly still as all those assembled awaited his decision. It was this fraught moment that the secretary chose to hazard another glance at the queen—and saw, to his astonishment, that she had been staring at him! They both averted their gazes immediately, returning their attention to Herod, who had risen from the throne. Without a word he went to Alexandra, and taking her by the hand, raised her to her feet. It was a brilliant performance on both sides, and all in attendance uttered a sigh of relief as the tension melted away and all suspicions seemed to vanish.

But it was a performance nonetheless, and soon both players reverted to their familiar roles as wary antagonists. Although Herod seemed to have healed the divisions within his family, he was not without suspicion that Alexandra might once again plot against him. So he commanded that she should dwell at all times in the palace, and that she should be closely guarded day and night so that nothing she did in private life could be concealed. Little by little these hardships put her out of patience, and she began truly to hate him. When it became clear that nothing would change she sent another secret letter to Cleopatra, entreating her assistance. Cleopatra's response was quick in coming, for developments that were damaging to Herod increased the likelihood that she would one day add Judea to her possessions. She advised Alexandra to flee secretly to Egypt, bringing her son Aristobulus along with her.

This advice pleased Alexandra, and she contrived to have two coffins made, one for herself and one for Aristobulus, and gave orders to her most trusted servants to have them carried away in the night, as if for burial. They would then be transported by road to the coast, where a ship awaited to take them to Egypt. But on the appointed day one of Alexandra's servants who knew of the plan happened to fall into conversation with a man named Sabion, one of Alexandra's friends, and spoke of the plan to him, thinking that he already knew of it. Sabion was a devious man, one whom Herod suspected had been involved in the poisoning of his own father Antipater. Hoping that this information would change Herod's hatred to favor, Sabion revealed the plan to the king.

Thus it was that the secretary found himself roused from sleep in the middle of the night by the king's chamberlain, and ordered to the royal apartments. There, in an antechamber, awaited the king. With him were two officers of the cavalry, Jucundus and Tyrannus, who were esteemed for their unusual height and strength and served as his most trusted bodyguards. But most astonishing of all was the presence of Queen Miriam herself, clad in a heavy robe and mantle. With the party assembled, Herod quickly led the way to the back of the palace, to a large loading dock in the basement where foodstuffs and other items were received for delivery. As Herod strode up, the dock's wide doors were being pulled open to the night air, and a large wagon bearing two coffins lurched forward.

"Halt!" Herod cried, and the two bodyguards ran forward with their swords drawn to block any further movement.

"What is this?" Herod demanded of the driver. "Who has died without my knowing it?"

The driver, too terrified to speak, simply shook his head.

"Well then, I suppose I must find out for myself," Herod said grimly, although it seemed to the secretary that he was laughing through his teeth.

"Open them," he commanded his bodyguards. "This one first."

The two bodyguards quickly set to work, prying open the lid of the first coffin with iron bars. The secretary risked a quick glance at the queen, who stood opposite him on the other side of the wagon, but her bewildered gaze told him that she knew nothing of what was about to happen. After a minute or two the nails had all been removed, the lid of the coffin loosened. The bodyguards gripped the sides of the lid and looked to Herod, who nodded.

The lid was lifted, revealing Alexandra's motionless body. For once her face was passive and silent, though the weird torchlight seemed to give it a supernatural animation.

Her eyes fluttered open as Herod bent over her, bringing his face to within a few inches of hers.

"Hello, Alexandra," he said, in a low, gurgling voice. "It seems that you have come back to life! And back to the palace, of course."

The royal secretary glanced again at the queen, but she had turned away in mortification and disgust.

"Jucundus, help the queen mother out of this wagon," Herod ordered. "Take her to my personal physician for a complete examination. She appears to have taken a sleeping elixir of some sort. A bit too much of it, perhaps."

"Yes, Majesty."

"As for him," Herod jerked his head in the direction of the driver, "you know what to do. As well as with all the others who had a part in this treachery."

"Yes, Majesty," Jucundus replied. "What shall we do with the other coffin?"

"Bury it, of course," Herod shrugged.

At this Alexandra cried out incoherently and struggled to sit up.

"Hmm, she seems to object," Herod said carelessly. "I suppose we should find out who's in it first."

The process of prying the nails and lifting the lid was repeated with the second coffin, revealing Aristobulus. Unlike his mother, his eyes shot open immediately and he sat bolt upright.

"The high priest of Israel, hiding in a coffin," Herod mocked. "Rather unclean, don't you think? Quite undignified, at any rate."

He turned to the queen, who by now was weeping profusely.

"Come, my dear," he said, leading her back into the palace. "We shall leave these two to recover from their aborted adventure, and to consider its consequences."

But it seemed that there would not be any consequences, at least not immediately, for Alexandra and Aristobulus were restored to their stations in life as if nothing had happened, and the royal secretary, the chamberlain, and the two bodyguards were warned never to speak of the incident. But that very night Herod purposed in his mind to put the young high priest out of his way forever, though he bided his time in the execution of his intention, that he might be better concealed in doing it. His plans for Alexandra were less certain, for he continued in his strange, symbiotic regard for her, and knew moreover that it would cause him no end of trouble with Cleopatra if she were accused. She would live many years more, conniving and plotting and leaving behind a record of disgrace and disaster, as future books of this history will reveal.

Joanna slowly rolled the scroll shut and gave her uncle a long, curious look. Up to now, it had never fully registered in her mind that he too had once enjoyed the vigor of youth, and all the passions and desires that accompanied it.

"Were you in love with her, Uncle?" she asked.

"There was not a man alive who could be in the same room as Miriam and not be in love with her," Aduel said wistfully.

"Perhaps it was that exquisite mouth of hers," Joanna teased.

"It was not just her mouth. Everything about her was

exquisite."

"Was she in love with you?"

"No, no, it was nothing so perilous as that," Aduel said. "She rarely spoke to me, or I to her. There wasn't occasion for it."

"But she did like you."

"I believe she saw in me an ally of sorts," Aduel explained. "In a palace overrun with Arabians and Egyptians and Greeks I was one of the few Hebrews in a position of importance. I was a very weak ally, of course. I had very little influence. I did as I was told, wrote what was dictated. I never dared to contradict or even to question—except for one instance, in the business with Cleopatra, as you will see in Book the Tenth. Still, if any in that pit of vipers could be trusted to understand her thoughts, at least a little, it was probably I. We were kindred spirits, of a sort, two headstrong souls sharing the same heritage and views about life but separated by a wide gap in station and situation."

"It's sad, sometimes, the way life works out," Joanna mused.

"It is, sometimes," Aduel said. "But I do not feel sad. I have been blessed by the Lord, wonderfully blessed."

He reflected a moment, then chuckled.

"You need not grieve for me, child," he said. "I was never meant for Miriam, nor she for me. She was royalty by birth and by nature, willful and demanding in every thought and every deed."

"But she was beautiful," Joanna reminded him.

"Oh yes." Aduel's voice sank back to a distant whisper. "I see her even now. She was beautiful. So very, very beautiful."

Chapter 15

The next morning Joanna lay abed for some time after waking, meditating lazily in the darkness. Her uncle's long-ago passion for Herod's beautiful queen had piqued her curiosity, and she speculated as to what might happen in the coming books. But presently her mind wandered to other things, particularly Aduel's offhand remark after the previous day's reading: *I was never meant for Miriam, nor she for me.* How did he know that? How could anyone know? She thought of the scribe. Was he meant for her, or she for him? She knew that her uncle considered him to be a brilliant match, and it was obvious that the young man cared for her deeply. And there were so many things to recommend him! He was kind, thoughtful, fearless, true. But was that enough? Would he ever stir her to the very depths of her soul? Would anyone?

Her doubt made her irritable and she sat up, ready to shake off her moody solitude. Far off, in the front of the house, she heard the door to the courtyard open and shut. She knew it must be morning, and wondered who was coming, or going. She swung out of bed and tested her leg. It felt much better; the swelling had gone down. Thanks to the myrrh—and the scribe.

She opened the door and stepped into the chilly morning air of the kitchen. No one was there, but she could hear voices in the front room. Her uncle was speaking to someone in an irritable, peremptory tone. At first she thought it must be Irijah, but the voice that responded, though familiar, was not that of the querulous old manservant. With her mind still clouded with the fog of waking, she foolishly ventured toward the doorway that opened from the kitchen to the front room to find out who it was. She saw a flash of blue, the briefest glimpse of an elegant robe, as someone sat down in one of the chairs before the hearth. She froze and stifled a gasp. She had almost blundered into the presence of the man she feared most.

Nicolaus of Damascus!

She shrank back immediately and tried not to breathe. He had not seen her, she was sure of that. But what was he doing here? She inched back closer to the corner, careful not to bang the crutch against the wall, and stopped to listen.

"I leave within the hour," Nicolaus was saying. "Before I go, there is something I must tell you. You must hear me out."

"Very well then, I shall hear you out," Aduel grumbled, grudgingly taking his own seat. "But first, where is it?"

"Where is what?"

"The gold."

"What gold?" The confusion in Nicolaus's voice was evident.

"My twenty-five talents of gold."

"Twenty-five talents of gold!" Nicolaus was flabbergasted. "Who promised you twenty-five talents of gold?"

"I thought you did," Aduel said. "If I am to be included in the list of Jerusalem's leading citizens, certainly I should have the trappings that go with it."

"I had nothing to do with that, Aduel," Nicolaus said, relieved that Aduel's demand for gold was simply an attempt at dark humor. "It was Herod himself who added your name to the list."

"Herod! Why?"

"I don't know. I questioned why you were included, but he would not explain it. The only thing I know is that in the weeks after you were brought to the palace to advise the king, his spies reported that you were seen several times at the Temple, making mysterious inquiries—eagerly seeking out some men while actively avoiding others. It was unusual for someone who had remained out of the public eye for so long."

"That was strictly personal business," Aduel said testily.

"I don't doubt it," Nicolaus said, "but Herod does. He knows that you have always despised him."

"Not always," Aduel said ruefully.

"Perhaps not, but Herod's doubts torment him night and day. The most innocuous comment or the most innocent action arouses suspicion. Even now the royal secretary is compiling additional lists, of all the leading men not only in Jerusalem but throughout Judea—for what purpose no one can be sure. The king suspects everyone, even the most loyal members of his court."

"Then you have taken a risk by coming here."

"Possibly."

"Why?"

"I thought it necessary to warn you." Nicolaus's voice took on a tone of urgency. "The king's condition is becoming more uncertain every day. He complains of a strange fire that glows within his belly, and pains in his intestines, and yet his appetite is insatiable. He has repeated convulsions, and when he sits upright he has difficulty breathing, and that itself is utterly loathsome, due to the stench of his breath. Word of all this has begun to leak out; the people have become restive. The stability of the government is at risk. Herod has changed his will several times recently. Since the illness set in, he has lost all sense of emotional balance."

"He lost all sense of emotional balance some time ago," Aduel grumbled.

"Perhaps, but now we await messengers from Rome who will tell us whether the crown prince is to be executed. Herod may be dying, but—"

"Herod is dying, you may be sure of that," Aduel interrupted.

"We cannot be sure yet," Nicolaus contradicted. "The force of life is strong in him, stronger than any I have ever seen. He craves life, he wills it! Even now he prepares to go to Callirrhoe to take the waters, and one never knows. It may work."

"Nonsense, Nicolaus," Aduel scoffed. "Let him go to Callirrhoe. It's a very long way on a fool's errand, all the way to the other side of the Dead Sea! Try what he may, he shall go the way of all the earth, and the sooner the better. I take it you are to accompany him."

"Yes, I and all the rest of the court and two thousand of his personal troops," Nicolaus said. "That is why I have come to you now. I do not know when I will return to Jerusalem, if ever. And if Herold should die with the succession undecided, there will be a power struggle within the city, perhaps throughout the land."

"And you think I have something to fear from all this?"

"As a former official of Herod's court you would be vulnerable. You live in this house at the pleasure of the crown. It's impossible to say how long that would continue after Herod is gone."

"I can find another house," Aduel muttered.

"Yes, but you don't seem to understand," Nicolaus insisted. "If you remained in Jerusalem, you would no longer have protection from your enemies."

"Enemies! I have no enemies."

"None that you know of. But you know how men are. Once they are freed from restraint they will have vengeance for the slightest of reasons, or no reason at all. You must be prepared to flee Jerusalem at a moment's notice. Even better if you were to leave now."

"Leave now!" Aduel exclaimed. "Based on speculation? Where would I go?"

"To Alexandria, of course," Nicolaus said. "It's the most Jewish city in the world outside Judea. There are synagogues throughout the city. The whole of the Delta district and half the Beta district are occupied by Jews."

"Are they Jews who would welcome a former official of Herod's court?" scoffed Aduel.

"Not all of them," Nicolaus admitted. "But I have many friends there. They would offer you safety."

"But to leave Jerusalem!" Aduel protested. "Who even knows if I would be allowed to leave?"

"I know of no travel prohibitions currently in place," Nicolaus answered.

"Not currently, but what about tomorrow, what about an hour from now?" Aduel argued. "You said yourself that the royal secretary is compiling additional lists. What are they for?"

"I don't know," Nicolaus shrugged. "But if you think it necessary, I can obtain a safe passage for you. With the privy seal, it would override any proscription issued by the royal secretary."

There was a long silence.

"Alexandria is a beautiful city," Aduel wavered. "Better to die there in peace than here in a bloodbath. But all of this is so sudden."

"You must consider it," Nicolaus urged. "Think of the risk to yourself and your household! If it's money you need, I will supply it."

"I have no need of money," Aduel growled. "I have lived quite frugally these many years."

"Of course. But you will consider it?"

"I will give it all the consideration an old man can muster."

"Very well, then." Joanna could hear Nicolaus rise from the chair. "The king's caravan will depart any minute now. I must not be missed. I will obtain the safe passage and write the letters of introduction to my friends in Alexandria when we arrive at Callirrhoe. I'll send them to you by special messenger. You may never need them, but you will have them nonetheless."

"I will be here to receive them," Aduel said. "Goodbye, Nicolaus."

Joanna heard the door open and the rustle of fine linen as Nicolaus exited to the courtyard.

"Nicolaus," Aduel said.

"Yes, Aduel."

"Why are you doing this?"

"Because I have owed you a debt these many years. I should like to repay it."

"You owe me no debt, Nicolaus. You never have."

"Perhaps not," said Nicolaus. "But I should like to repay it nonetheless.”

Joanna heard the courtyard’s outer gate open and shut, but it was a long time before Aduel closed the door to the house. Too late she decided that she should retreat to her room and pretend that she was still asleep; Aduel had come into the kitchen. She tried to look as if she had just woken up, grabbing a couple of raw figs from a basket that hung near the window and nibbling at one. But Aduel was not his normal genial self; he made no inquiries of her. He merely nodded absently and murmured something in the way of a morning greeting before turning around and making his way to his underground lair.

She did not see him for two hours. In the interim she made herself useful, crushing an enormous number of olives to collect the oil, and spreading the pulverized fruit over a hunk of rough bread that Edna had baked the previous day. Now she was seated in her assigned place, in the chair before the fire with her leg propped up, the myrrh dutifully applied. The idle life of an invalid, seemingly so carefree, was proving intolerable to her. Aduel appeared and wordlessly settled himself into his chair. She looked up hopefully, grateful for the distraction, but her uncle seemed sunk in his thoughts.

“Well?” he said presently. “Shall we go?”

“Go where, Uncle?”

“You know where. Alexandria.”

She blushed, embarrassed that he had known all along that she had been eavesdropping. But it was the very question she had just been pondering. Alexandria! At first she had rejected the idea outright, but within minutes she had begun to entertain it. A city ten times larger than Jerusalem! She could not even imagine it, but she was intrigued. Hers was a cautious soul, but not without a spirit of adventure. And there was another consideration: In a city of that size there would be bright young scribes by the dozen—perhaps even one superior to her suitor in Jerusalem. It was with twinge of guilt that she considered her uncle's question.

"Do you really think it will be dangerous for us in Jerusalem after Herod dies?" she ventured.

"It will be a time of upheaval, as Nicolaus has said," Aduel replied. "But how great an upheaval will it be, and when will it begin? What will be the outcome? And what of Alexandria? Who knows what we would find there?"

"A lighthouse," Joanna said brightly. "And a famous library, with more books than you could ever read! And a great hill with a spiral path, with views of every part of the city for miles around."

"The landmarks and the buildings, yes, they will be the same. But what of the people? Thirty-five years ago I was welcomed there. I was a person of some importance then, a foreign dignitary of sorts. What would I be now? A powerless old man too fearful to remain in his own land."

"But we could go just for a time," Joanna suggested. "If things did not go well with us, we could return to Jerusalem."

Aduel shook his head.

"If we leave this place, we will never come back," he said. "I won't, at least. You, perhaps. It's very hard to know at a time like this. We think that we can see the future, that it will continue very much like the past and the present, but events beyond our control can change everything in an instant."

He sighed a great sigh.

"For the time being we will remain in Jerusalem," he decided. "If Nicolaus is true to his word, I will have letters of introduction within a few days. If necessary, we will make use of them. But only if necessary.”

Joanna settled back into her chair, at the same time relieved and disappointed. The two of them sat in silence for some time before Aduel worked a scroll out of his sleeve and held it out to her.

“Shall we replace the doubts and worries about the present with the doubts and worries of the past?”

With a smile of gratitude Joanna wordlessly took the scroll. She unrolled it carefully, and after making herself comfortable in her chair began to read:

“Herod: A Secret History, by Aduel of Sepphoris. Book the Ninth.”

Herod’s envy of his young brother-in-law lay dormant for several months, until the Feast of Tabernacles in the autumn of that same year. Both Herod and the general citizenry were merry throughout the days of the feast, and it seemed that a time of tranquility had come over the land. However, at the end of the feast days Aristobulus, who was now seventeen years of age, went up to the altar to offer the sacrifices in accordance with the laws. He was a good deal taller than most men, and had the beauty of countenance common to his sister Miriam. Dressed in the high priestly vestments and ornaments, he provoked a great outpouring of warmth and affection from all the people. They mingled their good wishes with shouts of acclamation, and rashly proclaimed that life had been better when his family had held the throne. At this an evil spirit of jealousy overtook Herod, and he resolved to abandon his restraint and to do away with the young high priest at the first opportunity.

When the festival was over, the king and his court made their way to Jericho for additional feasting. There Alexandra entertained him at her estate near the city. Herod was very pleasant to the young Aristobulus, even playing games with him in a juvenile and ludicrous manner. At that time it was hotter than usual, especially as Jericho is far lower in altitude than Jerusalem, and all those present went outdoors to gain some relief. There were large fish ponds about the house, and on a sudden caprice many of Herod's acquaintances, and even his servants, plunged into the water to cool themselves. At first Herod and Aristobulus were only spectators, but after a while the young man, at Herod's instigation, went into the water among them. By this time it had grown dark, and upon a signal from Herod, those whom he had appointed dunked the young high priest under the water, as if in sport, and held him there until he drowned.

When news of this calamity was carried back to the women, the joy and goodwill of the occasion were shattered, and there was hysterical lamentation at the sight of the dead body. Herod fell into tears also, and exhibited a real confusion of the soul, for his conscience was overcome at the sight of the young man's lifeless face. He took great care that the funeral should be magnificent by making extensive preparation for the sepulcher where the corpse would be laid, and providing a great quantity of spices, and burying many expensive jewels with him. All Jerusalem was deeply grieved, and even the women of the young man's family who were in such deep sorrow were astonished by Herod's efforts and received some consolation from them.

However, no such things could overcome Alexandra's grief, which was deep and obstinate. She had been made aware of Herod's role in the plot and sent an account of it to Cleopatra, who took up the cause with relish. She would not give Antony a moment's peace over it, but demanded that he punish the crime, reminding him that Herod, who had been given by Antony a kingdom that did not belong to him, had committed a horrid crime against one who was indeed of royal blood. Antony was persuaded by these arguments, and he sent for Herod to appear before him in Syria. Letters from Antony were typically placed directly into the king's hands, so the royal secretary accompanied the messenger to the audience chamber where Herod was holding court.

When the king read the letter his face turned ashen, and he ordered the chamber cleared except for his closest advisors. They all stood before him, wondering what might be wrong, since none yet knew of Alexandra's letter to Cleopatra.

"I have been summoned to appear before Antony in Syria," Herod began.

"Whatever for, Majesty?" asked Corinthus.

"To stand trial," Herod said grimly. "For the murder of Aristobulus."

"Murder!" exclaimed Corinthus. "But the young man's death was certainly an accident."

"Yes, an accident," Herod muttered. "But some seem to think differently."

"Who?" demanded Corinthus.

"There is only one person who could cause Antony to take so unexpected a step," Herod replied.

All those assembled immediately grasped Herod's chain of reasoning, following it from the murdered youth to his mother to the Egyptian queen.

"You must not go," Corinthus declared. "Cleopatra wants Judea, and once you are out of the way she will certainly have it."

"What am I to do, then?" Herod snapped back. "Remain here and defy Antony? That would assuredly bring destruction."

"There is always Parthia," Corinthus suggested.

"Parthia!" Herod growled. "Better to die a noble death than to engage with that pack of liars. No, I'll go to Antony as he has commanded. I have no choice. Cleopatra has wanted my kingdom for many years, but she hasn't gotten it yet. We'll see if I can outwit her again."

He said this last with a grim smile, but it was evident that he was badly shaken, and fearful. For it was widely known that Cleopatra had herself ordered the deaths of possible claimants to her own throne, namely her brother and sister.

"Joseph!" Herod barked. An older man, the husband of Herod's sister Salome, stepped forward. "You will be responsible for the public affairs of the kingdom in my absence."

Joseph, who was already the chief administrator of the government, bowed and stepped back.

"Corinthus! You will organize the journey. We will travel with a small contingent, but with gifts worthy of the occasion. The minister of finance will withdraw half the gold and the best of our valuables from the treasury and prepare them for transport. We leave on the morrow."

Corinthus bowed his acknowledgment. The marching orders had been given; there was no time to lose. But Herod had one more commission in mind.

"You," he pointed at the royal secretary, whom he never addressed by name, "will remain here. Choose one of your scribes to accompany me and handle my correspondence during my absence. Wait afterward for your instructions."

Herod clapped peremptorily.

"Go, then! What are you waiting for? We depart at noon tomorrow!"

The royal ministers quickly dispersed. The secretary remained, as did Joseph, the trusted advisor and brother-in-law. Herod beckoned the secretary closer.

"While I am away, you will write to me each day with an account of all that transpires," Herod said. "Your letters will be placed directly into my hands. I have chosen you to remain here because you seem to have no difficulty distinguishing fact from fiction. I trust that you will not fail me."

"Never, Majesty."

"Good. Go, then."

The royal secretary bowed low, disappointed that he would not be an eyewitness to Herod's desperate attempt to mollify Antony. But he would soon come to realize that equally important events would take place in Jerusalem. As he slowly retreated from the chamber, he could hear Herod's grim instruction to old Joseph.

"In addition to the daily affairs of the government, you will have a special task to undertake," he muttered. "But only if Antony should order me killed."

"Yes, Majesty."

"If that should happen, then you will kill my wife Miriam immediately," Herod continued. "My bond with her is particular and unique, and if I shall not have her, no other man shall have her either. Especially Antony, for I know that her mother has sent him her portrait, and I have been told that he greatly admires her beauty."

"Yes, Majesty. It shall be as you say."

With the seeds of trouble so foolishly sown, Herod departed for Syria the next day. In the weeks that followed Joseph faithfully administered the affairs of the kingdom, and for that reason was frequently with Queen Miriam, both out of respect for her and because business required it. Joseph was by nature a garrulous man, and though he never allowed himself to chatter in front of Herod he showed less restraint in the presence of the queen. Thinking to perform the king a service, he often allowed his discussions of the affairs of state to wander into discourses about Herod's kindness. But the women, especially Alexandra, who was never far from her daughter's side, would invariably rebut him with strident arguments and objections. The queen herself would often catch the eye of the royal secretary, who was standing by in his official capacity, and through expressions and gestures, would indicate her irritation at the old man's pointless digressions. The unfortunate Joseph, not realizing that it was useless to refute the raillery of Alexandra or the annoyance of the queen, instead tried still harder to contradict them, until finally, at his wits' end, he revealed Herod's secret command. To him it was an obvious indication of the king's affection for the queen, and of his unwillingness to be separated from her even in death, but Miriam and her mother saw it in a different light. Their natural dismay soon turned to fury, and from that point onward they constantly harangued the poor old minister with angry accusations and threats of their own.

About this time a report went about Jerusalem, spread by Herod's enemies, that Antony had tortured Herod and had put him to death. At this there was a great panic within the palace, for there were rumors that a rebellion was imminent, and that Herod's enemies would slaughter everyone associated with him. With tears and threats and much shouting Alexandra endeavored to persuade Joseph and the king's other ministers to evacuate the palace, and to flee to the Roman legion that was encamped outside the city. Salome, the king's sister, was privy to all these discussions, much to the disgust of Alexandra and Miriam, who said that she was of lower birth than they and should have no place in them. Yet she remained, thanks to Joseph's support, and argued just as strenuously that until they were sure that Herod was dead they should not leave the palace, for it would be an abdication of the throne, and would precipitate yet another civil war. Joseph, knowing what Salome said to be true, and knowing also that Alexandra promoted her scheme in hopes of receiving the kingdom from Antony, resisted at first. But under the persistent onslaught of Alexandra and the queen his resolve began to crumble. Just as these deliberations—if they could be called that, for they consisted mostly of angry screaming by women who hated each other—were reaching their climax, a messenger was announced.

"What is it?" Alexandra snapped as the man was escorted into the council chamber. "We have no time for messages."

"I come bearing letters from His Majesty, King Herod," the messenger announced.

"What!" Alexandra was stunned. "Give me those!"

But Joseph signaled to the messenger, who placed the letters in his hand before Alexandra could snatch them.

"We will all together hear what the king has written," Joseph said. "The royal secretary will read the letters aloud to all in this chamber."

The secretary, who had been a silent spectator throughout the tumultuous meeting, stepped forward and sorted through the letters. Some of them were addressed to the queen, some to others in his family, and one was addressed to Joseph. The secretary selected this one, broke the seal, and began to read.

"'To my queen and those who govern Judea in my absence, greetings. There is excellent news to report from Syria. After much discourse with Antony, and after presenting him with the copious gifts we brought from Judea, I have fully recovered the good opinion of this great man. He has stated that it is not good to require of a king an account for the acts of his government, for such a king would be no king at all. Moreover, he has reminded Cleopatra that it would be best for her not to meddle in the acts of my government.

"'Since my arrival I have had many honors from Antony; I dine with him daily and frequently sit with him to hear petitions and cases that are brought before him. I no longer have any apprehension of hard treatment from him, and I will soon return with firm assurance of his favor in my management of public affairs.

"'There is also no longer any reason for uneasiness about Cleopatra, for Antony has given her the territory of Celesyria, north of Galilee, and has thereby pacified her and gotten clear of her persistent entreaties for additional possessions.

"'I trust that all remains calm in Jerusalem and I eagerly await my reunion with all who govern in my absence, especially my beloved queen, who no doubt rules with all of her customary grace and compassion.'

"Thus ends the letter," the royal secretary concluded.

A stunned silence prevailed in the council chamber. Alexandra, whose countenance had changed from disbelief to sullen hatred as the royal secretary read the letter, arose and left the room without a word. Miriam followed.

"And so the royal family remains in the palace," Salome scoffed. "Rescued from destruction by the commoner Herod once again."

After this there was nothing left to do but await Herod's return, and during that interval the tension between the factions within the palace continued to simmer. After his arrival, both his mother and Salome wasted no time informing him of Alexandra's intention. Salome added, although it was not true, that Joseph and the queen had engaged in criminal conversation regarding plans to usurp Herod's throne. Herod was enraged at this, and at once sought out the queen, who was in the palace garden, along with Alexandra and some other women of the court.

Having dismissed the others, Herod immediately took his wife to task. Both were unaware that their conversation was not entirely private, for the royal secretary was also in the garden, where he had been taking a moment of leisure in a quiet alcove in the wall that separated one part of the garden from the other.   Due to the warmth of the day he had fallen asleep, lulled by the knowledge that his beloved queen was near, and when he awoke he could plainly hear her engage in the most intimate of discussions with her infuriated husband. It was a moment of trepidation for the royal secretary, who had neglected to include the queen in any of his reports to Herod in Syria, fearing that a mention of even the slightest incident or conversation might arouse the king's insane jealousy. Now he barely dared to breathe, for the conversation on the other side of the wall had placed him in a most compromising position.

"I have even been told that you and Joseph plotted together," Herod was saying in a voice that trembled as he spoke, "and when you found that I was not executed by Antony, nay, that I was alive and would return to Judea, the two of you laid snares for me that you would have the kingdom to yourself nonetheless."

"What!" Miriam was genuinely shocked. "Who told you such things?"

"Never mind that," Herod growled. "I only wish I could believe that it were not so."

"Of course it isn't! How could you say such a thing? Your wife intriguing with Joseph, an old man and your sister's husband besides? It's absurd! And deeply insulting!"

"Then you deny it on your oath?" Herod demanded.

Miriam did deny it on her oath, and repeatedly, saying all the things that an innocent woman could say in her own defense. Little by little the king left off his anger at her, and finally made an apology for seeming to have believed the scurrilous reports. Soon he was overcome with his passion for her, professing the extraordinary affection he had for her, until they both fell into tears and embraced one another most tenderly. But Herod endeavored to draw her into a similar profession, giving more and more assurances of his belief in her fidelity, until finally Miriam made a dreadful mistake.

"Yet did you not command," she demanded through her tears, "that if any harm came to you from Antony, that I, who had not been the cause of it, should perish also?"

Herod cried out with an inchoate roar, and angrily leaped up.

"So it's true!" he shouted, loud enough for those in the nearer part of the palace to hear. "You were plotting against me! What more evidence do I need? Joseph would never have uttered what I told him unless there had been a firm confidence between the two of you, and great familiarity as well! Oh yes, great familiarity. I know it all now! Such intimate conversation is a criminal act, nothing short of treason! I know the price of treason, even if you and Joseph do not, and you both will pay it! I will see to it!"

And with that he fled from her, leaving her weeping, and as he passed through that part of the garden where the royal secretary remained hidden, scarcely breathing, the secretary could see him tearing his hair with his own hands.

But Herod, overcome with love for his wife, did not order her to be slain. He did give the order for his brother-in-law Joseph to be executed immediately without trial or even the opportunity to defend himself. As for Alexandra, he ordered her bound in chains and kept in custody as the cause of all this mischief.

"And thus concludes Book the Ninth," Aduel said.

Joanna shook her head as she closed the scroll.

"How could he be so wicked?" she said, her anger rising. "To murder the high priest and prince of Judea! And then Salome's husband!"

"This was but the start of it," Aduel said. "There will be others."

"But how could he not be punished?"

"He will be," Aduel assured her. "Salvation is far from the wicked, for they do not seek the will of the Lord."

"Yes, but if only Antony had not confirmed him in the throne!"

"Antony, and all those around him, were easily corrupted," Aduel said. "Antony valued Herod's loyalty far more than he cared for justice. Herod knew that, and above all Herod was a survivor."

"Thankfully he will not survive much longer," Joanna said. "If what you say is correct."

"I am sure of it. No man can defy death forever."

"The sooner the better, then."

"Not exactly," Aduel said. "Not until the letters of introduction and the safe passage arrive from Nicolaus. Only then can we safely pray for an end to this dark chapter in our nation's history."

Chapter 16

The next morning Joanna woke early. She assumed that she would lie abed in the darkness for an hour or two, drifting in and out of sleep as she had the previous morning, but her restlessness grew until she could stand it no longer. She swung out of bed and stood up without the crutch, taking a few hesitant steps in the darkness. There was no pain, and even the nagging numbness she had expected was gone.

She went into the kitchen, where morning light streamed through the small window. Edna was nowhere to be seen but she heard Aduel stirring the hearth in the front room. He looked up in surprise as she entered without any trace of a limp.

"Where is your crutch?" he asked.

"I don't need it anymore. Nothing hurts."

"But your leg," Aduel objected. "Is it still swollen?"

"No. It's bruised, but the swelling has gone down."

"Ah," Aduel nodded. "The myrrh. Which reminds me: It seems only right to thank the young man who gave it to you."

Joanna nodded. She had been thinking the same thing but was not sure how to go about it. Thanks were indeed in order, but any sort of communication with her inscrutable suitor would be fraught with complications.

"I will take the crutch back to the Temple this morning," Aduel said. "On the way back I could visit the young scribe and convey our gratitude. Or, if you prefer, I can send him a written message."

"I would like to go."

Aduel was surprised.

"To the Temple?" he asked. "After what happened before?"

"I'd like to see the old woman again," Joanna said. "I'd like to thank her."

"I'd like to thank her myself," Aduel mused. "And ask her certain questions concerning her visions and prophesies."

"Then we can go together," Joanna said. "I can be ready in a minute if you want to go now."

"Now!" Aduel exclaimed. "Certainly not! You heard what the doctor said. Two weeks indoors, with no stairs or steps of any kind. And certainly no venturing out on the bumpy streets of Jerusalem."

"No, Uncle," Joanna said firmly. "I can't sit idle all day when there is no longer any injury, and I can't avoid the Temple forever because of one incident. Besides, it will be far less dangerous now that there isn't any eagle to cut down."

"True," Aduel said, "but it's too soon. You will remain indoors today, and I'll consider it. Perhaps we'll go tomorrow, if it seems right. Meanwhile, what of your response to the young scribe? Shall it be in writing, or would you like me to thank him personally?"

"I don't know."

"Well, you have some time to decide," Aduel said. "I'll go to the Temple tomorrow, whether you are able to accompany me or not. As for the scribe, I suppose it can't hurt to have him pining one more day."

"Pining! Uncle!"

"I was a young man once," Aduel said waggishly. "If I had spent a month's pay on myrrh for a maiden, I would have wanted to know what became of it."

"A month's pay!" Joanna's mood suddenly turned serious. "It wasn't that much, was it?"

"Probably."

"Then he may be more foolhardy than I thought."

"Smitten, anyway," Aduel teased. "Driven from his senses."

"Uncle, stop," Joanna admonished. "This is serious. You must help me decide."

"Decide? About what? Whether to deliver your thanks in person or in writing?"

"About all of it."

"You mean the marriage contract."

"Yes."

"I cannot help you with that. You are of age, and quite able to think clearly. You must decide."

"But everything is so uncertain," Joanna fretted. "What will happen if Nicolaus's fears about Jerusalem come true? What if we were to leave suddenly for Alexandria?"

"Once signed, a marriage contract cannot be broken," Aduel said. "You would be expected to return to Jerusalem and fulfill your vow, come what may: Insurrection, war, famine, disaster. That is why you must make your decision carefully. It will likely be the most important of your life."

Joanna closed her eyes and sighed, overwhelmed by the enormity of it.

"You need not decide today," Aduel reminded her. "You need not decide any day until you are ready. Meanwhile, get yourself something to eat and drink, and I will fetch something to read. Your friend Cleopatra figures prominently in Book the Tenth. She will help us to pass the time."

Twenty minutes later they had settled themselves in their customary places before the hearth. By now it was understood that Joanna would do the reading. She unrolled the scroll and took a moment to glance over the first panel.

"Herod: A Secret History, by Aduel of Sepphoris. Book the Tenth."

Herod's troubles with Cleopatra were not yet finished, for she was insatiable for gain, and she nagged at Antony continually to deprive other monarchs of their territories. It was not surprising, therefore, that great portions of Syria were added to her dominions. Yet after this she was still not satisfied, but demanded Judea as well. Antony yielded to her in this, though not entirely, for being ashamed to appear completely enslaved to her he gave her only the part of Judea near Jericho. Still, this decision sorely vexed Herod, for it was one of the most valuable regions in his kingdom. It was the only place where grows the balsam tree, from which is produced medicine prized throughout the world, and moreover it is known for another kind of tree, the palm, which had been a symbol of Judea's political independence for over a century.

To make matters worse, Cleopatra had decided to visit Judea and inspect her new possession. Herod met her there, and entertained her lavishly, and although he was accompanied by the essential advisors of his government he was careful to leave the women of the court, particularly Alexandra and the queen, in Jerusalem. Though seemingly prudent, this precaution proved to be a source of great difficulty for the king, for Cleopatra immediately set out to seduce him, making little effort to conceal her intentions. Herod was appalled by these overtures, and in his consternation convened a secret council of his most trusted counsellors and friends. They met before daybreak in a windowless chamber of the king's winter palace, around a large table intricately crafted of marble. Not even Herod's personal guard was allowed inside the room, but instead was posted outside the heavy oaken door. Not until he was confident in the complete secrecy of the proceedings did Herod call the meeting to order.

"I suppose you all know why I have brought you here at this hour," he began.

"Cleopatra," said Achiabus, Herod's first cousin and one of his most trusted confidants.

"Exactly," Herod replied. "Since the day she got here she's been making a run at me, every time we're together. In the palace, in the balsam grove—in full view of everyone!"

"We've noticed," Achiabus said dryly.

"It's shameless!" Herod continued. "She's mauling me constantly! And the things she whispers into my ear! But that voice! It's almost like a musical instrument, the way she employs it. Even the simplest sentence is a beautiful, mysterious song. I can begin to understand how Antony is bewitched."

Herod's counselors murmured their agreement.

"But what is the meaning of it?" Herod asked. "Do you suppose there is really some attraction?"

He seemed simultaneously flattered and disgusted by the thought. It was obvious to everyone that there was no such attraction, but only the ulterior motive of a woman widely known for her scheming. But none dared say it, for fear of wounding the king's pride.

"Whether there is or not, for you to return her affection, or even give the slightest indication of it, would be a mistake," Achiabus hedged.

"Why?" Herod demanded. "Two can play at that game, you know. If I can find out what she's planning, perhaps I can turn the tables. What might come of it?"

"Death," said a voice from the corner of the room. All around the table turned to stare, for this word had come from none other than the royal secretary, who never spoke at such meetings unless something had been inquired of him.

"A dissenting voice," Herod said irritably. "Spoken by one usually wise enough to keep his own counsel."

"Apologies, Majesty," the secretary said hastily. "I meant nothing by it."

"Nonsense," Herod snapped. "You obviously meant something. Explain yourself."

"I cannot be certain, Majesty," the secretary squirmed, "but Cleopatra does nothing without an eye to gain. It seems likely that these advances are nothing but a snare for you."

"To charge me before Antony with indecent acts," Herod said grimly. "Acts which I could not then deny."

Again there were murmurs of agreement all around the room.

"Then I have no choice," Herod said. "It must be done."

Herod's counsellors looked at one another blankly, for they could not conceive what solution Herod had hit upon.

"What must be done?" Achiabus ventured.

"If one of us must die, let it be her," Herod said calmly. "I must kill her now, this very day, while she is in my power."

"But Majesty, she is the Queen of Egypt!" Achiabus stammered. "There is no woman of higher rank in all the world!"

"She is a meddlesome pest, irksome to all," Herod replied. "I will never have a better opportunity to rid the world of her, and thereby save everyone around her a multitude of evils."

"But Majesty!" Achiabus protested. "What of Antony?"

"Antony will understand," Herod said confidently. "I'll write to him, as one man to another, and explain it. He'll be angry at first, but he'll be better off without her. Eventually, he'll see that."

Herod's advisors were stunned. They shifted uncomfortably, not knowing what to say. Finally one spoke.

"He will regard it as insolence of the highest degree, and he will waste no time dispensing the appropriate punishment."

It was the royal secretary again. All eyes turned to him, including Herod's.

"What do you know of Antony?" he demanded irritably. "Have you ever spoken with him?"

"No, Majesty," the royal secretary replied evenly. "But I know him to be a man completely besotted with this woman, pestilent though she may be, and it seems evident that anyone that would deprive him of her company through violence and treachery, though it eventually be for Antony's advantage, would quickly meet his own end."

"Nonsense!" Herod scowled. "If she runs at me now to gain possession of my kingdom, he cannot expect her to be faithful to him, or to stand with him in a time of need. He'll see that when I explain it him."

The secretary left off the argument, for he had already ventured far beyond his place, but the others had begun to take courage.

"No, Majesty, what the scribe says is true," said Achiabus, as the others nodded agreement. "You would be risking the utmost danger, and for nothing more than personal satisfaction, and that itself would be short-lived."

The others concurred, admonishing him vigorously. This surprised Herod, for no king expects opposition from his subordinates, but rather acquiescence and servile flattery.

"Then what am I to do?" he complained angrily. "I am to see her today, and again tomorrow. How can I put up with it? Those breathy whispers, her lips touching my ear. And that suffocating Egyptian perfume!"

"Her advances are no doubt most loathsome to the king," Achiabus observed, "but up to now you have rejected them honorably. If you had not, then your plan to make an end of her would be your only hope. But for now you must continue in your virtuous course, for if she were ever to lay any charge against you, you would be able to refute it with an honest face and an untroubled conscience before Antony."

"Before Antony!" Herod growled. "As if Antony would ever believe anything I should say against the word of that cunning viper!"

But Achiabus continued to confute him, and all those present added their objections, citing all the hazards it would create, until finally he became concerned, even frightened, at the thought of any harm that might come to Cleopatra while she was in Judea. So he resolved to continue to treat her kindly, and this he carried out, even going so far as to bargain with her to return the lands around Jericho to his control for an annual payment of two hundred talents. Thus she remained unharmed, and when she finally decided to depart, seeing that she could not entice him, he conducted her on her way to Egypt, parting from her with insincere declarations of goodwill—and many presents.

It was the last time the two of them ever met, but Herod kept a wary eye on Cleopatra. She continued to covet Judea, and neighboring Arabia as well, and persisted in strategies that would allow her to add one or both of these kingdoms to what Antony had already given her. Her opportunity finally came a few years later, when the simmering conflict between Antony and Octavian came to a boil. This was the result of resentments that had been building for some time, not least of which was Antony's abandonment of his wife Octavia, who was Octavian's sister, in favor of Cleopatra. Partisans in Italy also took it ill that Antony had seen fit to bestow upon Cleopatra and the children that she had borne him various Roman territories of the East, to rule as their own. Loyalty throughout the Roman world, which had been uneasily shared between the two rulers, was now openly divided between East and West, and it became clear that one leader would be vanquished, and the other would rule.

With civil war looming again, there was never a question but that Herod would back Antony. In the preceding years Judea had enjoyed great prosperity, and Herod had collected an enormous amount of tax revenue, which he now spent raising and equipping an army on Antony's behalf. But Antony, who had an army of his own consisting of one hundred thousand foot soldiers and twelve thousand horse, declined Herod's assistance, instead directing him against his neighbor, the King of Arabia. This was at the insistence of Cleopatra, who fully expected Antony to be the victor in the civil war and anticipated that by setting Judea and Arabia against each other, one or the other would be shattered, and afterward added to her kingdom.

Herod needed little encouragement to undertake this assignment, for he had been at odds with the King of Arabia for years over money borrowed and never repaid. Moreover, Herod was by nature a man who thrived on action, bravery, and daring—a man better suited to conquering than to governing. The first engagement was a victory for the Judeans, but the Arabians soon regrouped at the village of Cana. Herod marched against them, and as he approached the place he selected a site for his army to camp, so that he could formulate a strategy of attack at the time of his choosing. But as he was giving the order to fortify the camp, his soldiers, puffed up with their earlier success, clamored that he should not delay, but lead them immediately against the Arabians. Inspired by their fervor, he led them on, with all his regiments following in rank behind him. The Arabians lost courage, and most fled without putting up a fight. They would have been destroyed except for the treachery of Athenion, the general of the troops of Cleopatra. These troops had ostensibly been sent to aid Herod, but Athenion had openly quarreled with the king, and when he saw that Herod's army was successful, he unleashed his own fresh troops on them. Caught unprepared, the Judeans were easily beaten, especially in the stony places where cavalry was of little use. With this turn of events the Arabians took courage and returned to capture the unfortified Judean camp, where all sorts of slaughter took place. Herod, realizing that his army was shattered, nonetheless rode to the assistance of those who remained, although he could in no way change the outcome of the battle. He quickly marshalled the remnant of his forces and retreated into the mountains, from which he made raids on several parts of Arabia, being careful to avoid a pitched battle, while at the same time caring for the wounded and reviving the spirits of those who remained fit to fight.

But just as Herod's army had begun to regroup and take heart, an earthquake, as great as any that has ever been recorded in Judea, struck in the night. The army, lodged in the field, sustained little damage. But as reports trickled in from Jerusalem, Sepphoris, Jericho, and other places, it became evident that the destruction was catastrophic. Over ten thousand men and their families had been killed by the collapse of their houses, with much livestock also wiped out. When the Arabians heard of this they gathered their troops on the other side of the Jordan River for a final assault against Herod's diminished forces, who in their state of utter despair gave no thought to resistance.

But Herod refused to be beaten. He moved among his commanders, emboldening and encouraging them, and when he had convinced many of these that there was still a chance of victory, he prepared to persuade the rank and file.

"The men are downcast and restless," Corinthus cautioned him. "There's much talk of abandoning the field to the enemy and returning home. Do you think it wise to try to rally them for another battle?"

"I think I have no choice," Herod said grimly. "Abandoning the field will mean the end of Judea, for the Arabians will surely overthrow the government. How can I claim to be king of a nation when I cannot convince men to fight to protect it?"

And so the troops were assembled, and Herod, standing before them, gave one of the great orations of his long career:

"You are well-acquainted, my fellow soldiers, with the many unexpected calamities that have put a stop to our glorious success. Even the most courageous among you can hardly keep your spirits up. But all these reversals can be overcome, and since we cannot avoid fighting if we wish to preserve our nation, I stand before you to remind you why it is necessary to persevere. The men who now oppose us are among the most treacherous of enemies. Under a flag of truce I have sent ambassadors to sue for peace; they have beheaded these ambassadors. Are these the kind of men you will allow to march into Judea unopposed, to do as they will with your wives and your families and your possessions?

"Furthermore, consider recent events. We were conquerors in the first battle, and when we fought a second time they were not able to oppose us, but ran away. Is this an example of their manhood? It was only by the treachery of Cleopatra's army, which made war upon us without declaring it, that we have come to the distress we are under, and Cleopatra's army is no longer here. If the miseries that have been thrust upon us by the earthquake have frightened anyone, let him consider that this very thing will deceive the Arabians, who will think we have sunk too low to fight! When we boldly march against them we will shatter their insolent conceit, and repay them for their treachery, for they must be taught to behave as civilized men, though they will always be inferior to you in valor!"

With this a great shout went up from the troops, who now clamored for battle. Before their enthusiasm could wane Herod led them across the Jordan. As he had predicted, the Arabians were astonished, and despite their far superior numbers were decisively defeated in battle, being so thoroughly routed that a great many of them were trampled to death by their countrymen as they fled to a nearby fortress. This place Herod immediately besieged, and as there was no water within the Arabians quickly sued for peace. But after the murder of his own ambassadors by the Arabians, Herod would receive none of theirs, but insisted on terms of unconditional surrender. Four thousand Arabians were thus taken captive and sold into slavery. Those that remained thought it better to fight, but could in no way sustain the battle due to their thirst, and about seven thousand of them were killed. Having once again turned the bleakest of circumstances into improbable triumph, Herod ended his glorious expedition and returned to Jerusalem to rule over his expanded domain.

But while all this was happening, a far greater struggle was taking place in another part of the world, off the western coast of Greece near a place called Actium. It was here that the forces of Antony and Cleopatra met those of Octavian in a struggle for control of the Roman world. Although Octavian had for many months been quietly building his forces in the West, it was Antony who had the larger and more seasoned army, with one hundred thousand foot soldiers to Octavian's eighty thousand, and superior experience in strategy and command. Yet this great general was persuaded to risk all on a naval battle, rather than a land engagement, at Cleopatra's insistence. Their navy, consisting of five hundred ships bedecked with great banners and many ornaments, as if for a triumph rather than a battle, was twice that of Octavian's. But Antony's ships, though powerful, were large and cumbersome and severely in want of competent sailors, being manned in large part by harvest laborers, common travelers, ass-drivers, and young boys who had been captured in nearby Greece and pressed into naval service.

The ships were drawn up in battle array, but for four days the sea was so rough that they could not engage. On the fifth day Antony ordered his fleet forward and the battle began, with Octavian's smaller, nimbler vessels pressing around the larger ships of Antony with spears, javelins, and missiles of fire, while the latter used catapults to fling down stones from wooden towers. But with the battle about equal and the fortunes of the day undecided, Cleopatra's sixty ships, which had been placed in the rear of the engagement as a reserve, hoisted sail and put out to sea in full flight, going through the thick of the battle and putting Antony's fleet into disorder. As soon as he saw her ship sailing away, Antony abandoned all those who were fighting for him and followed her, soon disappearing from sight and putting a sudden end to the struggle.

After they reached Alexandria, Antony and Cleopatra spent the winter in revelry and feasting, as if nothing were amiss. But as spring arrived, Octavian began his inexorable march from Syria. With the few forces that remained to him, Antony won an initial skirmish with Octavian's troops, and the next day took a stand on a hill outside the city. From there he could see Cleopatra's navy sail out to meet the approaching ships of Octavian, but as the fleets approached one another Cleopatra's sailors saluted Octavian's ships with their oars—and then came about to join ranks with them. Antony's cavalry immediately deserted him, and his foot soldiers were quickly defeated. Retreating to the city, he cried out angrily that Cleopatra had betrayed him to the enemies he had made for her sake. Fearing his wrath, Cleopatra retired to a fortified tower she had built next to the temple of Isis, where she had stored all her treasure, including gold, silver, emeralds, ebony, ivory, and cinnamon. Lowering the doors, which were strengthened with bars, she sent messengers to Antony to tell him she was dead.

Hearing this Antony impaled himself on his sword, but the wound was not immediately fatal. Cleopatra sent word that she was still alive, and Antony demanded to be carried to her. She refused to open the doors of her tower, but instead let down ropes and cords to which Antony's servants fastened him, though he was all covered in blood. Then Cleopatra, along with the two ladies in waiting who were the only others in the tower, managed, with great effort, to haul him up through the tower's high window, and he breathed his last in her arms.

Cleopatra engaged in negotiations with Octavian, mostly concerning the fate of her children, but ultimately poisoned herself rather than be captured and taken back to Rome as a trophy in Octavian's triumphal parade. Many say that it was done through means of an asp, the method that Cleopatra had selected as the quickest and least painful way to die after much experimentation on condemned prisoners. However, no such creature was found in the building after her body was discovered, and some believe that it was accomplished through poison that she had hidden in an ornament in her hair.   Thus ended Cleopatra, at thirty-nine years of age, and the kingdom of Egypt as well, for this great nation, which had dominated world affairs for over three thousand years, was now designated a province of Rome, which it remains to this day.

"And thus concludes Book the Tenth," Aduel said.

Joanna sighed as she rolled up the scroll, feeling a little fatigued. The history she had just read had been vaguely familiar to her, and on this sketchy foundation she had conceived a primitive admiration for Cleopatra. But never had she heard it in such detail, and Aduel's account had given her cause for reflection.

"So," she said. "Herod did get the better of Cleopatra."

"Really?" Aduel seemed surprised at her conclusion. "How so?"

"Well, he never actually outwitted her. He never got part of Egypt. But in the end she died and relinquished her kingdom, while he lived and retained his."

"True," Aduel admitted. "And he retains it to this day, almost thirty years later."

"I wonder what would have happened if he had tried," Joanna speculated.

"Tried what? To outwit her?" Aduel asked. "What would have happened had he played at her game of seduction and deceit? Why certainly he would have been drawn into her web and destroyed."

"Which you and his cousin unfortunately prevented."

"It was unfortunate for Cleopatra," Aduel shrugged. "But probably better as far as Judea is concerned."

"I don't think so," Joanna said stonily.

"You would prefer to live under the rule of a heathen queen

rather than a Jewish king?" Aduel asked.

"Herod is an Idumean," Joanna reminded him.

"Yes, but his primary interest has always been Judea," Aduel said. "For all his faults, Herod has done great things for our nation. For him it isn't just another territory in a larger empire."

"Herod's primary interest has always been himself," Joanna said irritably.

"Indeed," Aduel chuckled. "But is that not the way of all men and women?"

"It doesn't have to be," Joanna snapped. A jumble of rebuttals sprang to mind: Her mother, toiling from sunup to sundown in their little hovel in Jericho: errands, chores, spinning wool into thread to eke out a meager living for her two children with never a lament or a complaint. The soldiers who fought Herod's battles and won Herod's wars and died nameless and forgotten on some dusty field far from home. The farmers who worked the land throughout the kingdom, scratching out an existence under the merciless sun to feed the nation—and paying extortionate taxes on their crops at the city gate so that Herod could do great things for Judea.

"The whole thing just seems so tragic," she complained.

"The romance of Cleopatra and Antony?" Aduel asked gently.

"All of it. It gives me much to think about."

"About the dreadful things people do in their quest for power?"

"I suppose." Joanna was silent for a moment, as the great injustices of life yielded to a more pressing question. "But do you think Antony was meant for Cleopatra, and she for him?"

"I can't really say," Aduel reflected. "By all the accounts I have heard and read, certainly the answer would be yes. But I myself never saw them together. One could always speculate that on her side it was all a strategy, and on his a failure of morals."

"I think it was more than that," Joanna said resolutely.

"Well, you're probably right," Aduel nodded. "She was a complex woman, and often in a perilous position, while he was in many ways a simple man, a drunken soldier who held the whole world in his hands and didn't know what to do with it."

They both remained silent for some time, lost in their thoughts.

"But what of our business?" Aduel said finally. "Have you decided?"

"About what?"

"About your response to the scribe. Shall it be delivered in writing or in person?"

"It shall be both."

"Very well, then," Aduel said. "I would like to write it while the daylight remains. What would you like it to say?"

"Thank you, Uncle, but that won't be necessary. I will write the message myself."

Aduel raised an eyebrow.

"Are you certain? There are many men who would disapprove of a woman who writes."

"Better that I should know that now," Joanna reasoned. "In fact, that is the thing I would like to know most of all."

Chapter 17

After the midday meal Joanna made her way carefully down the gloomy, narrow stairway to the subterranean chamber. All that afternoon and into the night she remained there, bent over Aduel's writing desk—working out the wording, scratching out the letters, using a prodigious amount of papyrus and burning through Aduel's stock of candles as if they cost nothing. She had never given much thought to her penmanship but now she was greatly displeased with it, for it was plain and blocky and not nearly as elegant as the scribe's. But it was legible, and as the last of the candles burned low she made her way back up the staircase, the finished document in hand.

Morning found her at the writing table again, reviewing her work, silently criticizing its possible faults, when she knew in her heart that it was perfectly satisfactory. She had even gone so far as to personalize it, badgering Aduel persistently until, with many misgivings, he had revealed the scribe's name. She debated whether this was too bold a step—whether she should not take the time to carve out another square of papyrus and create yet another revision with a more generic salutation. But her uncle was waiting upstairs, impatient to go to the Temple and make detailed inquiries of old Anna, and she knew that if she rushed she would achieve nothing more

than a shaky, blotted mess. Her heart jittered as she read it a
final time:

She smiled slightly. Even now, after so many drafts that
had all conveyed the same sentiment, the message surprised
her. She had always been cautious by nature, but this note
was a gamble. It was audacious, it was impertinent, it was
unconventional. In the wrong hands it could be construed as
something shameful, intolerably immodest, so she had made it
ever-so-slightly ambiguous. And yet she knew that there was
nothing truly wrong with it. Aduel had reminded her that this
was probably the most important decision of her life; she would
not make it in darkness. She and the scribe would decide
without intermediaries or interference—a luxury few couples
enjoyed in a society defined by tradition and family ties. This
note was a precious opportunity to speak to him directly. Its
few words would tell the young scribe all he really needed to
know about her, and his response would tell her all she needed
to know about him. They would unite as equals or not at all.

She folded it carefully and sealed it with a dab of plain wax.
Back upstairs she handed it to Aduel, for even though they
would be calling on the scribe together it would never do for
her to be seen handing a message to a young man. Aduel was

waiting, pacing impatiently near the door with the crutch, and as soon as she had laced her sandals they set off briskly along the familiar route: down the hillside, up the long market street, across the plaza, up the many stairs, through the portico, and across the Court of the Gentiles. In the Court of the Women they paused, surveying the courtyard for the old woman, but she was nowhere to be seen. Joanna took the lead, guiding Aduel to the inconspicuous wooden door in the recesses of the north portico.

"Is this her chamber?" Aduel asked.

"Yes."

"I never knew what was behind these doors," Aduel said. "I assumed it was where the priests kept their concubines."

"Uncle!"

Aduel chuckled and rapped quietly with the crutch. There was movement within, and after a moment the door opened slightly. But to Joanna's surprise it was a middle-aged woman who peered out at them.

"Apologies," Aduel said, flustered. "We were looking for Anna."

The woman said nothing, but opened the door wider and stepped aside for them to enter. Surprised, Joanna followed her uncle, and gasped. In the opposite corner of the little room, on the pallet-bed where she had lain just a few days before, now lay Anna. The old woman's eyes were closed and her breathing was labored. With a cry Joanna pushed past her uncle and knelt beside the low bed, taking one of Anna's hands in hers.

The old woman's eyes fluttered open. She peered uncomprehendingly at the girl, who pushed aside her veil.

"Ah, maid," the old woman said.

"You saved me from the soldiers," Joanna said, doing her best to hold back her tears.

"Yes, of course."

"I came to thank you."

"To know you are safe from Herod, that is my thanks," the old woman rasped. "And the young man?"

"Yes, he is safe too."

The old woman closed her eyes. Aduel knelt next to the girl.

"I too have come to thank you," he said quietly. "The maiden is my niece. She is my ward and my responsibility."

The old woman made no response.

"You are ill," Aduel continued. "I will not trouble you for long. But there is one question I must ask you. The maiden has told me that you have seen the Messiah."

At this Anna's eyes opened wide and she managed to raise herself a little.

"Yes. Yes!"

"What can you tell me about Him?" Aduel pressed.

"He is our salvation," Anna said. "He is the salvation of Jew and Gentile alike!"

"Jew and Gentile?" Aduel asked incredulously.

"He is our salvation," Anna repeated, sinking back.

Aduel stared at her, perplexed. Anna's attendant, who had been standing silently behind them, stepped forward.

"It's time for her to rest," she said.

"We shall trouble you no further," Aduel nodded.

He leaned forward, close to Anna's ear.

"Is there anything I can do for you?" he asked.

The old woman grasped his arm firmly and tried to speak, but her words were stuttered and indistinct. Joanna could make out nothing, but after a moment Aduel began to recite quietly:

"The Lord is my shepherd. I shall not want.

"He makes me lie down in green pastures. He leads me to still waters. He restores my soul.

"For His name's sake He guides me in the paths of righteousness.

"Even though I walk through the valley of the shadow of death, I fear no evil. For You are with me. Your rod and Your staff, they comfort me.

"You spread a table for me before my enemies. You have anointed my head with oil, and my cup runs over.

"Your goodness and mercy have followed me all the days of my life.

"And I shall dwell in the House of the Lord forever."

With a deep sigh Anna relaxed her grip on Aduel's arm. Her breathing became deep and steady. Joanna sobbed quietly as Aduel led her from the room.

"I just saw her three days ago," she said tearfully as they walked across the Court of the Women. "She was so full of life."

"Our days are like the grass," Aduel said. "We blossom like the flowers of the field; a wind passes over us, and we are gone."

"But surely this is not a sickness unto death," Joanna protested. "It isn't, is it?"

Aduel did not reply.

"She cannot die, Uncle!" Joanna implored. "She cannot!"

"It is the way of all the earth, child," Aduel sighed.

"But I have so many things to say to her!"

"And I as well," Aduel said. "So many questions. The

Messiah, a Savior of Jew and Gentile? Perhaps she was delirious. Although...although...Isaiah himself did prophesy such a thing centuries ago."

Joanna barely heard him. At the moment Isaiah and his prophecies meant nothing to her. She followed her uncle blindly across the Court of the Gentiles and down the many stairs in the stone tunnel.

"We'll return tomorrow," Aduel comforted when they reached the plaza below. "Perhaps she will have recovered, or at least have regained some of her strength. Only the Lord knows. He sees what we do not. Come, this is the way to see the young scribe."

"We can't go to him now!" Joanna protested.

"We must," Aduel said firmly. "He will want to know Anna's condition."

"Yes," Joanna reconsidered. "Yes, he will. But let us say nothing of the other."

"As you wish," Aduel nodded. "We'll save your message for another time. But I will thank him for the balm."

They turned into a winding lane tucked into the looming shadow of the Temple Mount. At a low building Aduel stopped in the doorway and said something to someone inside. A moment later the young scribe appeared. He bowed low, maintaining his usual impassive expression although he was clearly surprised to see them.

"I have come to express my gratitude for the balm you provided for my niece," Aduel began. "As you can see, it has effected a swift recovery."

The scribe nodded and cast a quick glance at the girl—the same quick glance he had allowed himself the first time they had met.

"There are additional things to be said in that respect, but we will save them for a future day," Aduel continued. "Today we bring sad tidings. Old Anna has taken to her bed. She is gravely ill."

"Old Anna?" The scribe's expression changed slightly. "The woman at the Temple?"

"Yes."

"I had no idea."

"Nor we. We have just come from there. She inquired after you."

"I will go to her at once. Thank you for the information."

The two men bowed to one another, and Aduel turned away. There was another quick glance between the girl and the scribe—a glance that Joanna found both tantalizing and completely unsatisfying. Then she followed her uncle home in silence, slightly ashamed that thoughts of Anna were drowned out by her disappointment over the undelivered message. She sought relief by busying herself in the kitchen, assisting Edna with tasks that required no assistance, but her efforts were so moody that the old woman soon suggested that she take some fresh air in the courtyard. She brushed past Aduel, who had just emerged from the concealed doorway to his subterranean chamber, and seated herself on the wooden bench outside the door, hoping that her peevishness would melt away with the spring sunshine. Through the door, which she had left slightly ajar, she could hear Edna and Aduel in conversation.

"Is there a problem?" the old housekeeper asked.

"We've just been to the Temple," Aduel explained, "to see old Anna. She is gravely ill."

"Old Anna?" Edna asked. "Wasn't it she who saved the maid from disaster?"

"Indeed. Saved her from some rough treatment at the hands of Herod's soldiers, at the very least."

"She's an inspiration to all of us in the Court of the Women, old Anna," Edna said. "She has been all these years. I see her there every time I go to the Temple. Did you know that she is eighty-four years old?"

"I did not. And I thought I had reached a ripe old age."

"You and I are but children in her eyes," Edna replied. "Widowed after seven years of marriage, they say, and that was early in life. She has spent all the time since at the Temple, praying and fasting. Some say she is a prophetess."

"So I've heard," Aduel said. "Tell me, Edna, are there any prophecies of hers that you know of specifically?"

"None specifically," Edna said. "I've never spoken to her directly. I always meant to, but it never seemed to be the right time. Would it be possible for me to go now?"

"Yes, go," Aduel said firmly. "Say to her what you have just said to me. She may not be able to respond, but she will hear you."

A minute later Edna emerged from the house. Nodding to Joanna with a forced smile, she hurried across the courtyard and through the gate. The girl sat a few minutes more, wondering how she would pass the rest of the day, before going back into the house. Aduel was not at his usual place before the hearth, but instead was standing near the window with a scroll. He looked up as she entered.

"I'm sorry, Uncle, I'm just not in the mood for reading today," Joanna said curtly.

"I understand," said Aduel. He went back to the scroll.

Normally Joanna would not have interrupted him, but today her irritability overcame her manners.

"Especially not a book that long," she said. "Is it Book the Eleventh?"

"No. It is the Book of the Prophet Isaiah."

"Oh." Joanna thought for a moment. "What does it say?"

"Many things."

"Yes, but what are you reading about now?"

"I was trying to recall the prophecy I mentioned earlier. And I have found it. The Lord says, 'I will come to gather all nations and races, and they will come and see my glory. I will perform a sign among them…and send them to the nations…distant coasts and islands that have never yet heard of me.'"

"Then Anna was right," Joanna marveled.

"It seems so," Aduel admitted.

"If she is truly a prophetess, then why are her prophecies not written down?" Joanna wondered.

"I don't know," Aduel shrugged. "Perhaps she has no one to write them."

"I could write them," Joanna suggested. "I will go to her, tomorrow, and tell her. I could sit with her, as she recovers, and she could recount the visions she has seen."

"We'll see, child, we'll see," Aduel said. "It may be some time before she is strong enough for that."

"But still, I would like to go to her and tell her."

"We shall both go," Aduel promised.

He gave her a brief smile and returned to his scroll.

"Uncle?"

Aduel looked up.

"Yes?"

"When you've finished Isaiah, could we read Book the Eleventh?"

"Certainly. But I thought you didn't want to read."

"I don't know what I want," Joanna admitted. "My thoughts are everywhere, and none of them happy. I think it would be soothing to hear you read."

"Very well," Aduel said. "Fetch me Book the Eleventh, and I shall read it. We'll see where it takes you and your turbulent thoughts."

Five minutes later the two of them were seated in their usual places before the hearth. Aduel took a final look at the Book of Isaiah before rolling it up tightly and tucking it securely in his lap. As he unrolled the other scroll, Joanna closed her eyes, as her uncle always did when she was the reader, and allowed the gentle rhythm of his elegant intonation to wash over her.

"Herod: A Secret History, by Aduel of Sepphoris. Book the Eleventh:"

Herod had but little time to celebrate his conquest of the Arabians, for word of Antony's defeat at Actium spread quickly. The king's quandary was intense. After Actium, Antony and Cleopatra, who were now married, fled to Egypt and lived for several months more, as described in the preceding book of this history. During this period Herod remained in Judea, and Antony wrote to him requesting the military support he had previously dismissed. The letter was a plaintive one, and in some ways pathetic for a man who had so recently ruled the greater part of the Roman world. Herod considered for several days how to respond. Finally he called the royal secretary to the council chamber, with only his cousin Achiabus and Sohemus, one of his closest and most loyal advisors, in attendance. Fidgeting upon his throne Herod began to dictate.

"I must reply to Antony," he began. "I have put it off long

enough."

The three courtiers nodded their agreement.

"Herod, King of Judea, to Antony, hmm, how should I address it?" Herod said to the royal secretary. "Put that into proper form, something that won't inflame Octavian should it fall into his hands."

"Yes, Majesty," the royal secretary said.

"Good," Herod said. "To continue:

"I am aware of your reversal at Actium and you for your part may have heard that my campaign against the Arabians was successful, despite the treachery of Cleopatra's troops. I have reconstituted my army and I now offer it for your assistance in the war against Octavian, along with money and the security of the fortresses of Judea. However, there is one condition: You must kill Cleopatra. For it is against her that Octavian declared war, not you, and without the threat of her influence it is likely that you will be able to sue for clemency and resume your place in the affairs of Rome. Without this condition my assistance is useless, for my soldiers will fight half-heartedly on behalf of this avaricious queen, or perhaps not at all. I trust your decision will be a wise one, and I await it with humble gratitude for the many honors you have conferred upon me."

Herod stopped and considered for a moment.

"Is there anything else?" he inquired of his advisors. "It says what needs to be said, does it not?"

"Indeed, Majesty," sympathized Sohemus. "A most difficult letter to compose."

"Yes, telling a man he must kill his wife—it does complicate things," Herod mused. "I wagered all on Antony. I was a fool not to hedge with Octavian, at least a little."

"Not so, Majesty," flattered Achiabus. "No one in the court would have predicted Antony's defeat."

"And what you have said is true," Sohemus added. "The men would be hard pressed to fight for Cleopatra, even with you to lead them."

"Still, difficult to make such an outrageous demand on an old friend," Herod said.

"But prudent," Achiabus said.

"Yes, and the time for being prudent is now upon me, if not already past," Herod muttered.

"I think the king worries needlessly," Sohemus said. "If Octavian is the eventual victor, as seems likely, you would still be his only choice to rule Judea. There is no other."

"But there is another," Herod said testily.

"Who, Majesty?"

"Hyrcanus."

"Hyrcanus!" Achiabus was flabbergasted. "Majesty, Hyrcanus is over eighty years old now, and has no interest in the affairs of government. He never has."

"Still, he would provide a convenient alternative, should Octavian decide to depose me."

The three courtiers were dumbstruck at the king's sudden fears about Hyrcanus. The former king and high priest, mutilated by Antigonus and carted off to Parthia as a prisoner of war ten years earlier, had been treated kindly by the king of Parthia and greatly honored by all the Jews in that region. When Herod had won back the kingdom from Antigonus, he had readily welcomed Hyrcanus back to Jerusalem, receiving him with all possible respect, giving him the place of honor at public meetings and feasts, and calling him father. These demonstrations of affection were applauded by the populace, and in the ensuing years Hyrcanus had lived quietly and contented himself with all that was afforded him. He hardly seemed worthy of suspicion.

Achiabus finally found his voice.

"If His Majesty truly fears the wrath of Octavian, would it not be better to delay this response to Antony," he asked, "and wait for some communication from Octavian?"

"I might be waiting a long time," Herod replied irritably. "In the meantime, Antony deserves a reply, even one so unsatisfactory as this."

Achiabus bowed his acknowledgment.

"Tie it up with all the usual niceties, but remember, nothing too incriminating," Herod ordered the royal secretary. "Have a messenger stand by."

The royal secretary bowed, but before he could leave the grand doors at the front of the chamber swung open.

"I thought I told you His Majesty was not to be disturbed," Sohemus snapped at the guard.

"A citizen requests an audience with His Majesty," the guard said nervously. "He claims to be here on urgent and important business."

"What citizen?" demanded Sohemus.

"Dositheus, attendant to Hyrcanus," the footman said.

Herod leaned back with a look of smug satisfaction and raised a finger for the royal secretary to remain. The three courtiers traded amazed glances. Dositheus was well known to them—not only as a longtime friend and close confidant of Hyrcanus, but of Alexandra as well. He had no reason to bear the king any good will, for Herod had slain two of his kinsmen in political purges, and he himself was under suspicion if for no other reason than his close ties with the previous royal family.

"Let him come forward," Herod said, in a voice of cool calculation.

The doors shut behind Dositheus as he entered the chamber.

He was a middle-aged man of aristocratic bearing—but obviously terrified. He stopped before the throne and made extended obeisance to the king.

"Well, well, rise, my good man," Herod said good-naturedly. "What is it you've come to see me about?"

"A letter, Majesty," Dositheus quavered. He looked about nervously at Achiabus and the other two.

"You may speak," Herod said. "What is this letter?"

"It is from Hyrcanus, Majesty," Dositheus said. "Written to the ruler of Arabia."

"And do you know the contents of this letter?" Herod asked smoothly.

"Yes, Majesty."

"Well, then, what are they?"

"Perhaps Your Majesty would care to read it himself," Dositheus said, holding forth a sealed parchment.

"Ah, you have brought the letter itself!" Herod said, pulling back his lips in that wolfish smile that was not a smile. "How very convenient. Let's see what it says."

He broke the seal and perused it quickly, grunting disapprovingly as he did.

"So," he said, looking up, "Hyrcanus requests an armed escort from Judea to Arabia, with the intent of forming a rival government there."

He handed the letter to Achiabus, who shook his head as he read it.

"Please, Majesty, spare Hyrcanus your wrath!" Dositheus begged. "The letter is not of his making. It was Alexandra who put him up to it."

"Of course!" Herod chuckled. "Alexandra, that lover of strife. It could be no other."

The king was clearly enjoying himself now.

"Tell me, Dositheus," he asked, "what did Alexandra say to convince the old bird to commit himself to such a rash scheme as this?"

"She reminded him of your injurious treatment of their family, and accused you of further wicked designs, and said that surely Octavian would not allow a friend of Antony's to occupy the throne of Judea," Dositheus recounted. "She spoke of it night and day, and would not desist, until he finally gave in. So you see, one could hardly blame Hyrcanus. She is a very contentious woman."

"To put it mildly!" Herod laughed. "But the letter. How did you come into possession of it?"

"I have been entrusted to deliver it to the ruler of Arabia," Dositheus said.

"But instead you have delivered it to me," Herod smirked.

"To preserve the tranquility of the nation and the honor of your throne," Dositheus gabbled. "Your Majesty realizes, of course, that there is no real threat from Hyrcanus. I know you will manage the matter discreetly. I beg of you, Majesty, say nothing to Hyrcanus about my deviation from his instructions."

"Your deviation!" mocked Herod. "Your treachery, more like! But fear not. Treachery toward a friend is, well, treachery. Treachery toward the king is treason. So it was well for you to bring this to my attention. By doing so, you and your family have been restored to my good graces."

"You are most gracious, Majesty, our most gracious king!" Dositheus fell to his knees and bowed his face to the floor with a great many more attestations to Herod's greatness.

"But what to do now?" muttered Herod, ignoring him. "What to do now?"

"I will fetch Hyrcanus at once," Sohemus declared indignantly.

"He will stand before you to answer for this crime."

"Not yet," said Herod. He motioned to the royal secretary for Hyrcanus's letter, which the secretary had just finished reading.

"Dositheus, rise," Herod commanded. "You will convey this letter to the ruler of Arabia, as planned. Then you will return to me with his reply. So you see, there will be no deviation from Hyrcanus's instructions, simply an additional stop here and there. Do you understand?"

Dositheus again bowed low.

"Good," said Herod, handing him the letter. "Affix a new seal and be on your way. I am already anticipating your return."

Dositheus did return, in less than two weeks' time, with the reply. Once again he was received in the closed council chamber, and once again Achiabus, Sohemus, and the royal secretary were shown the intercepted letter. In it the Arabians promised Hyrcanus everything he had asked for. It was, as Dositheus had said, a clear threat to the tranquility of Herod's regime, for the people of Judea were desirous of a change in government and had a sentimental preference for the previous royal family.

Herod immediately summoned Hyrcanus to appear before him. The inquisition was brief and painful to watch. The old, mutilated man was his usual passive self, and seemed never to have suspected that Dositheus might betray him. He seemed more befuddled than frightened, and Herod showed his letter to the Sanhedrin and quickly pronounced a sentence of death. And thus did Hyrcanus, who had endured many changes of fortune throughout his life, come to an end that he did not deserve. Both Herod and his father Antipater had come to greatness by means of Hyrcanus's mild disposition and passive nature—a nature that was not, unfortunately, passed on to his daughter Alexandra. For it was by means of her scheming that her father met his end, although

Alexandra herself, despite her part in this plot, suffered no punishment. For Herod, though constantly under the threat of her intrigues, seemed to enjoy the opportunity to outwit her, which he had done repeatedly with the aid of turncoats and spies.

With Hyrcanus out of the way, Herod considered his options. It was now clear that Antony had no intention of following Herod's advice to have done with Cleopatra, so the king decided upon a bold gambit: He would sail to the Greek island of Rhodes, where Octavian had established his winter headquarters as he prepared to march against Antony. This would occasion another lengthy absence from Judea, similar to the one five years earlier when Antony had summoned him. Recalling the conflict that had erupted within the palace on that occasion, Herod took the precaution of separating the two warring factions of his family. To the fortress of Masada, southeast of Jerusalem, he sent his mother and his sister Salome, under the care of his remaining brother Pheroras (his other brother Joseph had been killed some years earlier in the war against the Parthians). To the fortress of Alexandrium, to the northeast, he sent the queen and her mother Alexandra, under the watchful eye of his loyal friend Sohemus. Yet seemingly Herod had learned nothing from his previous experience, for he gave Sohemus the same charge that he had given his brother-in-law Joseph five years earlier: Namely, that if any calamity should befall him Sohemus should kill the queen (and her mother as well), and turn the kingdom over to Pheroras.

With these things undertaken the king set sail for Rhodes, accompanied by many of his court officials and a small detachment of his personal guard. At his audience with Octavian, Herod put off none of his royal dignity, for he had decided to appear not in the role of an offender or supplicant, but as a potential friend and ally. He did, however, take the precaution of laying aside his royal diadem, before he launched, undaunted, into an unapologetic account of his actions. He said that he had been a friend to Antony, and that even after Antony's defeat at Actium he had not deserted him, but had been a faithful counsellor, and had demonstrated to him that the only way to save himself, and not lose all his authority, was to slay Cleopatra. He stated further that he was not ashamed to own his friendship with Antony, but instead was proud to demonstrate the kind of services he could render a benefactor, and now proposed to remain in the same capacity, simply substituting the name of Octavian for the name of Antony.

Octavian, seated regally as Herod stood before him, had at first eyed his petitioner coldly. He was less imposing in appearance than Antony—a bit shorter, with curly, yellowish hair, small, uneven teeth, and eyebrows that joined together above his nose. By nature he was less impulsive than Antony, his countenance more inscrutable, but as Herod had spoken it had gradually softened. When Herod concluded by pointing out that he had laid aside his diadem to indicate his submission to Octavian's will, the latter's doubts seemed to melt away completely. Moreover, he was aware of Herod's reputation for valor and military success, and as a shrewd strategist realized that Herod, if rejected, could prove an impediment to his final conquest of Antony and Cleopatra. Taking the diadem, he placed it back on Herod's head, and confirmed him as King of Judea, and encouraged him to be as great a friend to himself as he had to Antony.

With his crown settled upon him more firmly than ever, Herod returned triumphant to Judea. By boldly confronting the potential danger from Octavian, he had acquired an even greater reputation than before. However, when reunited with the scattered elements of his family in Jerusalem, he found his house in disorder. Queen Miriam and Alexandra were quite uneasy, for they knew that they had not been put into a distant fortress for their own safety, but instead for the purpose of isolating them and removing any power they held, not only over others but over their own affairs as well. Miriam remembered the command Herod had given to Joseph, and grieved that he would not allow her any hope of surviving him, concluded that his love for her was nothing but a sham, conducted for his own advantage. To confirm her suspicions she had worked subtly during her house arrest, in league with Alexandra, to win over her keepers, especially Sohemus, with gifts and many kind words. That foolish man, forgetting what had happened before, was gradually persuaded—and further, anticipating that Herod would be dethroned by Octavian, thought it best to ingratiate himself with the two women who would then be likely to hold the power in the kingdom.

So it was that when the king arrived at the palace, and hurried to his wife so that she alone would be the first to hear his joyful news, she greeted his report with a groan. She said she was rather sorry for it, and afforded him many signs of her dissatisfaction. Herod did not know what to make of it, for he had no reason to suspect that Sohemus would be so foolish as to reveal his secret commands. But the open hatred his wife now bore to him troubled him greatly, and he alternately raged at her and reconciled himself to her, while she remained aloof.

This state of affairs persisted for several weeks, and days that should have been marked with celebration and feasting were instead plagued by unbearable tension. Among those who sought to turn the king's anger to advantage were Herod's mother and his sister Salome. The longtime hatred of these two toward Miriam and Alexandra erupted into a relentless campaign of verbal warfare, as they provoked Herod to wrath with long, spurious tales of Miriam's disloyalty. In return the queen, who had inherited too much of her mother's contentious nature, wasted no opportunity to insult her antagonists, openly mocking the inferiority of their birth and their other shortcomings with unmitigated malevolence.

Just when it seemed that the situation could not continue for another day, with Herod swinging abruptly between love and hatred for his wife and always overcome with one passion or the other, news arrived that Octavian was victorious in Egypt, and that Antony and Cleopatra were both dead. Leaving his domestic troubles behind, Herod hurried away to Egypt. There he was hailed as a great friend of Octavian, who was now sole ruler of the united Roman realm, for he had already proven his loyalty to his new patron by turning back a troop of gladiators who were coming to Antony's aid from Asia Minor. Herod received some of the spoils of Cleopatra's shattered kingdom, including her personal bodyguard of four hundred Galatian warriors and some of the more valuable attendants of her court. Indeed, Octavian returned to Herod all the lands of Judea that Antony had given to Cleopatra, and gave him additional territories besides, including Samaria and several coastal cities. Hoping that these new triumphs would somehow quell his domestic troubles, Herod returned to Jerusalem even more glorious than before. But the seeds of conflict had been sown and diligently nurtured, and in the coming months they would ripen into a final clash with disastrous consequences.

"And thus ends Book the Eleventh," Aduel said, rolling up the scroll.

"With Herod murdering yet another member of the royal family and gaining more power and possessions because of it," Joanna said sourly.

"Yes, Herod was adept at turning Roman politics to his own advantage. Throwing over Antony in favor of Octavian was a

difficult decision to make, but he calculated correctly. With
Hyrcanus out of the way, Octavian had no viable alternative."

"How long did Octavian rule Rome?"

"Quite a long time," Aduel said. "In fact, he still does."

"He does? I've never heard of him."

"You know him by a different name: Augustus Caesar."

"Oh. Why did he change it?"

"He didn't, really," explained Aduel. "Augustus is a title
the Roman Senate gave him a few years after his victory over
Antony. It means, roughly, 'His Reverence.' It's one of his
many titles: First Citizen, Supreme Commander, Chief Priest,
and so on, but it's the one he has come to be called by most
often."

"How can we have a high priest in Jerusalem if the Romans
consider Augustus to be chief priest?" Joanna asked.

"Oh, the Romans are rather careless about matters of
religion," Aduel replied. "Unlike us, they are not too particular
about their gods and their worship."

"Hmph!"

Joanna folded her arms and stared straight ahead, looking
at nothing. The discontent that had plagued her earlier had
returned in full force. The paradox of such a powerful nation
that paid only token respect to God irritated her all the more.

"I wonder where Edna is," Aduel remarked. "She's been
gone some time."

Joanna said nothing. Aduel shrugged and got up.

"Well, I suppose I'll return these books to their place," he
said.

Joanna heard him make his way carefully down the
concealed stairway. A sudden knock at the door roused her.
She looked up in panic. It was a measured knock, not the

intemperate pounding of a soldier, but it was terrifying nonetheless. She did not know what to do. Edna and Irijah were both out, and her uncle obviously had not heard the knock. She got up and opened the door a crack.

"Aduel of Sepphoris?"

It was not a soldier, but a messenger who peered at her in the twilight.

"This is his house," Joanna replied.

"A message," the man said, thrusting a folded piece of papyrus at her.

She examined it as she closed the door. Her uncle's name was written on the outside, in handwriting that looked very much like Hilkiah the scribe's. Her heart pounded. What could it mean?

She went to the top of the stairway and called down:

"Uncle?"

"Yes?"

"A message for you."

"A message! From whom?"

"I'm not sure. A messenger just delivered it."

"Already? Praise the Lord! Bring it here, child."

She descended the steps carefully, blinking as her eyes adjusted to the near-darkness. At the bottom of the stairway her uncle peered up eagerly. The late-afternoon gloom reminded her of her earliest days in Jerusalem, a time of her first tentative hours of formal education, a time that seemed so far away, though it had been but a few weeks ago. How much things had changed since then! How much she had changed!

She handed Aduel the message. As soon as he saw it his face fell. He opened it and read it quickly.

"I'm sorry, child," he said sadly. "When you said it was brought by a messenger I thought it was good news. I thought it was from Nicolaus. But instead it is bad news. It is from Hilkiah, the young scribe. Anna is dead."

Chapter 18

The next day Joanna awoke early. She had expected a fitful night, but instead she had fallen into a deep slumber. Now, despite all that had happened, she felt an abiding peace as she contemplated the events of the previous day. After receiving the scribe's message she and Aduel had hurried to the Temple, but Anna's chamber had already been vacated. Their inquiries had directed them to a burial place outside the city, and proceeding there by torchlight they found Edna praying near the burial chamber. Anna's body had already been laid to rest.

Now she stared into the early-morning darkness, trying to make sense of what little she knew about Anna's life. The end was so sudden, so unexpected! But as she probed deeper, she realized that her sorrow was more for herself than for Anna. In the few brief days since she had encountered Anna she had begun to think of the old woman as a substitute for her mother—a wise and powerful presence to guide her in her final few steps toward womanhood, in ways that Aduel could not. Since the riot at the Temple she had enjoyed a quiet friendship with Edna, but Edna was a simple soul—pious, to be sure, but whose thoughts focused in most part on the routine domestic details of maintaining a household. She had sensed in Anna something deeper, something unshakable, and she had yearned to know more. Here was a woman who had penetrated the mystery of the eternal God, at least a little—at least enough to be entrusted with prophecies! What did it take to have that kind of faith?

Her thoughts wandered to the scribe. She learned from Edna that he had gone to Anna's chamber and had insisted on remaining there during her final hour. He had then hastened away to arrange for a tomb while the women prepared the body for burial. It all had been accomplished in keeping with the Law—at his own initiative and apparently at his own expense. The more she thought about it, the more it awed her. Her lingering doubts about the betrothal had faded. If he would have her, she would have him; there was no more time for misplaced amorous mooning. The only questions that remained were how soon the matter could be decently broached, and how to go about it. She could follow Aduel's original plan, and ask her uncle to arrange the matter in conformity with tradition. But something urged her to adhere to the alternative she had chosen—to give the scribe the message she had composed, even though it was now somewhat stale. Because even though she now felt that she knew his mind well enough to make her decision, it seemed only right that he should know her mind equally well.

She heard Edna moving about in the kitchen outside her door. It was time to get up, yet she continued to lie still, staring up at the darkness. But now Edna was speaking to someone in low tones, and a voice was replying: Aduel! She quickly swung out of bed and felt her way through the darkness, opening the door quietly.

Aduel and Edna were in the kitchen, putting on cloaks. The first light of dawn filtered through the window. They were going out, and the girl knew where.

"Would you leave without me?" she demanded.

They looked at her sheepishly.

"We thought it would be better for you to sleep," Aduel said.

"I'm going with you," Joanna declared. "Just a moment. I won't be long."

They made their way through the awakening city and arrived at the tomb just as the sun was rising. The rough, arid terrain of the burial place, its weather-beaten vegetation so forbidding in the eerie torchlight the night before, seemed a different place in the warm light of day: serene, welcoming. They prayed together in solemn mourning outside the whitewashed stone of the tomb until Aduel offered a final benediction. Then they made their way back up the rocky path back to the city.

"It seems so strange that we are her only mourners," Aduel remarked. "Perhaps I should hire some."

"No, Uncle," Joanna said firmly, recoiling as she thought of the professionals who mourned for a fee. "She would not want them."

"No," Aduel said. "She would not. At least she had the young scribe to care for her. I shudder to think..."

His voice trailed off.

"What, Uncle?" Joanna pressed.

"I shudder to think what would have become of her had he not been there," Aduel said grimly.

"Why?" the girl asked. "What would have happened? She would have been given an honorable burial, would she not?"

"Hard to say," Aduel muttered. "Just as likely she would have been taken to the Valley of Hinnom."

"With the trash?" Joanna gasped.

"A pauper's burial," Aduel shrugged. "And if nothing else, Anna was certainly a pauper."

"But wouldn't the Levites—"

"The Levites care for the Temple, not necessarily the people in the Temple," Aduel interrupted. "As for the rest of us—well, I for one wish I had paid more attention. As one always does when the time for paying attention has passed."

Joanna was reminded of her own intention, to sit with Anna and record the old woman's prophecies so that they might be known throughout the land. It was hardly her fault that her project could not be carried out; Anna had died before anything could be done. Still, it gnawed at her.

"I suppose her prophecies will never be known now," she mourned.

"Why not?" Aduel countered. "What of your plan to write them down?"

"I only heard one. And the scribe and I are the only ones who heard it."

"You can't be sure of that," Aduel shrugged. "Perhaps there were others. We can inquire. But even if you and the scribe are the only ones to have heard this strange thing, you will have the opportunity to tell what you have heard."

"But when?" Joanna demanded. "Who will listen?"

"That I do not know," Aduel admitted. "But I do know this: You will have the opportunity."

Joanna considered this as they trudged along. She suspected that her uncle was only attempting to lift her spirits.

"But how do I know that what Anna said is really a prophecy?" she objected. "There are true prophets and false prophets."

"There are," Aduel agreed, "but the Law reminds us that

it's really rather easy to distinguish between them. The prophecies of true prophets come true, and those of false prophets do not."

"Then Anna could not truly have been a prophet," Joanna said sadly.

"Why not?"

"Because she said the scribe and I would see the Messiah return in glory."

"And so you may."

"But you said that Herod had slaughtered all the infant boys in the region of Bethlehem."

"Yes, I did say that," Aduel confirmed.

"Then surely the child is dead now."

"Perhaps," Aduel said. "But recall that there was a delay in sending the troops to Bethlehem, because the magicians did not return to Herod as they had been ordered. They returned home another way, and thus there was a time during which the child and his parents might have escaped."

"Then Anna's prophecy could be true," Joanna murmured.

"Yes, it could," Aduel agreed. "And remember, the Lord does no great work without giving his servants the prophets knowledge of His plans."

Back within the city walls the three mourners parted ways, with Edna returning to the house while Joanna and Aduel made their way to the Temple to see what more they could learn about Anna. Their inquiries led nowhere. The woman who had accompanied Anna on her deathbed was nowhere to be found, and the Levites who tended Temple affairs professed to know little. One of them, a very old man, recalled that Anna had prophesied that the Messiah would be called a Nazarene, but this seemed so absurd that everyone had discounted it immediately, and those in the Temple hierarchy had preserved it as a favorite joke. In general the Levites seemed to regard Anna's residence on Temple grounds as a nuisance, as Aduel had surmised, and to be relieved that she was gone. Additional queries in the Court of the Women yielded no further information, instead provoking bewildered or emotional responses that only brought unwanted attention. They returned home empty-handed, with Joanna greatly dejected.

They found Edna busy in the kitchen, where a hearty aroma was beginning to arise. The old housekeeper had prepared a meal the previous day, and now it was simmering in a large cauldron over the kitchen hearth. Soon it was ready. Joanna's senses had not deceived her: It was lamb, prepared as a stew with lentils and vegetables and seasoned to perfection. It was a rare treat; meals in Aduel's household were seldom more elegant than a simple porridge. Joanna ate greedily, admonishing herself each time she refilled her bowl that she had gulped down enough, while at the same time marveling at how the right food at the right time could be so comforting. Even after she had stuffed herself she found herself mopping up the last bit of gravy with a hunk of coarse bread. After washing it down with a long draught of water she leaned back against the wall and closed her eyes, for she suddenly felt very sleepy.

When she opened them again she found that both Aduel and Edna had risen from the low table where they had taken the meal. Her uncle was in his chair before the hearth, just beginning to unroll a scroll, while Edna was handing a large bowl of stew through the doorway to Irijah, who immediately began to slurp it greedily in the courtyard. Joanna roused herself to action—but she only got as far as the hearth, where she plopped into the chair next to Aduel with a sigh.

"Perhaps you should lie down in your bed," her uncle suggested. "Rest for an hour or two."

"No," said Joanna, who by now was feeling a little queasy. "I need to sit up."

"As you wish."

"Is that Book the Twelfth?" Joanna asked.

"It is."

"May we read it?"

"I think we may," Aduel smiled. "Reading is no longer hard work, is it? Rather a restful and relaxing activity. In Book the Twelfth you'll meet someone you have already encountered."

"Encountered in the other books?"

"No. Here, in Jerusalem."

"Who?" Joanna demanded.

"You'll see," Aduel smiled. "I presume you would like me to read."

"If you don't mind, Uncle, I would like to read. I think it would help to occupy my mind."

"Very well."

Aduel handed her the scroll. It was one of the shorter ones, and after unrolling it to the end and glancing over it, Joanna began to read:

"Herod: A Secret History, by Aduel of Sepphoris. Book the Twelfth."

After his triumphant meeting with Octavian, Herod had brought back more from Egypt than additional territory and four hundred soldiers. Several of Cleopatra's courtiers had also accompanied him, for after the death of Cleopatra and the annexation of Egypt to Rome, the Egyptian royal court no longer existed. Many of these courtiers remained in Jerusalem for only a short time before drifting off to other employments, but some affixed themselves permanently to the royal establishment of Judea. One of these was Nicolaus of Damascus, an accomplished scholar who had, among his other duties, served as the tutor to Cleopatra's younger children. Tall and austere, he professed himself a Jew, but like so many in his position his outlook was that of a worldly Greek. In time he would rise to a position of prominence in Herod's court, serving as court historian and philosopher, and even as Herod's chief counsellor in matters of policy and diplomacy.

But those things were in the future. During his first months in Jerusalem the maturing philosopher was not entirely sure how to conduct himself in Herod's palace, for despite his enormous learning Nicolaus still clung to the mistaken notion that the caprices of human nature could be tamed by logic and reason. At this time he was around thirty-five years old, about the same age as the royal secretary, and the two became friends—as much as any two persons could be friends in such an environment, for the atmosphere of a royal court is invariably poisonous, a breeding ground of suspicion and mistrust. From time to time they encountered one another—usually while waiting for the king—and on these occasions they would often converse, with the philosopher always eager to debate some aspect of universal truth while the royal secretary tended toward more practical topics such as court politics.

The latter were becoming more and more volatile during the philosopher's early days in the court. The hatred that had simmered during Herod's absence in Egypt was again coming to a boil. The queen, perhaps too confident of Herod's passion for her, continued to provoke his mother and his sister Salome with rough language and stinging insults, and unwisely ignored the patience with which they bore these remarks—for they were hardly cringing before her, but instead were biding their time as they prepared a plot against her. Toward the king himself she continued her saucy attitude, and continually referred to him, often in his presence, as 'my grimy little soldier.' At first Herod took this with good humor, for he was exceedingly adept with both the javelin and the bow and prided himself on his military prowess above all else. He hoped that this new epithet signaled the grudging end to the acrimony of their relationship, but he soon perceived that it was not meant as a term of endearment.

All of this continued for the better part of a year before the queen took a liberty that precipitated the disastrous climax, as was later related by the eunuch who attended the royal bedchamber. One day around noon the king was lying in his bed, taking his rest when he called for the queen. She came in accordingly, but would not lie down next to him, and when he was very desirous of her she ridiculed him.

"What is that to me?" she retorted. "Go to your Arabian dog for that."

Herod was stunned. Not only was this an insult to his first wife, Doris, who had been put out of the palace in favor of Miriam, but to his mother Cypros, who was also of Arabian descent. Yet the queen went so far as to provoke him further, saying that she had no regard for his feelings, for he had caused her grandfather Hyrcanus and her brother Aristobulus, the handsome young high priest, to be slain. Thus rejected, the king went into a wild fury, openly threatening violence toward the queen, who mockingly dared him to make good on his threat.

He did not, but his anger continued unabated throughout that day and into the next. Seeing that he was even more disturbed than usual, Salome set her plot in motion. She sent the king's cupbearer, who had been co-opted into the scheme in advance, to tell Herod that the queen had requested his assistance in giving Herod a love potion. When Herod inquired what was in this potion, and what its effect would be, the cupbearer said he did not know, but thought it best to bring it to Herod's attention and let him decide what to do.

This false information had its desired effect, for Herod flew into an even more violent rage than before. Rejecting all sensible attempts to discover the truth, he instead ordered that the eunuch who was the most faithful to the queen, and without whose knowledge she did nothing, be tortured. When this man was under the utmost agonies he still could say nothing about the false charge, but cried out that so far as he knew the queen's hatred for the king was occasioned by something Sohemus had said to her. As soon as he uttered this Herod leaped up and cried out that Sohemus must have seduced the queen during her confinement in the fortress while Herod had gone to Rhodes. Sohemus, who had been promoted to a position of even greater power in the government at the queen's urging, was arrested and put to death at once, without trial or a defense of any kind.

The queen, however, was brought to trial. That very day Herod convened a proceeding in his audience chamber, choosing as a jury all the courtiers and friends who were most faithful to him. Also in attendance, as spectators, were the remaining courtiers and ministers, including the royal secretary, along with many others, including Salome, her mother, and the queen's mother Alexandra. Herod himself took the roles of prosecutor and judge. As Miriam stood before him, her hands bound in golden chains, he laid out an elaborate accusation concerning the love potion and its composition, though he produced no actual evidence of it, merely the report of the corrupted cupbearer. But he was in too great a passion to temper his charges with any semblance of fairness, and when he had concluded, the jury, after token deliberation, passed the sentence of death upon the queen. They did, however, recommend that the sentence be commuted, and that the queen be imprisoned in one of the mountaintop fortresses of the realm.

Joanna put down the scroll.

"But what of her defense?" she asked angrily. "Surely they could see that it was all a lie."

"There was no defense," Aduel sighed. "None was allowed."

"How was that fair?" Joanna demanded.

"When the king conducts a trial," Aduel explained, "the procedure and the verdict are whatever the king wants them to be. Besides, I doubt she would have made a defense even if she had been given the opportunity. She would have thought it beneath her dignity."

"She should have said something," Joanna insisted.

"By that time she hated Herod so, she would not even afford him the pleasure of a retort," Aduel said. "Perhaps we should pause for a bit."

"No," Joanna said resolutely, shifting uncomfortably in her chair. "I want to read."

"Very well."

Herod took pause, and seemed ready to commute the sentence, still not willing to part forever from the woman he loved so viscerally. But immediately there was an objection from the gallery. It was Salome, who labored strenuously to have the queen put to death. In her arguments she could not conceal her utter hatred for Miriam, and her statements were so strident, mocking the queen's beauty and her royal bearing, that it became clear that her case was motivated by a most insidious jealousy. But when she pointed out that an imprisoned queen would become a rallying point for Herod's enemies within the realm, he wavered. The others of Salome's party, including Herod's mother, took up the cause, shouting down any opposing point of view, while Herod sat gloomily silent through it all—for the first time in his life, unable to decide.

At length the furious debate subsided. All eyes turned to the king, awaiting his verdict. Yet still he hesitated, the agony of his soul clearly revealed by his imploring gaze at his condemned wife. A single beseeching glance would have saved her, but she refused to give it, and instead looked steadfastly away.

Finally the king spoke:

"She shall die today."

He buried his face in his hands as the guards approached the queen to lead her away. But suddenly the sickening hush that had settled over the chamber was shattered in a most shocking way. Alexandra, the queen's mother, leaped from her place with a loud cry, but instead of cursing Herod she rained down reproaches on her own daughter, shouting that had been ungrateful to her husband, and was deserving of her punishment. She went on like this for some time, and was even so outrageous as to tear her hair, and it quickly became obvious that this indecent behavior was nothing more than an attempt to save herself from a similar fate. Yet throughout it all Miriam said not a word, but looked at her mother with a concern that manifested the greatness of her soul. She was led away to her death with unshaken composure, thereby demonstrating to the spectators the true nobility of her lineage. Thus died Miriam, a woman of excellent character, who had all that could be asked for in beauty and royal bearing, and was lacking only in the ability to hide her true feelings, and to moderate her words in perilous circumstances.

Again Joanna put down the scroll, but this time for a different reason. As she had narrated the account of the trial there had come over her an unpleasant sensation, part indignation and part terrible certainty, and now she felt her cheeks begin to flush. She felt a little short of breath. She looked at Aduel and noticed that there were tears in his eyes.

"But…Herod didn't really have her executed, did he?" she asked.

"He did," Aduel replied quietly.

"That very day? There was no reprieve?"

"Within the hour," Aduel whispered.

"How awful," Joanna said. "It's just so awful."

She closed her eyes and made an effort to wish away the overpowering sensation welling up within her, but she could not. Aduel looked away as she leaned over the side of her chair and vomited the entirety of her huge midday meal onto the stone floor. Edna rushed in, and a few moments later the door from the courtyard opened and Irijah appeared, carrying a bucket. He wordlessly handed her the rag that he carried with him as he did his daily chores. Joanna realized that he had been sitting on the bench just outside the door, listening to her read, just as she had eavesdropped on the conversation between Edna and Aduel the day before. After she had wiped her face Edna led her away, and Irijah dropped to his knees, looking rather queasy himself as he began to mop up the mess.

Chapter 19

After her moment of illness both Aduel and Edna insisted that Joanna take the precaution of remaining in bed for the remainder of the day, and although she no longer felt sick she was too humiliated to object. The next morning she rose with the dawn, and after reassuring herself with a few mouthfuls of bread and water that she was no longer at risk of nausea she padded quietly down the stairway to her uncle's underground study. She intended to find Book the Twelfth and finish it, but instead she found Aduel, kneeling on his prayer mat near the window. She turned around quietly, hoping to steal back upstairs without attracting his notice, but he had already risen.

"Well, my child, you're up early," he said. "Feeling better?"

"Much better, Uncle."

"Come, then, let's go upstairs and find you something to eat."

"I've already eaten."

"Then let us rejoice in this day that the Lord has made," said Aduel. "What do you propose to do with the gift?"

"I was hoping I might finish Book the Twelfth."

"After what happened yesterday?"

"I'm sorry about that, Uncle," Joanna said. "Nothing like that has ever happened to me before."

"Perhaps because you've never heard a story like Herod's before."

"Or Miriam's. Do you think he really loved her?"

"Oh, without a doubt. His passion for her was beyond my power to describe it. It was the kind of great love story the Greeks tell so well in their epics and fables."

"Then how did it go so wrong?"

"Strangely enough all great love stories seem to turn out badly," Aduel shrugged. "In Herod's case it was more than love; it was obsession. It was his great misfortune that it collided with his other obsession."

"Power?"

"Herod's greatest curse," nodded Aduel. "His supreme concern was his throne, superseding even his love for Miriam."

"She seemed so noble," Joanna mused. "In many ways more than Cleopatra."

"If that is your conclusion, then I have done my work well," Aduel smiled.

"Will there be any more about her?"

"No, she disappears from the story now, except in her role as the mother of the young princes."

"Oh. Do they play a part?"

"In fact they do. But I warn you, their story is another one that ought to be read on an empty stomach."

"Is it soon?"

"Soon enough," Aduel said.

He drew a scroll from the shelf and motioned for her to take the stool, while he stood near the window.

"Now," he said, "I shall read what remains of Book the Twelfth. And then perhaps, if your stomach consents, we'll venture a bit further."

With the queen gone it seemed reasonable to expect there would be peace in the palace, but in fact the opposite took place. No sooner was Miriam dead than the king's affection for her was kindled in a more outrageous manner than before. His love had never been of a calm nature, and even after eight years of marriage it had never been within his power to manage. Now it seized him so violently that he would search throughout the palace day and night, sometimes leaping out of bed and running about in a wild manner, always calling for the queen and wailing in lament, and sometimes speaking to her as if she were standing in front of him. To divert his mind he convened great assemblies and feasts, but these accomplished nothing, and he continued his raving, even going so far as to order his servants to call for her. Many in his court despaired for his kingdom, for he was incapable of managing the affairs of the government while in this disordered state, which seemed to be permanent. Some of them, particularly those who had come over from Egypt, proposed to take bold measures— namely, to make the king accept, by force of reason, the reality of his decision.

While this remedy was still being debated, two of these men, Nicolaus of Damascus and a colleague named Eustochius, encountered the king in a corridor on one of his wild rants through the palace, and were so bold as to attempt it themselves.

"Majesty," Nicolaus said calmly, "who is it that you seek?"

"I seek the Queen," Herod snapped. "Surely she is here somewhere! I just spoke to her a moment ago."

"Are you speaking of Her Majesty Queen Miriam?" Nicolaus asked.

"Of course I'm speaking of Miriam!" Herod retorted. "Who else would I be speaking of?"

"Majesty, let us review the facts of the situation," Nicolaus continued patiently. "It is a sad truth that the queen no longer—"

At this point he was interrupted by the royal secretary, who had come upon them just as the discussion commenced.

"She may be in the garden," the secretary said in a low voice. "I often see her there. Come, let us look for her."

Taking both Nicolaus and Eustochius by the arm, he attempted to guide them away from the king. Nicolaus regarded him with surprise, but seeing the look in the royal secretary's eyes and trusting him as a friend, he did not resist. Eustochius, however, broke away with a look of annoyance and took up Nicolaus's argument.

"Majesty," he said. "Let us speak plainly. The queen is dead."

"Dead!" Herod exclaimed. "She is not dead! She can't be! I just spoke to her!"

"No, Majesty, you did not speak to her," Eustochius said. "She is dead. Completely and irrevocably dead."

"But how did she die?" Herod demanded.

"She was executed, Majesty."

"Executed! On whose authority?"

"On your authority, Majesty."

"Lies!" shrieked Herod. "Lies! Guards! Guards! This man speaks lies about the queen and the king. He speaks treason! He shall be executed at once!"

Eustochius began to protest, but it was no use. The two guards who had rushed up drew their swords and roughly hustled him away. Nicolaus stared in disbelief as the royal secretary hurried him out of sight.

"Arrogant fellow." The royal secretary shook his head. "He thought he could reason with a lunatic."

"You—you saved my life," Nicolaus gasped.

"I preserved a brilliant scholar for further service to the crown," the royal secretary shrugged. "Think no more of it."

"No," panted Nicolaus, "I will always think of it. I will remember it as long as I live."

After this Herod's affliction grew worse, for a pestilential disease broke out throughout the country. A great many died, including some of Herod's close friends, and most in Judea attributed it to divine vengeance for what the king had done to Miriam. As a final resort Herod forced himself into the wilderness, on the pretext of going hunting, and there afflicted himself by tormenting his own flesh. After a few days he fell ill, with inflammation and a terrible pain in the back of his head that only increased his madness. The doctors despaired of him and broke off all treatment, fully expecting him to die.

Hearing this, Alexandra, who had remained free after her daughter's trial, hatched her final plot to wrest away the throne. She began by endeavoring to get possession of the two fortresses that guarded Jerusalem, and thus take control of the city. But her attempts to persuade their commanders that it was best for her to take control, since she was the prospective guardian of Herod's two young sons with Miriam, were angrily rejected. One of these commanders, Achiabus—Herod's cousin and most trusted advisor—sent messengers to inform Herod of Alexandra's design. The king, tormented by pain and madness and more ready than ever to inflict punishment, sent orders for her to be seized and executed immediately, which she was. In the following months Herod gradually recovered his health and his sanity, and having rid himself of the root cause of so much turmoil within his household, enjoyed a period of domestic tranquility, though plots and rebellions would reappear on the horizon soon enough.

Aduel rolled up the scroll.

"Thus ends Book the Twelfth," he said.

"Finally we have done with Alexandra," Joanna commented.

"Yes, after so much scheming, Herod finally put her away," Aduel replied.

"I just don't understand why he allowed her to remain so long."

"I never fully understood it myself," Aduel said. "On the one hand, she was the mother of the queen. On the other, she was a constant source of discord. Of course, Herod could be blamed for much of that."

"Two people grasping at one prize," Joanna observed.

"But Herod always with the upper hand."

They considered this for a few moments.

"At least I finally understand the debt that Nicolaus always talks about," Joanna said.

"Yes. But as you could see, it was a very small act on my part."

"But was Eustochius really executed?"

"Oh yes. Immediately."

"Then it wasn't a small act. You did save Nicolaus."

"I suppose," Aduel chuckled. "Poor Nicolaus. He turned quite pale after the incident, and remained so for several days. He normally has a rather ruddy complexion, you know."

"But he does owe you a debt," Joanna concluded. "You should let him repay it."

"I intend to," Aduel said. "The king's caravan will have reached Callirrhoe by now. If Nicolaus has sent the letters he promised, they will arrive soon. Once they do, all our options will be open to us. If necessary, we can flee to Alexandria."

At this Joanna's face clouded over.

"But you don't think that will really be necessary," she said. "Do you, Uncle?"

"Hard to know, my child, hard to know," Aduel said. "Jerusalem has been on edge for some time now. It's impossible to say what will happen when Herod finally dies. We must be prepared for any outcome, and to decide at a moment's notice. Ah! I do believe I hear Edna upstairs. Perhaps she has brought us something wonderful from the Valley of the Cheesemongers."

Chapter 20

Tragically Edna had not gone as far as the Valley of the Cheesemongers that morning, but she had something almost as good to show for her errand: bread fresh from the baker, still warm on the inside. On fine mornings Aduel took his breakfast in the courtyard and today Joanna joined him, taking for herself a second breakfast, for the bread was irresistible and she was still hungry.

They sat side by side on one of the rough wooden benches and ate in silence. Aduel closed his eyes after he finished, basking in the sunshine, and seemed to slip into meditation. Joanna attempted to imitate him, but her thoughts were too restless. She alternately concluded that her uncle had overstated the danger of turmoil in Jerusalem to spur her to readiness—and then that he had understated it to reassure her. As much as she detested Herod, his impending death frightened her. He had been king of Judea since long before she was born, and although he was hated and feared, life under his rule was familiar and predictable. It was hard to know how things would change after he was gone. Would there really be violence and upheaval as her uncle and Nicolaus of Damascus seemed to fear? And would it affect more than just a few political adversaries grasping for the throne?

Despite the sunshine the morning air was chilly, and she

began to fidget. Sensing her agitation, Aduel opened his eyes.

"Take a few turns around the courtyard," he suggested. "I don't expect you to sit still all morning like a worn-out old man."

"We could walk to the Temple," Joanna hinted.

"Not now," Aduel demurred. "I need to stay here, in case the letters from Nicolaus are delivered."

"Couldn't Edna or Irijah could wait for them?"

Aduel shook his head.

"It's too important," he said. "I need to stay."

"Then what about Book the Thirteenth?" Joanna prompted. "Is it a long one?"

"Actually, it isn't," Aduel said, "even though it covers a period of nearly twenty years. But they were twenty years with relatively little conflict, which makes for dull reading. So I did my best to summarize. We can skip it if you like."

"I want to read it," Joanna insisted.

"A good way to pass the time," Aduel agreed. "Fetch it now, child, and we'll begin."

"Here in the courtyard?"

"No indeed," Aduel said. "If a passerby should hear us, and catch wind of Herod's name—"

He shook his head ominously.

"Spies are everywhere," he said in a low voice. "We'll read inside—far enough from the window that the words will not carry."

A few minutes later they were seated in their chairs before the hearth. Aduel had indicated that Joanna should read. Thankful for the distraction, she dove into the text:

"Herod: A Secret History, by Aduel of Sepphoris. Book the Thirteenth."

After a long convalescence Herod's mind regained its clarity, and with the opportunities for war and conquest at a low ebb he began to cast about for other ways to demonstrate his greatness. He constructed a theatre in the middle of Jerusalem, and an enormous stadium on the plain outside the city. These he covered with inscriptions of the great acts of Octavian, now Augustus, also adorning them with trophies of the nations that Rome had conquered, all made of pure gold and silver and decorated with precious stones. He established a regime of athletic games, to be celebrated every five years, as well as a similar competition for musicians, and spared no expense to attract the most accomplished performers in all these pursuits from nations far and wide. In the stadium he instituted a program of races, featuring chariots drawn by two, three, or four pair of horses, with significant prizes. Additionally he collected a great number of fierce and exotic beasts, particularly lions, which were made to fight with each other, or with condemned prisoners.

These expenditures indeed impressed the foreigners in Judea, but to the native Jews they seemed a flagrant violation of venerable laws and customs, particularly the throwing of men to wild beasts for the delight of spectators. After some deliberation, ten of the most pious contrived a plot of assassination. Armed with daggers, they awaited Herod within the theater on the occasion of one of the performances there. But just minutes before the attack was to take place, one of Herod's spies discovered their intention, and after initially dismissing the report, the king reconsidered and returned to the palace. There he summoned the ten conspirators, for they had been identified by name, and when they arrived they were immediately placed under arrest. Seeing that there was no hope for them, they revealed their daggers and stated their purpose plainly.

The conspirators were immediately put to death, but when the incident became known to the people, the spy who had exposed the plot was seized and torn to pieces, and then fed to the dogs. This event was witnessed by many of the citizens, but no one would reveal who had done it, until Herod in his fury had a great many of them tortured. Some of them finally confessed what they had seen, and Herod ordered the execution of not only the perpetrators but their families as well, for his wrath, which in earlier times had been subject to moderation, had become implacable.

With these difficulties overcome and the threats to his rule receding, Herod, ever active, set about making improvements throughout his realm. It was at this time that he built the fortress called Herodium, mentioned in an earlier book of this history, to commemorate his victory over the partisans of Antigonus as he fled Jerusalem at the onslaught of the Parthians. He built additional fortifications in Galilee and Perea, for he was forever thinking of ways to enhance his own security. In the west he rebuilt the city of Samaria, in the region of the same name, which had been awarded to him by Augustus after the downfall of Cleopatra. This city he fortified with a wall of great strength, and within it he built a grand temple dedicated to Augustus, and in addition changed the name of the city to Sebaste, which translates as Augustus in the Greek. This was one of the many pagan temples Herod built in the parts of his kingdom that were not Jewish, and these created no little unease among the pious Jews, though Herod tried to make excuse for himself, and insisted they were built only to maintain the favor of Augustus.

After his success at Sebaste, Herod undertook an even more ambitious project, which was to make a great seaport from a run-down city near the sea. He rebuilt the city all of white stone, and adorned it with a theater and an amphitheater and palaces for the aristocracy, as well as a sophisticated sewerage system that carried all runoff to the sea. But most remarkable was his vision for a haven built up from the sea itself. This was achieved, at enormous expense, by lowering huge blocks of stone imported from Italy into water twenty fathoms deep. Over ten years a wall more than one hundred twenty cubits wide emerged from the sea, and on the top of this were built towers and arches, as well as docks for ships and lodging for mariners. At its completion this haven was the largest of its kind in the world, exceeding even that of Athens, and at its entrance was a temple of polished stone that housed a colossal statue of Augustus. The city itself was renamed Caesarea, in honor of Augustus.

These cities were but two of the extensive building efforts Herod undertook throughout Judea. In all these new places, and throughout the rest of his realm as well, Herod instituted an extensive network of spies, because people everywhere murmured against him, uneasy at the rapid pace of his innovation and resentful of the heavy taxes that paid for it. Herod commanded them to keep their minds on their work, not permitting the citizens to meet, to eat together, or even to walk together. There were spies everywhere, watching at all times both in the cities and on the roads, and any who were suspected of conspiracy were taken, either secretly or openly, to the desert fortress Hyrcania, and there put to death. From time to time Herod himself took part in these efforts, going out in the night disguised as a private citizen and attempting to trap conspirators in their talk. He also required all the multitude to swear an oath of loyalty to him, and those that resisted were done away with, although Herod made several exceptions, most notably for the Pharisees, because their leader Shemaiah had long ago spoken on Herod's behalf in his trial before the Sanhedrin.

In the midst of all this prosperity there occurred only one interruption, when a severe drought, stretching over two years, struck Judea and the surrounding region. The resulting famine and pestilence were severe. Throughout the land people resorted to eating all manner of things that were not typically eaten, down to the roots of the grass, and the violent distemper that followed caused the deaths of many. The king himself was in distress, for the bulk of his revenue came from taxes on the harvest and his monumental building projects had emptied his treasury. However, he resolved to assist his people, so he cut up all the fine furniture in his palace and melted down the gold and silver it was made of, sparing not even those items that were the most elaborately crafted. The resulting funds he sent to his friend Petronius, prefect of Egypt, where the famine was not so severe, and thus procured a great quantity of grain. Herod instituted a careful system of distribution to prevent hoarding, even going so far as to instruct the bakers to provide bread to those who were too old or infirm to make their own. He also provided fabrics and clothing for the winter, because all the sheep and goats had been consumed in the famine. In all these things he took care to make known to the people that he was responsible for this relief, and thereby won over many who had hated him, and when prosperity was restored he went still further, cutting taxes by one-third.

These judicious policies cleared the way for Herod's most daring project of all, the rebuilding of the Temple in Jerusalem. The original Temple had been built by Solomon nearly nine hundred years earlier and then rebuilt by Nehemiah, in a smaller configuration, after the Babylonians sacked Jerusalem. Herod's stated goal was to rebuild Nehemiah's temple back to Solomon's original dimensions, but it was really much more than this. Herod intended to make the reconfigured Temple a showpiece for Jerusalem, a monument to match the magnificence of anything in Alexandria or Rome. This rekindled the suspicions of the citizens, who feared that despite his generosity during the famine, he would pull down the existing structure and then be unwilling or unable to complete the new one. But the king promised that he would not begin work on the structure until he had assembled all the necessary building materials, and he made good on his word. For the Temple itself he imported enormous white stones, twenty-five cubits in length, twelve wide, and eight tall, and despite the enormity of the work the structure was completed in eighteen months. This was all the more remarkable because the work was completed by priests who had been recently trained as masons and carpenters, since only priests were allowed to enter the Temple. After this the Temple grounds were greatly enlarged by building up the south slope of the Temple Mount with a vast amount of rock fused together with molten lead and rods of iron. This allowed for the creation of a vast new plaza, the Court of the Gentiles. The majestic porticoes that bounded the complex on each side, thirty-six cubits tall, required another eight years. The work has continued to this day, as Herod continues to supply funds for the continual embellishment of this remarkable structure.

In an effort to enhance his reputation throughout the Roman world, Herod also supplied funds for other projects far beyond the borders of his own kingdom. He built gymnasia in Tripoli and Damascus, theaters in Sidon and Damascus, aqueducts in Laodicea, and enormous fountains in Ascalon, plus temples to the pagan gods of Rome in several places. His donations throughout Syria and Greece are too numerous to mention. Upon finding out that the Greek Olympic games were to be cancelled for lack of funds, he sponsored lavish prizes—not only for the winners, but for second-place and third-place finishers as well—and even went so far as to compete himself in some of the military events.

During this time Herod's household was remarkably tranquil.

The two young princes who lived in the palace, his sons by Miriam, were sent away to Rome to be introduced to Augustus and educated in the sciences. In addition, Herod took an interest in a young woman of Jerusalem, noted for her beauty, who was also named Miriam, the same as his former queen. The family of this young beauty, though of the priestly line, was too inferior to be allied to him, so he remedied that problem by making her father high priest, after abruptly deposing the high priest who held office at that time. In this way Herod took to wife a second woman named Miriam, who was nearly as beautiful as the first, though in no way a match for her in purity of character or greatness of soul.

Joanna looked up, surprised. She had come to the end of the scroll. Aduel supplied the concluding punctuation:

"And thus ends Book the Thirteenth."

"Really?" Joanna was annoyed. "That's all?"

Aduel was puzzled.

"Did you think there should be more?" he asked.

"Well, yes," Joanna complained. "The whole book is nothing but praise for Herod. He could have written it himself."

"I tried to tell things the way they actually happened," Aduel said patiently. "Herod was capable of doing great things when he didn't feel threatened."

"And horrible things when he did."

"Yes. And don't worry, there will be more of those in the books that remain. By the time we finish your disgust for Herod will be in full bloom again."

"Are there many more books to read?"

"Only two."

"When can we read them?"

Aduel's response was interrupted by a soft knock at the door. He got up eagerly to answer it. Outside was a stranger in a heavy hooded cloak. Despite the bright morning sun his face was hidden in shadow.

"The Lord detests the way of the wicked," the stranger said.

"But He loves those who approve righteousness," Aduel replied.

The hooded stranger drew a sealed message from his sleeve and handed it to Aduel. Without another word Aduel closed the door. Joanna watched in wonder as he unsealed the papyrus and scanned it quickly.

"Who was that?" she demanded, disconcerted at the worried look on her uncle's face.

"A messenger," Aduel muttered distractedly.

"Did you know him?"

"No."

"But what did you say to him?"

"He quoted me a bit of a proverb," Aduel explained, still not looking up. "I gave him the appropriate response."

"That's why you wanted to wait here."

"Yes. Without it, he would not have given me this letter. It's a common precaution among scribes."

"Did he bring the letter from Nicolaus?"

"Yes," Aduel said. "Unfortunately it does not include the letters of introduction, nor the safe passage."

"Why not?"

"I will read to you what it says," Aduel said. "'Friend:'"

"Friend!" Joanna said hotly. "He does nothing of what he promised and yet he calls you friend?"

"He has taken the additional precaution not to address me by name," Aduel explained. "In case the letter should miscarry."

"Hmph!"

Aduel resumed reading:

"'Friend:

"'I have not yet had the opportunity to compose the letters of introduction or to obtain a safe passage for you and your household. There is no privacy in this wretched place, and all those who are here have nothing to do but watch each other for any sign of treachery, real or imagined, while the king still lives. Trustworthy messengers are scarce and I dare not send anything to you by royal courier.

"'The baths here at Callirrhoe have done nothing to improve the king's health. The physicians recommended that his whole body be bathed in a vat of warm oil, but when he was lowered into it his eyes failed him and he came and went as if dying. However, such a tumult was made by his servants that he revived at the sound of their voices.

"'I believe that he has now given up hope of recovery, for he has distributed fifty days' wages to each of the two thousand soldiers in his personal guard, with a great deal more given to their commanders and his friends. Tomorrow we return to the winter palace at Jericho, where I am likely to have the opportunity to provide you with the letters I have promised. Make preparations now.'"

"Make preparations!" Aduel snorted. "What does he think I'll be taking to Alexandria? All the baubles in the royal treasury? Two changes of clothing and some bread for the journey, that's all I have to take. And my scrolls, of course. I'll part with all of it before I'll part with those."

He noticed the girl's troubled look.

"And you, child, have even less," he grumbled

apologetically. "All your worldly possessions could fit into a pauper's bundle. Well, I'd never have been able to provide you a life of luxury, and I suppose it's for the best. You'd be leaving it all behind."

"You really think we're going, then," Joanna said quietly.

"Nicolaus is not prone to panic," Aduel reflected. "I hope to remain, but his warnings disturb me. I suppose it can't hurt to be ready."

"I would like to write to the scribe," Joanna blurted.

"Oh! The scribe." Aduel looked at her keenly. "I had forgotten about the scribe. Certainly you may write to him. What will you say?"

"I don't know yet," Joanna said. "Do you have the other message I wrote to him?"

"Yes, here." Aduel fished the little square of papyrus, still sealed, out of a pocket in his sleeve. "Why not send this? It would save time. I can deliver it to him now if you like."

"No. I wish to write another."

"Very well," Aduel said, handing her the first note. "But don't take too long. If Nicolaus's fears are realized..."

He shook his head ominously.

"Don't take too long."

Chapter 21

Determined that her revised message to the scribe would match the simple brilliance of the original, Joanna worked late into the evening and all the next morning at her uncle's writing table, re-composing and re-copying. By midday she dared delay no longer. Selecting her preferred version from the many scraps of papyrus that littered the table, she folded it carefully—then unfolded it to read it a final time. In content it was very much like the previous version, and its purpose would be the same: To convey as much of her essence as could be expressed in a few veiled words. But Anna's death and the uncertainty that now hung heavy over all Jerusalem had dampened the bright, hopeful tone of the original:

> *Most Excellent Hilkiah,*
>
> *As before, I write to convey my lifelong gratitude for the balm, which worked wonderfully to heal my injury and soothe my soul.*
>
> *Your care for Anna in her final hours and afterward was fitting repayment for her great compassion and courage in a time of need. I pray that some day I will be able to do as much.*

She folded it a final time and sealed it with a dab of wax—not plain wax this time, but a bit of her uncle's more expensive and elegant red. Upstairs she found Aduel not in his usual place before the hearth, but peering expectantly through the window lattice.

"Uncle?"

"Yes, child," Aduel said distractedly.

"I have completed my message to the scribe."

"Ah, your message to the scribe," Aduel said. "I'll have Irijah deliver it."

He stepped away from the window and called for Irijah.

"On second thought, why not summon the scribe here?" he asked. "Perhaps he could read what you have written and make some immediate reply. Too much back and forth could lead to delay."

The girl's heart skipped a beat as she nodded her agreement. She did not trust Irijah; it would be much better to see the message delivered herself. It might be an awkward encounter, but she would have an answer, or at least an indication, before the day was out.

Irijah entered from the courtyard. After receiving his instructions he departed without comment. Aduel returned to the window, then seemed to realize the futility of it.

"No sense standing here staring stupidly all day," he grumbled. "That won't accomplish anything, will it?"

Joanna smiled weakly, trying to think of something that

would soothe his anxiety.

"We could read," she said diffidently.

"I thought you might say that," Aduel smiled. From a pocket in his sleeve he produced a scroll. Although the weather had become too warm now to require a crackling fire in the hearth, the two of them settled into their accustomed places before the slow-burning embers, and Joanna began to read.

"Herod: A Secret History, by Aduel of Sepphoris. Book the Fourteenth."

One of the most notable among Herod's many construction projects was the new palace he built for himself on the western edge of Jerusalem. The opulence of this place can scarcely be described. Within its walls were groves of trees with long pathways for walking, as well as numerous courtyards, all lush and green, that were populated with bubbling fountains in the form of brazen statues. Once inside, an awestruck visitor would hardly believe the number and size of the rooms. There were banqueting halls that could feast more than one hundred guests at a time, and every chamber was adorned with precious stones and vessels of silver and gold. It was so large that it included several suites of royal apartments for the king's family members, but it was not large enough to diffuse the envy and hatred that ran between them.

The trouble began soon after Herod sailed to Rome and returned with the two princes, who had been sent there about ten years earlier. The young men, now about twenty years of age and of royal bearing, quickly became favorites of the multitude, for as the sons of the slain Queen Miriam and the great-grandsons of Hyrcanus they were the last living link to the dynasty that had ruled Judea for more than a century. Salome and those who had supported her in the false accusations against Miriam deduced that they would be punished for their wickedness when the young men rose to power, and immediately a campaign of calumny began. But it was cleverly done, for Salome and her party did not take their lies directly to Herod but instead spread them about quietly, so that after a time they carried to Herod without any record of their origin.

Disturbed by these reports, Herod soon left off the kindness he had shown the two youths, but he did arrange a suitable marriage for each of them. The elder, Alexander, was wed to Glaphyra, a princess of Cappadocia whose father Archelaus was a particular friend of Herod's. The younger, Aristobulus, was married to Bernice, the daughter of Salome. By this latter union Herod hoped to patch up the destructive rivalry between the two branches of his family, although it turned out to have the opposite effect. Salome worked actively to snuff out Herod's hopes of reconciliation, continuing to spread lies of the young men's murderous designs against their father. The young men, for their part, were sadly unschooled in matters of intrigue, and openly accused Salome and her allies for the injustice done to their mother, thinking it only honorable to declare their minds in a deliberate manner. The claims and accusations of both sides became widely known throughout Jerusalem, but Salome's subtle methods were far more effective, and most believed the narrative that claimed the two princes were plotting against their father.

To protect himself against these alleged plots, Herod introduced into his court a rival to the two princes: Antipater, the son of his first wife Doris. These two were officially recognized as Herod's first wife and first son, but they had been put out of the palace when Herod married Queen Miriam. Named for Herod's father, the young Antipater had all the shrewdness and self-interest of his illustrious namesake, but none of his nobler qualities. A dark-eyed, shifty sort of fellow, he perceived that his changed circumstances might eventually lead to the throne, and soon surpassed Salome in his cultivation of rumor and false information. He began to conduct himself as the equal of the two princes, despite their obvious pre-eminence both in birth and popularity, and when they complained of it, Antipater made certain that their reproaches were carried back to the king. Over time these tactics had their desired effect, as Herod gradually elevated Antipater higher and higher in favor among the court, finally sending him to Rome to be introduced to Augustus as the presumptive heir to the throne.

While in Rome Antipater continued his campaign of agitation, sending to Herod report after report that he hoped might grieve Herod against the princes. Upon receiving one of these, the most recent in a sequence that had continued over a period of several months, Herod shoved it back at the royal secretary, who was waiting for his dictated response.

"That does it," Herod growled. "We're going to Rome."

"Yes, Majesty." The royal secretary, who was not entirely surprised at this turn of events, bowed his acknowledgement. "Will there be any response to Antipater?"

"Not now," snapped Herod. "Tell your friend Nicolaus to prepare for the journey. Yourself as well. Plus Achiabus, Olympus, the others of my ministers whose advice I trust."

The royal secretary bowed again.

"Corinthus!" Herod barked. "Inform Alexander and Aristobulus that they will sail with me to Rome. If they complain or resist in any way, put them in chains. Go! We leave on the morrow."

The caravan departed the next morning for Caesarea, the beautiful city Herod had recently rebuilt on the coast of the Mediterranean. The two princes, not entirely sure of Herod's intentions, came along peaceably under a sort of mobile house arrest, though Herod made it plain that he would have no dealings with them. The entire journey, which took about a month, was tense and awkward—though most agreed that it was a relief from the constant strife in the palace.

Shortly after their arrival in Italy, a hearing was convened for Herod to present his case before Augustus. Appearing before the assembled courts of Judea and Rome, the king launched into a furious screed: that his sons were enemies to him, that they would take away his life to obtain his kingdom, and that they must be requited for their actions—preferably by the cruelest punishments that were ever known to mankind.

All eyes turned toward the youths, who were in tears, and uncertain how to respond. To refute their father forcefully would seem indecent, and only inflame him further. But Herod's passion was spent, and all the rest of the onlookers, including Augustus, seemed aware that the two princes were in no way guilty of the accusations that their father had laid out.

Finally Alexander, the elder of the two, composed himself and spoke:

"O Father, the benevolence you have shown us is evident, even in this grave judicial procedure, for it was in your power, both as a king and as a father, to punish the guilty. However, by bringing us to Rome, and making Augustus himself a witness to what is done, you indicate that you mean to save us.

"For you are well aware that all young men have ambition, and a lust for power, and are therefore subject to suspicion. But suspicion alone is not enough to prove an intent to murder. Let any man say whether we have actually attempted any such thing, and say it now! Can anyone prove that a poison has been prepared, or that there is a conspiracy in place, or a corruption of servants, or letters written against you? Indeed there are none of these things, except those manufactured by rumor.

"If indeed we murdered you, could we expect to obtain your kingdom? Our pious nation would not allow it, nor would Augustus himself. A royal family that is at variance with itself is a terrible thing, so let it be known that life is not so desirable to us that we should plead for it if it should tend to the harm of our father."

When Alexander had spoken, Augustus gazed with furrowed brow at Herod, who was a little confounded. All in attendance were anxious for the young men, since Alexander had made their defense with dexterity and prudence. Having no real evidence, Herod seemed to be casting about for some excuse for making the accusation, but he could think of nothing to say. After a silence, Augustus spoke:

"I believe, King Herod, that these young men are entirely innocent of the crimes of which they are accused."

There was audible relief throughout the chamber. But Augustus, demonstrating that it was not by accident that he had managed to take and hold power in Rome's far-flung dominions, continued:

"However, they are to blame," he said, "for failing to demean themselves before you so as to prevent the suspicions that have been spread about them. Now, I exhort you, Herod, to lay these suspicions aside, and be reconciled to your sons, and not give any credit to future reports about them. Repentance on all sides will heal these breaches that have arisen between you, and will improve your good will toward one another."

He beckoned to the young men, who crossed the room and fell down before their father. He raised them up, embracing each one distinctly, and all three of them were in tears, as was everyone else in the chamber, including Augustus himself. After this Augustus gave Herod permission to divide his kingdom as he liked upon his death.

"I will do it this moment!" Herod exclaimed. "Each of my three sons here shall have his part."

"No," said Augustus, who perceived that such an arrangement would precipitate a civil war in Judea. "I did not give you leave to deprive yourself of the power over your kingdom, or your sons, while you are still alive. Only in death may you appoint a successor, or divide your kingdom among many."

With this conclusion they all went away together, including Antipater, who pretended to rejoice at the reconciliation. Before leaving for Judea Herod honored Augustus with a gift of three hundred talents of gold, and Augustus reciprocated by giving Herod control over Rome's copper mines on the island of Cyprus, including half the revenue.

But the revenue from the copper mines would be realized only over time, and when Herod returned to Jerusalem he found his treasury bare. To remedy this, he embarked upon a scheme that he had considered for some time, but had never had the courage to attempt. At the urging of Ptolemy, his minister of finance, Herod decided to raid the sepulcher of King David. In this structure, an extensive monument that included several chambers hewn deep into the rock of the Lower City, it was rumored that great treasure had lain untouched for nearly a thousand years.

The mission was planned with the utmost secrecy, and Herod's royal secretary knew nothing of it until Nicolaus of Damascus appeared in his office and shut the door.

"I have just come from the king," he said hesitantly. He seemed unsure how to proceed.

"Yes?" the royal secretary prompted.

"An expedition has been planned," Nicolaus went on. "To remove the treasure from David's sepulcher."

"David's sepulcher!" the royal secretary exclaimed. "Don't tell me Herod is actually going through with it! The people will revolt."

"That's why it will be done in the dead of night," Nicolaus said distastefully. "We embark from the palace in the middle of the third watch."

"We! What do you mean, 'we'?" the royal secretary demanded. "Surely you're not involved in this."

"Unfortunately, I am," Nicolaus said mournfully. "I tried to convince the king what a terrible idea it is, how dreadfully wicked. But he became so much annoyed that he appointed me to accompany them. At least it will be of some historical interest."

"But Nicolaus, consider the meaning of this! You'll be a common grave robber!"

"If the king commands it, I will be a common grave robber," Nicolaus said defensively. "As will you."

"Not I!" the royal secretary declared. "I have no part in this."

"But you do," Nicolaus said. "The king wants a scribe to record the event and make an inventory of everything he finds. A scribe with discretion. He sent me to enlist you."

"No." The royal secretary shook his head. "I will not do it."

"But the king has commanded it!" Nicolaus argued. "You can't refuse an order from the king!"

"I never have, up to now. But I will not set one foot in David's sepulcher."

"But what should I tell Herod?"

"Tell him what you like," the royal secretary said, "but I will not do it."

That night the royal secretary lay awake in his chamber in the palace, staring into the darkness as the minutes melted slowly away. David's sepulcher was within the city walls, not far from his quarters in the palace. There was still time to respond to Herod's summons, but every fiber of his being rebelled against it. He tried to meditate on the example of Daniel, who had defied the King of Persia with quiet confidence, but the conviction of that great prophet eluded him.

Suddenly there was a soft knock at the door. It swung open a crack, and the torchlight from the corridor revealed Nicolaus's tall, austere figure.

"Come to fetch me, have you?" The royal secretary swung his feet onto the cold stone floor and lit a candle. "Well, you can save your breath. I haven't changed my mind. I won't go."

"We've already gone," Nicolaus whispered. "It's almost morning."

He stepped into the room and closed the door. The royal secretary realized that he had fallen into a deep, dreamless sleep, and had awoken with that elusive peace that he had always attributed to Daniel.

"So!" The royal secretary could not resist the urge to taunt Nicolaus a little. "You've returned from the land of the dead."

"Yes." Nicolaus's voice trembled. Even in the light of the single candle the philosopher's face seemed unnaturally pale.

"Well?" the royal secretary prompted. "What of David's treasure? How much did you get?"

"Nothing," Nicolaus sighed. "No money, at least. There was not a talent to be found. But there were many precious goods, as well as furniture of gold. Herod's men took it all away."

"At least he has something to show for it."

"Yes, but he wanted more," Nicolaus said. "He sent six of his soldiers deeper into the sepulcher, to conduct a more diligent search, even as far as the burial crypts of David and Solomon."

"And what came of that?"

"Something horrible," Nicolaus moaned. "We waited only a short time, and then a great cry erupted from deep in the sepulcher.

Moments later, four of the soldiers came running for their lives. They said that a great fire had burst out upon the two men at the front and consumed them."

"Really!" The royal secretary was intrigued. "What did Herod say to that?"

"Herod said nothing. He turned and ran as fast as he could, out of the sepulcher and up the steps to the streets of the city. I've never seen him so frightened."

"I've never seen Herod frightened at all," the royal secretary commented. "But what did he do with the things that had been removed? Did he put them back?"

"No. The soldiers took them to the palace. Much against their own inclinations, I think."

"No doubt," the royal secretary smiled. "It's a pity there was no one there to take an exact inventory."

"But there was," Nicolaus said darkly.

"Who?"

"Herod called for Diophantus, your chief scribe, to act in your place."

"Ah! An evil man for an evil errand."

"Yes, but I fear it was for more than a single errand," Nicolaus replied. "Diophantus has been appointed royal secretary in your place."

"What!"

"I tried to make excuse for you," Nicolaus apologized. "I told Herod you were indisposed, but he did not take it well. He said that you were standing in judgment of him."

"Perhaps I was." The former secretary took a moment to digest this. "And I now have an appointment with the executioner, I suppose."

"No," Nicolaus replied. "Herod said that you would remain in his service as a common scribe, under the authority of Diophantus. He knows that a man like that will lord it over you and make your life as intolerable as he can. It's his way of punishing you, though I think he still has regard for you."

"Possibly," the former secretary shrugged. He began to rummage among the papyri and parchments on his writing table. "I suppose I'll be moving to simpler quarters."

"The sooner the better," Nicolaus said. "That's why I have come to you at this wretched hour. It will be one less indignity you'll have to endure."

"Nicolaus," the former secretary said gently, "after so many years in Herod's service, indignity is nothing new to me."

"Yes, but now Diophantus claims the exalted position you have enjoyed for so long," Nicolaus said reproachfully. "You are under his supervision now. You are now nothing but a scribe who must do his bidding. You will have no direct access to the king, no opportunity to bend his ear should the need arise. Do you not see the folly of it?"

"I see it completely," the former secretary said. "Yet I also see the shame of having a hand in the desecration of a tomb, especially the tomb of Israel's greatest king. Let Diophantus make sport of me. Let him report me to Herod for treason, that I may be condemned to torture and death. It would be better than to live a single day with such regret."

"Oh, a fig for shame and regret!" Nicolaus exclaimed. "Such things are easily overcome. Instead, you have bargained away something for nothing. You did not prevent the desecration of the tomb. You could not, and you knew it. You have accomplished nothing with this act of rebellion!"

"You are a learned philosopher, Nicolaus," the former secretary said. "But life is more than a series of transactions. Perhaps some day you will come to believe that."

He gathered his few possessions and made his way into the deserted corridor. Nicolaus hurried after him.

"You'll remain in the palace, won't you?" the philosopher asked.

"Who knows?" the former secretary shrugged. "We'll see what other unsavory tasks Herod has in store for me."

"We can hope for leniency," Nicolaus said, "and that you will one day be restored to your position. But I daresay we will function in different spheres from now on."

"Yes, your star has risen to the top of Herod's firmament, while mine has come crashing to the Earth."

"I hope I may still call you friend," Nicolaus said.

"You may if you see any benefit to it," the former secretary replied. "But for your own sake, you may want to do it quietly. Goodbye, Nicolaus."

"And thus concludes Book the Fourteenth," Joanna said quietly. She gazed at her uncle as she slowly rolled up the scroll, but Aduel said nothing.

"So that was the way it ended," she remarked.

"Not exactly," Aduel said. "My service to Herod continued for another five years, in the capacity of a common scribe, as Nicolaus indicated."

"But you were never again the royal secretary."

"Correct."

"Do you think Nicolaus really tried to help you?"

"I have no doubt of it," Aduel said. "At that point I still considered him a friend."

"But you didn't later."

"No."

"What about now?"

"I don't know what to think now," Aduel sighed.

"Then obviously something happened."

"Yes."

"Can you tell me?"

"That tale is told in detail in the final book of my history," Aduel smiled.

"Can we read it now?"

Before Aduel could answer there was a knock at the door. Aduel rose to open it.

The girl's heart leaped. It was Hilkiah, the young scribe. In her excitement she rose from her chair and took a step forward. But before Aduel could greet him, the young man cut him off.

"I cannot enter," he said solemnly.

"You cannot enter!" Aduel was surprised. "Why not? Are you ill?"

"No, but I am unclean."

"Unclean!" exclaimed Aduel. "Oh, because of Anna. Because you have been in the presence of the dead, perhaps even touched the corpse, or the tomb."

"Yes, all of those."

"Well, never mind that," Aduel cajoled. "In many circles such things are rarely observed. In the palace, for example. A little dip in the mikveh, and all is well. So come in, please, come in."

"No," the scribe insisted. "It would defile the house, and all that are in it."

He glanced at Joanna.

"Very well," Aduel said. "I have summoned you here because we have a message for you. Except that I myself have no idea what it says. It is from the maiden. It replaces a message she wished to give you earlier, the day that Anna died. She did not think it appropriate to deliver it then."

A brief look of surprise flitted across the scribe's impassive face. Aduel held out Joanna's message, but the scribe made no move to take it.

"Of course," Aduel said. "Unclean."

He stooped to place the note on the rough stones of the courtyard. The scribe picked it up.

"My thanks for your summons," the scribe said. "In four more days I will be cleansed. After that I will respond."

Aduel took a deep breath.

"I hope and pray that we will be here to receive your response," he said. "But in the coming days we may be required to leave Jerusalem for a time."

"A wise precaution for one of the king's partisans," the young man nodded.

"Ah, you know about that, do you?" Aduel said irritably.

"All the scribes know of it, sir. Your service to the king and the way that it ended is legendary among us."

"Hmph!" Aduel scoffed. "If you know the way that it ended then you should know that I do not consider myself one of the king's partisans."

"My apologies," the scribe said. "My words were poorly chosen. I beg your forgiveness."

"Yes, yes, of course," Aduel replied brusquely. "Well. Until we meet again."

Joanna watched intently as two men bowed solemnly to one another. The scribe's countenance was impassive, as always, but he was fingering her note nervously, turning it over and over again, the way she had when she had received his. Then, unexpectedly, he turned to her and bowed deeply.

Their eyes met, without embarrassment, and she bowed slightly in return, betraying no emotion except her own surprise. Then he was gone.

Aduel shook his head as he bolted the door. Joanna was suddenly crestfallen.

"Couldn't he even come in for one minute?" she lamented. "Could he not even set foot in the house?"

"Everything he said was in strict accordance with the Law," Aduel answered. "He will be sprinkled with the water of purification on the third day, today, and then again on the seventh. Then he will be clean again and his life will resume as it should."

"We had such customs in Jericho," the girl groaned. "But they were never so strictly enforced."

"Nor are they strictly enforced here anymore," Aduel replied. "Unless you happen to be dealing with a scribe or a Pharisee."

He placed his hands on the girl's shoulders.

"Are you sure that you want to bind yourself to such rigidity?" he asked.

"How do you know that I want to bind myself?" Joanna was suddenly suspicious that her uncle had examined the drafts of the message she had left on his writing table overnight. "Did you read my note to the scribe?"

"No," Aduel said. "I read your eyes."

"Uncle!" Joanna blushed.

"Be it as you wish, then," Aduel smiled.

He leaned to kiss her forehead.

"Scribes!" he sighed. "If only their piety were directed toward more worthy things!"

Chapter 22

Aduel's household passed the night in a state of uneasiness, with Aduel himself hoping that some new communication from Nicolaus would arrive any moment, and Joanna hoping that it would not—at least until the scribe's four remaining days of ritual purification had been completed. All Jerusalem waited with them, with fascination and dread, for word from Jericho. There was no shortage of news, which surged in quiet ripples from shop to shop and house to house. The fact that almost all of it was false only quickened its spread. In Aduel's house it was Irijah who provided a steady stream of supposition and rumor. The old manservant continued to perform his daily chores around the city, fetching water and wood and other daily essentials, but he seemed to spend most of his time gossiping in the marketplace. What information he brought back was of little practical use, but it was so morbidly compelling that he felt no need to season it with his customary gloomy predictions.

Joanna shivered as she descended the ladder from her morning chores on the roof. The sun was shining and the spring air was warm, but still she found herself chafing her arms to drive away the chill. A dark foreboding hung over the city; she could feel it even though she had not ventured beyond her uncle's courtyard for days. Herod's death had been rumored for weeks, even months, and these reports had been taken up as truth by the credulous—with disastrous results. But now the feeling was different. A sense of inevitability loomed.

Yet still there was nothing official.

Back inside Aduel was in the same place she had left him twenty minutes earlier—beside the window, peering through the lattice at an angle, trying to get a better view of the street.

"Uncle?"

"Yes, child."

"When the scribe was here, yesterday…"

Joanna paused, to see if her uncle was paying attention.

"Yes?"

"He spoke of your service to the king, and the way that it ended. What did he mean?"

"As to my service to the king, you need no explanation," Aduel said. "At this point you know more about that than anyone, except possibly Herod himself. As to the way it ended, well, it ended rather abruptly. And rather perilously, I might add. That sequence of events is described in the fifteenth and final book of my history. I doubt we'll have time to read it before we bundle it off to Egypt."

"Maybe we could read it now," Joanna suggested.

"I'm too anxious to read now. I'd be stumbling over every third word."

"I could read," Joanna said.

"No, no, it's not the right time," Aduel fretted, waving away the suggestion. But just as quickly he changed his mind. "Oh, why not? It will help us to get through this excruciating wait. Go fetch the fifteenth book, child. It won't be in the usual place, but you'll find it."

At the bottom of the cellar stairway Joanna stopped short. Aduel's secret room had scarcely changed—there was very little to change—but the element that defined it was different. The shelves above the writing table, which had always held his scrolls, were empty. Instead there was a sturdy wicker basket on the writing table. She opened it and carefully unfolded the leather sheet that lined it. The precious scrolls were tucked inside, protected from the elements. She gazed at them longingly. Each of them seemed to promise a new revelation; each called out to her, demanding her careful consideration. But there was no time for that now; the letters from Nicolaus would arrive soon. She dug to the bottom of the basket until she came to the books of her uncle's secret history, innocently mingled with the Scriptures. She found Book the Fifteenth and packed the other scrolls back in the basket, feeling a little breathless.

Upstairs she wordlessly took her seat before the hearth. Unrolling the scroll, she began to read it silently. Unable to resist the temptation of hearing his work recited, Aduel grudgingly wandered over from the window and sat down. Joanna returned to the beginning of the scroll and began to read aloud.

"Herod: A Secret History, by Aduel of Sepphoris. Book the Fifteenth."

Despite their emotional reconciliation in Rome, Herod's relationship with the two princes deteriorated quickly once back in Jerusalem. Antipater and Salome, working both independently and in concert, resumed their campaign against the princes. Salome took advantage of her position of mother-in-law to Aristobulus, the younger of the princes, quietly undermining the marriage and persuading her daughter to spy on her husband, and to report things that he and his brother said in private. Antipater worked in other ways, continuing to spread subtle accusations. When these worked their way back to Herod, Antipater would pretend to intervene on behalf of his half-brothers.

It was not long before one of the subtle lies spread by Antipater found its way back to its intended target. The king was told, by an unknown informant, that his three favorite servants—his cupbearer, his steward, and the master of the bedchamber—had been corrupted by Alexander with great sums of money. When questioned, these men said they knew of no mischief afoot against Herod, but the king was not convinced. He gave them over to the torturers—who were under the supervision of Antipater. Still they gave no information about any sort of plot, but when they were in utmost agony, with howls and shrieks that could be heard throughout the palace, Antipater ordered the racks to be stretched further, and one of the victims began to babble. He said that Alexander hated his father, and that he was now ready to take the kingdom, because Herod would not live much longer, and even went so far to dye his hair black to conceal his advanced age.

This embarrassing revelation filled Herod with anger and fear, and his suspicion and hatred alighted on those closest to him, supposing that they had the greatest power to hurt him. He turned his network of spies inward, and a reign of terror began within the palace. If anyone was accused on the slightest evidence, or no evidence at all, Herod thought himself safer if they were destroyed, and all at random seemed doomed to destruction. It came to such a pass that his servants fell to accusing one another, imagining that he who first accused another was more likely to save himself. Yet those who succeeded with this strategy were hated, and were accused themselves, and many who used it to settle private scores later found themselves facing the same fate as their victims.

As the palace sank deeper into chaos great numbers were savagely tortured and killed. Among the accused were Jucundus and Tyrannus, masters of the horse who had once been Herod's most trusted bodyguards. These men had become friends with Alexander and now they were arrested and tortured. After enduring it for a great length of time they said that Alexander wanted them to kill Herod while he was hunting wild beasts and claim that he had fallen from his horse and run himself through with his own spear. Others gave similarly bizarre testimony. One of the youngest to be tortured, to save himself, cried out that Alexander had conceived a plan of rebellion with the help of the King of Parthia, and that he had prepared a poisonous potion.

To this accusation Herod gave credit, and put Alexander in prison, but though he busied himself with a search for the potion he found none. Just as the matter seemed to have come to a standstill, it was revived by none other than the accused himself. From prison, Alexander sent four letters to Herod, which were read aloud before the court at Herod's command. In them, Alexander confessed to plotting against his father, and said there was no need to torture anyone else, and that all in the court agreed that they should do away with Herod, so that they could get clear of the continual fear they were in. He particularly named Pheroras as his chief ally in the plot, and implicated Ptolemy, the minister of finance, as well. In a separate letter the prince said that several times Salome had come to him by night in his imprisonment, and forced herself upon him whether he would have her or not, an accusation so lurid that many in the court had trouble stifling their laughter.

But after making a fool of Herod in front of everyone Alexander remained in prison, and the palace was continually filled with terror and trouble. Even the most intimate friends fell to attacking each other, with no defense or refutation allowed to anyone, and night and day the cries of the doomed echoed through the corridors as the torturers went about their sinister work in the dungeon. Herod's own life was entirely disturbed, for he trusted no one, and began to imagine that Alexander stood near him with sword in hand, ready to slay him. His mind was intent upon this vision night and day, and he revolved it over and over, completely ignoring the affairs of the kingdom in the throes of this distraction.

There then arrived from Cappadocia an ambassador who wished to look into the charges against Alexander. In a miserable spectacle, Alexander was interrogated and confessed that he and his wife Glaphyra had planned to flee to Cappadocia at the first opportunity, to escape Herod's wrath. But he insisted that they had no evil designs against the king, and Glaphyra confirmed it. Although this seemed only a mild sort of disobedience, Herod took it as convincing evidence against the princes, and wrote a letter to Augustus, accusing them of conspiracy. When he received it, Augustus washed his hands of the matter, stating that Herod would now have complete authority to punish the two princes however he saw fit, for he had grown weary of controversies involving Herod, especially in the matter of his sons. But he further advised that Herod should convene a tribunal in the Roman city of Beirut, which Augustus himself had founded, and that he should choose one hundred fifty jurors to counsel him on the fate of the princes.

This Herod did, but like most of the trials he convened the outcome was predetermined. Herod presented his case in a ranting and disordered fashion, and no rebuttals or defense were permitted. Unlike the trial conducted before Augustus, the two princes were not allowed to speak—or even to be present. As for the accusation that they had plotted against him, Herod made almost no mention—having very little evidence—but made great ado over the many insults he believed he had received from them, saying that these were a heavier punishment than death itself. When no one contradicted him, he begged them to pity him, as if he himself had been accused. After this pathetic display the jurors perceived that there was no room for equity or reconciliation, and to please Herod they voted as he wished, finding the princes guilty. Each in turn was asked to recommend a sentence, and though the most distinguished voted for the milder penalty of imprisonment, the majority voted for death.

The decision was still Herod's to make, and he took the princes to Caesarea, the magnificent city he had built along the coast. A large portion of the court went with them, and the scribe who had formerly been the royal secretary was among them. As they came to Caesarea and settled into the palace Herod had built for himself there, a terrible fear came over the city that the princes would meet the same sad fate as their mother and uncle and grandfather. No one dared speak of it, or even hear it spoken of, for fear of reprisal, and the city was unnaturally quiet.

Herod's palace at Caesarea was smaller than the one in Jerusalem and the city itself was a rocky, sandy sort of place near the sea with little vegetation. Nicolaus of Damascus had just returned from an embassy to Rome concerning Herod's latest dispute with the Arabians, but the scribe had not yet spoken to him because there was not much opportunity for clandestine conversation. But when the scribe noticed Nicolaus leaving the palace grounds alone he followed at a distance, and caught up to him at the nearby city gate.

"Ah, friend, how good to see you again." Nicolaus feigned surprise for the benefit of the guards. "I'm going to look at the new theater. It's here, just outside the city walls. Would you like to see it? I believe it was not completed when you last visited Caesarea."

"You're right, Nicolaus. I was just going to see it myself."

The open-air theater was a large masonry structure not far outside the wall. It was currently deserted, and once inside its shadowy concourse Nicolaus dispensed with pleasantries:

"Tell me of the trial in Beirut," he said in a low voice.

"It was a sham, like all such trials," the scribe whispered back. "The conclusion was reached even before it began. Herod gathered all his friends and they delivered a verdict of guilt, exactly as he wanted."

"It seems impossible that so many should have voted for death," Nicolaus said mournfully.

"Does it?" the scribe asked. "Many voted that way only to flatter Herod, because that was the outcome he favored. But others chose it out of sheer hatred toward him."

"Hatred?" Nicolaus said. "I don't understand."

"They want to see Herod bring even more opprobrium upon himself by killing his sons," the scribe explained. "They want all the world to see just how loathsome he can be."

At this Nicolaus merely grunted.

"What of you, Nicolaus?" the scribe asked. "I'm told that your efforts in Rome were successful."

"More successful than you know." Nicolaus spoke in an even lower voice. "Augustus was so pleased with my diplomacy that he resolved to hand Arabia to Herod."

He shook his head disgustedly.

"But then the letter arrived with Herod's rambling tirade about the princes," he continued. "The emperor read it and changed his mind."

"So after all these years Herod had Arabia within his grasp and then lost it?"

"Correct," Nicolaus confirmed. "With all this disgraceful wrangling he has cost himself a great addition to his domain. But I have not told him this yet. It would put him in a dreadful temper about the princes, and that is something we must avoid while there is still hope of saving them."

The scribe nodded his agreement.

"Fortunately, I was able to report to the king what his friends in Rome think of the situation," Nicolaus continued. "Almost unanimously, they believe that the princes should be imprisoned, rather than executed, so that no irrevocable mistakes will be made."

"And what did Herod say to that?"

"He became silent and fell into a great thoughtfulness."

"That's something," mused the scribe. "But—what's that noise? Who's shouting?"

"It sounds like someone inside the city," Nicolaus said.

"That's odd," the scribe replied. "Perhaps we should investigate."

They hurried back into the city. Even Nicolaus, who seldom walked any faster than a stately stride, was agitated. In the street leading to the palace a crowd had gathered, and as they pushed their way forward the scribe could see a soldier, grizzled and stout in full military garb, crying out before the multitude.

"Truth is dead!" he shouted. "Justice has been stolen from us! Lies and hatred prevail!"

By now hundreds of men had gathered, and among them there was universal approval for the old soldier. A murmur of agreement began to swell, though no one was so bold as to add publicly to his statements.

"Who is that?" Nicolaus asked one of them.

"Old Tero," the man replied. "One of the king's oldest and most loyal captains."

"Justice is trampled underfoot!" Tero cried. "The king must know of it! The king must hear! I demand to see Herod!"

The scribe looked expectantly at Nicolaus. But the philosopher shook his head, indicating that he had no intention of taking a hand in this unexpected turn of events.

It did not matter; Tero's demand to see the king had provoked a fevered discussion among the guards. A messenger was sent, and a few minutes later Tero was escorted into the palace, and on into Herod's audience chamber. Nicolaus and the scribe followed, along with a great number of the multitude, as well as spectators from other parts of the palace. Soon the chamber was filled to overflowing. Tero had already begun to address Herod and he spoke with unbounded liberty—speaking as one soldier to another, rather than as a subject to a king:

"Truly, Herod, I think you are the most miserable of men," Tero was saying, "to listen to the most wicked wretches against those who ought to be dearest to you. Where has your reason gone, and left your soul empty? Where has your genius gone, by which you have won so many victories? Would you slay these two young men, born of your queen, who are accomplished in every virtue to the highest degree? How many times have you said that Salome and Pheroras should be put to death, and yet now you believe them against your own sons? Will you leave your entire kingdom to Antipater? Don't you realize what you're doing? Perhaps you should take the temperature of your army, for the common soldiers all commiserate with the two princes, and many of the captains show their indignation openly against those closest to you who have perpetrated these lies."

He went on to identify the disaffected captains, whose names Diophantus, the evil royal secretary, hurriedly wrote down. To bring these men into the matter was a rash gambit, but at first it seemed a brilliant stroke. Herod knew each of them personally from their long years of service and seemed moved by the appeal. Nicolaus glanced at the scribe with a look that was at the same time incredulous and hopeful, and they both awaited Herod's response with bated breath.

But there was no response, because Tero, like so many old soldiers, did not know when to stop talking. His speech continued at such length, and with so much vulgarity and so many digressions, that his initial advantage was entirely squandered. The hope that had brightened Nicolaus's face slowly dimmed as Tero's diatribe went on, and Herod became by degrees uncertain, then annoyed, and then angry.

"Enough!" he cried finally. "Bind this man and put him in prison! And all that he has named as well!"

"Yes!" shouted a voice from the crowd. "Put him in prison and put him to death! He is a traitor to the king!"

The crowd gasped as a man leaped forward to stand before Herod. It was Trypho, the king's barber!

"This man tried to persuade me to cut your throat with my razor when I trimmed you, Majesty!" Trypho declared. "He promised that Alexander would give me large presents if I did so! He is no friend of yours!"

"What!" Herod roared. "He said this to you and you did not report it?"

Trypho stood speechless, frozen by his folly.

"Not true, Majesty!" Tero shouted. "This man's testimony is an obvious lie—"

"Silence!" Herod bellowed. His face was one of the darkest fury. Nicolaus closed his eyes in despair.

"Rack them both," Herod said to the commander of the guard. "Tero's son, too. We shall have the truth about this."

Under the torture Tero held fast to his story, as did Trypho. But Tero's son, seeing his father in such a deplorable condition, called out that he would tell all if the king would free him and his father from their torments. When Herod agreed to do so, he said that an agreement had been made that Tero should lay violent hands upon the king, and though he would probably suffer death for it, it would be an act of generosity in favor of Alexander.

As with so many of the other accusations that had come before, there was no way to tell whether this one was true. But it did not matter. In Herod's unbalanced mind the princes' guilt was now firmly established. He ordered all his court officials, along with all the men of the city, to the theatre outside the city walls where Nicolaus and the scribe had earlier met in secret. Then he produced Tero, his son, Trypho the barber, and all the captains Tero had named, and accused them before the multitude. The crowd, provoked to the same sort of madness that had reigned for so long in the palace, picked up stones and pieces of wood and whatever else was at hand, and pelted all the accused until they lay dead. Then Herod pronounced the sentence of death upon the two princes, saying that they would be taken to Sebaste, about a day's journey from Caesarea, and strangled there.

After this the crowd dispersed. Nicolaus and the scribe went back to the palace, where they sat in Nicolaus's quarters in silent dejection. Before long, Diophantus, the evil royal secretary, came knocking. He was looking for the scribe.

"Nicolaus, have you seen—" he began. His obsequious tone turned imperious as he spotted the scribe. "Oh! There you are. Why aren't you at your work?"

The scribe looked balefully at the royal secretary but said nothing.

"Well, never mind that," Diophantus said. "Go there now and write the king's decree."

"What decree?"

"The decree condemning the two princes. I take it you were in the theater just now."

"I was there," the scribe said stonily.

"Then you heard him pronounce the decree."

"I heard it."

"Well, obviously it must be written and sealed for it to be carried out in Sebaste."

The scribe simply shrugged, which infuriated Diophantus.

"Well, what are you waiting for?" he demanded. "Go now to your table and write it."

"No."

"What do you mean, no?"

"I cannot."

"You cannot or you will not?"

"I will not."

"That is an act of defiance. I must inform His Majesty."

"You must do what seems right to you," the scribe replied.

"I will indeed," Diophantus said with smug satisfaction. "I will indeed."

Nicolaus and the scribe sat silently for a few moments after Diophantus departed. The scribe sighed deeply and arose from his seat.

"Where are you going?" Nicolaus asked sharply.

"After Diophantus," the scribe replied. "Herod might as well hear it from my lips as from his."

Nicolaus scrambled to his feet.

"No, my friend." He lay his hand on the scribe's shoulder. "Herod is in a barbaric temper right now. The very sight of you will be enough for him to condemn you to torture and death."

"At least he will hear what I have to say," the scribe answered.

"What you have to say!" Nicolaus exclaimed. "What can you possibly have to say that hasn't already been said?"

"I will recount all that has gone before," the scribe said. "I will remind him how weak is the evidence that has been produced against the princes, especially some of the documents. I am sure that many of them are forgeries."

"It doesn't matter," Nicolaus said forcefully. "Herod has banished away anything that might help him to reason better in this matter. He will ignore you. You are nothing to him now. A mere scribe of the government, one among many."

"True, but even a common scribe has his story to tell," the scribe argued. "An old soldier has had his say before the court and the multitude. Why not an old scribe?"

"Because we saw what happened to the old soldier," Nicolaus pointed out. "His counsel to the king resulted in a gruesome end for the counsellor."

"Still, I will speak," the scribe said resolutely. "I will say what needs to be said in support of the princes. I should have said it before now."

"No, my friend, I will not allow it," Nicolaus said. "Your refusal to write the king's decree will be trouble enough, but it can be managed. You may speak to him if you will, but only after his savage temper has subsided."

He stepped into the corridor.

"Guard!" he called.

Two soldiers came hurrying up, for within the palace Nicolaus wielded a great deal of authority.

"Confine this man to my quarters." Nicolaus pointed to the scribe. "Keep him here until I return."

Nicolaus did not return until well after nightfall. As soon as he dismissed the guard, the scribe brushed past him without a word, retiring to the humble quarters where the palace servants took their rest. All that night he tossed on his simple bed, awaiting the terrible summons that he knew must come. It did not take long. The next morning two soldiers escorted him to the audience chamber, where the king and his court were waiting. Herod was in his judgment seat, paring an apple and cutting it into slices—a habit he often occupied himself with during the humdrum business of minor court affairs.

"Ah yes, it is the scribe," Herod began. "The recalcitrant one."

The scribe said nothing.

"Tell me, scribe," Herod said, "how long have you been in my service?"

"These forty years, Majesty."

"Yes, since the very beginning, and at my side for most of those years," Herod mused. "And yet with all that you have seen, and all that you know, you do not fear me. You have never feared me. Why?"

The words of King David, written a thousand years earlier, leaped to the scribe's mind:

In God I trust and shall not be afraid. What can man do to me?

But the scribe knew better than to quote these words to Herod at such a moment, and he remained silent.

"Here I sit, with a knife in my hand, a very sharp knife," Herod continued, deftly spearing a chunk of the apple and lifting it to his mouth. "You know that at this moment I could hand it to any one of these men, who would strike you down without a second thought. And yet you stand before me calmly. You have seen what happens to men who defy me. Yet you do not fear. Why?"

Here the scribe perceived that silence would no longer be to his advantage.

"I know that Your Majesty's apple will taste sweeter unmixed with the blood of his servant."

"Ha!" Herod grunted. "Even when I threaten your life you speak to me without fear! You have taken my measure these forty years, scribe. You look me in the eye and you understand me, perhaps better than I understand myself. Perhaps it was a mistake for me to remove you when you defied me in the matter of the tomb. Perhaps things would have been different with a different man at my right hand. Perhaps you should be my first counsellor in place of Nicolaus."

"Nicolaus far excels me in the matters of the world, Majesty," the scribe said.

"Yes, but I believe that you excel Nicolaus in the matters of the soul," Herod replied. "I believe that you excel all these who serve me. Kings take pleasure in honest lips, you know. They love a man who speaks the truth."

The scribe nodded in recognition of the proverb.

"And yet you defy me," Herod went on. "You defied me once, all those years ago. More than once! You defied me at the beginning, in that letter to Hyrcanus. Ah! It surprises you that I remember so small a thing from so long ago. Of course I remember. A king must always remember. He must remember every single thing that has been done, for good or for evil. And yet that was for my good. It was for my good, just as it was in the matter of Cleopatra. And now you have defied me again. I suppose you think it for my good. Would you have me rescind my command concerning the two princes? Because even though you would not write it, it has been written, you know. Written by another and sealed by me. Well? What of it? Would you have me rescind what I have commanded?"

The scribe tried to recall the defiant speech he had spent the entire night rehearsing, but he could not remember one word of it.

Herod's philosophical mood seemed to shift. He leaned forward and spoke in a menacing tone:

"It matters not. It is done. Whether for good or for evil, I hardly know, but it is done. But there is something that I do know, something I know clearly: a king cannot tolerate a servant who continues to defy him."

The scribe waited with resignation for the fatal words to fall. But instead the king leaned back and sighed a deep sigh.

"You will leave my service," Herod said. "You will retire in Jerusalem on half pay."

The scribe bowed low, overcome with astonishment and relief.

"My most humble thanks, Majesty," he mumbled.

"My steward has procured a house for you not far from the palace," Herod continued. "He says it is a modest place, but it will suit you."

"That is most gracious of Your Majesty." The scribe again bowed deeply. And then he lost all composure and began to babble:

"But I had hoped to one day return to Sepphoris—"

"No," Herod interrupted. "You will abide in Jerusalem. You will remain close at hand, in case I should require the counsel of honest lips. Now go. If there is anything you require, Nicolaus will see to it."

"If I may, Majesty..."

"Yes, what is it?"

"There are two domestics who served me here for in the time that I was the royal secretary—"

"What, the old man and the old woman?" Herod snapped. "Yes, Nicolaus has mentioned them. Take them with you. What use could they be to me? Now leave my sight."

The scribe bowed deeply again, then backed away quickly before Herod could change his mind. And thus ended a lifetime of service in the government of a man who had grasped for greatness, and attained it, and then lost it through his fear of losing it. Favored by fortune, he was encompassed by a myriad of dangers and got clear of them all, but once he had achieved absolute authority he used it wrongly in case after case. Surrounded by foreigners who understood little of our nation, undone by those who should have been closest to him, he abandoned the holy God of Israel and all other decent things in a quest for magnificence—a quest that ended in sorrow and misery. So powerful a place, the throne, and yet so precarious!

Chapter 23

Joanna had come to the end of the scroll. She looked up at Aduel, unwilling to concede that his monumental history had reached its end.

"And thus concludes the story of Herod," Aduel declared with a flourish. "A history carefully hidden away—one that will likely never be read, but that needed to be written nonetheless."

Joanna nodded wordlessly. She took her time scrolling Book the Fifteenth to its beginning. When she finally spoke, her first remark was an unexpected one:

"You were right about Nicolaus," she said quietly. "He doesn't owe you anything. He hasn't for years. You saved his life, then he saved yours."

"What, by keeping me captive in his quarters when I wished to speak to the king?" Aduel asked. "Hmph!"

But his indignation quickly subsided.

"It's possible, I suppose," he sighed. "Perhaps Nicolaus was right that day. I never thought of it that way. How is it, child, that you perceive these things? That young scribe of yours will find in you a worthy foil."

Joanna blushed.

"If I ever see him again," she said quietly.

"Now, now, it may not be as bad as all that," Aduel

comforted. "If things go smoothly after Herod dies, we may not have to leave Jerusalem after all."

"But it seems it would be better to leave, if Antipater takes the throne," Joanna said. "Is he not still the crown prince?"

"He is still the still the crown prince, though he may not be for much longer," Aduel said. "He is now in prison, thanks to Nicolaus."

"Nicolaus!" Joanna was shocked. "How did that happen?"

"There have been three years more of treachery and intrigue since I left Herod's service," Aduel said. "Antipater has found himself entangled in a web of his own spinning. The particulars are tolerably well known to me, though I did not witness them first-hand."

"Then you should add a book to your history," Joanna said. "When I came to the end of Book the Fifteenth, I felt as though there was part of the story that hadn't been told."

"The story continues as long as Herod lives," Aduel agreed. "But my history is told from my vantage point inside the palace. To write of the things that have happened in the three years since I left would be no more than to transcribe the common gossip of Jerusalem."

"Still, you must write it," Joanna insisted.

"No, child, no," Aduel said. "I worked for more than two years writing my history, and not until I finished all fifteen books did I realize that it was very likely that no one would ever read them. You are the first, and for that I am grateful, though you are also likely the last. But I am finished with Herod. If there is a sixteenth book to be added, someone else will have to write it. Perhaps you yourself."

"Me! But I don't know any of what has happened in the last three years."

"Then I will tell you of it on our journey to Egypt," Aduel said. "When we arrive you can set it down on papyrus if you like. But I doubt you'll find time, once you've encountered the library at Alexandria. Thousands of works of every kind, to satisfy that prodigious curiosity of yours! Most of them in Greek and Latin, of course, but we'll start your studies in those languages immediately. And there are many texts in our own language that you'll be able to read from the first day."

"I would like to read them," Joanna said thoughtfully. "In fact, I think the thing I would like most to read would be…"

She hesitated, wondering how her uncle might react.

"I think I would like to read Scripture," she said finally. "If you think it appropriate."

"Of course you should read Scripture," Aduel said. "Why should you not?"

"I'm afraid I wouldn't—well, that I wouldn't understand it."

"Nonsense!" Aduel contradicted. "You read as well as I do. Your vocabulary is enormous, your grasp of grammar remarkable. You will have no trouble understanding it."

"No, I mean…" Joanna's voice trailed off.

"Ah," Aduel said. "You mean that you wouldn't interpret it correctly."

Joanna nodded.

"Well, there is certainly the possibility of that," Aduel said. "Learned men with far more training than you have been doing that for hundreds of years."

He thought for a moment.

"Perhaps a small test will help us to determine your level of spiritual maturity," he continued. "I will pose to you a question that is vigorously debated by the great spiritual leaders of our nation. Do you feel ready to answer such a question?"

Joanna considered this. Her first impulse was to demur, but her ability to read had given her a boldness that she had not possessed before.

"I suppose," she shrugged. "Yes, why not?"

"Good," Aduel said. "Then here is the question: A stream of water is poured from a container that is ritually pure to one that is ritually impure. Does the ritually pure container from which the water is being poured become ritually impure by its contact with the impure container that is receiving the water?"

Joanna's face took on a look of pure consternation, which gave way to dejection.

"I—I don't know," she sighed.

"Come now, you must answer," Aduel insisted.

Joanna remained silent for several moments. Her newfound confidence had vanished; her face burned with shame. A simple question, with only two possible answers, and she could not perceive which one was correct.

"I don't know," she repeated irritably. "What does it matter?"

"Ha!" Aduel cried, clapping so loudly that it made her jump. "Ha! The Lord be praised! Out of the mouths of babes you have rebuked the mighty!"

Joanna was so startled by his outburst that she did not comprehend the words. In a moment her frustration had turned to fury.

"It's a stupid question!" she cried, her eyes blazing. It was the first time she had ever been angry with her uncle. "Why do you mock me?"

Now it was Aduel who was shocked.

"No, child, no! You misunderstand me!" He placed his

hand on her shoulder. "You have answered correctly! You are a girl, a young woman now, but a young woman with no formal education, and yet you understand more of the ways of the Lord than the most prominent teachers of our nation. You see past the ridiculous quibbles that have captivated them. They all proclaim that they will lead the nation in the way of truth and righteousness, but they devote their entire attention to the most trivial part of the Law, and things that are not even in the Law, while ignoring the most meaningful! The teachers of Israel, arguing and fighting over jars of water! What could be more foolish?"

Irijah burst through the door, startling both of them.

"Master, Master!" he exclaimed breathlessly. "There is news from the marketplace, shocking news!"

"What news?" Aduel asked irritably. "Am I to be told again that Herod is dead, but not really?"

"No." Irijah shook his head as he attempted to catch his breath. "No. Herod still lives. He has issued a proclamation."

"What proclamation?" Aduel asked.

Edna, who had been cooking in the kitchen, came in to see what was the matter.

"A proclamation from Herod was read, and posted for all to see," Irijah said. "All the leading men of Judea are to attend the king in Jericho!"

"How long can this go on?" Edna wailed. "How long can he live?"

"Now, now, it will be over soon enough," Aduel soothed. "This doesn't concern us."

"But it does!" Irijah contradicted. "You are on the list!"

Joanna was astonished—not only by the news itself, but by the look of shock on her uncle's face.

"Irijah, are you certain?" Aduel asked slowly.

"I heard it clearly," Irijah confirmed. "Aduel of Sepphoris, former secretary to the king."

"There must be some mistake," Aduel said.

"It's posted in the marketplace," Irijah insisted. "You can see for yourself."

"No, no need," Aduel said slowly. "I've been included on the roster of leading citizens once before. It seems I find myself on that list again."

"But what does it mean?" Joanna asked. "Why does he want you in Jericho?"

"I don't know," Aduel considered. "I don't. Are we to be held captive for another ranting speech deep into the night? Possibly. But possibly for another reason. Jericho is a long way to travel just to listen to the ravings of a madman."

He pondered for a moment.

"I have decided," he said finally. "We will leave Jerusalem. It's too late to go tonight. Without the safe passage, we would be stopped before we even got to the city gate. We'll go in the morning. We can mingle with the travelers who are making their way home before the Sabbath."

"Who will leave?" Irijah asked suspiciously.

"All of us," Aduel replied. "You, Edna, the maiden, and myself."

"All of us!" Irijah said querulously. "Do we all need to accompany you to Jericho?"

"We're not going to Jericho."

"Where, then?"

"Alexandria."

"Alexandria!" Irijah was stunned. "But you've been summoned to Jericho!"

"Yes," Aduel said testily. "Which is why I'm going to Alexandria."

"But the king has decreed death for those who do not obey his summons!" Irijah protested.

"By the time I am missed we'll be halfway to Egypt," Aduel said.

"I have a cousin in Hebron," Edna offered. "It would be on the way. We could wait there, out of view of the spies, until Herod has died."

Irijah shook his head emphatically.

"I'm not going to Egypt!" he declared. "I know no one in Alexandria. Jerusalem is my home."

"The streets of Jerusalem may soon run red with the blood of the innocent," Aduel said brusquely. "You'll be better off out of the city than in it. We'll come back when things have settled down."

"Come back!" Irijah argued. "We'll never come back."

Aduel did not reply.

Irijah stared angrily for a moment, then turned abruptly and went out, banging the door behind him. Joanna and Edna exchanged worried glances. Aduel got up and patted the old housekeeper's hand.

"It will be for the best," he assured her. "He'll see."

He sighed and went to the window, where he stood, peering silently through the lattice, seeing nothing.

A minute later there was a knock. Aduel hurried to the door. It was another stranger—again cloaked in anonymity, but even in the limited light from the doorway Joanna could see that he was different from the first. She watched, fascinated, as the familiar sequence took place.

"The Lord is righteous," the stranger said. "He loves

justice."

"The upright will see His face," Aduel replied.

The secret message was produced suddenly, as if by magic; it was handed over silently; Aduel closed the door swiftly without so much as a nod of acknowledgement.

Joanna looked on eagerly as her uncle unsealed the message. But her heart sank when he shook his head.

"Still no letters of introduction," he said darkly. "Or anything else."

"But what does he say?" the girl demanded.

"What does he say?" Aduel repeated. "What does it matter? Oh, I'll read it to you. At least the part I can make out.

"'Friend:

"'I am constantly attending to matters here in Jericho. I have not been able to obtain a safe passage for you. The privy seal is continually in the possession of Ptolemy, who himself is under the watchful eye of Salome. No one is inclined to grant favors of any sort. I know of no travel restrictions, but Herod has little to occupy him except the reports that are brought daily from spies throughout the kingdom.

"'Today a bizarre sequence of events took place. The king asked for an apple, and was paring it with a sharp knife as is his custom, when he suddenly raised the knife against himself. Achiabus rushed to stay his hand. There was a very great lamentation throughout the palace, and Antipater, in his prison cell, assumed that the king had died, and attempted to bribe his jailers to release him. But the chief jailer informed the king, who cried out more loudly than any thought possible, and beat his own head even though he is at death's door. He then ordered that Antipater be executed at once. That treacherous scoundrel has now been slain, as was his due, and

Herod has ordered that the court scribes be brought so that he can change his will again. The end will not be long now. I will make every effort to send you the letters I have promised. You must be ready to leave at a moment's notice.'"

Aduel ceased reading but continued to peer at the letter.

"Is that the end?" Joanna asked.

"It's the end of the original letter," Aduel said. "But here, below, is another paragraph that evidently was added later. Look how small the lettering is. It must be something compelling for Nicolaus to squeeze it into this small space, but I don't know if these old eyes can read it. Hmm, let me see."

He held the papyrus up to his eyes. Squinting, he began to read again:

"'The king has summoned all the leading men of Judea, from every city, town, and village, to come here to Jericho. He has not stated the purpose of it, but I fear that it is not for their benefit. He is now in constant agony and his temper is one of fierce rage. I pray that no one whose life you value was included.'"

"But I was included, Nicolaus," Aduel murmured. "I was on the list."

Chapter 24

The great journey had begun; Aduel and his little household were on their way to Egypt. Shimmering in the distance was the Great Sea, the one the Romans called Mediterra. They were not the only ones fleeing Jerusalem. The dusty road was crowded with travelers, all headed away from the city. The throng was so great that Joanna had become separated from her uncle and his two old servants. Amidst the crowd of strangers she had once again attracted the attention of the man with the onions; he was carrying the same large basket of them. Again he insisted on selling her some, but he could not seem to name a price that made any sense. She looked around nervously, hoping for a familiar face, when someone ahead called out that there had been a mistake—that they were travelling east, not west! What she had thought was the Great Sea was really a river: The Jordan! Everyone pushed forward, but their excitement gave way to consternation when it was discovered that the river was in full flood. Joanna looked about desperately for her uncle—or any familiar face—because there was no way to cross and she could not swim. A young man who looked like the silversmith's son brushed past her, but he vanished before she could attract his attention. Suddenly there was a shout from behind: Herod's men had followed them! They had fallen upon those in the rear, and were hacking at the defenseless stragglers with daggers and swords. And the king was among them! He was not on his deathbed; it was all a trick! All those around her rushed forward and plunged headlong into the river, carrying her with them. Flailing hopelessly, she felt herself sinking to the depths. As the darkness closed in, she summoned all her strength for a final frantic burst toward the surface—and with a terrible cry sat bolt upright, bathed in clammy sweat, her terrified eyes straining for succor in the chilly darkness of her tiny bedchamber.

Her frantic gasps quickly receded as she discerned where she was. She lowered her feet gingerly over the side of the bed. The first touch of the frigid stone floor, the morning ritual she usually dreaded, was the most welcome sensation she could imagine. Opening the door a crack, she was relieved to find that the shutters of the small kitchen window had begun to glow faint purple with the predawn light.

She padded quietly to the front room, where she found that she was not the only one who had spent a fitful night. Aduel was seated in his usual place before the hearth, staring blankly at the smoldering embers of the dying fire. This was unusual enough at such an early hour, but even more unexpected was the sight of Edna, who never allowed herself the luxury of sitting in a chair, seated next to him. The two of them were so completely motionless that the girl backed quietly away, convinced they were in some sort of waking trance. But Aduel's voice checked her retreat:

"You're up early, child."

"Yes," Joanna said, a little confused. "Are you preparing for the journey?"

"No," Edna said, in a voice foggy with frustration and exhaustion.

"Edna awoke in the night and found that Irijah had not returned," Aduel explained. "I myself awoke two hours ago. Found I couldn't sleep either—a strange, uneasy feeling. Peculiar dreams."

"Yes," Joanna said.

"You too, eh?" Aduel stirred himself. "Well, dawn has come; the terrors of the night are behind us. Let's hope that the day holds no terrors of its own."

"Are we still going to Alexandria?"

"Yes, child, yes," Aduel reassured her, rising stiffly from his chair.

"But what about Irijah?" Joanna pressed.

"Yes, what about Irijah?" Aduel repeated irritably. "With the light of day comes the opportunity to inquire, and I shall be about that now."

He made his way slowly up the stone stairway to his bedchamber on the second floor, returning a few minutes later in his cap and heaviest cloak.

"I will return by the third hour," he instructed Edna and the girl from the doorway. "If a messenger from Nicolaus arrives, you must implore him to deliver the letter to you, even if you cannot give the countersign. If he refuses, tell him to come back at the third hour."

"But where will you go?" Joanna asked.

"Who knows?" Aduel shrugged. "I'll look in all the obvious places, I suppose."

Joanna looked at him questioningly.

"At the moment all I can think is that Irijah's absence is the result of strong drink and he's sleeping it off somewhere," Aduel explained. "If that turns up nothing, I may have to visit some old acquaintances."

"What acquaintances?" Edna asked sharply.

"Men who will know if Irijah has somehow fallen afoul of Herod's henchmen."

"No, Master, no!" Edna implored him, tugging at his sleeve. "You must not go near such men!"

"With any luck I won't have to." Aduel patted her hand. "Don't fret now, Edna, don't fret. I'll take care."

The two women's eyes met as he went out. Edna could not restrain her fury.

"The old fool!" she cried bitterly. "The old fool! He'll answer for this, he will! He'll answer to me!"

She disappeared into the back of the house and returned in a moment with her own cloak and shawl.

"Edna, no," Joanna implored her. "My uncle is already searching. Don't you go too."

"Your uncle is a man of gentle manners," Edna replied. "There are places he might not think to look, places where I will look. I'll find that old fool, you mark my words."

Joanna saw that it was no use arguing.

"Please, not too long," she implored the old woman. "If my uncle should come back with Irijah—"

Edna brushed past her before she could finish. Joanna closed the door and bolted it. It was a bad start to a crucial day, an ill omen to be sure. She looked around, uncertain what to do. She had never been alone in the house. Now was her chance to explore the rooms she had never seen—Aduel's upstairs bedchamber, and the converted stable on the opposite side of the courtyard that served as the living quarters for Edna and Irijah. But she felt no particular curiosity about those things. Instead she went to her own room and sat on the bed, silently contemplating this place she might never see again. It was nothing but a musty storage closet, gloomy even with the door wide open and barely big enough for the bed, but it was hers—a place of privacy, which was not such a common thing in the close-packed towns and cities of Judea. She wondered if she would be lucky enough to have anything like it in Alexandria.

Next to her on the bed, all that she owned was carefully packed: A second tunic, a shawl, a mantle, a blanket, and an extra veil. With this bundle sat a small leather pouch, modestly embroidered with precise needlework and fitted with a sturdy leather strap. In it were her most prized possessions. She took them out and spread them lovingly over the bed: A dried flower, beautifully preserved by her mother to commemorate some occasion that would now remain forever forgotten. A silver ring that had belonged to her father and been passed down to her brother, and then on to her. A locket of her brother's hair. A tiny kerchief of beautiful linen that her mother had worn on her wedding day. Three silver shekels that had been given to her, to spend however she liked, on the day she reached her majority. It was a breathtaking sum, equal to twelve days' wages for a common laborer, and she had considered many frivolous purchases—but had instead hoarded it with some vague foreboding of future necessity.

Suddenly there was a quiet rapping: Three quick knocks. She gasped. It was the messenger! She hurried to the door, terrified at the prospect of encountering a mysterious stranger and wondering how she might convince him to give her the message. If only she knew the Scripture, even half as well as her uncle, she would be able to give the countersign. But she knew hardly a word! Oh, why had she not studied it sooner? And why had Irijah picked last night of all nights to go out and get drunk? But there was no time to think of these things now. She unbolted the door and threw it open, wider than she had intended.

No one was there.

She gaped in consternation. Surely she had heard a knock! But perhaps—perhaps she had imagined it. She stepped outside and surveyed the courtyard. It was deserted. She even went so far as to climb the ladder to the rooftop, but it too was empty. Puzzled, she walked slowly back to the door, taking a last look around the courtyard. There was nothing out of place, just a piece of papyrus that had blown up against the wooden bench next to the door. She picked it up and examined it, but it was blank on both sides. It must have blown in on a gust of wind—odd, but hardly alarming. She shrugged and went back into the house, bolting the door behind her. She crumpled the papyrus and tossed it at the hearth, but it missed and rebounded across the floor. As she picked it up again she reconsidered; a blank bit of papyrus might be come in handy for practicing her penmanship. Back in her bedchamber she absentmindedly stuffed it into the leather pouch along with the treasured mementos of her past life in Jericho.

Again there was a noise at the door, a loud rattling that made her jump. There could be no mistake this time; this disturbance was protracted and insistent. She hurried to the front of the house.

"Who is it?" she called. "Who's there?"

"It's me, child." Joanna breathed a sigh of relief at the sound of her uncle's voice. "Let me in!"

Joanna fumbled with the bolt and opened the door. It was indeed Aduel, but Irijah was not with him.

"Uncle! You're back so soon!"

"Yes," Aduel muttered.

"But where is Irijah? Did you find him?"

"I did not find him," Aduel declared. "Instead I found my common sense. Why should I be roaming the streets in clear view of Herod's spies when I am in defiance of his order to report to Jericho? No, child, no. I could not justify it. It would put our entire journey in jeopardy. Irijah has chosen his course. He must bear the consequences."

Joanna was relieved. She felt a pang of sympathy for Irijah, but it was a mild one.

"Do you have your things ready?" Aduel asked.

"Yes."

"Good. We leave at once. Where's Edna? She's ready, I hope."

"Edna isn't here," Joanna said. "She went looking for Irijah."

"What!" The grim resolution that had galvanized Aduel seemed to leave him all at once. He sank wordlessly into his chair. Joanna regarded him fearfully.

"What can we do?" she asked.

"We can do nothing." Aduel shook his head. "We can do nothing but wait. I can justify leaving him. I can't justify leaving her."

He sank into a deep and troubling silence.

"I'm sorry, child, I'm sorry," he said finally, in a mournful voice that seemed far away. "We should have left at first light. Instead, we remain. And all for the sake of what? A refractory servant? It was a foolish mistake. I've put us all in danger."

"No, Uncle, no." She laid her hand on his to comfort him, just as he had comforted her so many times. "Edna won't be long. I told her to hurry! You'll see. We just need something to occupy ourselves until she gets here. You said that you would tell me the part of Herod's story that has happened since you left his service. Why not get started now?"

"There isn't that much to tell," Aduel demurred. "More intrigue and treachery within the palace, you can be sure."

"Then that's perfect," Joanna reasoned. "By the time you get to the end, Edna will be back."

"No, no, I don't think it's a good idea," Aduel grumbled. But immediately he changed his mind. "Well, why not? You might as well know the rest of it. Hmph! My thoughts are so disordered that I can barely think. Where to begin?"

"Start with Antipater," suggested Joanna. "After the deaths of the two princes, he was the only one who remained."

"He was hardly the only one," Aduel corrected, warming to his task. "Pheroras, Salome, Doris—and there were others, as well. It was a whole nest of vipers, each waiting to strike. But chief among them was Antipater, and in prime position to do the most harm. The people hated him, but Herod didn't. He delegated many things to him, and in many matters he and Antipater shared equal authority. And even though most in the army detested Antipater, it did not matter, because the army was still loyal to Herod. All Antipater had to do was wait. But he was not content to wait. He was afraid, afraid of the children."

"The children!"

"Yes, the children of the two princes," Aduel said. "Their fathers had been slain, but they had not, and Herod had taken them under his protection. They were young, but they were growing up. Antipater called them 'the heads of the Hydra,' and feared that if Herod did not die soon, the young lads would become so powerful that they would have the kingdom. Since there was little chance Antipater could induce Herod to murder his grandsons as he had his sons, he concluded that his only hope for the throne was if Herod were to die soon.

"Of course, this had to be done in such a way that Antipater could not possibly be suspected, and that cunning monster soon had crafted a plan. The tool he chose for the king's destruction was poison, and the instrument for its delivery was to be none other than the king's own brother, Pheroras."

"Pheroras!"

"Yes. That poor wretch, you see, was already in Herod's ill graces because he had refused to divorce his wife to marry the woman Herod had picked out for him—not once, but twice. And under the greatest pressure from the king."

"He must have truly loved his wife," Joanna remarked.

"He was certainly devoted to her. You might even say enslaved. He could refuse nothing she demanded of him, and everyone knew it, Antipater most of all. He decided to use this knowledge to complete his scheme. Antipater's mother Doris had been put out of the palace when Herod married Miriam, but lately she had been brought back, at Antipater's insistence, and he enlisted her in the plot. She cultivated a friendship with Pheroras's wife, his mother-in-law, and his sister-in-law, and soon those four women were thick as thieves. Pheroras became the slave not just of his wife, but of all of them. They met together frequently, and Pheroras and Antipater often with them, though for what purposes no one knew.

"In all the palace there was but one who dared to oppose this faction, but that one was a formidable antagonist. It was Salome, the king's sister, who had once enlisted Pheroras in her own evil plans to slander the two princes but who had regained Herod's good graces after the princes were executed.

Although she had no definite information, she reported her suspicions to Herod. Herod again called upon Pheroras to divorce his wife, and even went so far as to accuse her of captivating him by means of love potions.”

“Love potions!” Joanna exclaimed. “Did Herod really say that?”

“He did, before all the court,” Aduel confirmed. “But Pheroras again refused to leave his wife.”

“So Herod had him executed, right?” Joanna anticipated.

“No, Herod sent him away from Jerusalem, along with his wife, where he ruled a territory east of the Jordan called Perea.”

“So that ruined Antipater’s plot against Herod,” Joanna predicted.

“Yes, but not right away,” Aduel said. “Knowing that Herod’s suspicions had been aroused, Antipater went to Rome, under the pretense of delivering a copy of Herod’s will to Augustus. But many months later, while Antipater was still in Rome, Pheroras was taken ill and died in Perea. That was when Antipater’s plot began to unravel. Two of Pheroras’s freedmen went to Herod and claimed that Pheroras had been poisoned.”

“I thought it was a conspiracy against Herod,” Joanna objected.

“It was, but be patient,” Aduel said. “You’re getting ahead of me. Now, where was I? Ah, yes, the death of Pheroras. To investigate these claims of poisoning, Herod tortured all the female servants of Pheroras’s wife, and while in the utmost agonies one of them cried out that her mistress was innocent, but that God should send such agonies to Doris, Antipater’s mother, who was the root of all these miseries.

"Herod now had an important clue. It was never determined whether Pheroras actually did die from poisoning, but Herod wasted no time widening the scope of inquiry with additional torture. It was found that Antipater's steward had actually procured a poison from a physician in Egypt, which was intended for Herod and was handed to Pheroras's wife for safekeeping until an opportune time. Herod sent for Pheroras's wife and promised that she and all her servants would be pardoned if she confessed. Whereupon she did confess that she had the poison, and promised to bring it, but when she was allowed to go into her house to retrieve it, she instead threw herself down from the housetop."

Joanna gasped. Aduel paused, then continued.

"However, she did not die but was only rendered unconscious. Herod came to her, and comforted her, and when she had recovered her senses she produced the flask with the potion in it, and the box that it was in, and said that Antipater had prepared it for the king. This was confirmed on the testimony of those who had brought the box from Egypt, who were Antipater's servants and relations, and it was further discovered that Herod's third wife, the second Miriam, was aware of all these things but had concealed them."

"Let me guess," Joanna interrupted. "This time someone was executed."

"No, but Herod divorced her immediately, and blotted out their son, who was second in the succession after Antipater, from his will. And while all this was happening, a freedman of Antipater's came from Rome, and was found to be carrying another poison, which was to be administered to Herod if the first one did not suffice."

"Antipater certainly was thorough," Joanna remarked.

"Yes, too thorough by half," Aduel continued. "But while in Rome he was unaware of all that was transpiring in Judea. Even though there were many in the palace with knowledge of these things, Antipater did not hear of them, for Herod ordered that the roads be closely guarded, and anyone who might know of the situation or might be delivering news of it was detained. The guards even intercepted a letter from Doris, Antipater's mother, warning him that all was lost.

"Thus when Antipater returned from Rome and landed in Caesarea it was clear that something was amiss, for all those who had saluted him and expressed their good wishes on his departure now shunned him. But now there was no turning back, as all methods of escape were under Herod's control.

"So Antipater proceeded to Jerusalem, appearing at the palace clothed in the royal purple. Upon his arrival, the guards at the outer gate allowed him in, but shut out all those in his entourage. Antipater now understood fully the trouble he was in, but he put on a bold face and proceeded to the audience chamber. Herod was sitting in judgment along with Varus, the Roman governor of Syria, who happened to be visiting Jerusalem at the time. But as he approached his father, Herod turned his head away and held out his hands to keep Antipater at arms' length, and cried out that Antipater should not touch him unless he was cleared of the charges that had been lodged against him.

"Antipater's trial took place the next day, with Varus presiding. The outcome could not be predicted, for even though the evidence against him was strong, Antipater was allowed to speak in his own defense. He did so at length, with much weeping, about all the things he had done on his father's behalf, and reminded those assembled of the weakness of evidence obtained by torture. At the end of this performance those assembled were moved to pity, and it seemed that Antipater might yet win his freedom. Even Herod was moved, and was too overcome to proceed with the charges. He thus delegated the prosecution to one of his most trusted associates, a man who was not likely to be swayed by appeals to sentiment or emotion."

"Nicolaus of Damascus!" Joanna interjected.

"Exactly.   Nicolaus proceeded to make a lengthy and detailed case, bringing in many witnesses who had never been tortured yet nonetheless confirmed various details of Antipater's schemes.   Nicolaus concluded with the most serious charges, the conspiracy to poison Herod.

"When Nicolaus was finished, Varus asked Antipater to refute the charges. But Antipater had nothing specific to say in his defense, and instead appealed to God for some sign of his innocence. But when no sign came—"

"As if he could really expect one!"

"When no sign came," Aduel continued patiently, "Varus ordered a criminal condemned to death to be brought from prison. He then ordered that the liquid that Antipater's freedman had brought from Rome—the alleged poison—be produced. He explained to the prisoner that the substance might be poison or it might not, but if he should drink it down and survive, he would be freed."

Aduel paused, seemingly lost in his thoughts.

"Well?" Joanna prompted. "Did he drink it?

"Yes," Aduel said. "He did drink it. He drank it down, and died on the spot."

Joanna shuddered. A sickening feeling, like the one she had felt at the execution of Herod's beautiful queen, came over her, magnified by the tension that had been building for the last two days.

"Death! Death! Always death!" she burst out. "Everything to do with Herod is death!"

She got up and walked distractedly around the room, trying to quell the queasiness that gripped her. Finally, her stomach settled, she faced her uncle.

"Well?" she demanded. "Then what?"

"Then Varus got up and left the proceeding without a word, and departed from Jerusalem the very next day," Aduel said. "Herod put Antipater in prison, where he remained until just a few days ago. We know from Nicolaus's most recent letter what happened then."

"Antipater was executed in Jericho," Joanna said.

"Yes," said Aduel. "Requiring Herod to change his will yet again."

"But if he's gotten rid of all his sons, who will be king after him?" Joanna asked.

"Oh, there are other sons," Aduel said. "Herod has had ten wives, you know—not just the three I told you about."

"Ten!"

"That's rather modest by kingly standards," Aduel smiled. "The scholars tell us that a king of Israel should be allowed up to eighteen wives. I never mentioned Herod's other wives in my history because I never imagined they would be of any consequence."

"But now they are," Joanna said.

"Possibly," Aduel shrugged. "In any case, that concludes the account of what has happened in the reign of Herod since I left his service—a rather robust summary, I think."

He sank into a moody silence.

"And yet after all that Edna has still not come back," he mused. "I hoped at least we might have something more from Nicolaus by now. Are you sure no one came while I was out searching for Irijah?"

"No, Uncle," Joanna said. "I thought I heard someone knock, but I was wrong."

"You heard someone knock!" Aduel exclaimed. "Why didn't you tell me? Why didn't you answer it?"

"I did answer it," Joanna said defensively. "But there was no one there."

"There was someone there!" Aduel cried. "That was the messenger!"

"But there was no one!" Joanna protested. "I looked all around the courtyard. I even looked on the roof!"

"He was there!" Aduel insisted. "He was!"

Joanna was astonished. Her placid old uncle was animated now, almost frantic.

"Why didn't he wait until you came to the door?" Aduel muttered. He was pacing now, wringing his hands. "And why hasn't he returned? I was here well before the third hour. It's nearly the fifth hour now. Why would he wait so long? There must have been some danger. Tell me, child, tell me: Are you certain that when you opened the door there was nothing there, no message of any kind?"

"No, Uncle."

"There was nothing at all, then?"

Joanna thought for a moment.

"Nothing," she said. "Just a scrap of papyrus lying on the ground."

"A scrap of papyrus! That was the message! The message was delivered and you didn't think to tell me? The message we have been awaiting for hours?"

"But there was no message!" Joanna's lip trembled. "There was no writing! There was no mark of any kind! I examined it closely."

"Tell me you haven't destroyed it." Aduel's voice took on a peculiar calm. "Please, child, tell me that you have not destroyed the message."

"No, Uncle," Joanna said, alarmed that she had made some grave mistake. "I saved it for our journey. I thought I could use it, perhaps."

"Then where is it?" Aduel roared. "Where?"

By now the girl was genuinely terrified. Her hands trembled as she rushed to retrieve the leather pouch and dig out the crumpled papyrus. She held it out to Aduel.

"I'm sorry, Uncle," she cried, her tears flowing freely. "I'm sorry! I shouldn't have crumpled it. I didn't know. I didn't know!"

"No, child, no, there is nothing to fear." Aduel smoothed the papyrus carefully. "As long as you did not destroy it."

He grabbed a candle from a basket near the door and lit it in the glowing embers of the hearth. Joanna watched, puzzled, for there was no reason to waste a candle in the light of day.

"What are you doing?" she asked. "Are you going to burn it now?"

Aduel shook his head.

"An old scribe's trick," he explained. "If a soldier or a common spy were to see this, he would think it a worthless scrap, just as you did. But I know what to do with it."

He held the papyrus over the top of the flame, moving the candle in a gentle circular motion. After a few moments, to the girl's astonishment, tiny brown letters began to emerge from the blank papyrus. The message contained but two words.

Flee now.

Chapter 25

Joanna and her uncle looked at each other in alarm.

"Get your things," Aduel muttered. "We're leaving."

"But what about Edna?" Joanna objected.

"We'll worry about Edna later," Aduel said. "But we must go. I've been wasting precious minutes prattling about Antipater while danger has been closing in. I'll get my scrolls and my—"

The door, which was not bolted, swung open abruptly. In the doorway stood Irijah, but the gaunt old man was not alone. With him, holding him roughly under the arm, was an officer of the king's guard—the same sneering brute who had come for Aduel on the girl's first night in Jerusalem.

"So, you are here," the soldier jeered at Aduel, "just as the old fool said. Summoned to Jericho, but you remain in Jerusalem. Looks like you'll finally be taking that journey to Jericho after all."

"I was just preparing to leave," Aduel said calmly.

"Yes, with a side trip to Alexandria, I'm told!" the soldier mocked. "Oh, you needn't act surprised. This old fool has talked! Yes, he talked quite a bit last night while he was in his cups. The king may be dying, but did this nitwit think his spies were dying too? Quite a surprise for him, waking up in the king's dungeon! I knew him at once when I saw him. Remembered I had seen him here before, and came here straightaway.”

“Well, now that you’ve found the place, you can leave him here,” Aduel said testily.

“Of course I’ll leave him here!” the soldier roared. “It’s not him I want, it’s you!”

He gave Irijah a mighty shove. The old manservant, who had been looking rather dazed, stumbled and fell. Joanna gasped. Aduel rushed to Irijah’s side, examining the bleeding wound on his head.

“Look what you’ve done!” he said angrily. “I’ll need to get a doctor.”

“Never mind that!” the soldier said. “You’re going to Jericho.”

“Yes, yes, I’ll go to Jericho,” Aduel snapped. “As soon as I’ve seen to it that this man has a doctor.”

“You’ll go now, and you’ll go with me! The king still lives, and while he lives he’ll be obeyed! I have my orders to take you to Jericho, immediately. They’ll pen you up in the hippodrome there with all the other cattle that have been milling about, waiting for the slaughter.”

“What are you talking about, man?” Aduel snorted.

“Haven’t you heard?” the soldier grinned. “Herod knows that no one will mourn when he dies, and he wants all Israel to mourn. His last decree is that all the leading men of the nation will die with him, and that way there will be mourning aplenty. That’s why he has gathered them all in Jericho. Come on, then. You need to be there when the old goat kicks the bucket. Wouldn’t want to miss the fun.”

He pulled Aduel to his feet with the same rough grasp he had used on Irijah and dragged him into the courtyard. Joanna followed behind, tugging at her uncle’s sleeve.

"No, child, do not resist," Aduel implored her. "Take care of Irijah, if you can. When Edna comes, tell her to fetch a doctor."

He broke away from the soldier's grasp just long enough to face her, and to take her hands in his.

"It's a fitting end to a lifetime with Herod," he said. "That story is in your hands now. Do what you will with it."

The soldier yanked him away and hustled him roughly through the courtyard gate as Joanna watched helplessly. In her last glimpse of him he looked back, just for a moment, with a defiant smile.

She stood alone in the courtyard for a long time, too stunned even to think. Slowly she became aware of something unusual in the sleeve of her robe. Puzzled, she pulled out two pieces of folded papyrus. They were the letters from Nicolaus of Damascus, which Aduel had deposited there by some undetected sleight of hand.

Chapter 26

Twenty minutes after Aduel's arrest, Edna had returned to find Joanna weeping in the courtyard, but it was not until she saw Irijah's prostrate form inside the house that the old woman fully comprehended the depth of the catastrophe that had taken place. She had rushed away again, this time to find a doctor. But when the man arrived he pronounced Irijah's condition beyond his power of healing, since there was swelling inside the skull, and said that only time would reveal his fate. The two women had done their best to make the old man comfortable, covering him with blankets and propping his head on a cushion. He had remained there, moaning and shivering through the night, while Edna and the girl drowsed fitfully in the two chairs before the hearth. Now it was morning, and Irijah had lapsed into a deep, heavy slumber, though whether it was sleep unto life or unto death the women could not tell.

A sharp rap at the door roused them. Joanna shot Edna a terrified look, but the old woman shrugged.

"I don't think it could get any worse," she said stoically.

She got up stiffly and unbolted the door, opening it a crack. Although only a sliver of the visitor was visible, Joanna recognized the lanky figure and ruddy countenance at once.

Nicolaus of Damascus!

Edna opened the door. Nicolaus was alone. He stepped inside with a hurried, furtive look and glanced at Irijah.

"What happened to the old man?" he asked.

"He talked too much in front of Herod's spies," Edna said reproachfully. "This is the work of one of your soldiers."

Nicolaus grunted with disgust.

"They are not my soldiers," he said. "He needs a doctor. See to it at once."

He pressed a coin into Edna's hand.

"A doctor has already been brought," Edna said.

"Then bring a better one," Nicolaus said. "And gather your things. You should be ready to leave this place at a moment's notice, with the old man or without him. I cannot predict what will happen in Jerusalem once Herod is finally dead. He still lived when I left Jericho at midnight. It cannot be much longer, but he clings to life with a grip like none I have ever seen."

"Perhaps he knows what awaits him," Edna retorted.

Nicolaus eyed her icily, then turned to Joanna.

"As for you, maid, your uncle was taken to the hippodrome in Jericho and imprisoned there last night. Why did you not flee? Don't you know what will happen to him?"

Joanna looked down and did not answer.

"We've heard of Herod's monstrous plan for the captives in the hippodrome," Edna spat. "Why don't you do something?"

"I hold no sway with Herod's soldiers," Nicolaus said irritably. "There are thousands of them there, all straining for the thrill of the slaughter. That is why I have come here, to do what little I can. The maiden will come with me."

For the first time Joanna faced him.

"No."

Nicolaus's eyes widened at this adamant rejection. But

there was no anger in his gaze, only surprise.

"You needn't worry," he explained patiently. "My intentions for you are noble, in more ways than one. It is the least I can do for old Aduel, after what he once did for me."

Joanna shook her head resolutely.

"You must not remain here," Nicolaus insisted. "There will be upheaval in the city when Herod dies. There is no predicting what will happen then. Women often are not spared. I will not be able to help you. Neither will they."

Joanna glanced at the two old servants. Edna, bent and frail, returned her beseeching look with a hopeless stare. They both knew that Nicolaus was right: there would be no help in a time of chaos. She wavered. To put herself in the power of Nicolaus was the thing she feared most, and yet suddenly it seemed the most prudent course of action. She thought of Hilkiah, the young scribe. His week of purification would be complete tomorrow. He would undergo the rite of cleansing—the sprinkling with the ashes of the red heifer—and would be ritually clean. Surely she should wait until he came for her. But what if he did not come? What if the violence in Jerusalem erupted first? Her thoughts raced wildly. She knew where to find him; she could go to him if necessary. But then what? Without a marriage contract she could not expect him to accept her. Such a thing would be scandalous, unthinkable.

She prayed for wisdom. Surely there was some passage of Scripture that would direct her! But she had not had time to study Scripture. Life had overtaken her too soon. Reluctantly she nodded, slightly.

"Good. We must leave at once." Nicolaus gestured toward the door. "I will take you to the palace. You will be safe there. A wise choice, Joanna."

The girl's mouth dropped open. Nicolaus smiled his slight smile.

"It surprises you that I know your name," he said. "A minister of the king knows many things. I would not be wasting time with you if I did not think you were worthy. Come."

Joanna could control her tears no longer. Her eyes, already brimming, now overflowed freely. Nicolaus glanced at her as she dabbed at her cheeks, his pale eyes flashing with surprise and admiration.

"Ah! Here is something I did not know."

He had grasped her wrist lightly and was staring at her hand. Joanna pulled it away, but Nicolaus had already seen the ink stain on her index finger.

"A maiden who writes," he mused. "You are indeed worthy of a noble destiny."

Epilogue

Many weeks later, on a warm, cloudless afternoon late in spring, an old man stood in the courtyard of Aduel's little house, rattling the bolted door.

"Edna, open the door!" the old man cried. "Open the door, child!"

It was Aduel, safely returned from Jericho. The door swung open abruptly. But it was not Edna or the girl who stood in the doorway. Rather there was a middle-aged man, swarthy and scowling.

"Who are you?" the man demanded. "What are you doing here?"

"I might ask the same of you," Aduel said, stunned. "This is my house."

"No it isn't," the man retorted. "It may have been once, but it isn't now. I live here at the pleasure of the crown."

"Ah," Aduel said, comprehending the situation at once. "Just as I did, when the crown rested on a different head."

"I know nothing of that," the householder said haughtily. "All I know is that I have been given this place for my service to the king, and you have no part in it. You would do well not to come back here."

"Of course," Aduel said. "But—there was a maiden who lived here. And an old servant couple. Where are they?"

"How should I know?" the householder demanded rudely. "Do I look like someone who takes an interest in another man's maidens and servants?"

"No, of course not." Aduel shook his head meekly. "Just one more question, if I may. Were there any manuscripts here when you took the house? Scrolls of papyrus?"

"There was nothing!" the householder exploded, clearly exasperated by now. "When I took the house, it was empty. Completely empty, and you'll get nothing from me!"

"I want nothing from you, friend," Aduel said placidly. "I beg forgiveness for troubling you. I'll apply to Nicolaus. He may know something of all this."

"Nicolaus!" the householder said suspiciously. "What Nicolaus? Nicolaus of Damascus?"

"Yes."

"If you're planning to ask Nicolaus of Damascus, you may be waiting a while," the man said sarcastically. "He's halfway to Rome by now."

"To Rome!"

"Yes, he sailed with Herod's son, Archelaus, over a week ago. They're trying to persuade Augustus to confirm Archelaus as king."

"Archelaus!" exclaimed Aduel. "Of all his sons, Herod picked Archelaus as his heir?"

"Unexpected to be sure, but it was a great benefit to me," the householder said. "But that was weeks ago. Herod changed his will just before he died, after he executed Antipater. Where have you been all this time?"

"If you must know, I've been sick with catarrh all this time," Aduel said. "In a wretched little inn halfway between here and Jericho, far away from the news of anyone or anything. I came to Jerusalem straightaway, as soon as I was able to walk."

"Catarrh," the man said, softening a little. "That's a rough go. Hey, wait a minute! You weren't one of the ones shut up in the hippodrome in Jericho, were you?"

"In fact I was," Aduel admitted.

"Then you're lucky to be alive at all, never mind the catarrh!" the householder exclaimed. "That was more strange business, wasn't it? I never would have thought Salome would trick Herod's soldiers after he died and set you all free. She doesn't seem like the type."

"No, she doesn't," agreed Aduel. "But perhaps we all have at least one good deed lurking within."

"All things considered you were lucky to have been stuck where you were," the man confided. "Here in Jerusalem there was rioting in the streets, people demanding revenge on Herod's officials and spies. More than three thousand were slaughtered."

Aduel nodded. There was nothing more to say. He turned away.

"Hold on there," the householder called grudgingly, belatedly remembering his duty under the Law to the wayfarer and the sojourner. "If you need a place tonight, you can stay in the stable over there."

He nodded across the courtyard, to the wing of the house that had once accommodated Edna and Irijah.

"If you don't mind sleeping with the animals," he added quickly. "I keep goats there now."

"Thank you, friend, for the offer of hospitality," Aduel said, without a trace of sarcasm. "But I cannot rest until I find those I am seeking."

"It may not be as easy as you think," the man warned. "There's been a great deal of upheaval in the last few weeks."

"The Lord's eyes are on the righteous," Aduel said. "He will direct my steps."

With a quick bow he turned again and closed the courtyard gate behind him, knowing that the Lord would lead him in the way that he should go.

Frequently Asked Questions

When does this story take place? Your timeline says the Magi arrived in Jerusalem in 4 B.C., but I thought Jesus was born in Year 0.

The events depicted in *Herod: The Secret History* take place in 4 B.C. As far as we can determine, Jesus was probably born in late 5 B.C. or early 4 B.C. (recall that for B.C., the years are counted backward).

The calendar era we use today did not come into being until about five hundred years after Christ's birth. At that time, there were a number of calendars in use—the Roman calendar, which counted from the year Rome was founded, the Hebrew calendar, which counted from the date of creation, and so on. But the dominant calendar in the sixth century A.D. was one that counted from the accession of Diocletian to the throne of the Roman Empire in 284 A.D. A Byzantine monk named Dionysius Exiguus thought it was absurd to honor an emperor who had actively persecuted Christians, so he came up with a numbering system in which Year 1 was the year Christ was born. (There is no Year 0 in this calendar or most others.)

Dionysius gave it his best shot, but the historical evidence now available indicates that his calculations were a little off. Nonetheless, the new numbering system became established throughout Christendom and is now the predominant calendar throughout the world. In recent decades, secular scholars uncomfortable with any allusion to Christ have substituted

"B.C.E" ("Before the Common Era") for "B.C." and "C.E." ("Common Era") for "A.D." ("Anno Domini", Latin for "in the Year of the Lord"), but the numbering for the two nomenclatures is identical.

Did Rome control Judea while Herod was king?

Pretty much. Throughout Herod's reign, Judea was a client kingdom of the Roman Empire. This relationship had prevailed since the Romans captured Jerusalem in 63 B. C., in the aftermath of the inconclusive civil war between Aristobulus and Hyrcanus. It was solidified by Antipater's arrangement with Julius Caesar in 47 B. C.

The Romans usually allowed their client kings wide latitude in the internal affairs of the client kingdom, so long as their decisions did not conflict with the interests of Rome. Internal matters that did bear upon those interests were subject to review; for this reason Augustus initially took a hand in Herod's succession planning for his kingdom (before finally washing his hands of the whole unpleasant matter).

After Herod's death, his son Archelaus assumed the title of King of Judea, as Herod had unexpectedly specified in his final testament. However, Archelaus's enemies (including Herod's sister Salome and another son, Herod Antipas) pointed out that Archelaus had taken power without the express consent of Augustus, and *The Secret History* closes with Archelaus hurrying to Rome to attain that consent.

How do we know so much about Herod?

Most of our information about Herod comes from Josephus Flavius, a Jewish aristocrat, priest, general, and historian born around 37 A.D., about forty years after Herod's death.

Josephus did not set out to write a biography of Herod, but rather sweeping works of history that covered centuries or even millennia. The first of these, *The Wars of Jews*, was written around 75 A.D. It extends from the conquests of Alexander the Great in the fourth century B.C. to the destruction of Jerusalem in 70 A.D. The second, *The Antiquities of the Jews*, was written about twenty years later and is an even more comprehensive work written in large part to explain Jewish history, culture and religion to the intelligentsia of Rome.

Both these histories include a wealth of information about the four-hundred-year gap between the canonical books of the Old and New Testaments, with special attention to the four and a half decades before the birth of Christ that comprised a brash outsider's rise to the throne of Judea and his subsequent descent into barbarity.

Was there really a Nicolaus of Damascus?

Nicolaus of Damascus was indeed a real person, and was very influential in Herod's court and decision-making in the latter part of his reign. He was widely recognized by his contemporaries as well as by historians in later centuries, and did actually tutor Cleopatra's younger children in his early adulthood.

In addition to his diplomatic and ministerial duties Nicolaus was a prolific writer. His works included a biography of Herod, a universal history of 144 books, a biography of Augustus, and an autobiography. Fragments of the latter two works survive. In his autobiography, Nicolaus (writing about himself in the third person) credits Herod with providing him the inspiration to write his universal history:

> *"[Herod] forced Nicolaus to study rhetoric with him, and together they practiced oratory. And then Herod was seized by a love of history… and encouraged Nicolaus to take up the task of history-writing. Nicolaus set about the task in grand style. He gathered together the whole of [world] history, and expended greater effort on it than anyone else… After this, Herod sailed to Rome to meet Augustus; he took Nicolaus with him in the same boat, and they philosophized together"* (Nicolaus of Damascus, Autobiography, fragment 135).

For additional frequently asked questions, as well as a study guide that provides references to the historical sources for the events in the story and the scriptural passages cited in the text, go to

www.HerodTheSecretHistory.com.